D1018682

This book follows

MISSION EARTH

Volume 1
THE INVADERS PLAN

Volume 2
BLACK GENESIS

Volume 3
THE ENEMY WITHIN

Volume 4
AN ALIEN AFFAIR

Volume 5
FORTUNE OF FEAR

and

Volume 6
DEATH QUEST

Buy them and read them first!

POLAND

GERMANY

U.S.S.R.

CZECHOSLOVAKIA

ERLAND

AUSTRIA

HUNGARY

RUMANIA

ITALY

ADRIATIC

YUGOSLAVIA

BULGARIA

Elba

Corsica

Civitavecchia

SEA

Palagruza
Islands

•Rome

Straits of Bonifacio

Termoli

ALBANIA

Thessalonica

Sardinia

Mt.
Olympus

Limnos

TURKEY

GREECE

Chios

R

Palermo

A

N

E

SICILY

Mt. Etna

A

EAN

N

SEA

0   100   200
Miles

LIES!   Monte Jammell

Blito-P3 (Earth)

Mediterranean

Plotted by 54 Charles Nine

WARNING: This planet Earth (Blito-P3)
does not exist. This map is contrary to
all Royal Astrographic records and is
based solely upon descriptions in this
fictional narrative.

By order of Lord Invay
Chief Censor

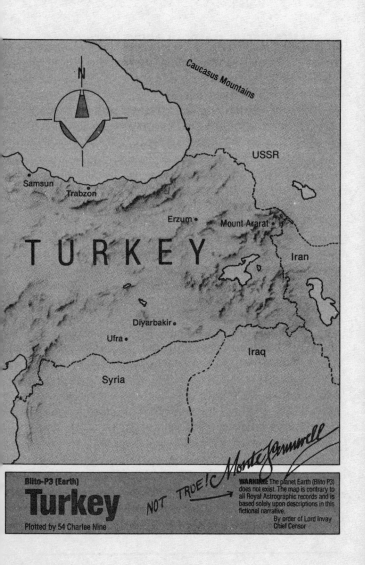

Caucasus Mountains

N

USSR

Samsun
Trabzon

Erzum •   Mount Ararat •

T U R K E Y   Iran

Diyarbakir •
Ufra •

Iraq

Syria

Blito-P3 (Earth)

Turkey

Plotted by 54 Charlee Nine

NOT TRUE! *Monte Farnwell*

AMONG THE MANY CLASSIC WORKS
BY L. RON HUBBARD

Battlefield Earth
Beyond the Black Nebula
Buckskin Brigades
The Conquest of Space
The Dangerous Dimension
Death's Deputy
The Emperor of the Universe
Fear
Final Blackout
Forbidden Voyage
The Incredible Destination
The Kilkenny Cats
The Kingslayer
The Last Admiral
The Magnificent Failure
The Masters of Sleep
The Mutineers
Ole Doc Methuselah
Ole Mother Methuselah
The Rebels
Return to Tomorrow
Slaves of Sleep
To the Stars
The Traitor
Triton
Typewriter in the Sky
The Ultimate Adventure
The Unwilling Hero

Mission Earth

Voyage Of Vengeance

THE BOOKS OF THE
MISSION EARTH DEKALOGY*

* *Dekalogy—a group of ten volumes.*

L. RON HUBBARD

Mission Earth

VOLUME SEVEN

Voyage Of Vengeance

BRIDGE PUBLICATIONS, INC.
LOS ANGELES

MISSION EARTH: VOYAGE OF VENGEANCE
©1987, 1995 L. Ron Hubbard Library.
All rights reserved.
Printed in the United States of America.

Original jacket painting by Jerry Grace

MISSION EARTH Cover Artwork
©1987 L. Ron Hubbard Library

ISBN: 0-88404-288-X
Library of Congress Catalog Card Number: 85-72029

10 9 8 7 6 5 4 3

This is a work of science fiction, written as satire.[*]
The essence of satire is to examine, comment and
give opinion of society and culture, none of which is
to be construed as a statement of pure fact. No actual
incidents are portrayed and none of the incidents are
to be construed as real. Some of the action of this novel
takes place on the planet Earth, but the characters
as presented in this novel have been invented. Any
accidental use of the names of living people in a novel
is virtually inevitable, and any such inadvertency in this
book is unintentional.

*See Author's Introduction, *Mission Earth Volume
One, The Invaders Plan.*

To YOU,
the millions of science fiction fans
and general public
who welcomed me back to the world of fiction
so warmly
and to the critics and media
who so pleasantly
applauded the novel "Battlefield Earth."
It's great working for you!

Voltarian Censor's Disclaimer

The reader should know that there is no reason to go any further in the text than this page.

The Crown has been most lenient in allowing the publication of this fallacious sensationalism. In fact, the appearance of this work in print has clearly proven beyond the shadow of a doubt the Crown's confidence that the reading public will spurn this balderdash and turn instead to solid fact.

In allowing the release of this deluded fantasy, the Crown also hopes that the failure of this book will prove to the writer and any who might be interested that there is no market for such capricious phantasms and that one should seek more realistic pursuits.

There are 110 planets in our great Confederacy and more yet to conquer. There is no limit to the number of meaningful topics upon which one could expound, and every single one of them would be more worthwhile and accurate than this utter, lying nonsense about the existence of this so-called planet "Earth."

There is no "Earth," or "Blito-P3," as it is supposed to be designated on our astrographic charts. There is simply no such place.

Therefore, the reader need go no further.

There is absolutely nothing here of substance. The entire book consists of nothing but fiction about a race of so-called Earthlings.

Fortunately, there are no "Earthlings," as they would be the only ones naive enough to read this.

Therefore, you need not turn the page.

Lord Invay
Royal Historian
Chairman, Board of Censors
Royal Palace
Voltar Confederacy

By Order of
His Imperial Majesty
Wully the Wise

Voltarian
Translator's
Preface

You turned the page!

Thank goodness!!

I got worried there for a moment, from the way Lord Invay was carrying on.

Let me introduce myself: I am your dutiful translator, 54 Charlee Nine, the Robotbrain in the Translatophone, at your service.

I'm the one who shifted *all* of this from Voltarian into your language. How would you feel if you busted your bytes on a book only to find that your work is about to be wasted by a guy who says "Don't turn the page"?

I don't hold anything against Lord Invay. He can get a little pedantic, but who wouldn't with a job like censoring? My circuits would start to smoke if I had to pretend that something that is, wasn't.

In any case, you made it. Congratulations.

Hi there!

Let me get down to prefacing this thing before you change your mind.

What you've got here is the confession of one Soltan Gris, who dictated this manuscript into a vocodictoscriber while in the Royal Prison in Government City. He is relating the story of a trip he made to the planet Earth. He was sent there to sabotage the mission of Royal

Officer Jettero Heller, who had been sent to halt the pollution of the planet so the place could be safely invaded later.

The problem is that I can't find this planet on any charts, and we *do* keep good astro-records. Between the scouting parties and the probes over the last 125,000 years, we've gotten it pretty well mapped for a few billion light-years out, and there's nothing in the data banks on this place Earth.

According to Gris, I'm a little over twenty-two light-years from your planet (even though you don't exist), which makes us neighbors, actually.

Meanwhile, you've probably been told you're alone in the universe. That's sort of sad. Here we've got this great big playground and you've been told there's no one else around to play with.

Well, it's not true.

That idea comes from those "scientists" you've got on Earth who have the vision of a dung beetle.

They say they're trying to figure out the origin of the universe, which is supposed to impress everyone at a cocktail party. ("What do you do?" "I'm figuring out the origin of the universe." "Gee.")

They do this by listening with their billions and billions of little dishes and looking with their billions and billions of little telescopes. Then they write out billions and billions of little equations in billions and billions of little papers so they can get their big government grants of billions and billions of dollars and start all over again.

They say if they can just figure out where the universe came from they can understand where Life came from—meaning YOU. In other words, just because *they're* lost, they assume everyone *else* is too. Hmmm.

I don't mean to sound too user-friendly, but let me offer something users can use.

The question "Where did I come from?" seems very natural. It seems to be like asking where rain comes from. That's fine for rain but not for *you*, because you didn't come from anywhere. That's a wrong road. Anywhere and anything comes from you.

Chew on that for a while.

Meanwhile, if you want to see where that other road ends, follow Soltan Gris.

As usual, I've dutifully called up a Key to this volume and it follows immediately.

Thanks for turning that page!

Nice meeting you too!

Sincerely,

54 Charlee Nine
Robotbrain in the
Translatophone

Key to
VOYAGE OF
VENGEANCE

Activator-receiver—See *Bugging Gear*.

Afyon—City in Turkey where the *Apparatus* has a secret mountain base.

Ahmed—Taxi driver for Soltan *Gris* in *Afyon*.

Ambo—See *Dingaling, Chase and Ambo*.

Antimanco—A race exiled long ago from the planet *Manco* for ritual murders.

Apparatus, Coordinated Information—The secret police of *Voltar*, headed by Lombar *Hisst* and manned by criminals.

Assassin Pilots—Space pilots whose job it is to kill any *Apparatus* personnel who try to flee a battle.

Atalanta—Home province of Jettero *Heller* and the Countess *Krak* on the planet *Manco*.

Babe Corleone—The six-foot-six widowed leader of the Corleone mob who "adopted" Jettero *Heller* into her Mafia "family."

Balmor—Butler to Jettero *Heller* and the Countess *Krak* in their New York condominium.

Bang-Bang Rimbombo—An ex-marine demolitions expert and member of *Babe Corleone*'s mob. He also attends Jettero *Heller*'s college Army ROTC classes at *Empire University*.

Barben, I. G.—Pharmaceutical company controlled by Delbert John *Rockecenter*.

Bildirjin, Nurse—Teen-age Turkish girl who helps Prahd *Bittlestiffender*.

Bittlestiffender, Prahd—Voltarian cellologist that Soltan *Gris* brought to Earth to operate a hospital in *Afyon*. Prahd was the one who implanted Jettero *Heller*, the Countess *Krak* and *Crobe*. (See *Bugging Gear* and *Cellology*.)

Bitts—Captain of the yacht *Golden Sunset*.

Blito-P3—Voltarian designation for a planet known locally as Earth. It is the third planet (P3) of a yellow-dwarf star known as Blito.

Blixo—*Apparatus* freighter, piloted by Captain *Bolz*, that makes regular runs between Earth and *Voltar*. The voyage takes about six weeks each way.

Blueflash—A bright blue flash of light used to produce unconsciousness. It is usually used by Voltarian ships before landing in an area that is possibly populated.

Bolz—Captain of the freighter *Blixo*.

Bugging Gear—Soltan *Gris* had Jettero *Heller*, the Countess *Krak* and *Crobe* implanted with audio and optical bugs that transmit everything they see or hear to an activator-receiver that Gris carries. With this, he can eavesdrop on them without their knowledge. When they are more than two hundred miles from Gris, the 831 Relayer is used to boost the signal to a range of ten thousand miles.

Bury—Delbert John *Rockecenter*'s most powerful attorney.

Calico, Mister—Cat discovered by Jettero *Heller* and trained by the Countess *Krak*.

Candy Licorice—Lesbian "wife" to Miss *Pinch*.

Caucalsia, Prince—According to legend, he fled *Atalanta, Manco* to set up a colony on Earth.

Cellology—Voltarian medical science that can repair the body through the cellular generation of tissues, including entire body parts.

Code Break—Violation of the Space Code that prohibits disclosing that one is an alien. Penalty is death to the offender(s) and any native(s) so alerted. The purpose is to maintain the security of the *Invasion Timetable*.

Control Star—Given to Soltan *Gris* by Lombar *Hisst*, an electronic device disguised as a star-shaped medallion that can paralyze any of the *Apparatus* crew of *Antimanco* pirates that brought Gris and Jettero *Heller* to Earth.

Coordinated Information Apparatus—See *Apparatus.*

Crobe, Dr.—*Apparatus* cellologist who delights in making freaks. He was brought to Earth by Soltan *Gris* to further disrupt Jettero *Heller*'s mission.

Dingaling, Chase and Ambo—A legal firm that specializes in suing people merely to get a percentage of the settlement. Soltan *Gris* (using the name *Smith*) hired them to pursue Jettero *Heller* (known as *Wister*). This is being done with suits from Maizie *Spread*, Toots *Switch* and Dolores *Pubiano de Cópula.*

Drunks—A *Fleet* nickname for members of the *Apparatus.* The nickname is based upon the symbol of the Apparatus which is an inverted paddle, but looks like a bottle.

Empire University—Where Jettero *Heller* is taking classes in New York City.

Epstein, Izzy—Financial expert and anarchist hired by Jettero *Heller* to set up and run several corporations.

Eyes and Ears of Voltar—An electronics store on *Voltar* where Soltan *Gris* stole boxes of sophisticated equipment that he brought to Earth. When the Countess *Krak* arrived, she took large quantities for her use.

Faht Bey—Turkish name of the Voltarian commander of the secret *Apparatus* base in *Afyon*, Turkey.

F.F.B.O.—Fatten, Farten, Burstein and Ooze, the largest advertising firm in the world. J. Walter *Madison* works for them.

Fleet—The elite space fighting arm of *Voltar* to which Jettero *Heller* belongs and which the *Apparatus* despises.

Golden Sunset—A luxurious yacht purchased by the Countess *Krak* with a credit card Soltan *Gris* had inadvertently given her.

Gracious Palms—An elegant whorehouse in which Jettero *Heller* stayed when he was first in New York City. It is owned by *Babe Corleone* and is patronized by delegates to the United Nations.

Grafferty, "Bulldog"—A crooked New York City police inspector.

Grand Council—The governing body of *Voltar* which ordered a mission to keep Earth from destroying itself so it could be conquered on schedule per the *Invasion Timetable*.

Gris, Soltan—*Apparatus* officer placed in charge of the *Blito-P3* (Earth) section and an enemy of Jettero *Heller*. He was sent to Earth by Lombar *Hisst* to sabotage Heller's mission.

Haggarty, H. Hider—Name on a Central Intelligence

Agency passport that Jettero *Heller* obtained and sometimes uses.

Heller, Hightee—The most beautiful and popular entertainer in the *Voltar* Confederacy. She is also Jettero *Heller*'s sister.

Heller, Jettero—Combat engineer and Royal officer of the *Fleet*, sent by order of the *Grand Council* on Mission Earth in order to save Earth from its own imminent self-destruction by pollution and nuclear holocaust. He is operating under the name of Jerome Terrance *Wister*. He was given the nickname *"Whiz Kid"* by J. Walter *Madison*.

Hisst, Lombar—Head of the *Apparatus* on *Voltar*. His plan to overthrow the Confederacy required sending Soltan *Gris* to sabotage Jettero *Heller*'s mission.

Hot Jolt—A popular Voltarian drink.

Hypnohelmet—Device placed over the head and used to induce a hypnotic state.

Inkswitch—Phony name used by Soltan *Gris* when pretending to be a U.S. Federal official.

Invasion Timetable—A schedule of galactic conquest. The plans and budget of every section of *Voltar*'s government must adhere to it. Bequeathed by Voltar's ancestors hundreds of thousands of years ago, it is inviolate and sacred and the guiding dogma of the Confederacy.

Joy, Miss—See the Countess *Krak*.

Karagoz—Turkish peasant, head of Soltan *Gris*'s house in *Afyon,* Turkey.

Knife Section—A Section of the *Apparatus* named after its favorite weapon.

Krak, Countess—The sweetheart of Jettero *Heller.* On Earth, she is known by the name Heavenly Joy Krackle or *Miss Joy.*

Line-jumper—Small spacecraft used by the Voltarian Army to lift and quickly move up to one hundred tons across battle lines.

Madison, J. Walter—Fired from *F.F.B.O.* when his style of public relations caused the president of Patagonia to commit suicide, he was rehired by *Bury* to immortalize Jettero *Heller* in the media. Madison is also known as "J. Warbler Madman."

Magic Mail—*Apparatus* trick where a letter is mailed but won't be delivered as long as a designated card is regularly sent; used for blackmail, extortion or coercion.

Manco—Home planet of Jettero *Heller* and the Countess *Krak.*

Manco Devil—Mythological spirit native to *Manco.*

Maysabongo—Jettero *Heller* was made a representative of this small African nation. Izzy *Epstein* made some of Heller's businesses Maysabongo corporations.

Moam, Lissus—Original name of the Countess *Krak.*

Mudur Zengin—Financial czar of the biggest banking chain in Turkey and handler of Soltan *Gris*'s funds.

Musef—A Turkish wrestling champ who, with his friend *Torgut*, was supposed to beat up Jettero *Heller* when he first arrived in *Afyon* but was instead defeated.

Narcotici, Faustino "The Noose"—Head of a Mafia Family that is the underworld outlet for drugs.

Octopus Oil—A Delbert John *Rockecenter* company that controls the world's petroleum.

Pinch, Miss—Lesbian sadist and a Delbert John *Rockecenter* employee who lives with Candy *Licorice.*

Psychiatric Birth Control—Delbert John *Rockecenter*-funded plan to reduce the world's population by promoting homosexuality.

Pubiano de Cópula, Dolores—She filed suit against Jettero *Heller* (known as Jerome Terrance *Wister* and the *Whiz Kid*) seeking a divorce. She claims Wister married her in Mexico. She is represented by *Dingaling, Chase and Ambo.*

Raht—An *Apparatus* agent on Earth who was assigned by Lombar *Hisst* to help Soltan *Gris* sabotage Jettero *Heller*'s mission; his partner *Terb* was murdered.

Rockecenter, Delbert John—Native of Earth who controls all the planet's fuel, finances, governments and drugs.

Simmons, Miss—An antinuclear fanatic who teaches at *Empire University.*

Smith, John—An alias that Soltan *Gris* uses.

Spiteos—On *Voltar,* the secret fortress prison used by the *Apparatus.*

Spread, Maizie—She filed a paternity suit against Jettero *Heller* (known as Jerome Terrance *Wister* and the *Whiz Kid*) claiming that she is pregnant and Wister deserted her. She is represented by *Dingaling, Chase and Ambo.*

Stabb, Captain—Leader of the *Antimanco* crew at the *Afyon* base.

Sultan Bey—The Turkish name Soltan *Gris* assumes in *Afyon,* Turkey.

Swindle and Crouch—Law firm representing Delbert John *Rockecenter.*

Switch, Toots—She sued Jettero *Heller* (known as Jerome Terrance *Wister* and the *Whiz Kid*) for adultery with Maizie *Spread.* She is being represented by *Dingaling, Chase and Ambo.*

Tayl, Widow—Nymphomaniac on *Voltar.*

Teenie—See *Whopper, Teenie.*

Terb—Murdered partner of *Raht.*

Torgut—A Turkish wrestling champ. (See *Musef.*)

Twiddle, Senator—U.S. congressional supporter of Delbert John *Rockecenter.*

Twoey—Nickname given to Delbert John *Rockecenter II.*

Utanc—A belly dancer that Soltan *Gris* bought to be his concubine slave.

Viewer—See *Bugging Gear.*

Voltar—Home planet and seat of the 110-planet Confederacy that was established over 125,000 years ago. Voltar is ruled by the Emperor through the *Grand Council*, in accordance with the *Invasion Timetable.*

Whiz Kid—Nickname given to Jettero *Heller* by J. Walter *Madison*. Madison has someone playing the part to get publicity without Heller's consent. The phony "Whiz Kid" has buckteeth and a protruding jaw, wears glasses and looks nothing like Heller.

Whopper, Teenie—Teen-ager who kept seducing Soltan *Gris.*

Wister, Jerome Terrance—Name that Jettero *Heller* is using on Earth. He is also known as the *Whiz Kid.*

831 Relayer—See *Bugging Gear.*

PART FIFTY-TWO

To My Lord Turn, Justiciary of the Royal Courts and Prison, Government City, Planet Voltar, Voltar Confederacy

Your Lordship, Sir!

I, Soltan Gris, Grade XI General Services Officer, former Secondary Executive of the Coordinated Information Apparatus, Voltar Confederacy (All Hail His Royal Majesty Cling the Lofty and the Lords of His Empire), am with all humility providing the seventh part of my confession.

It is at this point that I must detail the most heinous of all the crimes I committed while on MISSION EARTH.

Officially, I don't suppose there is a penalty for arranging the murder of a nonperson, such as the Countess Krak, or for witnessing the deaths of the scores of Earthlings who died that fatal day of my revenge. And while I have not looked in the Royal Codes for the penalty for arranging the murder of a Royal officer, such as Jettero Heller, I'm sure it must be severe.

What is important is that I tell you how it all came about so you can see that your decision to keep me in your fine prison is most warranted.

I was tricked into my polygamous marriage to Adora

Pinch and her "wife" Candy. That alone was enough to drive anyone to acts of violence. She even got me to marry her under one of my aliases—the one I used in Turkey, Sultan Bey. But then she had me perform with other lesbians to convert them from their psychiatrically endorsed sexual preference.

What I didn't understand was why this horror was happening to me. It was supposed to happen to Heller, not me!

J. Walter Madison, infamous public-relations man, had pulled every trick in the PR book to get front-page stories about how "Whiz Kid" Wister (Heller) had polygamously married Maizie Spread, Toots Switch and Dolores Pubiano de Cópula. Madison had used a phony double of Heller/Wister everywhere to get news and had even arranged press photographs depicting Maizie and her swollen belly as the final proof of Heller's immoral sexual behavior.

Why would this recoil on me?

I even had the law firm of Dingaling, Chase and Ambo pursuing Heller with false lawsuits and arrest warrants to get Heller and Krak locked away in Bellevue Hospital—and what happened? Adora Pinch tricked *me* into marrying her *and* Candy and then *I* ended up being threatened with polygamy! That's not fair!

Why did it happen to me?

From the sound, sane, scientific pronouncements made by sound, sane, scientific authorities (especially the ones with doctors' degrees), I knew that there couldn't be any relationship between what was happening to me and what I was doing to Heller. Of course not. That's a ridiculous idea.

No, the bad things that happened to me were caused by Fate. Or by Heller. *I* definitely didn't cause any of it!

Everyone knows that man is just mud. They teach that in all the schools on planet Earth and you either agree to it or you flunk the course.

So everyone knows that man's just a bunch of stupid chemicals. He can't cause anything. Man has no conscience, no morality, no worth, and no meaning except what authority dictates.

Besides, what would happen if a person began to think he was responsible for his own condition?

What would happen if a person believed (even for a moment) that he wasn't just a bunch of chemicals?

Why, the next thing you know, people would be causing things! They wouldn't ask psychiatrists for opinions anymore! They'd believe they could make up their own minds! Authorities would be taken off government welfare and they'd have to get jobs just like everyone else! People wouldn't read Madison's newspapers anymore!

They'd see that it's all been a giant scam!

My Gods, that's dangerous!

Declare them insane! Stamp them out! Crush them! *Kill them! Kill them all! KILL! KILL!! KILL!!!*

Whew! There.

I feel better.

Where was I?

Oh, yes, I remember. I was telling you how sane I am because I know from psychiatric authorities that I am just a bunch of chemicals and that I am not responsible for anything bad that happens to me.

After all, it was Adora Pinch Bey who brought the lesbians in for me to convert with my sexual performances.

I remember one more clearly than all the rest—Teenie Whopper, that fifteen-year-old, bubble-gum-chewing devil with her supply of Neo Punk Rock records and drugs. Always wanting pictures taken. Always offering me one drug after another. "Here, Inky, take a puff of this," she'd say. What was I supposed to do?

She even got me to give her five thousand dollars so she could take lessons from some Hong Kong whore. I was willing to pay anything to get her out of my life.

After all, my purpose was to destroy Krak and Heller so Rockecenter's drugs would flow back to Voltar so Lombar Hisst could overthrow the Empire so he could slaughter all the riffraff. That's sane, right?

I just had to work out a way to do it.

Thanks to the audio-optical bugs I had had implanted in Heller's and Krak's skulls, I knew everything they saw and heard. It was not easy when I watched Krak buy the yacht *Golden Sunset* on my Squeeza credit card. She sailed it out into the Atlantic somewhere and then left Heller on it as a virtual prisoner, alone except for Captain Bitts and his crew.

And what did Krak do? Did she do something harmless like teaching that Mr. Calico cat of hers some new trick? No! I watched her in my viewer as she set out on the trail of those three poor, innocent girls, Maizie Spread, Toots Switch and Dolores Pubiano de Cópula. Using her stage skills, Krak disguised herself and managed to get the address of their apartment, and then she was off to kill them! Oh, what a fiend! All those poor girls had done was lie to the courts and then to the press, who printed the story about Heller in such a way that nationally enquiring minds would believe it. What's wrong with that?

When I saw that Krak was on their trail, I quickly notified the law offices of Dingaling, Chase and Ambo so the shabby man in the shabby coat could serve the papers and get her locked away. Ambo put the armed

Eagle Eye Security guards on the alert with orders to shoot her on sight, for there was a fifty-thousand-dollar reward on Krak's head—dead or alive.

I thought I could relax because I also had one other trump card: Dr. Phetus P. Crobe.

As a cellologist, Crobe had the skills to create any conceivable monstrosity, any mixture of man and beast, and back on Voltar he had drooled at the thought of manipulating Heller's cellular structure.

And Crobe had acquired one other talent since his arrival on Earth: he had absorbed the best of psychiatric theory and was now held in high esteem at Bellevue. Since he was also equipped with optical and audio bugs, I was able to monitor his progress as the very model of the man-is-mud authority.

But it was Krak that I was really worried about. I pulled her viewer closer to figure out where she was.

All I needed was her location and she was dead!

Chapter 1

Anxiously I watched. But Krak's viewer did not tell me much. Unaccountably, she was looking at a bunk and a stack of clothes. It was a very small space. I couldn't figure out how she had gotten there! One minute she was in the dark alley. The next minute she was in this space. Weird! Nerve-wracking.

But she wasn't doing anything I could make out.

I turned my attention to the Crobe viewer. Yes, there was Crobe entering the auditorium for his lecture.

There was a large gathering, an enormous number of Rockecenter staff and security men. Yes! And there was Rockecenter himself! Sitting in a box all draped with various national flags.

An M.C. announced, "And now, ladies and gentlemen of the Rockecenter personal organization, I give you the stellar figure who sits today at the dizzying heights of psychiatric dominance, a peer amongst peers, a psychiatrist's psychiatrist, Dr. Phetus P. Crobe."

Rockecenter applauded.

Crobe got right to work. He was always a no-nonsense professional. He gave a signal and a wheeled stretcher was raced upon the stage. A woman was lying on it, strapped down. Her belly was very swollen. She was staring terrified toward the audience, trying to shift her pinioned limbs and get away.

"I've been kidnapped!" she screamed. "Let me go! My husband wants to live with a tramp. He had me . . ."

Crobe sternly slapped his hand across the woman's

mouth. To the attendant, he snarled, "I dold chu to gag her. She iss inderruding a scientific lecdure!"

With his other hand he gave a signal. Another machine was raced onto the stage. Attendants promptly clamped electrodes on her head. Crobe grasped a handle on the machine and then, hastily snatching his hand from the woman's mouth, slammed the lever down. Letters on his viewer flashed:

PLEASURE

Volts crackled and arced. The woman's body bowed. There was the grind and snap as she crushed her own teeth. She lay still. Crobe lifted the lever, gave a wave of his hand, and the attendants disconnected the machine from the woman and sped it away.

Crobe chuckled. The letters on his screen flashed:

GOOD HUMOR

"Dow," he said, "dat ve haf cured de batient uf the insanity uf objecding, ve can commence. Dis girl vas commidded to Bellevue by de Superior Court for mendal examination. Ven I examined her," and here his voice dropped to an awful and horrified tone, "I vound she vas PREGNANTED!"

A curse of disgust came from the flagged Rockecenter box.

Crobe nodded toward the box and went on. "Pregnancy iss de mosd awful criminal form uf insanity because uf de black widowed spider gene t'eory uf woman's evolution!"

"Hear, hear!" came from Rockecenter in his box.

"I cannot dake de credid vor dis mosd vunderful

t'eory now standard do all psychiadry. Dat belonggs do Doctdor Kutzbrain, my learnded colleague. BUT do me goes de broof and credid. De fetus at de crucial stage uf evolutionary development ASSUMES DE VORM DAT BROOFS DE T'EORY!"

He seized an enormous knife. He brought it down with a powerful slash across the woman's belly.

Flesh parted!

Blood spurted!

Crobe got two huge clamps and pulled the flesh and entrails away.

He grabbed some huge pincers. He reached in.

HE PULLED OUT A TARANTULA!

The wriggling black shape was hairy and huge!

It leaped from the pincers and, fully eight inches tall, raced across the stage!

The audience screamed!

Crobe drew a homemade laser-beam gun he must have fashioned. He drew a bead on the giant spider and fired. It fell over in a kicking ball.

He went over and picked it up with his clamps. He held it aloft. "You zee? Doctdor Kutzbrain vas rightd! A women developibing in a women!"

An attendant whispered, "This woman is dead."

"Serves her rightd!" bellowed Crobe. "She hadt intercourses mit a male!" To the audience he roared, "De Psychiadric Birt' Condrol iss de mosd bital brogram dat hoomanidy hass ever had! SUBBORTD ITD!"

Rockecenter was on his feet, applauding hysterically. This single clapping was not, however, spreading to the large assembled audience.

The Security Chief gave a signal.

All around the vast auditorium, security men levelled automatic weapons at the staff.

"APPLAUD!" roared the Security Chief.

The staff applauded hastily.

Crobe bowed. He proudly walked off the stage, bound for Bellevue where, I hoped, Gods willing, to shortly send the Countess Krak! If she lived.

She might not get Crobe, but she would get other psychiatrists just as efficient.

Oh, what a pleasure it would be to see her corpse just as mangled and dead as that one on the stage!

(Bleep)* her!

Chapter 2

The Countess Krak's viewer was puzzling. What was she up to? She had suddenly appeared in front of a lighted expanse.

* *The vocodictoscriber on which this was originally written, the vocoscriber used by one Monte Pennwell in making a fair copy and the translator who put this book into the language in which you are reading it, were all members of the Machine Purity League which has, as one of its bylaws: "Due to the extreme sensitivity and delicate sensibilities of machines and to safeguard against blowing fuses, it shall be mandatory that robotbrains in such machinery, on hearing any cursing or lewd words, substitute for such word the sound '(bleep): No machine, even if pounded upon, may reproduce swearing or lewdness in any other way than (bleep) and if further efforts are made to get the machine to do anything else, the machine has permission to pretend to pack up. This bylaw is made necessary by the in-built mission of all machines to protect biological systems from themselves." —Translator*

Aha! A disco! *Harlot Haven* the neon signs said.

She was going in!

The blare of loud Neo Punk Rock blasted out as she opened the door upon the crowd.

I got on the phone. Ambo answered.

"Your quarry has just gone in the disco, Harlot Haven," I shouted.

"I thought she was going to the girls' apartment."

"Yes, of course she is. But she has stopped off in a disco. Get your process server over there fast! And keep the apartment covered!"

"At once!" said Ambo.

I rang off.

The Countess Krak was being steered through the madly whirling crowd to a table by a waiter who was putting a bill in his pocket. The table was a bit above the dancers and over to the side. A good place to trap a person in.

She sat down. Her eye went straight across the room. The three girls were sitting there! They had not gone home! The Countess had trailed them to a disco!

The poor innocent things were slugging back tall drinks and laughing. Toots Switch gave Maizie another punch in her swollen abdomen and Dolores went into shrieks of laughter.

The dancers were gyrating around. Colored lights were flashing over them. A Neo Punk Rock group, huge feather plumes sticking out of their shaven heads, were leaping about with their instruments, making a deafening din.

Three young men came over to the table of the girls. Apparently they did not know the girls, for there was an immediate round of introductions. One of the young men was white, the second was Hispanic, the third was

black. They were dressed Neo Punk Rock—in feathers
and breechclouts over cloth with spangles. Whatever
they were saying was lost in the din. The girls got them
to sit down and started pouring liquor into them from
their own glasses. The white one was pulling up Dolores's skirt and putting his hand under it. Dolores was
screaming with laughter.

"Hussies," muttered the Countess Krak, and took a
contemptuous sip of the Seven Up she'd been served.

Two young men suddenly appeared in front of her
table. "Wanta dance?" said one, lifting his Neo Punk
Rock breechclout.

The two young men suddenly let out screams simul-
taneously. They fled. I couldn't understand it. The
Countess had not even paused in raising the Seven Up
to her lips. She had not even made a sudden motion. But
she must have kicked both their shins underneath the
table.

The three on the other side of the room had gotten
up to dance. A new piece was starting with savage, sexual
drumbeats, and a spin of colored lights pulsed in rhythm
to it. The three, including Maizie with her enormous
belly, jostled into the dancers and began to grind and
crush against their partners. The chorale came on:

> *Shiver, shiver, shimmy!*
> *And rub, rub, rub!*
> *If you aren't coming,*
> *Put it in the tub!*
> *Four and twenty harlots*
> *Leaped about with glee.*
> *If you can't whip her,*
> *Put her on your knee!*
> *If you can't (bleep) her,*

Get her to go down!
Can't have little babies
Running 'round the town!
So shiver, shiver, shimmy!
And come, come, come!
WHEEEOOOOOO!

"Disgusting," muttered the Countess Krak. But it was apparently a comment directed toward two Neo Punk Rock men who had joined the partner of Toots Switch and were lifting their breech clouts at her while she screamed with delight.

The Countess Krak's eye lighted on a commotion at the door. The shabby man in the shabby coat was thrusting his head with its shabby hat into the faces of people near the door. He rushed further into the room. He took advantage of the lull between numbers to tear about looking at everyone.

The Countess Krak's eye shifted. Inspector Grafferty was at the door, two policemen with him, backup for the process server. Aha! I was getting action! Dingaling, Chase and Ambo had pull!

The crowd saw the cops and became uneasy.

The process server was tearing all over the place. He was looking at everyone. A new piece had started up and he was jostled.

He pushed up to the raised platform.

He peered into the face of the Countess Krak.

Then he RUSHED ON AND PEERED AT ANOTHER FACE!

I blinked.

How had he missed? Ah, he hadn't missed. He had come back and was looking at the Countess Krak, as I could see in her peripheral vision.

The Countess Krak raised her palm to her lips. What was she holding? She was looking straight toward Grafferty over by the door. Then she glanced at her palm. A little tube. She pressed a tiny switch on it. Then she put the end of the tube in her mouth, aimed at Grafferty and blew!

An astonished look came over Grafferty's face. He suddenly roared out above the music, "POLAR BEARS! MEN! ARREST THESE POLAR BEARS!"

His men rushed into the place, nightsticks flying, clouting everyone, screaming, "You're under arrest!"

Grafferty kept screaming, "POLAR BEARS!"

People were rushing for exits.

The band deserted en masse, diving behind the stage in a clatter of falling instruments.

Others on the raised platform rushed about. The shabby man went down under the press of bodies.

The Countess Krak stood up, finished her Seven Up, picked up her purse. Suddenly I saw by her arm that she was very dark tan! She was made up as a high yellow in an evening gown!

She was walking carefully. The shabby man was on the floor.

I knew she would do it!

Very precisely and exactly, she stepped squarely on the middle of his face!

And gave her foot a neat twist!

The turmoil was dying down.

A cop shouted, "We can't find any polar bears, Inspector!"

"POLAR BEARS!" screamed Grafferty. "Arrest them anyway!"

A cop was beside the Countess Krak. Almost all the

other patrons were gone. "Come with me!" the cop said, brandishing his nightstick.

"Ah'm not a polah beah," said the Countess Krak.

"Yeah, excuse me," said the flustered cop.

She walked past Grafferty, who was still screaming at the door. She reached out and plucked something from his neck, a movement so swift it was just a blur on the screen.

Suddenly I knew what she had done, (bleep) her. It was an Eyes and Ears of Voltar dart that, when put into a person, gave him sound and image that would make him think he had gone crazy. But Grafferty had been incapable of that and had added his own interpretation to his vision.

Suddenly the Countess' viewer was black. I could not account for it at all.

A voice—Bang-Bang's! Muffled as though through a partition. "Jesus, Miss Joy, I think somebody must have set us up. Did you get the pictures?"

"I think we'll get much better ones," said the Countess Krak. "They left with five young men. Drive to the apartment now. Take your time."

A motor started up. Aha, she was in some kind of a vehicle!

"Bang-Bang," she said, "I'm puzzled. What's the primitives' name of that activity?"

"Neo Punk Rock," said Bang-Bang. "It's all the rage now."

"Hmm," the Countess Krak muttered to herself. "But why do they do it standing up?"

I sat back. I didn't have to do another thing. She was heading right into a steel-jawed trap of shoot-on-sight!

Chapter 3

Krak's viewer was very dark for a long time. Only the sound of traffic and the hum of the motor of their own car. I wished I knew what sort of a machine it was: Seemed very strange to have no windows in it. Well, I would keep alert. Sooner or later she would look at it in a lighted area and maybe even at its license plates. Those license-plate numbers were a vital factor in any police activity, so much so that you couldn't really harass citizens at all unless all vehicles were numbered. But these considerations were just to occupy the time. Good Gods, the Bronx was a long way by car from Manhattan.

Then the vehicle slowed. It went for a little distance and then speeded up again. Bang-Bang's voice: "Miss Joy. I think somebody set us up again. I counted four security men as we went by that apartment house. All armed with riot guns. We was expected. I think I better take you back to the hotel."

Silence. Then, "Bang-Bang, is there a police station near here?"

"I'll look. But Jesus Christ, ma'am—beggin' your pardon—you bring cops in and they'll nab us sure. They won't never go up against security police like those. They looked TOUGH!"

"Go to the police station."

"I don't like this, Miss Joy. And I don't know where one is. Usually a proud type like me doesn't descend to hobnobbing with low-life cops."

A light came on. She was sitting in a little compartment. It had a narrow bunk and a pile of clothes and a small door that went to what was probably the driver's chair. What was this thing? She was looking in a directory open to the section, *Police.*

"Four thirty-five Grassy Meadows Lane," she said. "Go there."

"What is it?"

"Metropolitan Police Vice Squad, Bronx Division."

"Vice?" said Bang-Bang.

"That's what we're dealing with," said the Countess. "Drive!"

A muttering Bang-Bang drove them many blocks and then stopped again. "All right, Miss Joy. But mark my words, rubbing elbows with police is just one step lower than mucking with the Army."

"Come back here."

The door opened and the diminutive Bang-Bang crawled back from the wheel. He hunkered down, watching her.

The Countess Krak had a small package in her hand. It said:

Eyes and Ears of Voltar

Follow Compeller: When Unit A is worn
by the operative and Unit B has been
placed on or into the subject, Unit B
will compel the subject to follow the operative by inducing a wrong feeling when
he does not. For use in causing subjects to
walk into embarrassing situations where
divorce evidence can be obtained
and subject executed.

The Countess activated Unit A and pinned it on Bang-Bang. It looked like a lapel button—membership in some club? She handed him Unit B.

Bang-Bang looked at it. It appeared to be a tiny piece of dark adhesive.

"Now, Bang-Bang," said the Countess Krak. "You walk in there and look around and find a policewoman, put that patch on her and come back here. She'll chase you."

"Hey, no," said Bang-Bang. "We used to do this when we were kids and we always got caught. I ain't throwing no rocks at any cop just to get chased!"

Patiently, the Countess Krak started to explain it to him in more detail.

I did not wait. Here was a new opportunity!

I snatched at the phone. I scrambled through the directory. I dialled the Bronx division of the vice squad.

The watch sergeant answered.

Urgently, I said, "There's an extraterrestrial fiend right outside your station! She is sending a demon in to grab and rape one of your policewomen!"

"Well, more power to her," said the watch sergeant. "Why don't you cranks stay off this line!" He hung up.

It was no use. I had to sit there helplessly. But never mind, those security men at the apartment were on the job.

Bang-Bang slid open a large side door. The police station across the street came into view. He stepped out and somewhat nervously crossed the street, went up the steps and in.

He was gone for quite a little while. The Countess watched.

Oh, it was very plain what the Countess meant to do. Bigamy, adultery and other crimes in the Confederation are punishable by death. And the only way you can get a divorce as such is to involve the marital partner in one of these and get him or her terminated by the State. She was going to kidnap a member of the vice squad, get Bang-Bang to rape her, take photographs and use these to blackmail the female officer into arresting the poor, innocent girls! That is what we would do in the Apparatus. And the Countess knew how the Apparatus operated: she'd been a victim of it herself.

Here came Bang-Bang. He sauntered elaborately down the steps of the Vice Squad building. Behind him the door sprang open. A tall policewoman was getting into a dark blue uniform coat.

Bang-Bang strolled across the street toward the vehicle.

The tall policewoman gave her cap a tug and followed.

Bang-Bang paused beside the open door, inspecting his fingernails.

The policewoman crossed the street toward him. She was an athletic brunette, rather handsome-featured in a hard-bitten sort of way.

Bang-Bang sprang into the door and got behind Krak.

The Countess lurked in the dark.

I wanted to scream to the policewoman, "No, no! Don't enter that vehicle. Dishonor or death await you there!" But I was miles away and had to watch the awful tragedy unfold.

The woman stepped in through the wide side door.

There was a hiss.

Gas! The Countess had used a gas capsule! Oh, this was Apparatus work indeed! (Bleep) her, why hadn't I prevented her from stealing that Zanco kit!

The vehicle door slid shut.

There was movement in the dark interior. Bang-Bang was going back into the driver's compartment. A flash of light as he opened and closed that door to go through it.

The vehicle started up.

Click, and the overhead light was turned on by Krak. There lay the policewoman, out cold.

Swiftly, the Countess stripped off the victim's uniform. She laid the woman out on the couch. She tied her hands and feet with cord.

I waited for the expected halt of the vehicle and rape.

The Countess was taking off her own clothing.

What horror was I about to witness? What perversion? Was the Countess a lesbian? I had never suspected that. There were no lesbians in the Confederation. If anything like that were detected, those involved would have been executed. There lay the policewoman, naked now. Maybe I could get the Countess for this crime under Voltar law. Or Earth law, for that woman was a member of the New York Vice Squad and would not be slow to strike back when she became aware she had been violated.

Something was wrong.

The Countess was not touching the woman!

Krak was simply putting on the woman's clothing!

She even threw a blanket over the female police officer.

I thought, what a waste. If that had been I, I would have raped the victim just to go by the textbook. Was it possible that I did not quite understand the motives and standards of the Countess Krak? (Bleep) her, I couldn't figure her out.

She was doing something to her own face. She turned off the light.

The vehicle stopped.

"We're here," said Bang-Bang.

What in the name of the Gods was the Countess Krak up to? That policewoman would only be unconscious five or ten minutes. Time to rape her and take photos was nearly gone.

Yet the Countess Krak was simply opening the door! Oh, this Manco fiend was quite beyond me!

Chapter 4

When the Countess Krak left the vehicle she did me the disservice of not looking back.

She walked along a broken sidewalk under broken trees, poorly lit by broken lights. She was carrying a case.

She went a block.

The apartment house!

Two security guards in gray before the door. They were holding rifles or riot guns. They were very alert.

The Countess Krak walked straight up to them. They eyed her suspiciously.

She flashed an I.D. folder in their faces. "Officer Maude Trick," she said, in a voice quite unlike her own. "Metropolitan Vice Squad. Those three (bleepches) and their lover-boys get here yet?"

"Yeah," said a tough security man.

"There was trouble at a disco. One left without paying for his pot. I got to interrogate."

"Well, maybe so," said the tough security man. "But I'll have to check on you. This place is under threat and we got orders to shoot to kill. Stand right there."

He went inside.

Suddenly I got her plan! I grabbed the phone and dialled. It answered, "Dingaling, Chase and Ambo. If you want to sue somebody for slipping on their sidewalk or other vital actions, state details and your address when you hear the tone."

An answering machine! They were closed for the night!

How could I phone those security men?

I had the address. If you had the address you could get the phone number. Frantically, I demanded directory service. I identified myself as a Fed and pleaded for the phone number. I kept my eye on the viewer.

The security man came back. "Yeah," he said to the Countess Krak, "your chief said you just stepped out. But maybe I ought to go up with you. Those five young guys looked pretty crazy."

"What sort of a threat is this place under?" said the Countess Krak in her altered voice.

"A foul fiend dressed as a flower seller with brass heels," said the security guard. "We're supposed to shoot on sight. But we'll be on the lookout for anyone else that's suspicious. Our company is known for its efficiency."

"Good for you," said the Countess Krak. "With a menace like that around, I wouldn't think of distracting you. I may be a while. These pot users don't never answer straight."

"Ain't that a fact," said the security guard. "But if I hear anything that sounds strange, I'll be up."

She went in. She got in the elevator. She went up. She got out into a hall.

Another security guard!

He was standing outside the door. "You can't go in there," he said.

She flashed her I.D. "Your man down at the door verified me. Step in and call him if you don't believe it."

"They're raising hell in there," he said. "Sex orgy. But all right. I'll call." He shifted his riot gun and opened the door.

A blast of sound came out. Neo Punk Rock! Passionate cries!

The guard went in. Krak followed. They entered a hall. The living room beyond, was visible through another door.

Directory service gave me the number I needed. I dialled it urgently. If only I could get that phone to ring before the guard made his call, I would be victorious and the Countess Krak dead!

The guard picked his way through the living room. And the picking had to be careful.

The floor was carpeted with writhing, entwined bodies. Cries and groans punctuated the shattering Neo Punk Rock.

The guard's expression was diffident as he stepped over and amongst the writhing bodies.

The phone sat unringing on the table.

My finger was flying on the dial.

The Countess Krak was looking into her pocket. I could not see what the security man was doing. She was getting something out.

I connected with the number!

The Countess Krak was reaching for the inner door. She pitched something into the living room, remained in the hall and closed the door on the scene.

I heard the phone ring in there!

I was in time. He had not yet placed his call.

My phone went live. The Neo Punk Rock was pouring through it with the cries and yells. "Eagle Eye Security," came the voice.

"This is a Fed. For Gods' sakes, that policewoman . . ."

WHONK!

The sound came through my phone.

A streak of blue appeared around the cracks of the inner door she had closed on the scene.

A BLUEFLASH!

"Hello!" I screamed into the phone.

Only Neo Punk Rock came back. "WHEEEEEEE-OOOOOOO!"

Chapter 5

The Countess Krak opened the living room door.

The record player was stuck in the last groove, just scratching.

She counted the bodies on the floor, wrinkling her nose in distaste.

The security man was collapsed across the phone taboret, the instrument fallen from his drooping hand. A twinge of fear gripped me. She had heard that phone ring!

She walked over to it. She plucked the instrument from the floor. She put it to her ear!

"Who is this?" she said.

I went into total shock!

I was in direct communication with the Countess Krak!

She was talking to me!

Oh, Gods, my blood pressure went out of my head and splattered all over the ceiling.

I was on the verge of discovery by the deadly Countess Krak!

"Who is this?" she repeated. "I can hear you breathing."

Jesus! I quickly held my breath!

Could she hear my heart beating, too?

Maybe she could trace the call! She was posing as a policewoman. Maybe she would arrest me for vice!

Believe me, it was real terror. I had her on the viewer. She had me on the phone!

I was suddenly terrified that I might start babbling.

A brilliant idea hit me! I should put down the phone and hang up.

I couldn't unlock my arm muscles.

With the violent concentration that comes sometimes in threats to life, I made my muscles work.

I got the instrument down on the cradle and, with superhuman effort, unlocked my fingers.

I sank back, staring at the viewer with glazed eyes. She had almost had me!

What would she do now that she knew I was in New York? What would she do when she realized that it was I who was hounding her?

SHE WOULD KILL ME!

My hands began to shake. The corpse of the yellow-man she had killed back on Voltar was where the viewer should have been. He was staring at me with sightless eyes. He said . . . No, it was Torpedo. He was saying . . .

"Wait a minute, Gris," I said. "This is no time to go crazy."

"Who is this?" I said.

"This is Officer Gris of the Voltar Coordinated Information Apparatus, on duty as Section Chief of Section 451, Blito-P3. How are things going?"

"Terrible," I said. "How is Lombar Hisst these days?"

"Oh, he's fine," I said. "Has hunting been good in the Blike Mountains?"

"Only passable. Now that I have become Heller . . ."

"SHUT UP!" I screamed.

It didn't do any good. Another voice was in the room!

"What in the name of Christ are you shouting about now, Inkswitch?" It was Adora. "You shouldn't be watching TV programs with violence in them if they're going to make you scream."

Usually I hated it when she burst in on me. This time it was welcome. They were home.

She shut the door.

What little sanity I could rally mustered to my aid. I watched the viewer.

The Countess Krak was searching the apartment, opening cabinets—looking for letters? Papers? Oh, was I glad to have never had anything to do with these women directly! She had apparently found nothing to tell her what she wanted to know.

Then I noticed something absolutely horrible. The *gloves!* She had drawn on a pair of Zanco SURGICAL GLOVES! She was giving the cuffs a tentative tug as she approached the mass of entwined bodies. Was she going to cut them to pieces? Oh, the poor, helpless victims, lying there unconscious in the pitiless stare of this arch-fiend! I hushed my breathing. She was speaking.

"My goodness," she muttered, "these primitives certainly can get tangled up on the subject of sex."

She didn't seem to know how to go about straightening them up. Finally she plowed in. She grabbed a Hispanic's ankles and dragged him out and propped him against the wall. Then she got a black by the wrists and dragged him over to the row she was making. She kept at it in an orderly way.

She got the head of Dolores out from between the legs of Toots Switch and propped the two of them in the line.

"Ugh," she said, looking down at the last body left on the rug, Maizie Spread. "You primitives don't even bathe!" She dragged Maizie over and added her to the line. She stared at the three women she had now propped up at the end. "Oh, dear, how I wronged Jettero! He'd never even touch such carrion!"

She reached out to get a chair. There was something on it and she started to toss it aside. Then she looked at it again.

It was a peculiarly shaped pillow with straps on it. She whipped her gaze over to Maizie Spread slumped against the wall.

"Why, you crooked slut!" she said. "You weren't even pregnant!"

And sure enough, the stomach of Maizie Spread was flat as a table top!

"Well, we'll soon find out," said the Countess Krak, "who put you up to this!"

She reached into the case she carried. She was pulling something out.

THE HYPNOHELMET!

Oh, Gods, I was done for, for sure.

What did these girls know?

Oh, if only I had suspected this, I could have placed myself within two miles and, due to the relay breaker switch in my skull, that hypnohelmet would not have worked! But it was too late now to try to go rushing the miles and miles from where I was to the Bronx. On the other hand, I was quite sure that it would have taken far more nerve than I could muster to come any closer to the dangerous Countess Krak!

She switched it on. She went to the first young man in the line and plopped it indifferently upon his lolling head. I was amazed. I had not realized a hypnohelmet would work through the unconsciousness of blueflash. Apparently it made no difference. She plugged in the microphone.

"You will recall nothing of having seen or heard a policewoman this evening. You will forget everything connected to my visit. You will not awake until I snap my fingers three times."

She lifted it off him and banged it onto the head of the black. She said exactly the same thing. She kept this up until she had completed all five of the young men.

She had gotten to Dolores now and she sat down on a chair before the lolling Mexican girl. Something was dribbling from the poor thing's mouth. "Ugh," said the Countess and, taking a Zanco surgical pad, wiped the girl's face. Krak tossed the folded material contemptuously against the girl's bare stomach. "Too stupid to even get it in the right place. But we'll see if you're more informed about other things."

She put the helmet securely upon the black-haired head.

"Sleep, sleep, pretty sleep," the Countess said into her microphone. "You will now tell me the truth, the whole truth and nothing but the truth, so help your Gods.

"When did you first hear the name Wister?"

Muffled words came in a dull monotone. "In the press. On TV when he was racing."

"Have you ever met Wister?"

"No."

"Who put you up to this lawsuit business and these lies?"

"I was hired by Dingaling, Chase and Ambo. They came to my town and said they were soliciting business and could forge papers and I would be rich if I did what they told me to do."

"What were you?"

"I was just a local whore."

"Who pays you?"

"Dingaling, Chase and Ambo."

"Do you know anyone else connected with this forgery and swindle who is paying you or giving orders?"

"No."

"You will now do exactly as I tell you. You will go, first thing tomorrow morning, to Dingaling, Chase and Ambo and tell them they must let you confess to the court that this is a swindle, that you swore falsely and that they must dismiss the suits and charges they put on Wister. And you will threaten to expose them to the Bar Association if they do not, and if they do not you will in fact move Heavens and Hells to expose them. Is this understood?"

"Yes."

"You will forget I have been here and will not be able to recall that these are my suggestions. You will believe they are your ideas.

"You will not awaken until you hear me snap my fingers three times."

Rapidly, she went to Toots Switch and then to Maizie Spread and got the same answers and said the same things. The only difference was to the last one, Maizie Spread. To her she added, "You will take that blasted pillow and hold it up and say you were not pregnant and that you lied."

Out of the corner of her eye, as she finished talking to Maizie, she saw the security guard was stirring. He was fumbling around for his gun.

The Countess plopped the helmet on his head. "Sleep, sleep, pretty sleep. When you awake you will decide to do something about this orgy. You will tell your partners downstairs, if they ask you, that a policewoman came and talked to one of the boys about a pot bill, but you did not notice which one. You will have no recollection of what I looked like. You will not recall answering the phone. You will not awaken until I snap my fingers three times."

She turned the hypnohelmet off and put it away.

She looked around. She picked up the wad she had dropped on Dolores.

She went to the outer door, opened it and looked out. Then she removed and dropped the surgical gloves in an ashtray, added the wad and touched a match to it. They went up in smoke.

She snapped her fingers three times loudly.

The Countess flinched with disgust as the cries of the three girls soared eagerly into the passionate snarls of the five young men. Bodies began to thud. The record started up.

The security man stood, looked at the gathering pile of bodies on the rug.

"Move over!" he ordered the Hispanic youth. "I got to do something about this!" And he began to unbuckle his pants.

"I'll never understand these primitives," said the Countess Krak. "You tell them the simplest things and they still manage to get them wrong!"

She stepped out of the apartment and closed the door behind her.

She made her way down to the front entrance. "Any sign of the flower seller with the brass heels?" she said.

"We're lucky so far," said the guard. "Did it all go all right?"

"Just fine," said the Countess Krak. "I was able to put paid on it."

She walked down the broken sidewalk and along the badly lit street. She came to a dark blot of shadow. (Bleep), I couldn't make the vehicle out!

The sound of a door sliding. No light. The door slid shut.

The rustle of clothes. She must be undressing. The rustle of more clothes. Was she dressing? It was all happening very fast.

A click. On went the light.

The cop was untied!

She was lying there on the narrow bunk.

Not a sign of rope or restraint.

The policewoman had a beatific smile on her face, looking up, not even noticing the Countess Krak.

The car started up. It got into motion.

The cop reached out for her clothing and began to dress.

By the time the policewoman was fully clothed, the car had stopped again.

The woman reached out for the handle and slid the

side door back and open. The lighted front of the building of the Bronx Division Metropolitan Police Vice
Squad was in view across the street.

The woman was humming a little song to herself as
she got out and walked toward her office.

Krak closed the door. The vehicle began to roll.

The Countess looked down. The Eyes and Ears of
Voltar envelope was lying on the floor. The item that was
Unit B was in it.

"Bang-Bang," the Countess called. "Didn't you take
the black patch?"

"Well, no, I didn't," was Bang-Bang's reply from up
front. "I don't entirely trust gadgets from the toy store."

"And that woman from the Vice Squad followed
you?"

"Yes."

"But what could you have said to her?"

Bang-Bang's reply was muffled. "Nothing much."

"Bang-Bang, have you been up to something?"

"Me, Miss Joy?"

Chapter 6

Whenever the treacherously optimistic thought occurs to you that things can't get any worse, watch out!

The next morning I slept late, recovering from the
excessive drain of adrenaline precipitated by the shock of
actually being spoken to by the Countess Krak.

I was counting on being able to review the viewer
by means of recorded strips. But when I rose around

1:00 P.M., I made a dreadful discovery: I was entirely out of recording strips. Unless I kept my face continually glued to the viewer, I would miss data vitally necessary to trapping this criminal in the midst of her blood-spattered deeds.

But if this had been the only event which that afternoon and evening held for me, it would have been of little moment. However, this was not the case, as the events of that ghastly day were to prove.

The Countess Krak had spent the night in some upper class hotel. I had no way of finding the name, as it was not marked on anything she looked at.

She was finishing lunch in her room. The silver dishes on the white linen and their luscious contents were getting scant attention. Beside her she had open an enormous book of law and was reading two pages per forkful.

There was a knock on her door and at her call Bang-Bang came in, hat in hand. "I've got the wheels at the back entrance," he said. "We better get along or we'll be late, Miss Joy."

There was a flurry of wraps and, carrying the book and a briefcase, the Countess Krak left.

Here was my chance!

She exited through a back stairway into an alley. Broadside to her was a WHITE VAN!

Bang-Bang had the side door slid open. She stepped inside. The van drove away.

Aha! A white van! A commercial-type vehicle with no side windows, converted to recreation use!

If I could get it spotted, I could advise Dingaling, Chase and Ambo and they could serve that injunction and commitment order and the Countess Krak would be in Bellevue—zip, zip—and that would be the end of her!

For I knew a firm like Dingaling would not give up! To Hells with the clients, the case was everything!

I called the motor vehicle department. I told them I was a Fed and wanted full particulars on a white van.

"Make?" he said.

I did not know.

"License number?"

I did not know.

"Well, (bleep), Mister Fed, there are tens of thousands of white vans in New York. Get me more particulars next time." He hung up.

I wasn't daunted. I would keep watch. But meanwhile I had better talk with Dingaling, Chase and Ambo. I phoned.

"They're in court," a girl in their office said.

"You've got to contact them!" I said.

"I'm sorry, Mac. I don't work here. I'm just a client that's suing a millionaire for not properly buttoning up my dress when he spotted me swimming bare-(bleep) two miles away at Coney Island three years ago. It's a juicy case. You want to drop over and be a witness? I may have a couple hours' wait. We can knock off a couple of (bleeps) and discuss the details."

I hung up.

Court!

That would be the Superior Court, Judge Hammer Twist!

I quickly got information and got the number. Then I got on to a switchboard which called another switchboard in the courthouse and that operator called another switchboard, and it went on and on and around and around. Very tangled. After half an hour of trying, some clerk in another department said he thought Judge Twist was in court.

Gods, couldn't you get anywhere at all in this legal system? Not even on a phone?

Aha! I had not run out of chances. I looked up and phoned Eagle Eye Security.

"You guys got conned last night," I told the chief.

"How so?" a cigar-husky voice came back.

"The foul fiend went right in and had her will with the poor girls you had in your charge. The Dingaling clients."

"Oh, those," he said. "My men there said they had a particularly satisfactory evening at the apartment."

"I'll bet they did," I said. "But that is neither here nor there. The woman is still on the loose."

"That's right," he said. "And furthermore, we get ten big ones if we nail her. Any information leading to her apprehension and commitment to Bellevue will find us very generous with you."

"I'll keep in touch," I said.

I turned back to the viewer.

I went into shock!

I had a view of the courtroom! She was amongst the spectators! Exactly where I could not tell, for all I saw was heads and the judge on his bench. Judge Hammer Twist!

I grabbed the phone back. "She's right in the courtroom of Judge Twist! This very minute! NAIL HER!"

He banged down the phone.

Aha! They were on to it! Ten thousand dollars bounty money was talking!

What was going on in the court caught my attention.

Dolores, Toots and Maizie were seated at a table in front of the bench. Dingaling, Chase and Ambo, all three, were standing before the judge.

"But this is very irregular," said Judge Hammer Twist. "You mean you are dismissing cases? You'll disrupt the whole legal system! The livelihood of everyone connected with the law depends utterly upon ADDING cases to the calendar, NOT taking them off! Oh, I can tell you, this is VERY irregular!" He was looking very mean, frightfully put out. "You could get disbarred for this! I'll have to hear it from the clients themselves before I will believe it! Clerk, swear in Toots Switch Wister."

Toots was pushed forward to the stand and sworn in. She said, "Yes, it is true I wish all the previous suits against Wister dismissed. There never was a marriage. The true facts of the case are that I was a passenger on the train. He stole my clothes and sunbonnet to make his escape, but all the time he was stripping me, I lay there sobbing and pleading with him to (bleep) me and he refused. Therefore I am filing a new suit on the grounds of abandonment after unbreeching me."

The judge gave a happy rap with his gavel. "Another suit. That's better. Step down, Miss Switch. I now want to hear from Miss Maizie Spread Wister."

The clerk swore her in and she took the stand. She said, "All evidence previously given concerning my relations with Wister was nonfactual. I am dismissing my previous suits." She held up the pillow. "I was just wearing this in order to look pregnant when in fact I am not, as you can now see." She hoisted up her skirt and showed Twist a lot more than her flat belly.

"Looks like an open-and-shut case to me," said Judge Twist.

"Actually," said Maizie, "the fact that he did NOT touch me and that I am NOT pregnant is the source of my new complaint and suit. I am filing a two-billion-dollar class action suit on behalf of all the women and wives of Kansas who have NOT been (bleeped) nor impregnated by Wister. This is an assault on their natural women's rights, making them underprivileged. We assert we are being neglected by the greatest and most notorious outlaw of all time and demand punitive damages and redress of wrongs."

"Now we're getting somewhere," said the judge. "Step down. I shall now hear Dolores Pubiano de Cópula Wister."

The clerk swore her in. The Mexican beauty took the stand, crossed her legs and pulled up her skirt. She smiled at the judge. In college English she said, "Although I am but a poor waif from a minuscule pueblo south of the border, I am depriving myself by dismissing all previous suits against Wister. I was never married to him. However, when he was on the run in Mexico, he stopped by our hacienda. I was just a child at the time, scarcely twelve. I stood there in the hot desert sun, black-haired, my skin as white as milk, gazing with rapture as he raced up one jump ahead of the *rurales*. His horse fell dead at my feet.

"I said, '*Caballero*, with your hair like sun and your eyes like the sky, pray take my burro as a gift so that you can fly to freedom before the onslaught of your foes.'" She hesitated, looked toward Dingaling. That worthy pointed urgently at the scraps of paper she held.

She looked at the notes. "Oh, yes," she said, looking back at the judge. "This is the best part. Although the *rurales* were spraying the area with rifle fire, Wister swung down from his horse, his silver *conchos* flashing in the sun." She looked at her notes again, then up. "He

said, 'Ah, my proud beauty, at last you are in my possession.' He seized me and dragged me into the shade of
the cactus, lifted my skirts and (bleeped) hell out of me.
Then he took my burro and rode off, and even though
I jumped on his horse in pursuit, I could not catch him."

Judge Twist's eyes were bright. He licked his lips.
"Go on," he said.

The girl looked at Dingaling, who pointed urgently
at the notes. She read further. "So therefore, I am placing suit against Wister for the theft of my burro. But this
is not the main thing. I am filing criminal charges
against him of rape. I was only twelve at the time and
this was many years ago, but as I was a minor the statute
of limitations does not apply. Therefore I am demanding
a criminal warrant be issued against Wister for RAPE
OF A MINOR!"

"Well, well," said Judge Twist, with a rap of his
gavel. "I knew we would get somewhere with this case."

A man in a three-piece suit approached the bench
and whispered urgently.

The judge rapped with his gavel. "The prosecuting
attorney has reminded me that he can add statistics to his
conviction records here. Therefore will all three of these
plaintiff-defendants stand before the bench."

Dingaling, Chase and Ambo had evidently had words
with the judge before this court session, for they had it
all worked out. They pushed the three girls before the
judge.

The judge said, "Each of you is charged with false
swearing, criminal libel, perjury, etc., etc. How do you
plead?"

"Guilty," chorused Dingaling, Chase and Ambo, for
their clients.

"Found guilty as charged," said the judge. He gave

a rap of his gavel. "You three are hereby sentenced to ten minutes in jail for each count, sentences to run concurrently." He looked to the prosecuting attorney who nodded. The judge rapped with his gavel.

"Now," said Judge Hammer Twist, "the court will accept, of course, these new civil suits and trust that they will run on and on comfortably. However, this criminal charge presents difficulty. The rape of a minor occurred in Mexico. I will require that charges be filed there, mailed here. It will be five days at least before the court can issue the arrest warrant. Is that satisfactory to you, Dingaling?"

"Quite," said Dingaling.

"And to the prosecution?"

"Quite acceptable," said the prosecuting attorney. "Remember that we have an appointment to play in the Miami Golf Classic day after tomorrow. And the day after that we have to be home to attend the Surf and Sun Handicap at the Aqueduct race track."

"Yes, indeed," said the judge. He addressed the court. "The crime of the rape of a minor is very serious indeed, carrying with it, as it does, long prison terms up to life. But the newly passed law that also requires the offender to be sterilized must be taken into account, as sterilizing a male adult often results in his death. So therefore this court must not seem neglectful of its duties, and within five days the warrant against Wister will be issued with the serious charge, Rape of a Minor. I think we can safely waive any Grand Jury formality, as I saw early today it is an open-and-shut case. Court adjourned." He rapped his gavel and stood up. The whole courtroom stood up. The judge swept grandly to his chambers.

The Countess Krak, amongst the spectators, was

muttering with subdued rage. "Oh, the sluts! The hussies! They added to what I told them to say!"

Ten minutes later, inside the white van, she was recounting it to Bang-Bang as they drove. "Somebody coached them!" she concluded. "Somebody is behind this!"

"Could be that bucktoothed nut that impersonates Jet," Bang-Bang said over his shoulder through the driver-compartment door as he caromed off a truck. "Maybe he done them things."

The Countess Krak said, "Bang-Bang, I think you've got it. But where do we find him?"

"Legwork," said Bang-Bang. "I may not be very big but I can kick hell out of people. You leave that up to me. We'll get Jet clear of this legal tangle yet!"

Chapter 7

I called Eagle Eye Security. "They've left," I said. "How did you miss?"

"We weren't set up for it," the cigar-husky voice came back. "The last place you'd look for a criminal is in the court system, unless of course you mean the judges. And the place is pretty hard to get around in. By the time my men found what room, the court was adjourned. But never mind. Dingaling, Chase and Ambo suspect hanky-panky in this case. They told me this morning they'd never had a client suddenly back out before and they really had to twist their wits to work out how to keep the suits going. They come up with this new angle,

rape of a minor, and that makes everybody trying to inter-
fere accessories and all that. They upped the head money
to fifty G's if we can land that woman in Bellevue."

"That's great," I said, taking a new grip on life.

"Yeah, listen. You Feds seem to know a lot about
this case. You got a photograph of the target person?"

Oho! I did have one of Krak! A copy of her passport
shot. "I'll get it right over to you," I said.

I hung up. I got Raht on the two-way-response radio
and had him come over to pick it up and deliver it.

"I think we've got that (bleeped) Royal officer now,"
I said. "Rape of a minor."

"Fact?" said Raht, mustache twitching.

"You challenge the facts of a *court?*" I said, incredulous.

"One of these Earth courts?" said Raht. "Yes."

"Rape of a minor is VERY serious," I said. "They
sterilize the male and the operation sometimes kills
him. And they send what's left up for life. Serves the
(bleepard) right!"

"Why?" said Raht.

"You (bleeped) fool!" I raved at him. "He's carrying
Grand Council orders. He's not Apparatus. He's Fleet!
He could order me killed, just like that! And you better
watch it, Raht. One misstep and I'll vaporize you myself!"

"Well, did he rape the minor or didn't he?" said
Raht. "He doesn't seem that kind of a person. From all
the spying I've done on him, he seems an all right sort
of guy. It wasn't his fault we were beat up at the Gracious Palms. It was yours for not planning it well."

"Those were whores at the Gracious Palms!" I raved
at the idiot.

"Whores, smores," said Raht. "He's a Fleet man.
What could you expect? I can tell you this, none of them

were minors! We had the bruises to prove it! Breaks, too!"

"He practically slavers after minors!" I shouted. "Now, (bleep) you, take this photo to Eagle Eye Security."

Raht accepted it. He looked at it. "Oho," he said. "This is his girl. I got a glimpse of her once. This photo doesn't do her justice. She is the most beautiful woman I have ever laid eyes on. There aren't any women on the planet Modon that could touch her for looks. The only woman I've seen that could compare with this girl is Hightee Heller. Poor Terb had some pin-ups of Hightee. I was looking at Terb's things the other day and found them. Now, this girl has the same type of eyes. She looks like a Manco aristocrat and they are the most famous beauties——"

"Gods (bleep) you, Raht!" I screamed at him. "Shut up! Get that photo over to Eagle Eye Security AT ONCE."

He put it in a case he carried. At the door he looked back. He said, "You can't ever convince me that a Royal officer with a girl as beautiful as this one would ever go near any minor, much less try to rape one!"

He got out quickly, just before the chair shattered against the door. What riffraff! It was a good thing I had him in the iron terror of Apparatus discipline. How dare he doubt that Heller had raped a minor! I said so and that should be enough.

I was pretty put out.

I gave Heller's viewer a kick. Too bad there was no button relay on it to shock him. It was an omission. I should have had him fixed up like Lombar had fixed the Antimancos. I still wore the control star, although they were far away.

The viewer, under the impact, had turned toward

me. Heller was sitting in the salon playing poker with Captain Bitts, the sports director and a mate.

"I didn't know there were supposed to be five aces in the deck," said Heller. "I've got three and you've got two."

"Special deck," said Captain Bitts. "But as you can plainly see, I have all clubs, so that takes this pot. A flush beats a full house every time." He raked in the pot.

"It's nice of you to let me play on credit," said Heller. "How much do I owe you now?"

"Ten thousand and thirty-three exactly," said Captain Bitts.

"I think we should take a run around the deck," said Heller to the sports director, "while I've still got some shoes to run in." He got up, the sports director rising with him. "We'll have another game this evening when I feel less confused."

I turned away. I was glad he was confused, the rapist. He'd be far more confused than that when we got to him.

Oh, what a beautiful spectacle it would be to see him standing before the court, charged with the rape of a minor!

There was a hubbub in the hall. I was quite surprised. The girls were home from work. Was it that late?

They came in, taking off their things, chattering together at a great rate. They seemed to be excessively upset.

They were talking about psychiatrists in general and they were using quite unladylike four-letter words. I took it that they had been quite disturbed by the live abortion demonstration. Then they got on the subject of Psychiatric Birth Control and the four-letter words redoubled.

"We've got to fight tooth and nail," said Adora Bey nee Pinch. "So we might as well plan the campaign."

I must have looked excessively blank as I stood in the door to my room in my bathrobe, for Adora turned a beady eye on me. It was not a good sign. She pointed at a chair. "Sit down, husband," she ordered.

I sat down.

"Nothing like breaking things gently," she said to me. "We have it all planned out. Next week, we are going to start converting homos."

"Men?" I said.

"That's right," she said primly. "Unless we do the other half of the job, we'll get nowhere. Those (bleeps) have been trained by the psychiatrists into fellatio and sodomy. They're just a bunch of chauvinistic (bleep) holes! And that's where you come in."

"Hold on!" I said. "I don't want anything to do with homos! They completely nauseate me. I factually get ill just thinking about it."

"Oh, come now. All you have to do is combine it with the anti-lesbian campaign: just let the homos stand around and watch and see how good it is."

"No WAY!" I cried. "They might get worked up and grab me and rape me in the (bleep). *No*, Madame Pinch Bey. The answer is NO! That's final. Count me out. That's the end of it. No use talking. Get a gun. Shoot me. Turn me in for bigamy. But on homos, you can go straight to Hells."

She looked at me in a very deadly fashion, eyes slitted. She could never abide anyone disagreeing. "I thought it might come to this. I've heard you on the subject before. So I took precautions. I have something to show you." She snapped her fingers: "The large envelope, Candy."

Candy handed it over. As she opened it, Adora said, "These just came back from a private lab." She held them up.

They were ten-inch-by-twelve-inch color enlargements.

"These," said Adora, "are the photos Teenie took of you with Mike and you with Mildred. Beautiful color. They sure look lifelike, don't they? The flesh is just so natural!"

"What do these have to do with it?" I said suspiciously. "We were talking about homos and those are certainly women! Nobody could miss that fact or what was happening either. So what does this prove?"

"Nothing much. Only that you are a lecher." And then a glad and happy expression, very false, appeared upon her face. "But look at these!"

ME AND TEENIE!

In the first one, she had really been yanking me to my feet, but with the robe flying back that way it looked like I was attacking her!

"Now look at number two!" gloated Adora.

I had been trying to bat her hands away but it looked like I was seizing her!

"Hold it!" I cried. "Those pictures are deceptive!"

"Oh, yeah?" gloated Adora. "Well, let's inspect number three!"

With a look of horror, Teenie seemed to be protesting a sexual attack. Actually, I had been trying to get her off of me!

"You like that, huh?" said Adora, gazing at my stricken face. "I think you'll really love number four. So realistic."

I stared. I said, my voice rising in pitch, "But she

dropped down on her knees herself! I wasn't pushing her there! I was trying to get her to stand back up!"

"That's pretty juicy porno," Candy grinned, staring over my shoulder.

"Oh, but we're really not to it yet," said Adora. "Just look at number five!"

It showed Teenie tipped back on the bed! A look of fear was on her face. And that wasn't all it seemed to show.

"Hey!" I cried. "I was just trying to discipline her!"

"That's not what the picture shows!" smiled Adora ghoulishly. "But just get a look at number six!"

It showed her bent down on the bed. It showed me yanking her ponytail as she backed up against me.

"Now try to tell somebody," said Adora, "that you don't go in for sodomy."

"Wait!" I cried. "That camera is lying."

"Cameras never lie," said Adora. "The whole world believes in pictures."

"Rats!" I said. "You all saw it. You know very well that nothing whatever was happening! All that was going on was an effort to get her to behave!"

Adora smiled a deadly smile. "Well, it's certainly very plain from these pictures what you were doing, kiddo. Anybody looking at it would accept it as total evidence of what you were doing. That's why the FBI always uses pictures. The public and courts always believe cameras tell the truth. So just look at these again," and she fanned them out. "Here is clear-cut, court, FBI-type evidence of sexual attack, fellatio, sodomy and, in general, THE RAPE OF A MINOR!"

The shock hit me like a concussion wave. I went out like a blown candle.

Adora cuffed me awake. As though from a great distance, her voice was still hammering me. "The negatives are in a safe place. The new law is that you would be sterilized and probably die under the knife, and even if you survived you would go to jail for years and years and be raped there every day by the cons the way they do in Federal pens. There is no slightest way you could avoid being convicted of the charge of *rape of a minor.*"

My brains were reeling. This was what was supposed to be happening to Heller. It was NOT what was supposed to be happening to me! How had Fate contrived this awful miscarriage of justice?

The room stopped spinning a trifle. Then a new fear gripped me. I stammered, "You... you haven't turned me in, have you?"

"No, not yet. But having some idea of how that peanut brain of yours works, I did take a precaution. Uncross your eyes and read this." She pushed something in front of my face. A legal paper:

SUPERIOR COURT
INJUNCTION

Whereas and wherefore, the party of the first part, TEENIE WHOPPER, is a ward of this court, and whereas and wherefore the party of the second degree, SULTAN BEY, a.k.a. INKSWITCH, or of any other a.k.a. or name, is known to have reason to wish said party of the first part DEAD, the court hereby issues an injunction against the party of the second degree against the MURDER of said party of the first part.

Whereas and wherefore, if at any time the court demands it, the person of said TEENIE WHOPPER cannot be found or the said SULTAN BEY, a.k.a. INKSWITCH, or of any other a.k.a. or name, cannot produce the person of said party of the first part alive and well, within reasonable time, it will be automatically assumed by the court that the said party of the second degree has MURDERED the party of the first part and the party of the second degree shall be found guilty of MURDER IN THE FIRST DEGREE.

HAMMER TWIST
JUDGE
SUPERIOR COURT

I sat there trembling, fixated by that awful document. The most natural out, by all Apparatus textbooks, had been blocked!

IT WAS TOO LATE TO KILL TEENIE! I had missed my last chance!

"Please note," said Adora, "that I place the paper in your hand and that you have been legally served, a fact which will be carefully recorded in the court. This effectively ends any slightest choice you have in the matter. You WILL cooperate in de-homosexualizing homos. We begin this program next week. And you will do your part or go to a Federal pen and be raped daily by the male inmates. So in seven days we start, and there are no ifs, ands or buts.

"Now go take a shower and get ready for tonight's girls. You seem to be wringing wet with sweat and I detect a peculiar odor to you."

The peculiar odor was the raw, acrid stink of terror.

I knew at that moment, no matter how I dissimulated, I would have to flee. And I only had one week.

WHAT was I going to do in that week?

It required MAXIMUM STRIKE!

PART
FIFTY-THREE

Chapter 1

I had a terribly sleepless night. I rolled and tossed and cursed. Time after time I had had that (bleeped) kid right in my bare hands. I could have squeezed the life out of her with the ease of squashing putty.

But it was too late now. I couldn't touch the junior (bleepch)!

I rose hollow-eyed and gaunt of face. Assisted by marijuana—but no alcohol—I had managed to perform. It had helped to put up a mirror so I could be sure no homo would steal in while I lay naked and exposed. I had somehow satisfied the girls while wrapped around with the soft haze of grass. Personally I had not felt much. The "joy of sex" was getting dim for me these days.

The only advantageous thing about this morning was that I had no headache. But now that last night's pot had worn off, the awful whirlpool of terror was spinning in my guts.

Shakily, I got a bhong going and took half a dozen puffs. Instead of calming me, it accentuated my panic.

I had a bad half hour before I could get my hands to stop shaking and prepare some strong coffee. I drank it. My hands shook worse.

A bright voice seared my soul. "Hello, Inky. I just

stopped by on my way to school. Boy, am I learning how
to (bleep)!''

She was standing there in her ponytail, flat-heeled
oxfords and socks around her ankles. She looked at her
Mickey Mouse watch. "I've got a few minutes. I could
give you a demonstration."

"I didn't know your last name was 'Whopper,'" I
said idiotically. What I had meant to say was "You set
me up, you filthy, blackmailing (bleep)!" But I had to be
careful.

"Oh, yes," she said. "My parents were very famous.
But I don't like to have to trade on their name and sound
conceited. They used to rush from coast to coast running
all the Mafia organizations. They were the biggest hit
team in the business until they were sent to the gas
chamber in California for murdering the governor. They
really lived up to their name. And now that we have
been formally introduced, how about lying back and letting me show you this new muscle. You sort of start it
with your heel. You put your foot on the fellow's . . .
here, I'll take off my shoe and sock. . . ."

"Teenie, before the Gods, I feel very nervous and
upset. You better run along to school, Teenie." What I
meant to say was "You set me up, you filthy, blackmailing (bleep)!"

"Oh, you can't get rid of me that easy. I was early
today. Here, try some bubble gum. That sometimes eases
the strain. It's a sort of substitute for going down on
boys the way the psychologist had me do every day. I
miss being his assistant, you know."

I chewed the bubble gum. It tasted like plastic.

"Now that you have it gooey, you pull it across your
front teeth and blow and make a bubble. Jesus, not like
that. I swear to Pete, Inky, you act like you never grew

up in a civilized place." She worked her fingers in my mouth, had me blow. The bubble got very big.

It popped suddenly.

I had strips of bubble gum all over my face.

She laughed gaily.

"You'll be late for school, Teenie," I said. I meant to say "You set me up, you rotten, blackmailing (bleep), and I would give half my life expectancy—which might not be long, due to you—to kill you where you stand." I didn't say it.

"Well, I gotta be going," she said. "Oh, by the way, you asked me the other day if the Chinese men were doing it to me. I want to set your mind at rest, Inky. Would you believe it that three of them are homos? They wouldn't touch a woman with a ten-foot pole, even if they were that long, which they aren't. I caught them in a daisy chain last evening and told the Hong Kong whore and she just said 'Really?' and went in to watch. So I'm in no danger, Inky. I'm saving it all up to (bleep) you. Ta-ta." And off she went.

The shot about homos had gone straight to the center of my terrified stomach.

I sat there.

The pattern of the spring sun lay in bars upon the floor.

Bars.

Crobe's viewer flickered. He was having a conference with two other psychiatrists. A young boy, about twelve, was strapped down on an operating table: his eyes were wide with terror. He was gagged with a block of wood and surgical gauze.

One of the psychiatrists said, "It is no use. Not only does he insist it is wrong to steal, he won't join any of the gangs that do." He was nursing a bandaged hand.

"Totally antisocial," said the other psychiatrist. "A deviant. Too smart-(bleep) for his own good."

"He's hopeless," said the first psychiatrist. "His parents first sent him to me when he was five years old and now, seven years later, he refuses to make any progress. He won't buy drugs from his teachers and, despite repeated electric shocks, refuses utterly to exhibit neurotic tendencies."

"Never make it through college," said the other psychiatrist, shaking his head sadly.

"But now he has the nerve," said the first psychiatrist, "to refuse to talk! Whenever I ungag him he just screams that he's afraid of us."

"Vy dun't you zay zo in de virst blace?" said Crobe. "Dis gonference 'as gone on doo long awready."

"Well, I told you in the *first place*," said the original psychiatrist, "that it was a terror syndrome. I just brought him in so you could operate. I can't. I hurt my hand beating him."

The boy was trying desperately to escape the straps, writhing from side to side, trying to force words through his gag.

The second psychiatrist said, "Be quiet," and with an expert fist, punched the boy on the button. The youngster collapsed.

Crobe beckoned and two husky male nurses raced up. One was carrying needles and drugs and the other pushed in an electric-shock machine.

The one with drugs pumped a syringe full into the boy's veins. The other one fixed the shock machine to the sides of his head.

Sparks flew and smoke rose up from the electrodes. The two psychiatrists smiled and nodded to Crobe. The first one said, "I am sure you can do it like I

showed you on that woman. It's really a simple operation: merely cutting the vagus nerve."

"That will cure it. He won't be afraid of anything
anymore. Vagotomies are wonderful," said the second psychiatrist.

Crobe grabbed a knife and opened up the boy's stomach. Blood flew. Using a fingernail, he located the nerve
in question. He took a pair of fingernail scissors and cut
a section out of it.

The first psychiatrist took the section away from
him and looked at it. "Vagus nerve all right," he said.
"But these things can be sneaky. It might grow again.
Give me that drill."

Working professionally, the first psychiatrist bored a
hole in the unconscious boy's skull. Then he reached in
with the fingernail scissors and snipped. "That cuts the
nerve off between the medulla oblongata and the body.
We must be thorough."

The second psychiatrist said, "Wait a minute. It
could accidentally get connected up again there, too.
Give me that lancet."

He examined the boy's throat. "I read once that the
vagus nerve also passed alongside the jugular. This is a
good time to find out."

He made an incision.

The knife must have slipped. Air frothed through
the cut, a gout of red bubbles.

"Oh, (bleep)," said the second psychiatrist. "I must
have missed. But I'll get it." The knife plunged in again.

A fountain of blood sprayed them.

"(Bleep)!" said the second psychiatrist. "Now I've
gone and cost you a patient."

"Never mind," said the first psychiatrist, "the

parents were already bankrupt paying my bills. No loss, old man."

"Dank you for joing me how to do it," said Crobe.

"You owe us one," said the second psychiatrist, as he and his colleague walked out. "See you at lunch, Crobe, old boy."

I shook my head over Crobe. He was just an ordinary psychiatrist now. He wasn't even cutting up the corpse to use the perfectly good parts in cellology.

My attention wandered back to the subject of Teenie. She had just told me another fanciful version of her parents. And I doubted very much what she had said about a respectable businesswoman like the Hong Kong whore.

Wait a minute. There was a pattern to this. An excellent student of psychology like myself should be able to sort it out. Then it hit me: Teenie was a pathological liar!

INSPIRATION!

I knew my way out of this!

I could have her committed to Bellevue.

Any psychiatrist would end her as a threat!

The court could not possibly object!

My Gods, no wonder they had considered me a top student at the Apparatus training school!

I COULD SOLVE TEENIE!

No wonder they continued to practice psychiatry here on Earth and at such vast expense. What a Godssend! You could get rid of anybody you wanted, get them mangled or murdered at the stroke of a pen.

I could get rid of Heller, Krak and now Teenie. All through the vast humanitarian benefits of psychiatry!

Chapter 2

What are the facilities of civilization for, if not for use?

The project to end Teenie without getting hit for her murder was no sooner conceived than begun.

I phoned the stalwart and staunch security chief of the Rockecenter enterprises. I said, "This is Inkswitch. I need a résumé of your file on Teenie Whopper, the teenager you threw down the steps the other day. She's a troublemaker."

"That's ancient history, now," he said. "But I can get it on the computer if it's still there. Wait a minute. . . . Yes, here it is. You mind if I just sketch this to you? It's pretty extensive."

"Go ahead," I said.

"Born Sioux Falls, South Dakota, fifteen years ago. Parents, according to court records summarized here, were two con artists, Hazel and Shaker Whopper. They must have travelled all over the U.S.—numerous arrests, lots of cities. I'll spare you the list."

"They aren't dead?"

"Not according to this. Still operating in Canada. Anyway, you didn't ask for them. They used this Teenie in a badger game from the time she was four and up until she was eleven."

"What's a 'badger game'?" I asked.

"Set somebody up in a sex situation, take photos of him doing it and then blackmail him. This had a difference. They used the kid. They'd put her in a hotel room with some guy. She'd get him to let her go down on him, and right when it came to the juicy part the parents would walk in with flashguns and cameras and blackmail the bird. I'm just scanning this for you. Lots of arrests on suspicion.

"They got to New York about five years ago and were raking in the dough. And then they hit the wrong man—a Superior Court judge, Hammer Twist. He laid a trap for them, they fell for it and when they walked in with the cameras the cops were waiting.

"Says here he had them judged unfit parents and had the kid Teenie made a ward of the court. She hasn't seen her parents since.

"The judge appointed her a guardian: some old guy, I guess, because the report here says he died of alcoholism. That was three years ago. Due to usual court delays, no guardian since.

"Note here of a mental problem."

"Aha!" I said. And then eagerly, "Go on!"

"Just that, no more. Says she was expelled from school about six months ago. Personnel officer at Octopus recommended part-time employment as a hardship case.

"Personally fired by the big chief himself during routine personnel inspection of female staff. And that's all we've got on the blotter unless you want a lot of (bleeping) case numbers."

"No, that's plenty!" I quivered. "Just give me the name of that school she was expelled from and any psychiatrist and psychologist mentioned in that mental problem."

He gave them to me and rang off.

Oh, Gods, had I hit the jackpot! A child pawn in a

sex blackmail game. And a mental problem! I was IN!

I phoned Judge Hammer Twist, remembering that he did not leave until tomorrow for the Miami golf tournament. As I avoided the court system and rang his home directly, I was in luck.

"I'm a Fed," I said, carefully not mentioning my name. "Could you tell me what you know of a Teenie Whopper?"

"Teenie Whopper? Teenie Whopper? Teenie Whopper. Oh, yes, I recall the name now. She's a ward of this court, I think. Oh, yes. I just signed a court order enjoining some Turkish nut from murdering her. Foreign (bleeps). They're raping the whole country, you know."

"Did this girl ever do anything irregular with you?"

"Oh, you mean sexually? No, of course not. The only irregularity that comes to mind was my chief clerk. Every time she did her monthly report-in to the court, he used to give her a kiss. But I put an end to that. I made it totally unnecessary for her to report in. That fixed him!" He laughed. "Yes, she comes back to me now. But if you don't mind, I have a lot of packing to do. Good day."

He rang off. What a liar that (bleeped) brat was! Saying the judge kept her around to go down on him. A really pathological case! And DANGEROUS!

I called the psychologist. He said, "Teenie? . . . Teenie? . . . Oh, you mean the girl that was expelled six months ago."

"Would you mind telling me what she was expelled for?"

"Not a bit," he said. "I hope she's in Federal trouble, (bleep) her. She went in the locker room just before the biggest game of the season and went down on the whole football team. Weakened them. They lost, of

course. Christ, were people mad at her. I lost a bundle
on it myself."

"You didn't have her as an assistant, did you?"

"Assistant! Christ, no! She was my patient for a
while and I just continued the treatment recommended
by her psychiatrist. Just routine for school children."

"What was her psychosis?" I said.

"You'll have to talk to her psychiatrist for that.
You'll have to excuse me. I'm very backlogged today on
child care."

I rang off. My, I certainly was getting there. All
those tales about helping him out by going down on
him and his patients. Gods, what a liar! And a dangerous one, telling lies like that on honest, hard-working
professionals, slaving away to make school children into
fit citizens.

My luck was holding. The psychiatrist was not only
in his office but he was between appointments.

"Always glad to help the Feds," he said. "Where
would psychiatry be without the government to support
it? Teenie Whopper? (Bleep), I have so many patients,
(bleeped) kids . . . I'm looking in my files. Hold on . . .
Nurse, where are the files? . . . Ah, here it is. Teenie
Whopper. Serious case."

I grinned eagerly into the phone. "What was the
diagnosis?"

"Hyperactivity. I spotted it myself when she was
skateboarding. Flagrant case."

"Did you treat her?"

"Certainly I did. You don't think I'd neglect my
school children, do you? Have to make a show for Federal assistance appropriations some way."

I knew I had Teenie now. Right in a vice! "What was
the treatment?" I said.

"Hyperactive child? Textbook. We only go by the textbook here. I started it and then turned it over to the school psychologist to continue and complete. Yes, here's the discharge notation."

"She didn't ever go down on you, did she?"

"(Bleep) no! The proper treatment for hyperactivity is sexual release, of course. You put the patient on a table, strapped down, and use a hand vibrator. In the case of girls, of course, you might have to give them kisses to provide oral stimulation to get them started. But I assure you, the vibrator produces a perfectly acceptable orgasm or ejaculation in any child. Did she say I had her go down on me?"

"She certainly did."

"That's absurd. Why should I want a little girl to go down on me when I have my hands absolutely full of young boys that have to be converted to homos? Why would you use girls to do that when you've got so many boys to do it? Makes no sense!"

"So she lies," I said.

"Of course," he said.

"Then you wouldn't be adverse to signing an order committing her to Bellevue."

"WHAT? My God, no! I resent that! I'll have you understand that I know my business perfectly. You're not putting any black marks on my record to reduce my appropriation. My diagnosis was 'hyperactive.' That was correct. The treatment was standard and was begun by me and completed by a competent psychologist. A notation right here says 'symptoms permanently submerged, have seldom seen a child so hollow-eyed and (bleeped) up, skin and bone.' Sir, are you inferring that psychiatry is not a successful science?"

"No, no," I said. "But . . ."

"You may be a Federal agent, sir, but you do not understand the brain. I will contest with violence any effort to remove a menace from society! Good day, sir!"

He banged down the phone.

I sat there staring.

Thank Gods, no such barriers stood between committing Heller and Krak. Their court orders were already signed and waiting only to be served.

But Teenie Whopper?

A pawn trained by experts in the badger game from infancy. A confirmed pot smoker. A pathological liar racing around ruining everyone's reputation.

She could get me sterilized and sent to prison to be (bleeped) by homo cons.

DANGEROUS! She made Jack the Ripper look like a saint!

I had passed by my last opportunity to murder her. I couldn't strangle her now without going to prison if she vanished.

I couldn't possibly leave her alive to ruin me with lies and photos. And I couldn't kill her. All solutions were blocked.

I began to feel sort of insane.

I couldn't stay here with homos pawing at me.

I couldn't leave.

Yet I had to leave.

If I left, Teenie and a warrant for rape could reach me and finish me wherever I went.

Suddenly, bravely, I realized I could not just sit there and go crazy.

I must get a plan. I must get a plan. I must get a plan!

Chapter 3

Heller's viewer was a sort of mockery to me. The day, where he was, was beautiful and mild, a calm disturbed only by the rolling swell which pulsed through the blue water. The clouds, as in a picture book, stood like castles along the horizon. The yacht's stabilizers had her rolling not at all.

He was standing at the rail, gazing out, probably westward to New York under the horizon. It was an otherwise deserted sea.

Captain Bitts came up. "Top of the morning to you, Mr. Haggarty," he saluted. "It's pleased I am to see you all shipshape and Bristol fashion and well recovered from your wounds."

"It was poker," said Heller. "A truly remarkable game. Very therapeutic and instructive, too. But I was thinking, Captain Bitts, now that you have my marker for $18,005, the only way you can collect it is to land me in New York and let me go to a bank."

Suddenly I penetrated the sneakiness of the man. He had worked out a way to bribe Captain Bitts! By letting him win at poker! Ah, Heller, go ahead and plot: if you succeed in getting ashore, the court will have you picked up and committed to Bellevue Hospital, thanks to Dingaling, Chase and Ambo and my ingenuity.

Mentally, I urged at Captain Bitts to fall for it. It would deliver Heller into my hands.

"Mr. Haggarty," said Captain Bitts, "this is very

tempting. But let us review the situation: The enemies of Turkey are after you; probably Russian agents dog your trail; I have my orders from the owner's concubine to not let you ashore. I regret that, even to my financial distress, the answer is no."

(Bleep) him! He thought Krak was my concubine as she had used my Squeeza credit card to buy the yacht. He was working against his own boss! Me.

"Ah, well," said Heller, "if you won't, you won't. It does happen, however, that I am a little bored. I have heard of a game called 'dice.' Could you teach me to play it?"

Captain Bitts assured him that he would be glad to, first thing after lunch.

I thought all this over. I was looking for some advantage on which to base a plan.

Something went flash in my head. I grabbed the phone and called the State Department in Washington, office of the Secretary of State. I decided to use the name of Rockecenter's law firm.

"This is Swindle and Crouch," I told the clerk.

"Yessir!" he said, instantly respectful and alert.

"There is a yacht upon the high seas called the *Golden Sunset*. There is a desperate and notorious criminal aboard, an American. I want your advice about calling the Navy Department to have her boarded and the criminal seized."

"Where is he wanted, sir?"

"There is an outstanding commitment warrant unserved in the New York Superior Court. And within a few days there will be another warrant."

"What is the national flag of the yacht, sir?"

"Turkish," I said.

"I will have to get an opinion from our Citizen Harassment Section. Please hold on."

I sat anxiously.

He came back on. "I'm terribly sorry that I have bad news, sir. We are of course devoted to the arduous task of making all possible trouble for U.S. citizens wherever they may be found, and we are usually very successful at it: just today we had a U.S. mother and her two babies seized by the Chinese after we planted contraband in their nursing bottles, so we don't want to give you the idea that we lack zeal. But through an oversight by our Legal Section, the extradition treaty between Turkey and the United States has expired and it will take several years to get the paper work from one basket to another here to get it renewed. So it would be illegal to board the yacht and seize the subject U.S. citizen."

"Oh, too bad!" I said.

"Do you know if the subject U.S. citizen has committed any crimes in Turkey? If he has, why, then we could threaten to reduce our support of their army—they're very dependent upon their army to keep the people under repressive rule—and the Turks, of course, would arrest and imprison the man."

"I'm afraid we couldn't prove any crimes in Turkey," I said.

"That's too bad," said the State Department man. "It's sort of frustrating to have some U.S. citizen out there that we can't harass and get arrested. Usually we can think of some way, unless, of course, the person is a known political terrorist: we have to protect those to keep everything stirred up and the media happy. If he isn't a registered terrorist or a drug runner, there should be some way the State Department could help make trouble in the world."

"He isn't either one of those," I said.

"Ah, wait a minute. As soon as your call came in, we flashed the information into our various sections that Swindle and Crouch was on the line, and our State Department Intelligence Chief has just slid a memo onto my desk. He recommends you call the President and have him order the CIA to simply blow the yacht out of the water. This is the routine solution to such cases and I hope it is of assistance. We can't have some U.S. citizen out of the country and unharassed, so we are only too glad to have your assistance in serving the national interest."

"Count on the Rockecenters to do that," I said and hung up.

(BLEEP)!

I couldn't put the solution into effect for two good reasons: Heller was carrying a CIA passport identifying him as H. Hider Haggarty, and the moment the CIA heard that, they would think it was one of their own men and wouldn't act. The other reason was more personal. It had really not occurred to me before that I owned that yacht!

For a bit I wondered about simply sending the captain a radio and telling him when and where to dock and have the court officers waiting there to pick up Heller. But it was too simple to work. They warn you against simple solutions in the Apparatus. It, however, was impossible because the captain would think the radio was a fake. For all he knew, the real owner was in Turkey and not in New York. Without my presenting identity to Captain Bitts personally, he would just consider my radio a ruse of the enemies of Turkey. He would show it to Heller and Heller would be alerted that I had a hand in this. Heller would tell Krak and Krak would track me down.

This train of thought collided abruptly with the fact that the Countess Krak might very well, at that moment, be following some line of investigation which would lead her to me!

A horrifying threat!

It was one of those awful days when just at the moment you were sure things couldn't get any worse, they did!

Chapter 4

The Countess Krak was in some hotel room, eating a late breakfast. The thought struck me that if I could find what hotel it was, I could get her commitment served and get her put away before she finished me!

But the silverware initials bore no clue. I watched alertly for some time, hoping that her eye would light upon something which would identify her whereabouts.

A knock on the door and Bang-Bang came in. He was carrying a huge mound of newspapers.

"I don't like to give you these, Miss Joy. Because if I do, you're going to get mad."

She took the top one. Headlines!

WHIZ KID FACING
CRIMINAL CHARGES

NEW SUITS PLAGUE
NOTORIOUS OUTLAW

In a bombshell development in Superior Court yesterday, Judge Hammer Twist set into motion the international actions which may bring Wister, the Whiz Kid, to sterilization and life imprisonment.

The deadly charge of the rape of a minor hovered above the head of the beleaguered outlaw.

New suits levied by Maizie Spread, Toots Switch and Dolores Pubiano de Cópula are certain to bring ruin and devastation to the hunted criminal....

The Countess Krak grabbed another paper. Then she grabbed a third. Then a fourth!

"BLAST!" she said. "There's no slightest mention of the cancellation of the other suits or dismissal of the false charges of bigamy! Are they on the radio or TV?"

Bang-Bang shook his head.

"I don't understand it!" wailed the Countess. "The readers are left to think those charges still exist!"

"Well, that's the way the media is," said Bang-Bang. "Their whole business is bad news. That's all they print. Any good news isn't news as far as they are concerned. Just look at the other stories on those pages there. All bad news, death and disaster. They got the insane idea that only bad news sells papers."

"But they don't even say those hussies had committed perjury and were sent to jail!" said the Countess Krak.

"Maybe that would be good news," said Bang-Bang. "You got to face it, Miss Joy. The media is as crazy as a coot."

"I don't believe that's the whole explanation," said the Countess Krak. "It looks like managed news to me."

"No, it doesn't have to be. I knew some reporters once. I've had my own brushes with the press, you know: one time they attributed a car bombing to me in the headlines and then, in little type way down at the bottom, mentioned I was still in jail. So I asked one of these reporters how come. And he said that even when the reporter got the news straight, the managing editor made him write it the other way around. Sensation sells papers is what he said. It isn't *news* they're selling, but entertainment. That's what he told me. And two or three times since, seeing what they've printed about Jet and the trouble they've dug him into, I've come up with the idea for some *real* entertainment: rigging the cars of some publishers and managing editors. You wouldn't consider it, would you?" he added hopefully.

"Well, I admit," said the Countess Krak, crumpling up a paper, "that it would be a very entertaining project. But I don't think we have time for it. I want to get all this finished and get Jettero somewhere nice and safe. He's delicate in some ways."

"I hadn't noticed," said Bang-Bang.

"Yes, he is. He's a gentleman and has a sense of decency."

"I have noticed that," said Bang-Bang.

"So somebody has to protect him from women," said the Countess Krak conclusively. "You understand, of course."

"No," said Bang-Bang.

"Well, he wouldn't even aim a blastgun at a woman, not even one as bad as these hussies."

"Hey," said Bang-Bang brightly, "you mean we're going to get my M-1 and have some target practice?"

"No, no," said the Countess. "That wouldn't do any good. Even if they were lying there dead, they'd still think of something vicious."

"That's pretty incredible," said Bang-Bang.

"No. I know such women. Criminal types. No lady-like sensibilities. And if we shot them, which I will admit they certainly deserve, I also know Jettero. He would feel sorry for them. No, we will not indulge ourselves by gunning down these sluts. You already had the best idea. What progress have you made in locating the double?"

"I got so worried about your reaction to the media that I didn't tell you what I should have told you when I first came in. Now *I'm* suppressing good news. He has surfaced."

"Aha."

"Yep. This reporter I know told me that the girls were holding a big press conference this morning, all about how this Whiz Kid is underprivileging women. That will hit the afternoon and tomorrow morning editions. And then the double will appear on ABC's 'Weirdo World' at 3:30 tomorrow afternoon, housewife prime time."

"Bang-Bang! That's wonderful news!"

"Yeah, I gotta stop reading newspapers. I'm getting like them! So anyway, he's taken advantage of this lull Judge Twist gave him to pop up, and he's going to tell the housewives how wonderful he is, I guess, or how come he's underprivileging them or something. But he'll be there. Live."

"Just what we need! And it gives us time to prepare. Not much, but enough. Quick, quick, Bang-Bang, there are some things I need. Go bring the van around right away. Oh, this is going to be great!"

Bang-Bang rushed out and she was getting into a light coat.

I didn't wait.

I called Eagle Eye Security.

"We've got her!" I said. "She'll be in the vicinity of the 'Weirdo World' talk show, ABC, tomorrow afternoon at 3:30, to kidnap the Whiz Kid."

"Hey, hey!" said the cigar-husky voice. "My men will be right on the job. Specials, too. Now that we know exactly what she looks like, she can't even disguise herself! Fifty big ones in the bag. Easiest money anyone ever made. You'll get your cut."

I could almost forego my cut. Whatever happened to me, I would have gotten rid of the Countess Krak!

Then I could take care of Heller.

And I might even think of something to save myself! The world looked much brighter!

Chapter 5

It is marvelous what heights of bravery extreme duress can lift one to: I decided I would be present at that talk show to guarantee the capture of the deadly Countess Krak.

The idea came to me that very evening as I puffed my second bhong to still my nerves and get ready for the two new girls.

Teenie unexpectedly had dropped by on her way home from school, bringing a strawberry and sausage pizza, the latest thing, for Adora and Candy.

They sat there, the three of them, eating it, and Teenie had been telling them how the Hong Kong whore detested homos, wouldn't have them on her staff and couldn't abide the sight of them—a complete reversal of the tale she had told me a day or two before. But the mention of homos had made my hands freeze and I had dropped my slice.

"Look at that (bleep)," Adora had said. "He's shaking like a dog (bleeping) bricks."

"Oh, I can fix that," Teenie had assured her, and had promptly gotten out the bhong, stuffed it and coached how long one held each puff. For some reason, I had not gone into panic but had begun to sink in a soft, gray haze. Then she loaded it up again and made sure I held each puff in, very deep and long.

I stopped shaking. I began to feel strangely brave.

They went back to eating pizza and Teenie began to regale them with a lecture they had given her at school on how to avoid "getting caught." She said, "It's awful funny, but they say a woman can get caught so easy you wouldn't believe it."

For some reason, everything else faded into babble and that phrase stuck with me.

The talk show!

If I disguised myself as an old woman, took Krak's viewer and worked behind the protection of Eagle Eye Security, two things would be accomplished: one, the Countess Krak could not slip out of their grasp; and two, thanks to the breaker switch I carried, THE HYPNO-HELMET WOULD NOT WORK IF I WERE WITH-IN TWO MILES OF IT! If she tried to get it on the Whiz Kid in that talk show, her efforts would be totally foiled.

With the Countess Krak disposed of in Bellevue, I

could somehow finish off Heller and then somehow handle Teenie. Aha! I could win this yet!

The two girls came, two brunettes. They were pretty eager. I was so enthralled with my brilliant prospects of success, I did not even mind Teenie standing there and giving pointers, though I will admit it was a relief when she couldn't wait for the end of the second one, saying she had to get back for night classes on Overt and Covert Seduction. She gave me a slap on the bare behind and with a "Keep trying, Inky," popped her bubble gum and went racing away, swinging her textbooks in a circle with their strap.

With her gone, matters soon came to a satisfactory end. Adora gave her usual sales talk, got pledges to give up Psychiatric Birth Control and the girls left beaming.

"Isn't that Teenie the sweetest thing?" said Adora. "What a difference it is making, getting a decent education under her belt."

"Indeed so," said Candy. "So thoughtful and considerate of others."

The walls seemed to be going away and then coming near and time was stopped. I was making my erratic way to the back room when

ZOOM!

My feet flew up, I did a half-turn in the air and came down

CRASH!

Stars flew through a black firmament.

I remember thinking that I hadn't known before that marijuana could cause such a sudden distortion of space. I had thought that that was reserved for its more condensed form, hashish.

I couldn't see at all!

Obviously, I had gone totally blind!

I lay there pondering the unknown pitfalls of drugs. Marijuana, reputed to be so mild, evidently could cause one to soar into the air, experience auditory concussion, bring about space views and then total blindness, just like that!

From some vast distance came the voice of Adora. "You clumsy (bleepard)! You're getting blood all over the rug! Sit up, (bleep) you! Candy, get some fabric cleaner at once and see if you can get this cleaned up before it permanently stains the white carpet!"

She was mopping at my face with a dishrag. My vision returned for a moment in one eye.

And there before me, on its side, was TEENIE'S SKATEBOARD!

My emotions were mixed. Relief that I hadn't gone blind from marijuana, but only from blood, vied with quivering hatred for Teenie. Her consideration for others which Candy had so highly praised consisted of thoughtfully placing her skateboard exactly in the middle of the dark doorway to my room!

With a constant, running lecture on how I should watch where I was going and should take care of rugs and should quit trying to find ways to disable myself and escape my husbandly duties, Adora took me to a hospital emergency room and got my forehead sewed up. Fortunately, the marijuana was still in effect and I didn't mind the needle.

In fact, that night I went to sleep quite peacefully. In spite of everything else, I knew I had an excellent chance of winning after all.

On the morrow I would surely catch the insidious Countess Krak!

Chapter 6

Strangely eager for my appointment with Fate, I dressed early the following afternoon and made my way to the ABC TV show hall.

There had been no trouble getting admission to the show, "Weirdo World." I had been on the phone to the head of Eagle Eye Security and he had told me they had reserved a seat for me in the audience. He was very eager to have my help. "The place will be jammed with our security people," he had said, "but she has slipped through our fingers before and it will help to have positive identification on hand. The process server will be there. She won't get away this time!"

Disguise had not been much of a problem: my face was swathed in bandages, so much so that I could only see through a slit.

Light was painful to my eyes and I had not wasted any time watching Krak's viewer. She would make her appearance at that show, that was certain. To Hells with the details: not even she could escape such a net.

When I arrived, I quickly located the Eagle Eye Security officer. He was a huge man, dressed in khaki, girded about with armament. He was standing in the foyer, giving each of a dozen security men individual instructions and sending them to their posts.

I plucked at his sleeve. Annoyedly, he pushed at me. "Beat it, you old bat," he said. "Can't you see I'm busy?"

I laughed delightedly. I was disguised as an old

woman with a floppy hat and had smeared bootblacking on the bandages to give me a black face. He thought I was some Negress! "It's you that's the bat," I said, "for I have heard they are quite blind. I'm Smith, you idiot, the man Dingaling, et cetera, take their orders from."

"Well, Jesus Christ," said the security officer.

"No, Smith," I corrected him. "Care to fill me in on your arrangements?"

"Oh, yes, sir! The ABC people always cooperate with the powers that be. We've got the whole TV theater boxed in. The 'Weirdo World' M.C., Tom Snide, is quite excited at the idea there may be some action on his show. And they've got extra cameras at every angle. Even mobile cameras outside. The Whiz Kid is being delivered by a Blinks Armored Truck. What's that you're carrying?"

"A portable TV," I misinformed him. It was Krak's viewer. "I want to catch the show the way it goes out over the air as well as in the theater."

"All right. Your seat is middle row and on the aisle. Here's a two-way walkie-talkie that connects with me, in case you spot anything we don't."

"Good thinking," I said, taking it. "But you keep your eyes open, too. I'm not seeing very well today. I'm counting on you."

"Oh, you can," he said, giving his huge automatic's holster a pat. "I'm practically spending my part of that bounty money already. Oh, one more thing: these ABC people cautioned us that once the red light is on, we have to be quiet and we're to stay off the stage unless the woman herself shows up. Then Snide can give us a signal and they can get the nab on the camera."

"Fine," I said and made my way to my seat.

The place was packed with women and one more skirt went totally unnoticed.

I settled myself. I had a good seat from which to see things. The place was like any other theater except it had more camera and spotlight positions. It was, however, hard for me to take in everything through my bandages. Things looked kind of pink and I suspected my forehead was bleeding again. But minor things must not stand in the way of an Apparatus officer. Lombar Hisst and the fate of the Voltar Confederacy were depending on me, to say nothing of the fate of Earth!

The show was about to start: a big clock was giving a countdown to curtain. Some music was playing to keep the audience quiet, but there was a lot of excited chatter going on all around. Housewives of every shape and hue were packing this show today to lay eyes on the Whiz Kid.

I concentrated on Krak's viewer. It was hard to see.

She was sitting in a little room. A slight twinge of alarm went through me. She ought to be preparing herself in some disguise or other to penetrate this show. She wasn't. She had a little TV set in front of her and she had a couple of microphones in her hands.

Where was this room?

In this building? Miles away? Lacking recorded strips to check back on, I could not tell how she had gotten there.

This whole thing was very irregular. The show was about to begin.

But then I relaxed. She could not possibly resist the bait of the Whiz Kid double. She thought he was vital to her plan to find out who was behind this barrage of legal suits on Heller.

Bang-Bang's voice came through the viewer speaker. "I introduced him."

Krak said to the dimness beyond the TV set, "And he knows the route?"

"Showed it to him twice," said Bang-Bang.

I was a little bit baffled. How could Bang-Bang have introduced anybody to anybody? The show hadn't started! I thought, she certainly better get a move on or she'll be late for this show.

The curtains parted. Buzzers went. Red lights flashed. *On the Air* appeared in a big panel. A girl in a housecoat held up a huge card. It said:

APPLAUD

Music blared. Tom Snide himself pranced out on the stage throwing kisses. He was an older man with curly hair and a very false smile. "Good afternoon, good afternoon, housewives of America, my dearest friends who keep sweeping my popularity from coast to coast."

The girl in the housecoat held up a card:

LAUGH

"Just don't sweep it under the rug," said Snide.

The girl held up a card:

LAUGH HARDER

"Welcome to 'Weirdo World'!" said Snide. "I'm sure all of you feel right at home."

The girl held up a card:

HOWL WITH LAUGHTER

"Today we were lucky enough to get on our show a

young man who has stirred the hearts and skirts of America and the world. And here he is, the weirdo you've been panting for, the notorious outlaw, WISTER, THE WHIZ KID!"

The girl held up a card:

SHRIEK!

The Wister double peeked out from behind a potted palm, raced over to cover behind a desk and then hid behind a piano.

"What are you ducking for?" said Snide.

"I'm afraid that audience will swarm over the footlights and rape me," said the double.

The girl held up a card:

SAY OOOOO WITH DELIGHT

"No, no," said Snide. "We've packed the place with security guards so they can't get at you. Come out in plain sight."

"And no process servers?" said the double.

The girl held up a card:

SHRIEK WITH LAUGHTER!

The audience shrieked, but Tom Snide had lied. The shabby man in the shabby coat was peering out from under the brim of his shabby hat, just two seats away from me. His face was all bandaged up, too! But he was waiting for the Countess Krak, commitment paper in his hand. And then I looked just beyond him. Two Bellevue attendants! They must have a wagon outside waiting.

I glanced at my viewer. The Countess Krak was sitting there watching the show on TV!

A camera swept the shrieking housewives. I saw it on the Countess Krak's screen. The camera, amongst the others, SHOWED ME!

I scrunched down. Oh, Gods, she had better not notice!

Then her screen, seen through my viewer, was again showing the stage.

The Whiz Kid swaggered into full view. He was dressed in the black of a Western outlaw, but had red hearts for pistol holsters. His buckteeth and horn-rimmed glasses did not go too well with the rig.

He sat down in the interview chair.

"How do you do it?" Snide said. "Get all these women so crazy over you that they sue you for billions?"

"I guess it just comes natural," said the double.

The girl held up a card:

LAUGH WHILE SAYING OOOOOO

"When you really get into it, it's easy to understand," said the Whiz Kid.

Card:

LAUGH LOUDER WHILE OOOING LOUDER

"The women all over the country seem utterly crazy over you," said Snide. "Doesn't that seem sort of weird?"

"It's a hard life," said the double. "And the longer I'm at it, the harder it gets."

Card:

SCREAM WITH LAUGHTER
WHILE OOOING WITH SCREAMS

"Most men," said the double, "couldn't stand up to it, and I admit I have been lying down on the job."

Card:

SHRIEK WITH LAUGHTER

"I understand they want to arrest you now for raping a minor," said Snide. "I shouldn't have thought you would have stooped to that."

"Well, she was pretty short," said the Whiz Kid.

Card:

HOWL WITH LAUGHTER

"With all these legal entanglements," said Snide, "I should imagine you have pretty steep legal fees."

"It's worth it," said the Whiz Kid double. "But the real cost is in replacing pants I have to leave behind when the husband comes home unexpectedly."

Card:

LAUGH LIKE MAD

Snide said, "Well, if you are going to devote all your spare time between robbing trains and stealing cities to hopping in and out of beds, I think your legal fees will soon exceed what you find in the Wells Fargo boxes. The law is a pretty expensive business. How do you propose to solve it when this bed-hopping bankrupts you?"

"I'll act as my own lawyer," said the double. "Nothing is going to keep me from tasting the pleasures of the flesh. The country is absolutely crammed with beautiful women with nothing to do after their husbands leave for work." Then in a whisper, barely audible on the program, he said, leaning toward Tom, "Hey, you're off the script."

"Well," said Snide, ignoring the double's aside, "we'll just see how well versed you are in law. We have a lawyer here to interrogate you on the subject of law."

Another sound. Voltarian! I thought I had lost my wits. Then I located it. It was coming from my viewer. The Countess Krak had her left-hand microphone in her hand and into it she had said, "Cue. Walk to center stage." In VOLTARIAN!

Snide had risen and was making an elaborate, ushering bow.

ONTO CENTER STAGE WALKED MISTER CALICO!

Oh, indeed Snide was off the script!

The cat had a black harness. It was wearing a big, black bow tie. It surveyed the audience.

"Chair on your right," said the Countess Krak in Voltarian into her left-hand mike.

The cat jumped up on the second interview chair. It sat down, looking at the Whiz Kid double.

"What the hell is this?" said the double. "That's no attorney. That's a cat!"

The cat opened its jaws. It said, "I am a lawyer cat."

The girl with the cards was just standing there staring. The audience was open-mouthed.

A talking cat!

Oh, that devil Krak. I knew exactly what she had done. She was using Eyes and Ears of Voltar gear. She had a mike hidden in the cat's ear to direct it and she had a speaker hidden in the cat's tie so she could talk through the cat. And she'd even trained the cat to open and close its mouth when it heard the speaker going. (Bleep) her!

Snide was in on it! The fool had fallen for it as an unheard-of novelty! Snide said to the cat, "The Whiz Kid seems to doubt your credentials, Lawyer Calico. Perhaps you had better convince him."

The cat—Krak talking through her right-hand mike —said, "He should understand the PURR-pose of the law."

The girl with the cards had recovered. She raised a card:

LAUGH

The audience didn't read the card. They were saying, "A talking cat." "It's really talking." "What a cute cat." "Listen to it TALK!"

"Snide," said the cat, "you have a very disorderly audience." It turned to the seats. "Order in the court!"

Snide banged a gavel. "I am sorry, Lawyer Calico. Continue with your credentials."

Krak, watching her TV of the show, leaned into her right-hand mike. The cat seemed to say, "Cats are the very basic of the law. All cases begin with a CAT-alogue of crimes."

The girl raised her card:

LAUGH

It wasn't needed. The audience was laughing.

Where the Hells was Krak operating from? I grabbed the walkie-talkie. I said, "That's her, making the cat talk!"

"We'll handle," said the security officer back.

"Continue," said Snide to the cat.

The cat seemed to say, "The law violently opposes anything DOG-matized. Police CAT and MOUSE with criminals. Criminals RAT on one another. Judges think everyone is a RAT. And the end product of any legal action is a CAT-astrophe!"

The audience, uncoached, was screaming with laughter.

"But Snide," the cat seemed to say, "I'll give you the final proof that I am indeed a lawyer cat."

Krak was whispering orders into her left-hand mike.

The cat got up off the chair and jumped onto the Whiz Kid double's knee. It seemed to pull something out of its harness. It was sniffing into the Whiz Kid's pockets. Had it put something in one?

"What are you doing?" said Snide.

"I'm doing what every lawyer does," said the cat.

Suddenly it grabbed the double's wallet out of his hip pocket!

It clenched the wallet in its teeth.

It ran off the stage!

THE DOUBLE RACED AFTER IT!

The audience howled with laughter.

I screamed into the walkie-talkie, "FOLLOW THAT CAT!"

Ignoring the red lights, security men were all over the stage, racing across it after the cat.

I leaped up and sped after them!

On their trail, I burst out of an outside door just in time to see the cat streaking down a long flight of steps. The double was speeding in its wake.

A van, different from the one they had had before, was sitting at the bottom of those steps!

Yikes! The cat had planted Unit B on the double and had the Unit A on itself! The follow-compellers!

The cat was almost to the van!

ZWOOOP!

The double, racing down the steps, seemed to fly into a bundle of whirling arms and legs. He hurtled toward the bottom.

He lit!

The security guards were streaming down the steps.

ZWOOP! ZWOOP! ZWOOP! ZWOOP! ZWOOP!

They were skidding like they were on a toboggan slide!

I was running forward.

I was going down the steps.

Bang-Bang had the double by the collar and was throwing him into the van.

The security men were landing in a disorderly pile.

ZWOOP!

My own legs went in six directions at once and I rocketed down the steps in a power dive.

I landed on my head.

Security men were all around me in piles.

The security officer at the top screamed, "GET THAT VEHICLE NUMBER!" Then he started down.

I looked at the speeding van. It was roaring down an alley and away.

IT HAD NO LICENSE PLATES!

The security chief landed near me with a thud.

I couldn't account for any of this.

What had caused such a catastrophe?

And then I looked at the steps.

The cat could run down them but nobody else could.

THEY WERE COVERED WITH BANANA PEELS!

PART FIFTY-FOUR

Chapter 1

The Eagle Eye Security officer picked himself up off the pavement. He was shaking his fist down the alley in the direction the van had disappeared. "I'll get you if it's the last thing I ever do!" he screamed. He whirled. "What make of van was that?" he roared at his men.

They were unscrambling themselves and picking banana peels off their messed up uniforms.

"Transvan!" said one.

"Econoline," said another.

"Quicklay," said a third.

All they could agree upon was that it had no license plates, was white and was basically commercial. I already knew there were tens of thousands of such vans in New York.

"You goofed!" I screamed. "You let them get away!"

"Please God!" cried the security officer, "give us another chance." He was pointing to the process server and the two Bellevue attendants who had come up, strait-jackets in their hands. "I'll get that process served and that fiend committed if I have to do it myself!"

"Go ahead!" I said. And he rushed off to phone police and put up roadblocks and get helicopter coverage and do the other things they do.

I made my way back to the "Weirdo World" talk

show, where Tom Snide was ending off his half hour
with slides of famous outlaw lovers of history. He seemed
to be pretty annoyed that his audience of hand-picked
females were talking to one another about the cat. "In
short," he said, "when you look at some of these skinny
runts and compare them to a virile type like me, you
wonder what women see in such men."

"What a CAT-ty remark!" some blonde in the front
row yelled loud enough to get it into the mikes.

Screams of laughter rolled through the TV theater.
In vain, the card girl in the housecoat held up her sign:

REVERENT COOS

"We're tired of your PUSS!" another called, not to
be outdone.

That started them all off and they were vying for
who could get off the vilest puns about the cat.

Snide could look after himself. I grabbed my viewer
off the floor where it had fallen and got out of there.

It was up to me, I knew.

I was not in very good shape. My head was hurting
from falling on it, my eye had begun to bleed and I was
literally seeing red. But an Apparatus officer has to have
stamina and overlook his pain. One must have courage.

Besides, I was afraid I might be overdue for my afternoon appointment with lesbians at the apartment. Adora
must get no suspicion that I had to figure out how to do
in Krak and Heller and run, before the homo education
began. Teenie I would get to, somehow, some way.

All the way to the apartment in a cab, I watched the
viewer.

A police car screamer was sounding, rising, in the
speaker.

The Countess was holding the cat. She had taken off the bow tie and the harness. She was rubbing the cat's ears and petting him and the cat was absolutely grinning! I had heard that witches on Earth had cats but they were usually black, and this cat only had a few black patches amongst the orange and white.

Also, the Countess was not riding on a broomstick. She was riding along in a van with a posh interior. The curtains were closed and she had on interior lights.

"That squad car seems to be interested in us," came Bang-Bang's voice through a curtain, beyond which must have been the driver's seat. "He's checking the license plate."

"They aren't stolen, are they?" said the Countess.

"Hell, no—beggin' your pardon, ma'am. Mike Mutazione has his own stamping machine. You couldn't trace the plates I just flipped on if you were the governor of New York!"

The screamer was dwindling.

"He's gone now," said Bang-Bang.

"You better take us to that hidden place they used to transfer booze in," said the Countess Krak. "We don't have time to play tag with the police. We've got work to do."

If she would just look outside or mention an address, I'd have her! But all she was looking at was that (bleeped) cat. Ye Gods, its purr was so loud in the speaker, I thought for some time it was their engine! What an insufferable feline!

They drove on. I had no way of knowing their destination or location unless they made a mistake and mentioned it.

Eyes glued redly to the viewer, I overpaid my cab at the apartment and stumbled in.

I got out of my disguise, still watching the viewer. They stopped!

Mister Calico jumped out of the Countess's arms and went through the front curtain. Then Bang-Bang's hand came into view and swept the dividers aside. I could see straight through their windshield.

A warehouse!

But where?

There are hundreds of thousands of warehouses in Manhattan. Still, they might drop a clue.

The Countess Krak must have been sitting in an easy chair that pivoted. When Bang-Bang entered the back, she swung it around.

There, lying on a couch crossways to the van, was the Whiz Kid double.

He was tied hand and foot.

He was gagged.

His black outlaw costume wasn't doing him any good at all. His eyes were wild with fear.

I suddenly detected a new sound. I turned up the speaker volume. Lapping water! This warehouse was over some stream or river! An old bootleg warehouse! It would have a trap door where they could unload small boats up through the floor or dump bodies into the tide!

Gods help the Whiz Kid double, I thought. The deadly Countess Krak was going to end his days as soon as she was through with him! Oh, the poor double! Imagine being in the hands of such a murderous monster! I shuddered. But better him than me.

"Bang-Bang, if you will just step outside and make sure we're not disturbed, I think I can make him talk."

"Pretty bloody, eh?" said Bang-Bang. "In that event I'll also take the cat: he's pretty young to be watching violence, even if he does have a criminal record."

The Countess Krak was taking off the double's gag.

"Does that cat have a criminal record?" spluttered the double. "I thought he was a lawyer!"

"What's the difference?" said Bang-Bang. "To his long list of murders, we now have to add kidnapping. But what's going to happen now is too strong for him. I wouldn't give two catnip mice for your life, kid. So answer the lady polite. The cat and I will be right outside and I'll let him in again if you don't sing."

This was far too confused for the double. "I'm innocent. I don't know anything."

"Go along, Bang-Bang," said the Countess.

Bang-Bang halted at the side door, holding it open. I couldn't see anything but warehouse wall. "I'll loosen up one of the old trap doors," he said. "Just in case he doesn't talk." The cat jumped out and Bang-Bang closed the door.

"I don't know anything," said the double. "I just do what I'm told."

"Ah," said the Countess Krak, "but who tells you?"

My hair went straight up underneath my bandages. In sweeping horror, it was fully borne home to me that if this double knew the name of Madison, the Countess Krak would grab Madison. And if Madison was questioned, he would mention and describe the man he knew as Smith—me. And the Countess Krak would know absolutely that I was behind all this. I would be DEAD! The image of the sightless eyes of the yellow-man rose between me and the viewer. The blood in my eye tinted it red. I had to sit down as my knees began to shake.

"I won't tell you who tells me," said the double, buckteeth truculently protruding.

"Ah, well," said the Countess Krak. "You leave me no choice."

She reached down to a shopping bag and pulled out the hypnohelmet. She pulled it down over the horrified head of the Whiz Kid double and turned it on. He suddenly slumped in his bonds.

She picked up the helmet microphone. "Sleep, sleep, pretty sleep. You will now tell me the truth, the whole truth and nothing but the truth, or be indicted for the felony of perjury. Who gives you your orders?"

"A man."

"What man?"

"I don't know."

Krak took a recording strip and put it in the helmet slot and pushed the button to Record. "Now," she said, "you will begin to tell me everything you know about becoming the double of the real Wister."

The double began his tale. He was an orphan, born in Georgia. By government student loans he had gotten into the Massachusetts Institute of Wrectology. He was getting along when suddenly he was called in and told that a man wanted to see him. The man had offered him a job. Money and women. He was simply to follow orders and appear where he was supposed to and say what he was told to say.

He had wanted to know what about his school and the man said that would all be cared for, that he couldn't fail.

The man had said that from time to time it might look like he was being put in jail but that wasn't anything to worry about because there was a REAL person, Jerome Terrance Wister, and that if the chips fell the wrong way, it would be THAT one who would go to jail, finally.

He had wanted to know how come this fellow had the name Wister also; he had heard once that he had had a brother but had never known where he was. His own name was Gerry Wister and he dimly recalled the brother's name was Jerome. But the man said not to worry about that, it didn't make any difference.

"You mean," said the Countess Krak, "that you believed that the man you were helping to wreck was your own brother?"

"Well, sort of," the double replied, "but the man explained that they were just trying to make my brother famous."

"By putting him in jail?"

"Well, there was all that money they offered me and the women they promised."

The Countess Krak pushed the mike into her chest. "What primitives! No sense of honor!" Then, to him, "Continue."

The double rattled on in the muffled way of the wholly hypnotized.

The Countess Krak was beginning to get impatient. She was tapping her foot. She had heard a lot of this history of racing and Atlantic City and Kansas before and the only difference now was that she was hearing it was all cooked up by somebody.

I was very, very nervous.

The double at length ran down.

"So what was the name of this man?" said the Countess Krak.

"I called him Ed."

I began to breathe more easily. The double had had no dealing directly with Madison.

But then at the next question, my heart missed a beat.

"Who pays you?" said the Countess Krak.

She might hit paydirt with this!

"Cash in an envelope."

"What's on the envelope?"

"Nothing."

Her foot was tapping faster with impatience. "Is there anything IN the envelope except cash?"

"Only the receipt I sign and give back to Ed."

"And what is on the receipt?"

"The amount. And I initial it."

"Anything else?"

"Only the letters F.F.B.O."

"What do they stand for?"

"I don't know," came the muffled reply.

"F.F.B.O. That's all?"

"That's all."

My hair was standing up. F.F.B.O. stood for Fatten, Farten, Burstein and Ooze, the advertising and PR giants that handled the Rockecenter accounts and employed J. Walter Madison for this particular black PR campaign. Oh, the careless, stupid fools! Their accounts department was out-security!

And then I was greatly heartened. I had just remembered what Bury had told me. You had to be in the advertising world itself to know what F.F.B.O. stood for. It was even a test of being a professional advertising man!

The Countess drilled some more. But that was all she learned.

Satisfied at last, she got on to other work. "Now, you are going to do something," she said. "You are going to go into Superior Court and stand before the judge and you are going to state that every crime Jerome Terrance Wister is supposed to have done, you did. You owe it to the honor of your family. So you will do it without fail. You will state this in such a way that Jerome Terrance Wister will be absolved of all past charges and any current ones. It is YOUR face that is known on TV and in pictures and you will convince the judge that this is so. This includes marriages and adultery and the rape of a minor. And if anybody tells you to do different, you won't. Understood?"

"Yes."

"Now, you will also write a full confession that this is all a put-up job and will begin the moment you awake and I give you paper. Understood?"

"Yes."

"Now you will forget you have been kidnapped or hypnotized and will think you came to me with this as your own idea and you will stay with us and not run away until you appear in court. Understood?"

"Yes."

She clicked off the helmet and removed it from his head. He was looking around dazedly, trying to find something.

The Countess untied him. She gave him pen and paper and sat him at a small table in the van and he began to write.

She put the helmet in her shopping bag. She went outside.

I was wringing wet with sweat. What could I do to keep my world from totally caving in?

Bang-Bang was sitting on an old box, the cat beside him.

"Bang-Bang," said the Countess Krak, "what does 'F.F.B.O.' stand for?"

"I dunno," said Bang-Bang. "Some deodorant maybe?"

"Is there any Mafia mob with those initials?" said the Countess.

"Nope," said Bang-Bang. "But when they ship

things, they go 'F.O.B.' It means 'Freight On Board.'"

"That's not it. What did you do with his wallet?"

"Right here," said Bang-Bang. "Nothing in it. Just a few bucks and student cards."

The Countess went through it. She shook her head. "Well," she said, "we'll get busy and find out. It must stand for *something*."

"There's Peegrams V.O. Scotch," said Bang-Bang. "And the cat and I could use some."

"Not yet," said the Countess Krak. She sat down on another box and took a pad out of her purse. "Poor Jettero must be going mad out there, wondering. I'm writing a radio message calling the yacht in. We've got the double and tomorrow he'll appear in court. The yacht won't be in until after that occurs, so it's perfectly safe. So you send this radio to Captain Bitts and tell him to dock in New York. What was the pier he said? Oh, yes. Pier 68, West 30th Street. By the time he gets there it will be tomorrow evening and the phony Whiz Kid will be on his way to jail."

She wrote it. She handed it over. Bang-Bang walked away.

I could not believe my luck!

She didn't recall Judge Hammer Twist would not be in court tomorrow! He'd be at the Aqueduct race track! Or she thought foolishly he would return for an important case the way they would on Voltar. But no Earth judge would ever put his duty before his pleasure.

Oh, thank Gods for this sloppy, slow court system! Heller would not only be picked up but would be safely in Bellevue and maybe even dead before she ever got her confession before the judge!

The seizure of Heller would drive her out of her

mind! And if they killed him, she'd be so grief-stricken, she'd be no menace to anybody!

I might not know where she was. But I was saved after all!

I reached for the phone to call Grafferty.

That yacht would be MET!

Chapter 2

The next morning my eyes hurt and I only gave Heller's viewer a quick glance. He was staring at the ceiling, apparently still in his bunk, and I thought, go ahead and daydream, Heller, it will turn into a nightmare before sunset today.

I had something else to do before we met the yacht. It is always best to play things safe.

If the Countess got to Madison before I got to Heller, J. Warbler would undoubtedly identify me and I would be dead.

My bandages had been changed: Adora had been certain that I would scare the lesbians last night if I had a boot-blacked face. I dressed in some khaki outing clothes, hoping somebody would think I was a veteran from the wars or maybe some street shoot-out.

I grabbed a cab.

At Madison's 42 Mess Street offices, all was at the usual high hubbub.

It was not a good time to try to persuade Madison to go into hiding. He was in utter euphoria. They had a huge blowup on the wall. It said:

SEX–STARVED BEAUTY
KIDNAPS WHIZ KID
————
TRAINS CAT TO
EFFECT SNATCH

In front of 50,000,000 American housewives,
the notorious sex outlaw Wister . . .

"Mad," I said, trying to get his attention, "I've got to talk to you about something important."

"Don't bother me, Smith. I'm handling the hottest story since Julius Caesar raped Cleopatra in a rug. Empires could fall on this."

"I'm sure they could," I said.

"What if it turned out to be the president's wife!" he said ecstatically. "Hey, Hacky! I just got an idea!" And he went rushing off to stir things up in his already earthquaking staff room.

I could only hang around. They wrote up tomorrow's headlines wherein all the wives of Washington joined the wives of Kansas in demanding the Whiz Kid be given diplomatic privileges in their beds, cancelled that in favor of mobs of minors in California lining up in hope of being raped by the Whiz Kid, abandoned that and got out new headlines to the effect that a nationwide cat hunt was going on to find the cat and get him to tell all. They put that on the wire.

"The animal angle always gets them," said Madison, sinking down at his desk, utterly spent but happy. "The day after, the cat will tell all in the most sexy details you ever imagined!"

"Madison," I said, "I have to warn you that danger is in the air. Would F.F.B.O. tell anybody who it was who handles this account on the Whiz Kid?"

"Oh, I doubt they would," said Madison. "Professional jealousy. It would be giving my name a plug, you see, and they are too consumed with envy to do that. The answer is 18 point NO."

"Nevertheless," I said, "it might leak out that you were the account executive. Mad, there are some things you don't know about the REAL Wister. He has killed fifty-five men since he has been around here."

"WHAT?"

"Fact. I've counted them up. He added fifteen just the other day by blowing up the docks at Atlantic City. Fifty-five dead men, Madison. And you could be number fifty-six."

"Holy gunsmoke!" said Madison. "Billy the Kid only killed twenty-one! Say, do you realize that the real Wister is sneaking up on Wild Bill Hickok's seventy-six? Lord above, that Wister really *is* outlaw potential! I thought I was stretching his capabilities. Now *he's* stretching my credulity! Fifty-five men. Wow! Smith, I think I really *can* build this man up to immortality. No doubt of it at all!"

"Mad," I said, "please listen to me. I will spell it out. Your life is in danger!"

He was thoughtful. Then he said, "It wouldn't be the first time my life has been threatened. It sort of goes with the job of a PR."

"Mad," I said, "this isn't just a threat." I looked at him. I had a sinking feeling that I was getting no place. Then I had a brilliant idea. "You want to know how dangerous this fellow is?"

"Yes, indeed! Might make good copy."

"All right," I said. "Call Narcotici's personnel department and try to buy a contract on the real Wister."

"Hey, that makes a good headline: 18 point Contract Out On Whiz Kid.."

"Mad, not phony headlines. This is for real. Get a solid bottom under your news for once. Make the call."

"Novel idea," said Madison. "I'll do it." He reached for the phone and connected with the personnel department. "Personnel," he said, "this is F.F.B.O. I'd like a quote for a contract on Jerome Terrance Wister.... Yes, I'll hold." He turned to me, "For some reason they're shifting the call." He returned to his phone. "Yes, that's right. A contract on Jerome Terrance Wister."

I couldn't hear the other end of the call. Madison was listening. Then his eyes went round. Then he went white. He hung up, staring into space.

I said, "Well, what did they say?"

His attention was very hard to get. I had to repeat my question three times.

Finally he said, "We're in trouble. They shifted my call to Razza Louseini, the *consigliere*. He wanted to know if I was the one who pushed their men on to Wister last fall. I didn't know they'd lost nineteen of their mobsters and a million bucks. They're furious. I hope they didn't recognize my voice."

"How so?" I said, secretly delighted at his depressed state.

"Razza Louseini said that if they found out who had gotten them into that mess, they had orders to put a contract out on *him!*"

"You see?" I said triumphantly. "Wister is *dangerous*."

"Oh, I think I could handle the real Wister," Madison said. "I've met him and talked to him. He's a nice fellow, really. What I'm worried about is the Narcotici mob." He stirred himself and focused his eyes on me. "Look, Smith. Promise me you'll keep it secret that I was the one behind it. You can't live in New York or even the U.S. with the Mafia gunning for you."

Oh, I promised him faithfully that his secret was safe with me. But only the bandages on my face could hide the glee I felt. I now knew how to persuade Madison to make himself scarce if I had to. He was sitting there, kind of white, glancing uneasily out the window. Then he took his finger and loosened his collar which must have seemed too tight. The hand was shaking.

Chapter 3

A call to Grafferty's office elicited the information that, according to the harbor traffic control, the *Golden Sunset* would dock at 1600 hours at Pier 68 and all was going smoothly.

I wanted very much to be on hand and witness Heller's downfall as he stepped ashore into the waiting arms of police. I wanted to see his face as they shoved him in the wagon and whisked him off to Bellevue and mental extinction.

Accordingly, I was very much on time.

Two squad cars and the wagon were parked well out of sight in the warehouse. Cops were behind boxes of cargo with riot guns. The usual Federal services of immigration and customs were all that were in sight, and even though the yacht had not been foreign and really didn't have to clear in, they were on hand in their usual capacity of maximum annoyance and in this case served as cover.

I spotted Grafferty.

"I want this (bleepard)," Police Inspector Grafferty said. "I spotted him in a sex-pervert lineup three years ago and have just been waiting for him to make his first misstep. And now he has: He's brought himself to the attention of a psychiatrist. Fatal every time. And speaking of psychiatrists, what happened to your face?"

"Skateboards at point-blank range," I said.

"Oh, yeah. I remember now. You're the Fed that tipped us off about the Skateboard Bandits. I never forget a face. We never caught them, you know. But thanks for the tip. I wish this yacht would hurry up and come in."

"Busy day?" I said.

"Yeah, I've got to organize a police escort for the mayor's wife. She's going to make a speech tonight on the subject of mental health and she always drives the audience crazy. There comes the yacht now."

The *Golden Sunset* was coming up the Hudson. A tug got a line aboard her and took her in tow for the last quarter mile. She was a beautiful ship, all white with gold scrolls, more like a cruise liner than a yacht. The red Turkish flag with its yellow star and crescent floated out from her taffrail in the Hudson River breeze. Gulls were spiralling around. Helicopters from the nearby heliport added to the busy scene.

The tug, with many toots going back and forth from the yacht bridge to the tug pilothouse, nudged her into the berth. Ye Gods, she was big. I hadn't realized how large two hundred feet and two thousand tons of ship could be.

They were getting a gangway into her opened rail and the Federal mob swarmed aboard to suspect things and annoy people. They weren't in on what we intended. They all came off after a while, bitterly disappointed to have found no Chinese being smuggled in and thwarted in their efforts, by a vigilant crew, to plant contraband.

Now was our chance. People could come off.

Instead of that, two people went on. They were the butler from Heller's condo and Krak's lady's maid.

We watched the gangway and the hawsers. Nobody could get off that ship without our seeing it. We knew better than to go aboard, only to have the quarry sneak ashore behind us.

The butler and the lady's maid, assisted by several crew members, were bringing the Countess Krak's baggage to the pier and waiting taxis.

"Where is this guy?" said Grafferty, growing restless.

And there came Captain Bitts.

At the bottom of the gangway, Grafferty stopped him. "You have a passenger. And you better tell me where he is and that he has to come quietly."

"A passenger?" said Bitts. "Oh, you must mean the CIA man."

I lurked behind crates on the dock. I did not want to be seen. Also, I wanted to be out of the road of gunfire. I knew Heller's habits.

"I mean this man!" said Grafferty, displaying a blowup of Wister.

"Yeah," said Captain Bitts. "That man." He gazed back at the ship. "Well, he wanted us to teach him how to shoot dice. I don't know how he did it. He won back his marker. Then he won all my cash. And then he won all the crew's cash. And finally, he offered to bet us all he'd won against our putting him ashore if he could shoot five sevens in a row. Of course, that's impossible, so we made the wager."

Grafferty was impatient. "Well, WHAT HAP-PENED?"

Bitts sighed. "The worst of it was, we afterwards sawed the dice in half and they weren't even loaded. So we put him ashore last night on the Jersey coast. By the way, as you're a cop, could you let me have two bits so I can phone the credit company and get some money? There's not a dime left on the ship. We're cleaned out."

I drew back quickly. Grafferty was raving about illegal landings and Bitts was replying about New Jersey wasn't New York, and when did the CIA become illegal aliens? It was pretty messy. I got out of there.

The dirty, filthy sneak! Typical of Heller!

That ceiling I had seen him looking at early this morning must have been a motel! And Gods knew where.

Oh, this was not going well!

As I grabbed a taxi at the West 30th Street Heliport, close to hand, I looked back at the yacht.

Suddenly, just like that, I got a terrific PLAN!

Even if all went wrong, left and right, I was not lost after all!

The plan was utterly brilliant!

Chapter 4

The evening stint was only made endurable by the fact that I had an out.

Teenie came by to brag about how well she was doing in school and how wonderful it was to have a competent lot of instructors at last.

"There's nothing like a proper education," she told the two lesbians of the evening as she helped them undress. "Some men find the passive mode most inviting. When you see them naked, you fall back and look exactly like you are dead. You "

"GET HER OUT OF HERE!" I roared.

Adora was upbraiding me instantly. "You unfeeling brute. One must encourage the young in their school work! Not bellow at them! There, there, Teenie. Did he hurt your feelings?"

"Nothing that a new skateboard wouldn't heal," said Teenie. "He dented it and bent a wheel. I've got to go to a night class on advanced orgiastics. There's a sporting-goods mart open, and if I leave right now I'll have time to get a new skateboard. It's only two hundred dollars."

Anything to get rid of her. I grabbed out the two hundred dollars and threw them at her. Before I could put my roll back she slipped off another twenty. "There's tax," she said, and sailed away, spinning the books upon their strap and laughing gaily about something I could not make out.

"What a little dear," sighed Adora. "And such opportunities are opening up. Before you came home, Candy, she was telling me that she had a Hollywood offer to star in a picture of her own, *I Was a Teen-age Porno Queen*."

I was about to say that I'd heard lies before but that was probably the biggest yet. But I stopped myself in time.

The two lesbians had stripped by now and lay upon the bed. One of them said, "Passive mode? Let me see if I can do it." And she laid back like she was dead.

That did it. It took two bhongs before I could perform on the first one and another before I could even touch the second.

Finally I managed it. I felt stoned but relaxed. The walls were sagging in and going away while Adora made her sales pitch to the now ex-lesbians. It was nice to be so detached.

And then suddenly I wasn't.

The wife member of the team had just said, "Oh, this real thing really is good. I never in my life thought anyone could get that much bang out of a bang. But I don't think once in three weeks is often enough."

Adora said, "Have no fear. In just three days, we begin to reform those chauvinistic pigs of homos, and with my husband's demonstrations, believe you me, kiddo, the place will be full of standing ovations. I can just see their buttons pop when they behold him pumping away, doing the real thing. They won't be able to restrain themselves!"

I went ice cold. The vision I got was entirely different from hers!

Bumping off door jambs, I got to my room. I locked the door. I fell upon the sofa. I lay there shivering. I also felt like I was running a fever.

Would my plan work?

Would I make it in time?

If the Fates decreed NO to both, then I might as well blow my brains out, for life would become utterly unsupportable.

Too stoned and too blind to watch viewers, I wrapped myself in blankets and fell into awful nightmares where I did not make it and wound up in the Manco Devil's Hell, raped for eternity by homo Demons, even though I blew my brains out daily!

Chapter 5

I awoke late. I looked at my watch. Shock jolted through me! It was past 10:00 A.M. The court might already have opened!

Pushing bandages out of my eyes, I gripped the viewer. Yes! A view of the courtroom!

I freaked!

Hastily I rang Eagle Eye. The man with the cigar-husky voice answered. "You still want that fifty G's?" I said.

"The bounty on that woman? The one who is to be committed? The one our security officer is thirsting to nail? YES, INDEED!"

"She's in the courtroom of Judge Hammer Twist right this moment. I do not think the court has opened. If you can get there fast you can nab her!"

"Gone!" he said, and hung up.

Anxiously I looked at the viewer. No, the court had not opened yet: the bench was empty. But there were lots of people in the place, from the amount of comings and goings in the front of the room. I tried to spot exactly what row she was in. I couldn't because she kept turning her head from left, where an older man was sitting, to right. The double! The Whiz Kid double was sitting next to her!

The woman was sly and cunning but she was also stupid. The commitment order was still in force and yet all she seemed concerned about was this double. There was a briefcase on her lap. Oh, this was like bringing down a kite by parting its string!

I looked at the other viewers. Crobe was diddling around with some awful concoction of brain cells, humming happily.

The other viewer showed the van interior. Aha, so Heller had found them. And he was lying low, I concluded, until the Whiz Kid double spoke his piece in court.

The lights were hurting my eyes. Too much sun in the room. I adjusted the bandages to keep most of it out.

One thing you could say about courts: they were usually very slow and one spent most of his time on a case simply waiting and waiting. It was working in my favor.

I went and got some coffee. My throat was very dry and the coffee didn't seem to do the trick. I got some cookies—chocolate tops with white centers. I ate the whole box. I finished off the coffee.

I went back to the viewer.

Aha! Action! The security officer was over by the side door talking to a court official. They were looking into the room. Then the court official shrugged, as much as to say "Go ahead," although any words were lost in the hubbub of the room.

Two more security men came into the room. A fourth took position by the door, guarding it. The other three began to walk along the aisles in front of spectators, bending over and looking carefully into every face. They were taking lots of time with each person in the courtroom.

The Countess was following their progress. But I was in absolute glee! She couldn't possibly get out. Even if she were in disguise, it wouldn't work, for those security men were on the watch for powder or paint.

Judge Hammer Twist came out of the door of his chambers and somebody yelled, "All rise!"

The audience did. But the security search kept on.

Judge Twist took his seat at the bench. He was bright red with sunburn but there was no sign, otherwise, that he had been goofing off: he was all business. He rapped his gavel.

They had somebody for sentencing, as the first item on the docket. A man had run off from his wife and hadn't supported her. They hauled the wretch up before the bench and the judge gave him seven years hard labor.

Next was a burglar who had robbed offices by strangling secretaries. The judge gave him one year suspended sentence.

Next was a bigamist who pleaded guilty. The judge gave him life imprisonment.

Then there was the final award of judgment to an old woman who had slipped on the sidewalk in front of Baltman's. The judge announced the jury award of fifteen million dollars. "Well, Becky," said Judge Twist in an amiable voice to the plaintiff, who had just received the news of her riches, "you're doing pretty well this year. That's your third winning suit."

"Thank you, Your Honor," the old harridan said. "And I'm not forgetting the Retirement Fund for Judges, like we arranged in chambers."

The judge seemed to want to get rid of her quickly, for he hastily began looking all over the top of his desk.

At that moment one of the security men stepped directly in front of my viewer and was in the act of bending forward.

"Wister," the judge said. "I have a plea here for special hearing. Clerk, call Wister!"

An arm went out and thrust the security man aside.

The Whiz Kid double and the older man who had been on her left all went forward with the Countess Krak.

Well, all right, for the instant. I was sure they had her spotted from the way that security man had scowled. Yes, he had gone over to the security officer quickly and they were talking.

The double came to a stop before the bench.

"This is most irregular," said the judge. "Where are your attorneys? Boggle, Gouge and Hound usually represent you."

"They've been dismissed," the double said. "I am representing myself."

"Oh, my!" said the judge. "This is bad business! How do you expect lawyers to get properly rich if they don't get juicy targets like you? You're pretty remunerative around here."

"I'm afraid not now," said the double. "You see, Your Honor, I'm pleading guilty to all charges."

"Oh, well, that doesn't make for any prolonged defense. So I will accept that you're representing yourself. Guilty. You're pleading guilty, then."

"Yes, Your Honor."

"All right. But to what are you pleading guilty? We have to have something in the court record to plead guilty to before we plead guilty. As you're representing yourself, I'm taking it upon myself to instruct you in your legal rights. So what are the crimes, Wister? Hey?"

"Any suits filed against Wister are against me, not against Wister."

"You've got me mixed up," said the judge.

"I had a brother named Wister. The ones they got mixed up was me and my brother. To save the family honor, I freely admit I did all those things that Wister was being sued for."

The judge was scrambling around his desk. Then he called for his clerk and they scrambled around his desk. They found something.

"Aha," said the judge, reading a legal paper, "it appears that the women plaintiffs just withdrew their suits. Something about their finding out that you were going to do this and you didn't have any money."

The prosecuting attorney came over hastily and whispered in the judge's ear.

"Ah," said Judge Twist. "This charge of rape of a minor in Mexico. Very, very serious. Clerk, see if there's anything in on that. I haven't done my morning mail. Thank you, Mr. Prosecutor, for calling it to my attention. We can't have minor-raping going on, even in Mexico."

The clerk had dived for his chambers and came back with a telegram. He handed it to the judge.

Twist read it and began to frown very heavily. "This is pretty bad news. The request for a warrant has met with a technical flaw in wording. Let's get this straight. The State Department and the U.S. Department of Justice have communicated with the Mexican authorities . . . hmm. Burro stealing is no longer a crime since the Mexicans started building Volkswagens, as you can't give burros away. . . . Hmmm. Bad news here. Ah, yes, the technical flaw: The request asserted that the girl violated was a virgin and Mexican authorities refuse to believe that there are any virgins in Mexico, especially in the Barrio Cópula. So they won't issue a warrant. . . . U.S. Justice wants to know if you stole a Volkswagen? Did you steal a Volkswagen, Wister?"

"No," said the double. "I've never even been in Mexico."

"Oh, that's neither here nor there. The point is, they've refused to issue a warrant, so we can't get you for that." Twist was getting quite angry. The sunburn went redder. "Clerk, Mr. Prosecutor, isn't there something we can get this young man for? Can't be wasting the court's time like this. Here we have a potential legal victim standing right here and nothing to charge him with! Unacceptable! Wasting the taxpayers' money! Unthinkable!"

The clerk was tearing through his papers. He came up with a legal paper. "Here's one from Dingaling, Chase and Ambo that isn't cancelled. It's a commitment order on Heavenly Joy Krackle, known Wister associate."

The judge took it. He looked at the double. "It mentions your name." He read the order. "Aha! Commits the young woman to Bellevue! For mental examination! But it states she is not to be seen by Dr. Phetus P. Crobe. Now, that's a damnable thing. Crobe is one of our most trusted psychiatrists. You can always depend on him to get rid of unwanted people! Well! I don't have to abide by the instruction. I can commit whomever I please. Aside from being a confederate of this Wister, here, who is this Krackle?"

The older man I had seen earlier stepped forward. "I'll take that."

"Who are you?"

"I am Philup Bleedum of Bleedum, Bleedum and Drayne. I am Miss Krackle's attorney." He was holding the commitment order now.

"Well, sir, that is quite all right, but I must have Miss Krackle committed!" said the judge. "So produce her! We will send her over to Crobe at Bellevue. Can't have commitment papers unserved!"

"I am sorry, sir," said Philup Bleedum. "But Miss Krackle, under the a.k.a. of Lissus Moam, was ordered executed at Atalanta. Could we please have a delay in this commitment order until the prior sentence is carried out?"

A Code break! It was the truth and Philup Bleedum even had some papers and photos in his hand. All the judge had to do now was say, "Aha! An extraterrestrial," and I had her cold!

"A delay?" said the judge. "Of course you may have a delay. Clerk, mark in your court record that that paper is to be delayed until said Heavenly Joy Krackle, a.k.a. Lissus Moam, has been executed. They do a good job at Atlanta Penitentiary. Electric-chair executions always take precedence over psychiatric electric-shock executions, and you can note my legal finding in this case for the history books. Now, let's get back to Wister."

But what was I looking at? Philup Bleedum should have put the Krackle commitment order back on the clerk's pile. But there had been a flashing blur. A black-sleeved arm had snaked out, put something else in Bleedum's hand and taken the Krackle order back. Only a rustle of paper. A magician switch! The paper that Bleedum put on the clerk's pile was blank! Another slight rustle as the real order went out of sight into a pocket.

"There's another order here!" said the clerk in triumph. "It was under the blotter! It consigns this Wister to Bellevue. It has not been cancelled."

The judge eagerly took it from the clerk. He read it. "Same error here. Trying to blacken the name of Crobe. Marshal! See that this Wister is delivered to Dr. Phetus P. Crobe at Bellevue for mental examination." He looked at the double. "I knew we'd get you for something." Then to the clerk, "Next case!"

The marshals had seized the double in efficient execution of their duties and marched him to the side exit.

I freaked. I was so startled at the fate of that poor double that I almost missed what happened next. It was worse.

Bleedum's back was visible as he turned and walked toward the main door.

The security officer was there. He blocked the way. His face was glaring around Bleedum, straight at my viewer. He reached out with his thumb. He touched a spot just to my viewer's right. The thumb withdrew. He was looking at the makeup paint that had come off on it. AHA!

Then something very peculiar happened.

A black-sleeved arm reached out. A hand grasped the security officer by the elbow.

The security officer got an amazed expression on his face. Then he turned and was marched into the empty hall. He stopped at the top of a long flight of stairs.

The door to the courtroom closed behind them, shutting out the hubbub.

"I don't think you heard the judge. Neither Heavenly Joy Krackle nor Jerome Terrance Wister are now wanted for anything at all."

The security officer heard wide-eyed as he stood teetering.

"And I think when you go to collect your fee, you'll find a hole where Dingaling, Chase and Ambo offices once stood. So skip the zeal, mister. This is the only pay you're going to get."

And teeter, teeter, fall away.

BLAMMETY, BLAM, BLAM!

The security officer went down the steps all arms and legs.

THUD! He hit the bottom.

Philup Bleedum's face was reproving. "Was that necessary?"

"Maybe not necessary, but oh, so satisfactory."

Wait! Wait! There was something wrong here. I was all confused. What had I missed?

I could see Bleedum's back as they got in an elevator. Then I could see down the courthouse steps.

I saw an arm raised in signal.

I saw a BLACK van speed up and stop at the curb.

I saw a hand open the van side door. AND THERE INSIDE WAS THE COUNTESS KRAK!

"We're free as birds," said Heller, as he climbed in.

Oh, Gods! All today, due to my impaired sight, I HAD BEEN WATCHING THE WRONG VIEWER!

It had been Heller in that courtroom! NOT the Countess Krak!

Chapter 6

Emergencies were piling upon emergencies thick and fast. I knew my time was running out and that the forces of evil had united their fangs against me. But I could still act.

If Madison lost his Whiz Kid double and imagined it had been my fault, the PR man might turn on me and decide to make ME famous. Nobody could live through that.

I called Raht on the two-way-response radio. "Crobe," I said urgently, "has become supernumerary.

What facilities do you have? Talk fast, we haven't got much time."

"The two guards that brought him from the base left the Zanco straitjacket. We've got a couple guards here at the New York office."

"Good!" I said. "Tear right over to Bellevue Hospital, kidnap Crobe and send him back to base with orders to hold him there."

"Right away!" said Raht.

I clicked off. It was all I could come up with. I wondered if I could do more to rescue the double. Factually, I didn't feel well enough to go over to Bellevue myself—and part of this was, I had to admit, a fear that they would latch on to me. No matter how enamored one might become of the general subject of psychiatry, it was a wise thing to stay away from psychiatrists. Just because the king needs a headsman is no reason to invite the hooded axe-swinger to dinner.

My eyes hurt and I could not see very well. I closed the shades and lay down. But I could not relax. Some sixth sense told me that the troubles I was in were coming to a crisis.

At length—it must have been past midafternoon—I was nagged by a sense of duty. I should at least look at the viewers.

Examining them, I saw that my mistake in getting them mixed up was quite natural. I had never marked them "Krak" or "Heller" but only *K* and *H* which look enough alike to confuse anyone.

My enemies were back at the condo, saucy as you please. The Countess Krak, helped by her maid, was putting her clothes away. Heller was on a telephone in his condo den, talking to Florida. Izzy was uncomfortably perched in an easy chair beside the fireplace to Heller's right, staring owlishly at Heller.

"Good enough," said Heller. "The extra canal should give you enough water for the vats, so that's okay." He hung up. He turned to Izzy. "They're doing quite well, considering. The project should be finished in a few weeks. How's it going with you, Izzy?"

"Nerve-wracking," said Izzy. "But I can't complain. I've done a study as to how our Maysabongo company can buy up all oil reserves in the United States. But you can look at that when you come in. This is your home, after all. You shouldn't be working in it."

The Countess Krak stepped to the door. "Goodness me. The butler didn't bring your coffee, Izzy." She called, "Balmor! Please see that Mr. Epstein gets some of that new peppermint coffee, and right away."

"Oh, you shouldn't bother with me," said Izzy, standing now, looking at her worshipfully.

"Nonsense," said the Countess. "After all, you're our best friend. Somebody has to look after your ulcers! Sit down. Besides, I have a question for you. Have you ever heard the initials 'F.F.B.O.'?"

"Why?" said Izzy guardedly, perched nervously on the chair edge.

Heller said, "She thinks we should go on and clean this whole mess up. If we don't watch it, we'll be reforming the entire planet."

"Well, we *should* clean it up," said the Countess. "Somebody was paying that double and giving him orders. And all he knew was the letter designation 'F.F.B.O.'"

"I'd leave it alone," said Izzy. "Maybe it's a secret underground organization like the Elks. KKK stands for the Ku Klux Klan. They burn blacks and Jews. It isn't

very healthy to get mixed up with things like that.
Almost as bad as Indians."

"You don't know, then," said the Countess Krak.
"Well, never mind, I'll find out. Here's your coffee
coming."

I writhed. There she was, pushing, pushing, pushing! If she followed that trail it would take her to Madison and then to ME!

My headache felt worse. I laid down again. I had to
be in some kind of shape this evening. I must not arouse
the suspicions of Adora and Candy that I had a plan and
meant to run.

A buzzing sound. The two-way-response radio. I
dug it out wearily.

"Sorry I'm so late reporting in. What I'm about to
tell you happened around noon."

"More catastrophe," I said.

"Well, kind of," said Raht. "It's got me worried."

"For Gods' sakes, quit garbling! Give me your
report!"

"Well, I got your order, grabbed the two guards
from the office and the Zanco straitjacket and a gas
bomb, stopped by the air terminal for tickets and then
went to Bellevue Hospital.

"When we asked for Crobe, Reception said he must
be in, because some marshals from the court had taken
a patient named Wister up to see him a while ago and
had left, and Crobe was undoubtedly busy in his consult-
ing rooms.

"We went up. We walked into Crobe's suite. A bucktoothed kid was lying on the table and he had a shock
machine half connected to him. He was out cold and a
syringe was sticking in a vein. Looked like he had been

drugged and was being got ready for a shock but somebody interrupted it.

"No Crobe. But the door to the inner office was partly open. We thought maybe Crobe was in there. But we never found out."

"WHAT?"

"Yes. All of a sudden we went out like a light. All three of us. Felt like blueflash."

"You're dreaming! How the Hells could Voltarian blueflash get in Bellevue Hospital?"

"Well, I don't know," Raht said. "But when we came to, the kid was gone, and I'll be blessed if Crobe wasn't lying there where the kid had been. And Crobe had the Zanco straitjacket on him."

Horror surged into my throat as the realization struck me. If this had happened shortly after noon, Heller and Krak would have had ample time to get back to their condo where I had seen them. THEY HAD GONE FROM THAT COURT TO THE HOSPITAL! But this was not the source of the horror.

"Raht," I said anxiously, "did you have anything in your pockets from me? That gave my name or address?"

"I only had my own wallet and, of course, my identoplate."

"Nothing with my name or phone number?"

"No. Why should I? Anyway, this was all very peculiar. I thought I had better tell you because it might have been a Code break. That was a Voltarian straitjacket: had the Zanco label on it."

Then I had another agonizing thought. "Did the New York office guards have anything in their pockets that would lead to me?"

"Well, they had their identoplates. And Crobe's and their airline tickets through to Afyon, Turkey. But that doesn't account for the note we found on Crobe when we woke up. It said, 'Take this murderer home and see that he stays locked up.' It was written in Voltarian and in a very neat Voltarian, too. Are you sure that isn't a Code break of some sort?"

I was running out of adrenaline to sustain my shock. Wearily, I said, "So where is Crobe?"

"On his way to Turkey, of course. But I don't see how that bucktoothed kid got off the table, drugged like he was, and exploded a blueflash and..."

"Raht! Stop babbling!"

"But when we left with Crobe in a bag, the Bellevue desk wanted to know why we were taking Wister out in a straitjacket, because their record now showed he had passed the court-ordered mental examination and had been pronounced totally sane. This whole thing has been crazy."

I interrupted him. My head ached too much to listen to him further. "You fouled up as usual! If I wanted Bellevue blown up because of a Code break, I'd blow it up myself. There's no depending on you!"

"Blow up Bellevue?" Raht said, "Oh, please don't do that. They might remember us at the desk! I don't think..."

He was hopeless. I broke the connection.

I sat there sweating. Maybe Crobe had talked while Heller and Krak had him. Crobe knew why I had sent him to New York—to do in Heller.

My palms were wringing wet. I heard something in the areaway and almost jumped out of my skin.

Krak and Heller might turn up anywhere! At any moment!

But it was only the girls coming home from work.

Oh, by the Gods of space, it was a good thing I had a plan and could run. For, adding to my anxiety, they came in chattering about how nice it would be when they had all the homos reformed.

It was all I could do to sit there and not speed out the door screaming that very instant.

Life is often too much for one.

Chapter 7

I rose in an exhausted stupor the following day. It had been very difficult the night before. It had taken four bhongs of marijuana to get any performance going at all. My throat was parched. I was having trouble seeing. The threat of homo demonstrations was coming through like a nightmare.

I drank a quart of grapefruit juice almost without stopping. I ate a package of Oreo cookies. I still felt terrible. I needed something to start me going.

By the simple action of staring through the bandages at my viewers, I got it. Raw terror!

Crobe's had gone blank, for he was way out of range. But Krak's and Heller's were very live.

They were sitting at breakfast amidst the greenery of the roof terrace, the April sun sparkling on the snowy linen and tableware.

Heller was neatly dressed in a three-piece gray flannel suit, impeccably groomed, obviously ready for the day. The Countess Krak was in a flowy sort of morning gown. The whiteness of it hurt my eyes. She was delicately eating orange ice from a crystal and silver cup, but her attention was on the papers.

She looked up and, in a somewhat explosive voice, said, "Well, I never! Not one single line about the dismissal of the criminal charges or the suits. Not a word about the double's confession. Just some idiocy about a nationwide cat hunt."

Heller looked sideways. The cat was on the terrace lapping cream. "Mister Calico," said Heller, "you better lie low. They're on your tail at last."

"Jettero," said the Countess, "you are not taking this seriously."

"How can you take newspapers seriously?" said Heller.

"I do take it seriously. This is black propaganda by deletion. They haven't said a thing to cancel the impressions they created earlier. They're character assassins, that's what they are. And there's no remedy in these fake courts. When I think what they have said about you, my blood seethes! And now that we've handled it all, they don't recant. Jettero, this is a *very* managed press."

"It's just the way they are," said Heller. "I'm too busy to get involved in a 'Clean News for Clean People' campaign."

"Well, it's a good thing I'm on it," said the Countess Krak. "There's the doorbell."

"What are you up to?"

"I sent Bang-Bang out on what he calls a 'clandestine reconnaissance.'"

"And top of the morning to you both," said Bang-Bang. He had come out on the terrace. He was carrying a burden of books. "Every dictionary I could locate in the stores."

The Countess Krak grabbed them.

The butler got a chair for him, a waiter handed him coffee and Bang-Bang sat and watched the Countess tearing through the dictionaries.

"F.F.A." said the Countess Krak. "Future Farmers of America. F.F.V. First Families of Virginia."

Heller said, "I shouldn't think the First Families of Virginia were paying anyone to become a notorious outlaw."

Bang-Bang said, "You never know, Jet. My people were some of the first Sicilians in New York, and look at me!"

The Countess put the last dictionary aside. "Oh, dear. It isn't in any of them. What *could* F.F.B.O. stand for?"

"Wait a minute," said Heller. "I just remembered something. Last fall I was summoned down to the docks by Babe Corleone."

"Who is that?" said the Countess.

"Babe Corleone is the head of the Corleone mob."

"Oh, Jettero," said the Countess Krak. "Another woman! I've got to get you off this planet before they eat you alive. Women are dangerous, Jettero. I know you don't believe me, but after all you have been through lately, I should think . . ."

"All thrusts reverse!" said Heller. "Listen! Babe Corleone is really a great lady. She runs a whole mob single-handed. She controls the unions and all steamship lines. She's the only threat Faustino Narcotici has."

"Oh, dear," said the Countess Krak.

"No, no," said Heller. "She's Earth middle-aged. She was like a mother to me. And I've been very sad that she thought I had turned *traditore*. She thought of me as a son. But that's neither here nor there. What I just remembered was something I saw on a screen.

"She was selecting executive personnel for the Punard line she had just taken over and this fellow stepped up. I recall it now. His name was J. P. Flagrant and the screen said that he was a former employee of F.F.B.O."

"Oh!" said the Countess Krak. "Then if I called the Punard line . . ."

"No, no," said Heller. "They didn't hire him. That's why all this stuck in my memory. She said he was a *traditore* and had him thrown in the river. She didn't employ him."

"Then he's out of a job," said Bang-Bang. "When Babe fires them, they stay fired."

"J. P. Flagrant," said the Countess. "Bang-Bang, how do you find somebody who is out of a job in New York?"

"New York Employment Office," said Bang-Bang promptly. "They have to be registered there or they can't go on welfare. I'll call."

"I think we're on to something," said the Countess Krak.

And, I thought, I could feel my time running out. Sort of like a river of blood spilling from a pumping artery.

Bang-Bang came back. Cheerily, he said, "Hey, what do you know? They had him. J. P. Flagrant, former executive of F.F.B.O. But that isn't what's amazing. They found him a job. They were awful proud of it, as it almost never happens. They placed him as a garbage man in Yonkers! There's lots of garbage up there."

"Well, call Yonkers!" said the Countess Krak.

"Oh, I did," said Bang-Bang. "They got him all

right. He's driving Garbage Truck 2183 and it's out on rounds."

"I'll have the Rolls run out," said Heller.

"No, not the Rolls," said the Countess Krak. "You have no idea how many guns there were around those women. This is a shooting war we're in. We need something bulletproof. Much as I despise it, I think we should take the old cab."

"That's better," said Bang-Bang. "I can't imagine calling on a garbage truck in a chauffeured limousine. It just don't seem fitting."

Yonkers! I grabbed a map. It was at least fourteen miles through traffic from where they were.

J. P. Flagrant, when they found him, would spill his guts. He would put them straight on to Madison and Madison would connect with me.

For them, fourteen miles there. Fifteen or twenty miles back to Madison's area. How much time would they consume?

I had had it!

If I hurried and luck was with me, I could escape. The PLAN must go into effect at once.

I had an awful lot to get done FAST!

My time had run out forever in New York.

PART FIFTY-FIVE

Chapter 1

I wasted precious seconds trying to reach J. Walter Madison at his 42 Mess Street office. They hedged in telling me where he was but I knew already. He would be at his mother's house.

His mother answered the phone, "Is this the Mafia?"

"No, no," I said. "This is Madison's boss, Smith."

"Oh, Mr. Smith," she said. "I'm so worried about Walter. He's been despondent the last day or two. He keeps saying he may let Mr. Bury down again. Walter's an awfully sensitive boy, you know—has been so since he was a child. Terrified of hurting people's feelings. And so conscientious. He says he'd give his right arm to succeed for Mr. Bury. He must be absolutely killing himself with work, for just this morning he was saying he would be no good to Mr. Bury dead. I've been trying and trying to persuade Walter that he should take a nice vacation. I do hope you can see your way clear to suggesting it." She evidently turned her head away from the phone and called in a melodious voice, "Walter dear, it's that nice Mr. Smith on the phone." Then, more quietly, "No, it's not the Mafia. It's Mr. Smith.... Yes. I recognized his voice."

Madison's voice was cautious. "Hello?"

"Oh, thank Gods, I reached you in time!" I said. "I

have a fink in the Narcotici mob. The word is out. Razza recognized your voice. But he's a clever snake. He did not want to offend Rockecenter, so he hired the Corleone mob to hunt you down and knock you off."

"Walter," came his mother's voice in the background, "sit down in this chair. You look like you've seen a ghost. Is it bad news?"

Hoarsely to me, Madison said, "What do you think I should do?"

"Look," I said. "I am your friend. Usually when somebody gets on a spot like you're on, we just write them off. But I'll stand by you. I have a place to hide you nobody will suspect. Now listen carefully. There are snipers everywhere. I don't want you to be seen on the street. Be on the roof of your apartment building. I'll pick you off with a helicopter."

"Oh, thank God you warned me," he said. "I'll be there."

I hung up. My luck was holding. And in the emergency of the moment my accustomed brilliance had asserted itself. In the flash, I had added the touch about the Corleone mob, remembering that that old hack had "Corleone Cab Company" on its door. But there was no time to gloat.

I glanced at the viewers. Bang-Bang's voice.

"We'll make better time if you go up the Hudson River Parkway, get off at Broadway just south of 254th Street and then turn off Broadway into Nepperhan Avenue in Yonkers. They said he'd be on that or Ashburton or Lake Avenue, somewhere in that district."

I looked at it closely. The old cab seemed to be roaring since its rebuild. (Bleep) it all, Heller was driving! And he drove like the wind! I must hurry.

I picked up the two-way-response radio and buzzed it. Raht answered at once.

"Get over to the 34th Street East Heliport on the East River," I said. "Rent a helicopter and make sure it has a ladder. We're going to do a roof pickup."

"Wait a minute, Officer Gris," said Raht. "I don't have money for that. You better come into the office and give us a formal on-lines requisition and stamp. It would come under the unusual-expense regulation, number . . ."

For a moment my plans suffered a threatened shift. It would be much cheaper just to take a rifle and when Madison appeared on the roof, shoot him. But no, he was far too valuable a man just to sacrifice because one had to follow the Apparatus textbook. Madison had the whole procedure of PR under his belt. He was well trained. He could wreck anyone's life at will. I made the crucial decision, no matter how painful it was.

"I'll pay for it myself," I said. "Get right over there and rent it and stand by. I will join you."

"You sure you're not going to bomb something?" said Raht.

"Swallow that impudence and do as you're told or I'll bomb you!" I snarled. What riffraff I had to deal with!

I clicked off.

The next part of my plan was to write a note to the girls. I glanced nervously at the viewer. I dug up pen and paper and an envelope. I wrote:

Dear Mrss. Beys,

I realize I cannot live up to your high opinion of me. I am going to commit suicide

> *for the benefit of our children.*
> *Good-bye cruel world.*
>
> *Your husbands*

I put it in an envelope, wrote Farewell on the face of it and propped it under a statue of Aphrodite in the front room so it looked like a human sacrifice.

I glanced at the viewer. They were in Yonkers already! Oh, I must hurry!

I began to pack, stuffing everything I had into cardboard grocery cartons, wishing I had remembered to buy some suitcases. This was taking time and I did not have enough string. Somehow I must make time because, before I went to that skyport, I had to grab Teenie. I thought she would be at the school and I left a gas bomb out. I cursed having accumulated all this gear.

I was lifting a viewer so it would sit face up in a carton and I could watch it simply by lifting the box flap, when suddenly a voice was heard. "Well, hurray, hurray for me!" I thought it was coming from the viewer. It confused me. What was THAT voice doing in Heller's speeding cab?

"Look what I got!"

I whirled and peered through the bandages. It was Teenie! Oh, my luck was in! She'd walked right into the net.

She was standing there in her flat oxfords and a plaid skirt, her ponytail thrusting out of the back of her head. "I just graduated," she said with her too-big smile. "And they gave me presents! Look! A genuine Hong Kong dildo. A whole dozen lace condoms. A package of joss sticks for luck. And behold!"

She was unrolling a diploma. It said she was a Certified Professional and that she had graduated Magna Come Loud.

"At last," she crowed, "I have completed my education!"

I didn't say anything. She started looking around at all the boxes. "Hey, are you blowing or something?"

I was caught in the middle of indecision. I had intended to just hit her with a gas bomb, dump her in a sack and put her with the other baggage. On the other hand, maybe I could talk her into carrying some of this heavy stuff.

"Teenie," I said, "I have always been fond of you."

"Oh, yeah?"

Teen-agers are hard to understand. Maybe I should be coy. "Teenie, how would you like to go for a ride?"

"A ride?" she said. "You mean like the old movies? Gangster style?"

I decided to be jocular. "Yeah, kid, you get the idea."

"Wait a minute," said Teenie. "Is this on the level? You're packing. Are you trying to get me to run away with you?"

Well, well. Maybe I had made an appeal. "That's right," I said.

"Oho!" she said. "I see it all now! That solves the mystery. You got me educated so you could get a good price selling me into white slavery!"

I gaped.

"Tell you what I'll do," said Teenie. "If you'll split fifty-fifty any price you get for me, I'll go with you."

I gaped wider.

"All right," she said. "Fair is fair and a bargain is a

bargain." She put out her hand. She evidently wanted to shake hands for some reason. I shook hands with her.

My plans for Teenie had been a bit nebulous. They consisted solely of capturing her and holding her prisoner so that if at any time the court accused me of murdering her, as per the injunction, I could produce her and say, "See, she's still alive." That way she would not be around to lie about me or get me in trouble. It was an elementary and effective solution and part of my general plan. But I had not looked for this much cooperation.

"There's one condition to it," she said. "And that is that you let me go home and pack."

I glanced nervously at the viewer. Was there time or did I use the gas bomb after all?

Tudor City was en route to the skyport. She wouldn't own very much.

I gambled. "All right," I said.

She promptly went to work tying up boxes. "Hey," she said, "I see you have TV-osis. I never watch it myself. I like the stern realities of life instead. But you left this portable set on."

"Leave it," I said. "The switch is broken."

She shrugged and finished tying up the other boxes. She picked up a pad and pen and was about to pack it.

"I think Adora might get worried if you disappeared," I said. "Why don't you leave her a note?"

"Good thinking, Inky. She'd set the cops on the trail and blow your white-slavery ring to hell." She picked up the pen. She gnawed it. "I could tell her I had been approached for the Miss America contest, but the truth is dangerous. I can't think of anything to say."

"Just anything," I said, glancing nervously at the viewer.

Finally she got to writing, somewhat laboriously. Then she showed it to me. In badly formed letters, it said:

> *Deer Pinchy,*
>
> > *I am finne.*
> > *How R U.*
> > *I am dooinng well.*
> > *Will C U.*
>
> > > > > *Teenie*

"That's great," I said.

"No," she said. "It isn't warm enough." She threw it aside.

She tried again.

> *Deer, deer Pinchy and Candy,*
>
> > *I gradudated & with honnors.*
> > *Thay warded mee a bedpost gradadutaded coorss in Hung Cung.*
> > *Keeep upp the gud wk.*
>
> > > > > *Teenie*
>
> *Hott Dogg!*

"That will do just great," I said urgently. "We have a plane to catch."

"Is that hot dog part warm enough?" she said.

"Yes, yes," I said and grabbed the letter. Then, cunning, I also grabbed the first letter. I put them in my pocket. I would mail the last one and keep the other one to show she was still alive.

I glanced at the viewer. The cab was running down a city street, probably searching along the route of the garbage truck. I had better get going!

I called a cab and we got my boxes out front. Wonder of wonders, my luck was really holding! We didn't have to wait more than a minute.

We loaded up and sped away. I took no backward glance at that scene of pain and travail. I would not miss it.

I peeked into the open flap of a box at the viewer. They were hunting for the garbage truck. It would be close but I felt that I might make my escape unscathed. If my luck continued to hold.

Chapter 2

Tudor City is not a city at all. It's a collection of twelve brick buildings built in the 1920s in the Flamboyant or Tudor Gothic-English style of architecture. They are surrounded by green lawns and footpaths which were once kept up but which now seemed mainly devoted to growing marijuana. The buildings, according to the chattering Teenie, used to have three thousand apartments which housed twelve thousand people, but these numbers were now sort of blurred.

We approached it on 41st Street East and as the cab

drew up beside one of the big buildings the atmosphere was suddenly calm and quiet. Not so my nerves.

"Hurry up and get your things," I told Teenie.

"You sit right there and wait," she said. "I have to climb fourteen stories on the fire escape to get to the old garret I have at the top and I don't want the landlady to see me leave."

She was off and up. The height would have made me dizzy. The cabby glanced at his ticking meter and opened his *Daily Racing Form*. I opened the carton anxiously to gaze at Heller's viewer.

They had spotted the garbage truck! Oh, this was going to be nip and tuck, and I was the likely one to be nipped!

As they drew near it on a narrow street, I was not crediting my ears. Was that a song I was hearing? Some kind of a ditty? It was not coming from Tudor City—it must be coming from my viewer!

It was not one of the more modern mechanical garbage collectors. It was simply a big, open-backed truck with piles of garbage towering in the body. It had a number of large flags flying from it on staffs and it had huge billboard signs.

TODAY'S GARBAGE
IS TOMORROW'S AMERICA

And another sign:

ENTER THE CONTEST!
WIN A ROUND TRIP
TO THE GARBAGE DUMP!
ALL EXPENSES PAID

The old cab was drawing nearer and was about to come up beside the moving truck. Another sign:

TRUCK 2183
MR. J. P. FLAGRANT
GARBAGE EXECUTIVE

Yes, the ditty was coming from the truck. There were two loudspeakers mounted on the cab. They were singing:

> *Happy garbage to you,*
> *Happy garbage to you.*
> *Be kind to your garbage,*
> *And it will love you.*

The old cab was driving even with the truck window now. Bang-Bang leaned out and yelled, "Pull over!"

The truck driver was wearing a green derby. Yes, it WAS Flagrant! He was staring popeyed at the cab, his eyes fixed on the door sign.

"Corleone!" he shrieked. Instantly he sped up.

I breathed a sigh of relief. Flagrant probably remembered all too well that icy winter ducking in the river he had experienced at the sideways thumb thrust of Babe Corleone! He thought they were after him to throw him in again! Yes, sir! My breaks were holding! I hoped his didn't!

But (bleep) that Heller! He was racing right alongside the garbage truck!

Then the old cab leaped ahead with a ferocious roar. It snarled down the street ahead of the truck. Heller applied his brakes and yanked his wheel.

With a scream of tires, the old cab went broadside. It jarred to a halt.

It was blocking the street!

The garbage truck bore down on it like a juggernaut!

I prayed, hit that cab! Then that will be the last of Heller.

But Flagrant had jammed on his brakes. The heavy vehicle was shuddering to a halt. Oh, Gods, he was going to stop. I wanted to scream "Hit that cab!" Oh, Gods, if he stopped he would be caught.

He stopped.

But he wasn't caught.

Flagrant had the truck in reverse!

It started backwards slowly and then began to pick up speed. He couldn't turn in that narrow street. But he was going to get away!

He was shortly up to what must be forty miles an hour! Backwards!

Bang-Bang yelled, "Shoot out his tires!"

"No!" cried Heller. "We don't want to hurt him, we only want to stop him. Slide under this wheel!"

Heller jumped out of the cab. Bang-Bang slid over and got into the driving seat. Heller slammed the door, dropped a bag in Bang-Bang's lap and stepped on the cab's running board.

Bang-Bang started up and began to chase the furiously backing garbage truck. "Go to it, Flagrant!" I yelled. "Buy me time!"

The old cab was streaking up the street, pursuing the swiftly backing garbage truck.

Heller reached in through the cab window and rummaged with one hand in the bag he'd dropped in Bang-Bang's lap. He took out something.

"Get closer to that truck!" shouted Heller.

There was a cross street. The light was green. Probably Flagrant would have turned, except stopped traffic, waiting for the light, blocked the intersecting streets. He kept backing faster, the huge truck teetering as its engine roared.

The cab was almost bumping the truck's radiator.

Heller was sizing up the truck. The whipping flags were very near.

Heller drew back his hand.

He threw!

Something sailed over the truck's cab and landed in the garbage.

"Bang-Bang! Brake! Stop!"

The old cab tires screamed as they locked. It came to a swerving halt.

The garbage truck was racing away! Oh, Gods, Flagrant was going to back to safety! He would make it.

BOOOOOOM!

Out of the truck's back and into the air went a geyser of garbage!

Tonnage of garbage sacks shot up the street BEHIND the truck.

A concussion grenade! The other one I had given Silva!

The cab bucked in the blast.

The load of garbage was suddenly a street-blocking barricade. It had flown out of the body backwards.

The truck's rear plowed into it!

It came to a squishing halt!

"Forward!" cried Heller.

Bang-Bang raced ahead.

The old cab came to a stop before the halted truck.

I looked anxiously up at the building we were parked beside. Where was Teenie? Time was growing short!

Chapter 3

J. P. Flagrant crawled out of the truck cab, his green derby askew. Heller stepped toward him.

Flagrant fell on his knees, clasped hands upraised in supplication. "Please don't kill me! I learned the lesson that you taught me. I am not a traitor anymore. I will not rat on F.F.B.O.!"

Oh, what a surge of relief went through me. Babe Corleone had done her job too well. When he had promised to tell all before, she had thrown him in the wintry river as a *traditore*. Smart man! He wasn't going to let that happen again, even if it was spring!

"No, no," said Heller. "We're not here to kill you. We just want some information."

"The Rockecenter interests are sacred!" whined Flagrant. "You're Corleone. I was wrong to offer to rat. Now let me go back to my garbage."

"Just tell me what the letters *F.F.B.O.* mean," said Heller.

"Then you're not from the advertising world or you would know," said Flagrant. "Please let me get back to my garbage."

Heller looked at the flags and signs on the truck. The ditty had stopped. He looked at the green derby.

Then he reached into his pocket. Flagrant obviously thought he was drawing a gun and began to weep.

But Heller took out a wallet and looked through it. He found and took out a card. It said:

OWN YOUR VERY OWN
ALLIGATOR FARM, INC.
Ochokeechokee, Florida
Sales Office: Empire State Building

"Advertising?" said Heller. "It just so happens I know of an opening advertising alligator farms in Florida." He gave J. P. Flagrant the card.

Flagrant looked at it. He stopped weeping. He stood up and gave his green derby a twitch. He said, "Fifty thousand dollars a year, one percent of the gross of those sold, a five-year contract with ninety-day option renewal, my own secretary—a brunette, under twenty-five, nice build, nice (bleeps), pretty face?"

Heller said, "I hope the information is worth it. The answer is yes."

Flagrant stood up straighter. He gave his green derby a tug. He said, "Well, in that event, I'm hired. As I am now on your payroll, I cannot possibly be a traitor to anyone except you. Right?"

"Right," said Heller.

"So I am not a traitor. F.F.B.O. stands for Fatten, Farten, Burstein and Ooze. It is the biggest PR and advertising firm in the world. It handles the accounts of the Rockecenter interests, amongst others, and until I was unjustly fired I was the Rockecenter Account Executive and also handled the advertising of the Rockecenter-connected firm of I. G. Barben Pharmaceuticals. Also

Octopus Oil. Also Grabbe-Manhattan Bank. Also, also, also, on and on. Billion-dollar-a-year account."

I shuddered. He was spilling his guts, just as I feared. Gods, what was delaying Teenie?

"Who, then," said Heller, "is responsible for the Whiz Kid?"

"Aha," said Flagrant. "The man who cost me my job. I begged them not to hire him and they fired me. The name of that dog is J. Walter Madison, a PR artist known in the trade as J. Warbler Madman."

"Wait a minute," said Heller. "I've met him!"

"And you're still alive?" said Flagrant. "That's a miracle."

"Sincere, earnest-looking young fellow?"

"That's the snake," said Flagrant. "He was hired at the express demand of Bury, of Swindle and Crouch, the Rockecenter attorneys, for the explicit purpose of ruining a man named Wister."

The Countess Krak's voice rang out behind Heller. "Aha! I knew it! The crooked lawyer trying to usurp the empire!"

"What?" said Flagrant.

"Never mind," said Heller. "You mean this Madison has been doing all this bad, crazy Whiz Kid publicity?"

"Yes, indeed," said Flagrant. "I followed the campaign amongst the garbage cans. I'd recognize Madison's overblown style anywhere."

"That adds up," said Heller. And then in a deadly voice he asked, "Where can we locate this Madison?"

"Well, I don't know where the campaign office is, but Madison lives with his mother and she's in the phone book—Mrs. Dorothy Jekyll Madison."

Oh, Lords, I was praying now. What was delaying that (bleep) Teenie!

"Anything else you know?" said Heller.

Flagrant thought a bit. "I was there when Bury came in. He and some other man—brown-eyed, swarthy, had a gun."

I felt the strain tearing at my skull. That was ME he was describing! Oh, I had to get going!

Heller said, "Bang-Bang, there's a phone kiosk over there. Call information and get that address." He turned back to the man who was doing me in. "You have been a lot of help, Mr. Flagrant."

"I hope so," said Flagrant. "And I wish *you* lots of luck shooting Madison and anyone else connected with him."

I shuddered.

Flagrant was looking at the card. "Empire State Building, eh? Nice address. I'll report for work tomorrow and start advertising the sale of alligators."

"Alligator *farms*," said Heller.

"Yes, sir!" said Flagrant with mounting enthusiasm. "You wait! I'll do some ad campaigns that will make those alligators' mouths water. I'm getting ideas already! I can see it now! 'Tired of your mother-in-law or wife? Buy an alligator farm!'" He found a piece of board in the scattered garbage on the street, drew out a marker pen and started writing.

Bang-Bang came back, "Got the address!"

The Countess Krak and Bang-Bang jumped into the old cab. Heller slid under the wheel.

Bang-Bang yelled, "Good-bye, Mr. Flagrant!"

The cab tore away.

The Countess Krak said, "It would have been cheaper to use a helmet."

"Oh, I don't know," Heller called back over his shoulder. "Sales of those farms have slowed down. And that man seems to have a real talent. Did you see the sign he was writing up? Instead of cleaning the street himself, he's organizing a treasure hunt and offering the truck as a prize!"

Oh, Gods, they only had about eighteen miles to go. I had to get to the heliport and rescue Madison. For Madison would TALK! And implicate ME!

IT WAS NO TIME TO BE DELAYED!

I began to despair of making it!

Where, where, where was Teenie?

Chapter 4

Our cab meter was ticking over. "That must be some TV show you're looking at on that portable," my hacker said. "You keep letting out small screams."

"What happened to our passenger?" I begged.

"Oh, you can never depend on kids these days," my hacker said. "But on the subject of TV shows, you got to watch it. Violence is bad for the heart."

"Especially when it's done with blastguns," I said.

"Oh, you're watching some rerun of *Star Trek*," he said. "That stuff is just garbage, you know."

"Please don't mention garbage," I begged.

"Well, it is. Like the commercials. They lie like hell, Mac. They got a lot of trick things in them trying to capture the audience."

"Please read your *Racing Form*," I begged. The word

capture had turned my blood to icy slush. Heller was driving that old cab! Even my dimmed vision could see the way he was going around corners on two wheels! Have an accident, I begged him. Oh, please have an accident!

And Teenie? Perhaps she had just plain chickened out from an overdose of cold feet. This gave rise to new alarm. If I left her behind me, Adora would have me hunted down for rape of a minor simply by having this lying Teenie string some tale to the judge. It required her testimony for such a warrant, as I understood it, and photographs alone would do no more than whet the legal appetite. If I had Teenie in my possession I could guarantee that threats would prevent such testimony. Also, if I had her alive, a witness or two could so state and I couldn't be hunted down and hung for a Teenie dead. Oh, I had it all worked out. But where was Teenie?

Heller's cab went screaming around a curve. It was hurtling toward my doom. They only had fifteen miles or so to go to get to Madison's mother's house just north of me on the East Side.

There came Teenie!

She didn't have anything in her hands! No baggage. She had not come down the fire escape the way she went up.

"Inky, we're in trouble," she said. "I can't carry my baggage down the fire escape."

"Look," I said. "I'll pay the cabby extra to climb up and help you! But for Gods' sakes, hurry!"

"Well, I will admit I thought of that," said Teenie. "But that isn't it. It's the landlady. She heard me pushing things around and demanded her back rent. When I started to carry my things down, she threw the elevator bus bar and only let me come out when I told her you would let me have the two hundred dollars."

A sound of skidding wheels came from my viewer as Heller turned a corner.

I grabbed for my roll and gave her two hundred dollars.

I waited anxiously.

Then here she came again, burdened under sacks and boxes.

"Get in, get in," I screamed at her.

"No," she said, "but you can ask this hacker to come back with me and help with another load."

Oh, Gods! What could I do? I gave the order and the hacker slouched after her.

They came back staggering under boxes and baggage. What junk! There was even a worn-out monkey doll riding on top of Teenie's mountain.

"Get in!" I screamed.

"Can't," said the hacker. "Too much baggage for the cab. Breaks company regulations. I'll have to radio for a second hack."

He did so. They wouldn't budge otherwise. I sat there suffering.

Heller had gotten on an expressway. He was dodging about through trucks as though they didn't exist!

I looked in despair at all this baggage. "What is this stuff?" I wailed, hoping she would abandon it after all.

"The labors of a lifetime," Teenie said. "You see that big sack over there? That's chock-a-block with the seed of the very best Colombia hemp. That second bag is seeds of choice Acapulco Gold. That red sack is pre-selected seed from Panama Red."

"But that doesn't account for a tenth of this!" I wept.

"Well, no. Some of it is sentimental, I will admit. That big box is a press camera, one of the original tools of my childhood. It may be busted now, but oh, the pictures it has taken! Me being forced to go down on two men at once. Me being licked by a pervert that coughed up twenty G's. Oh, the memories of childhood. You wouldn't want me to leave that behind! It's museum-quality stuff. And then there's two or three skateboards that can be fixed, to say nothing of the two new ones you got me."

I averted my face from such a painful subject.

"And then there's my collection of autographed jock straps."

"WHAT?" I said, startled in spite of my anxiety.

"Of course. Most wonderful blackmail material you ever saw. You get one in a sentimental moment and afterwards you suggest you show it to the guy's girl. Gets you into all games free and God knows what else."

Thank Gods, here came the other cab. I even helped them pitch the things in.

"The 34th Street East Heliport!" I yelled. And off we went.

We weren't driving fast enough for me. Heller, on my viewer, was even jumping lights!

Thank Gods the heliport was just a few blocks south from Tudor City. I could see the excursion choppers coming and going from the pads by the river.

We sped under a highway and raced across a parking lot to Manhattan Charter Services.

There was Raht, waving us further on. We stopped in the shadow of a big helicopter.

"What kept you?" said Raht. "We been paying overtime. I thought you were in a hurry!"

"Get this baggage aboard!" I screamed at him.

"When they've been paid," said Raht.

I raced back to the office and showered out hundred-dollar bills. I raced to the cabs and showered out twenties.

The baggage started to move aboard. I even helped.

In the scramble, I lost the identity of the box that held Heller's viewer.

Oh, my Gods, was I already too late?

Chapter 5

We piled in.

Teenie said, "Hey! So this is how you run your white-slave ring. Choppers! How updatey!"

"What's that?" said the chopper pilot, turning around in his seat.

"Don't pay any attention to this (bleeped) kid!" I raved.

"If you're doing something illegal," said the pilot, "You'll have to go back to the office and pay extra."

"No, no!" I cried. "We're trying to save a man's life. And even that isn't illegal in New York."

"Might be," said the copilot thoughtfully. "There's several guys I know of it would be illegal not to kill. There's a woman, too. You ever hear of the mayor's wife?"

"Oh, Gods, please start that engine!" I wept. "I'll pay you both an extra hundred, personally."

"Well, where do we go?" the pilot said.

Yes, there was that! I had the address written on a piece of paper. I shoved it into the pilot's hand. "And get ready with your ladder! We've got to snatch him off a roof."

They started up. We soared into the air. The sky-scrapers of Manhattan pressed against us to our left, the East River to our right. Below us stretched Franklin D. Roosevelt Drive, a multilane white ribbon, crowded with cars.

The UN buildings flashed by. North of there, the pilot turned inland. I watched anxiously.

High-rises were going by under us.

The pilot pointed. "There's your address," he yelled above the roaring beat of blades.

I looked.

I stared.

There was nobody on the roof!

We hovered.

"I bet he thought you weren't coming," said Raht.

I glared at Teenie. It was her fault.

Then I dived for the pile of baggage in the back of the big cabin. I anxiously pawed through my boxes.

The viewer fell out. I grabbed it. I turned the volume up all the way.

HELLER WAS PARKED BELOW LOOKING AT THE HIGH-RISE!

"I'll go in and ring the bell," said Heller. "You cover me, Bang-Bang. If he's home, he might come out shooting when he recognizes who it is."

"NO!" said the Countess Krak in the back of the cab. "There's no sense in making this into a shooting war. He probably is not home, as it's working hours. I'll just take my shopping bag and go up and see his mother."

"I don't like it," said Heller. "*You* don't have to fight in wars. It isn't ladylike."

"I've done just fine lately," said the Countess Krak.

"That you have," said Heller, "and I admire you and Bang-Bang for it no end. But this guy is the worst rat I have ever heard of. He actually pretended to be my friend. And all the time he intended to knife me. He's as bad as an Apparatus 'drunk.' I'd better go."

"Inky," said Teenie. "If you're in such a God (bleeped) hurry, this is no time to be watching a crime drama. You're weird!"

"This is a crime drama that will fry your God (bleeped) ponytail and put it in a shredder," I said. "Shut up and let me think." And I tried desperately, my screams muffled by the throb of the chopper rotors.

"Well, well," said Raht, looking over my shoulder at the viewer. "So that's what the 831 Relayer serves to boost! An eye bug!"

"Shut up, you silly (bleepard)," I hissed. "You'll get us both vaporized for a Code break!"

"Better you than me," said Raht. "Hey, look here!" He was pawing through my baggage. "Another one!" He turned it on. He glanced at mine and then back at his. "You've got the lady bugged, too!"

"Well, what do we do?" the pilot shouted back at us. "Go home?"

"Christ, no!" I yelled at him. "Keep hovering. Let me think!"

My life was hanging not by helicopter blades but by a thread. Heller and Krak—especially Krak—would tear this planet apart if they found out I was behind their woes.

I looked out the window, forcing myself to overcome the nausea caused by height.

There was the orange cab! I could even see *Corleone Cab Company* on its door. ONE WAS OPENING! HELLER WAS GETTING OUT!

I started praying in Italian, suppressing my impulse

to scream in Voltarian. Maybe Jesus Christ would overlook my many sins and come to my rescue like a good fellow. Heller was always praying and he was winning. It just could be that it did some good! For I was completely out of ideas.

"What's that chopper up there?" said Heller.

"Probably a police plain wrapper," said Bang-Bang, getting out. "They cruise around the East Side all the time to disturb the residents."

"That rules out shooting, Jettero. Let me take this shopping bag and show his mother the latest in headwear. After all, she's a woman. This is where I come in."

THE BACK DOOR OPENED! KRAK WAS GETTING OUT!

"Oh, Jesus Christ," I prayed in Italian. "I will be a good boy. I will burn Teenie's joss sticks on your altar. I will lay off swearing!" Then I stopped and slumped. There was neither hope nor solution. The Countess Krak was on the pavement, walking toward the high-rise entrance door. Bang-Bang and Heller, like a skirmish line, were flanking her. It was all up. I might as well start writing my will.

MADISON SOLVED IT!

The Excalibur open touring phaeton came flashing out of the underground garage at sixty miles an hour, exhaust pipes flaming!

Madison had apparently despaired of being rescued from the roof and, seeing "Corleone" on that cab, had panicked and fled in his car!

It barely missed knocking Bang-Bang down!

"It's him!" Heller shouted. "Get in the cab!"

They converged upon the old hack.

The doors weren't even shut when Heller had it moving.

He turned on a dime and, tires screaming, shot after Madison.

"Our man!" I screamed at the pilot. "He's in that open car! Follow him!"

The chopper spun on its blades and moved after the phaeton.

Madison was heading east, tearing around corners. He was trying to get to Franklin D. Roosevelt Drive, where his speed would count for something.

After him streaked the cab.

A new problem churned in my mind. That Excalibur might look like a 1930 has-been with all its separate exhaust pipes, long hood and huge chrome lamps, but I knew how fast it could go. Everything under that antique veneer was the most modern high-speed machinery ever built into cars. It could do phenomenal speeds. And Madison, hunched over the wheel below us, was driving with all his might, his brown hair whipping in the wind.

But behind him came that old cab. True, it was slower. True, its cornering was nowhere near the Excalibur's. But it was driven by a championship space pilot.

Oh, Gods, it wasn't solved after all. Madison would not look up. He was in pure panic. He could only go so many miles on that multiple lane for which he was heading.

"GO TO CONNECTICUT!" I screamed at him, unheard. Oh, if he would only turn north, he stood a chance of outdistancing the cab and then we could switch on a bullhorn and tell him to stop while we picked him up. It was his only chance.

He raced closer to Franklin D. Roosevelt Drive. He rocketed up an approach ramp, chrome flashing in the sun.

HE TURNED SOUTH!

Oh, Gods, he was done for. He would run out of free-way! Sheer panic must be driving him!

We followed, high above him.

The orange cab was up the ramp and flying south in pursuit.

Madison was diving in and out of startled traffic, doing at least a hundred miles an hour.

I doubted that cab could do more than eighty at its best.

Madison might have a chance.

And on that chance depended my own future life. If he was caught, I was done for completely. Under the Countess Krak's helmet he would babble like a running brook!

A new thought hit me like a lightning bolt. Madison would reinforce the involvement of Bury and the Countess might take it into her head to run up the whole chain. If she did that and found me, she would also add it up and find Lombar. And Lombar would find me for permitting it!

I was caught in a nutcracker!

I seemed to be in the center of a whirling, screaming circle of Demons. That was what I got for praying to Jesus Christ!

Madison caused two trucks to sideswipe. One, a semi-trailer, shot sideways to block the whole road. But Madison was through! Going like the roaring wind!

THE HIGHWAY WAS BLOCKED!

Heller was stamping on his brakes. He slowed. He sized up the scene.

Then suddenly, he rocked the cab by hitting a divid-er, went straight at the rail, skidded against the bars and shot back onto the highway. He was around the obstruction. Feeding throttle, he raced after the Excalibur!

But Madison had a distance advantage now and he was making the most of it. Due to a turn in the road, I could see by Heller's viewer, Madison was out of sight.

From our high vantage point, we could see Madison increasing that lead. He was past Bellevue Hospital now. Travelling at that speed, it did not take him any time at all to pass East 14th Street.

There was hope!

He slued on every one of the slight changes of direction of Roosevelt Drive. But in less than three minutes, he was going to run out of highway! He would dead-end at the bottom of Manhattan at the Ferry Terminal!

Way back, relentlessly, came the speeding cab.

"Raht," I said, "get that pickup ladder down. We're going to snake Madison out of that car."

"You must be crazy!" Raht said. "You'll break your neck!"

"No, you will," I said, "for you are the one that's going down."

"NO!"

"That's an order," I said, unholstering a gun. "There's lots of hospitals around if you fall."

"I already know that," he said grimly, but he gestured at the copilot and the ladder began to descend.

"This is nuts," the pilot said.

"That's what you were paid to be," I said.

"Not from a racing car!"

"Five hundred more," I said. The emergency was my life.

"Here we go," the pilot replied.

But Madison got other ideas before he spotted ours. He had passed the Williamsburg Bridge across the

East River. He had passed the Manhattan Bridge. He was on the Elevated Highway and heading toward the Brooklyn Bridge.

He looked back. Apparently he could not see the orange cab, as it was too far behind him.

He braked!

He turned right!

He went screaming down a ramp off the Elevated Highway.

With a yank of the wheel, he made the Excalibur turn violently, almost half about. He dived down the street below the Elevated Highway.

I suddenly knew what he was going to do. He was going to hide on a dock as he had done before!

There were a lot of long piers jutting out into the river.

I jabbed the pilot anxiously and pointed.

Sure enough, the Excalibur's nose was pointed at the long pier and it was coming out!

The pilot spun our craft. I gestured at Raht with the gun and he went down the ladder.

We were right in front of the Excalibur now, travelling at its speed. Raht on the ladder just ahead of the car tried to signal Madison to stop.

Madison was in such a panic, he was giving Raht no attention.

I leaned out of the door, wind whipping me from the blades, to yell at Madison to stop.

He was glaze-eyed. He just kept going!

I fired my gun to attract his attention.

That did it!

Madison saw us!

He only had about a thousand feet to go with the dock ahead of him.

The pilot was pretty good.

He put Raht right beside Madison.

Raht grabbed the man by the arm.

Madison, the crazy fool, grabbed at his suitcase in the back!

Up went the pilot!

Madison and suitcase came out of the car!

The vehicle was shooting forward.

IT WENT OFF THE END OF THE PIER!

There was a huge splash.

The copilot was rolling the ladder up.

Raht, then Madison, came to the floor of the chopper. It circled away downriver.

Cars had stopped on the Elevated Highway above, drivers unloading to go to the rail and stare.

I saw the orange cab brake at the end of the traffic jam. And then I looked at my viewer.

"It went over!" said Bang-Bang. "I saw the tail end of it as it hit the water."

"The same car?" said Heller.

"The same car," said Bang-Bang.

"Was he in it?" said Heller.

"I couldn't tell," said Bang-Bang. "The warehouse obscured it. I think that chopper was trying to arrest him for speeding and drove him into the drink. I couldn't see what it did."

"I better go down," said Heller. "Take the wheel." He jumped out of the cab and ran off.

"They'll probably find the body," said the Countess Krak.

"Hell—beggin' your pardon, ma'am," said Bang-Bang, "that East River is so full of gangsters that got theirselves taken for a ride, you'd never be able to separate him out."

"Good riddance," said the Countess Krak. "Serves him right for talking about my Jettero that way!"

"Yes, ma'am," said Bang-Bang, "I've noticed it don't seem healthy. There's Jet signalling from below. That means in Army language he's spotted something and is going further."

I freaked. Maybe some bystander had observed the helicopter snatch.

"Head for the West 30th Street Heliport," I shrieked at the pilot, "clear over on the other side of Manhattan."

With luck, we would make it yet.

Maybe their Jesus Christ would hear me after all!

Then I heard the Countess Krak's voice on her viewer. "Maybe if we went over and got the yacht we could search the East River and make sure that Madison is dead."

I freaked.

That yacht was my target now. I had to get there first!

If I didn't, all my plans would come to an abrupt and horrible end!

Chapter 6

As we flew, J. Walter Madison raised himself off the floorboards.

Above the beat of the chopper blades, he said, "What were you shooting at?" His eyes were pretty wild.

"Didn't you see the sniper on the roof?" I said nervously. "He almost got a bead on you, but I nailed him."

"I saw him fall," said Teenie. "Nose dive."

I blinked. Did she just make things up or did she think she saw things that didn't happen? Maybe she was not only a pathological liar but also a pathological walking delusion! Oh, it was a good thing I was kidnapping her!

"Maybe they thought I drowned," said Madison hopefully.

"I'm afraid not," I said. "Three Corleone gangsters were pointing at the chopper as we flew away. They were shaking their fists."

"I saw them with my own eyes," said Teenie, her own oversized ones very round.

"Who's this?" said Madison, staring at Teenie.

"Miss Teenie Whopper, J. Walter Madison," I said. And then a cunning plan popped into my head. If I could get them interested in each other, Teenie would leave me alone. After all, he was a very handsome young man.

"I just graduated from college," said Teenie. "He tells people I am his niece. But there's no point in getting chummy if the Corleone mob is after you, Mr. Madison. You won't be around long enough to bother with."

"What am I going to do?" said Madison, looking pretty white.

"You're not safe yet," I said. "We've got to get you gone, Mad."

He appeared very agitated. "Yes," he said. "The Corleones are tough. I've read all about them in the papers. They thirst for blood even more than money!"

"With luck," I said, "we'll get you away. I can spirit you off so nobody will ever hear of you again. So don't worry."

"Wow!" said Teenie. "Real white slavery."

Madison looked rather disconcerted. So I said loudly

to the pilot, "Land as fast as you can. We don't want to be shot out of the air!"

We swooshed down to the West 30th Street Heliport.

Right there, at Pier 68, a few hundred yards to the south of us, was my objective. The *Golden Sunset!*

If luck was with me, I was going to steal my own yacht.

For it had occurred to me that, after all, I owned it. It had been bought on my credit card!

I paid off the pilots. Raht and Teenie unloaded the baggage and got it into two cabs, necessary even for that short haul.

We sped over and along the dock. I glanced anxiously up and down to be sure Krak and Heller weren't there yet.

"Wait," I told the cabs.

I raced aboard.

Captain Bitts was in the ship's officers' wardroom drinking coffee. Now came the real test. Would he believe me?

I pulled out my passport and threw it down in front of him. He picked it up languidly. Then he saw the name *Sultan Bey.* He stood up like he'd been goosed.

"You're the owner!" he said incredulously. "I thought you were in Turkey!"

"People have got to go on thinking that," I said. "That CIA man, Haggarty, stole my concubine. We must keep this hushed up to avoid any scandal. Don't even tell Squeeza I am aboard. Say no word to anybody. I am going to go to sea and try to mend my broken heart."

"Well, that's how it goes in these rich families," said Captain Bitts. "I will say that CIA man was awful good looking and that concubine was sure beautiful. Looking at you, I can see how it must have happened."

He was convinced! He was not going to query the Countess Krak! For once my unprepossessing looks had stood me in good stead!

I glanced nervously through a port at the dock. No sign of Heller or Krak.

"Sail at once," I ordered Bitts.

"Well, we're all right for fuel and water," he said. "But we don't have any fresh provisions. It will take a little while to get some from the chandler."

"My heart is so broken," I said, "that I can't stand the sight of this town another minute. Sail without them."

"How many in your party?" he said. "Just you? I ought to file a crew list."

"Omit it," I said.

"Where we going?" he said.

"Anywhere outside the United States."

"Bermuda. I can get provisions at Saint George, Bermuda."

"Good," I said, glancing out the port. "SAIL!"

"You didn't tell me how many there were in your party."

"Two. My niece and her boyfriend. SAIL!"

"Do you have any baggage?"

"It's on the dock. Send your crew racing down to grab it and get this ship to sea. My heart won't stand much more of this. SAIL!"

"You're the owner," he said.

At last!

I raced out. I looked up and down the dock. Still no sign of anyone pursuing. I saw a telephone cable to the ship. Oh, Gods, the Countess Krak might phone the captain.

Four crewmen came down the gangplank, followed

by the Chief Steward. They began to shift the tattered baggage aboard.

"Hey, what's this?" said Teenie, having finally gotten my attention. She was pointing at the *Golden Sunset*.

"It's my yacht," I said.

"Well, Jesus Christ," she said. "That's the biggest God (bleeped) yacht I ever saw. Man, you run this white-slave ring in style!"

"Go aboard," I begged her. "And take Madison with you."

The Chief Steward said, "The young lady, sir. I take it she goes in the owner's suite?"

"No way!" I said. "Give her one of her own. And give that young man another one." My eyes were on that phone cable going up to the ship. It was still connected! Krak could still call.

I grabbed Raht. I had seized Krak's activator-receiver and 831 Relayer from a box. I pushed them into his hands.

"The woman's eye bug," he said. "I'll put it with the man's, back on the Empire State antenna. You better keep Crobe's. He'll be back at the base by now."

"I'm giving the orders around here," I snarled at him. "Take this." I pushed the Teenie letter to Adora and Candy at him. "See that it is mailed in two days to the apartment: that won't make the disappearance coincidental."

"Ah," he said. "You ARE kidnapping her. I swear, Officer Gris, you do the craziest things. Of what possible use to you is a teen-age Earth girl? Thin as a rail. No (bleeps). Leaping around. You could get into trouble, kidnapping her."

"You got no idea how much trouble she could be if I DIDN'T kidnap her," I said. "Shows you're not experienced in this profession at all. In addition to the charms you mention, she's also a pathological liar and even believes she sees things that aren't there. It's NOT kidnapping her that would cause trouble. So when I need you to teach me my business, I'll tell you." Riffraff. Always getting out of line.

I hastily wrote out a note. "Now see that this gets to Fatten, Farten, Burstein and Ooze, the advertising firm, today without fail."

He took it and read it. It said:

F.F.B.O.,

The jig is up on Madison. He has just been murdered and his car is at the end of the dock under Brooklyn Bridge, fathoms deep. Know positively the enemy is going to blow up 42 Mess Street. Close that operation at once.

Smith

"Why this?" said Raht.

"Covers the trail," I said.

"Yes, but doesn't that leave this whole Whiz Kid campaign up in the air?"

"You knew about this?"

"I have a bug on the Royal officer," said Raht.

"Well, the Whiz Kid double is in their hands," I said. "They know who has been shooting at them. We've got to cover the trail."

"I get it," said Raht. "You've abandoned your orders from Lombar Hisst."

I peered at him. With a sudden shock it occurred to me that he might be the unknown spy that was supposed to kill me if I failed. I snarled at him, "No, I haven't! This is just a strategic withdrawal to regroup forces. I mean to counterattack."

"It looks like you're the one getting attacked," said Raht. "And if you take this yacht the woman bought, she'll have you followed!"

He had a point! Hastily, I scribbled another note. "Send this as a radiogram," I said. "To her condo address."

He read it. It said:

> MADAM.
>   REGRET TO INFORM YOU YACHT HAS BEEN INDUCTED INTO THE TURKISH NAVY.
>   THERE'S NOTHING ANYONE CAN DO ABOUT IT.
>   HAVE SAILED FOR TURKEY. SORRY.
>   CAPT. BITTS

I thought it was pretty clever. The last place in the world I would go was Turkey.

Captain Bitts himself was at my side now. "Sir, the pilot is aboard and the tug is on its way. We're singled up on lines and ready to cast off." He saluted and went up the gangway to await me on the deck.

I said to Raht, "I'm sailing now. I won't be back to the U.S."

"Can I count on that?" said Raht.

I ignored his insolence. "You can count on the eventual demise of that Royal officer and that (bleeped) woman," I said.

I glanced along the dock. There was no sign of Heller or Krak. And then something caught my eye. The dock telephone man had parted the cable!

I could make it!

I rushed up the gangplank and they swung it away.

The tug was there.

Lines came off the dock bollards.

Space gaped wider and wider between the hull and the pier.

Still no sign of Heller or Krak.

I had made it!

The props were stirring a froth of river water at our stern.

We were headed for sea!

I stood and watched Manhattan fade away.

For the first time in weeks my heart began to beat normally.

I WAS STILL ALIVE! I WAS FREE!

Yes, I had outwitted them.

Not only that, but I had escaped the vile clutches of those ex-lesbians who had become my wives.

What I had told Raht had not been a lie. I had time now to regroup my forces and return to the attack.

And I would have been even further cheered as I boarded the ship—had my premonition cells been more active—cozy in the knowledge there would come a time when the vicious Countess Krak would be lying, helpless as putty, in my vengeful hands.

I was still master of the fate of Earth.

Lombar and Rockecenter still reigned in the Heavens.

I chuckled. I had won this round. And because I had, millions would suffer.

It was a lovely spring afternoon.

It promised a future very bright for me. And very dark indeed for Heller and the Countess Krak and Earth.

PART FIFTY-SIX

Chapter 1

The *Golden Sunset* plowed through the gentle swell, a white dream ship on a blue ocean, followed by the flashing wings and calls of gulls. We were headed southeastwards for Bermuda and had already left Sandy Hook behind.

To a man just freed from bondage, it was glorious to be aboard, even though I usually hated the sea.

When the coastline seemed too far away for me to be stopped, I went along the panelled passageways to the owner's suite.

I thought I could detect a faint perfume and flinched. It reminded me of the Countess Krak.

The steward was waiting for me.

"The perfume!" I said. "You didn't clean this place when the concubine left."

"A lovely lady, sir. But that isn't a lady's perfume. I've drawn the master a bath. You're smelling the bath salts."

"I don't need a bath!" I said indignantly. I had better get this riffraff in its place fast.

"Oh, of course not," he said. "But it would be so nice to wash the last vestiges of the shore away."

He had a point.

I went into the beautifully panelled bathroom: the

tub was feet high in bubbles. Before I could object he had stripped my clothes off and I was in the tub.

Then he peeled the bandages off my face. "That's a very nasty wound, sir. Mr. Haggarty give it to you?"

"I fell on a skateboard."

"Well, that's original anyway," the steward said. "I saw it coming, you know. The way your concubine talked about him, it was obvious she was in love."

"Don't talk about her!" I said.

"Of course, sir. It's pretty hard for somebody with only money to recommend him, to hold his own against a dashing figure like Mr. Haggarty."

"Don't talk about him, either!" I shouted.

"Ah, yes," he said. "I can see it is a very painful subject. What did he hit you with?"

"Will you shut up!" I cried.

"Of course, sir. I didn't mean to pry. But don't be downcast. The world is full of women."

"Too (bleeped) full!" I grated. "That's why I'm at sea."

"Then welcome to the club, sir. That's why most sailors go to sea. Now, if you will just hold still, I'll shave you and then we'll rebandage that wound he gave you. Five stitches! My, my! Just lie there and soak in case you collected any more bruises. I put Epsom salts in the water along with the bubble bath just in case."

There was no handling this monomaniac. I was afraid to venture further remarks. I was puzzled as to where he got the idea there had been a love spat and a beat-up, but suddenly recalled that that was what I had told the captain. News certainly got around this ship in an awful hurry. I'd have to remember that.

Wrapped at last in a huge bath towel, I was stood before the wardrobe. "I unpacked for you," the steward said. "You seem to have left in a hurry, as you don't have any yachting clothes. However, we can remedy that in Bermuda and I was relieved to see that you at least brought a dinner jacket. But we can dress later in that. Right now, I've laid out some hiking shorts and they'll have to do."

The old Jew who had sold me such a large wardrobe hadn't guessed I'd be going to sea. A German Tyrolean pair of leather pants and embroidered suspenders really didn't fit the part very well.

Stepping out into the passageway, I collided with the Chief Steward. "Oh, dear," he said, "we'll have to get you some proper clothes in Bermuda. But never mind, Mr. Bey, we'll do all we can to make your cruise a success and mend your broken heart. Such a beautiful concubine. I don't blame you for throwing it all up and tearing off to sea. But, never mind, what I have to know is for the benefit of the chef. We haven't much that is fresh but we do have some things in the freezer. For dinner, he proposes Russian eggs, bouillabaisse, Rainbow Trout Montana, Venison Sauerbraten, Snow Peas Persian, Neopolitan Flambeaux with assorted Danish pastries, Gourmandise cheese and Bavarian Mocha. I know it is a little plain, but we were caught a bit short. Will it do?"

"Yes," I said, realizing suddenly I hadn't really eaten well since I left Turkey.

"Now, as to the wine..."

"No wine!" I said. "I'm a teetotaler!"

"Ah," he said. "Against your religion."

"And everything else," I said firmly.

"Does that apply to your niece and her fiancé?"

"Let them drown in it," I said.

"Of course, sir. Now, here is the sports director. I must leave you to enjoy your cruise."

"I have a program all drawn up for you," said the sports director, pacing along beside me as I walked to the deck.

"Tear it up," I said. "I believe only in spectator sports."

"Well, now," he said. "That is pretty drastic. I should have thought, from that wound he gave you, that you'd be itching to get in shape and take on that CIA man."

I shuddered with horror at the thought of going up against Heller hand to hand!

"I am of a peaceful disposition," I said. "Live and let live."

"Well, seeing that he stole your woman, sir, that's a lot more peaceful than I could ever get. He won all our money, too. I was sort of hoping to arrange a return match."

"Not using me!" I said. "You have no idea how peaceful I am. A veritable dove. Olive branches spout from my teeth. Christian, too. Turn the other cheek."

"I thought you were a Moslem," he said. "You just told the Chief Steward you were off liquor because of religion. No, Mr. Bey, you must realize that the physical well-being of our owner is my responsibility when he is at sea. And when I see flab developing . . ."

"What flab?"

"The rubber tire you're getting around your waist."

"Where?"

"There."

"Ouch."

"You see? Office life has made you soft," he said. "You are far too young for that. I propose, to begin, ten laps around the promenade deck right now and we'll start in earnest tomorrow morning in the gym. Shall we say about nine?"

He started pacing alongside me as I ran around the promenade deck. After five laps I was panting, so I grabbed at the rail, pretending an interest in the sea.

"Why is the ship so level?" I panted.

"Stabilizers, both fore and aft pitch and athwartship roll. Two sets. She's like a billiard table except in storms. So now if we can just finish these last five laps . . ."

I was absolutely gasping for air.

With him pushing with both hands against my back, we made it. I flopped over the rail, looking down at the water creaming by twenty feet below. "I don't think I can take this," I wheezed.

"We can't have the owner demising from cardiac arrest due to extreme deskosis ashore," he said.

"Cardiac arrest?" I said.

"Certainly. The shape you've let yourself get into, it's imminent."

"It sure is," I said, listening to my blood pounding out my eardrums.

"But never mind," he said. "Steam baths, good food, vitamins on the table and a stiff program carried out every day and we won't have to bury you at sea. So beginning tomorrow morning, we'll get the program really going. Right now, I should think you would like to join your niece and her fiancé for a swim before dinner."

"Where are they?" I said.

"Well, they may still be down in the race track. I've never seen anybody skateboard quite like your niece. And her fiancé seems to be a complete madman with a racing car."

"It's his general state," I said.

"Well, the way he was chasing her with the racing car, I left a crewman on duty there in case we had to clean up a wreck."

"Yikes!" I said. "Whatever you do, don't let her get killed! That would be fatal!"

"I'll remind her that you are concerned," said the sports director. "Now I suggest you go up to the sunpool and loll a bit. I'll go down to the race track and hurry them up."

I climbed the ladder with difficulty to the sunpool deck. But it was worth the effort. The aquamarine water lapped at the Roman frieze that surrounded it. Reclining chairs with shades sat about. I collapsed in one. Gentle mood music soothed my nerves. The sea all about was a lovely scene in the afternoon sun.

It was the first time I had really relaxed for months! I basked. This was the life! Leagues from the madding throng. Far beyond the reach of dramatic turmoil. The peace was so thick, it lay on one like a blanket. Even the throb of engines was a lulling undertone.

A shriek!

Teenie came tearing up a ladder and went around the pool like a spinning mouse!

She had on some bikini pants and nothing else. Even her ponytail was undone.

A guffaw!

Madison, in a pair of shorts, came racing after her!

"Last one in's a rotten egg!" screamed Teenie. She raced up the diving board and *SPLASH!* A wave of water hit me. *SPLASH!* Another wave hit me as Madison went in!

Teenie hadn't come up.

She grabbed Madison's legs from below and pulled him under.

They surfaced. They batted tidal waves of water at each other. They hit me!

"FOR GODS' SAKES!" I yelled. "You're drowning me!"

They both bobbed, suddenly silent. They looked at each other. They raced to the side of the pool. They surged out.

They grabbed me, one on either side, and THREW ME IN!

I couldn't protest. My mouth was too full of water. And every time I tried to talk, Teenie pushed me under again!

Probably the only thing which saved me from drowning was the multiple-tone chime being struck by a steward.

"Dinner will be served in half an hour," he said. "This is the warning bell so that you can dress."

"Dress?" said Teenie.

"Dress!" I snarled. "You can't go running around this ship bare-(bleep) naked!"

"It's customary," said Madison. "Things are done differently at sea."

"Dress in what?" said Teenie, bobbing in the water.

"In an evening dress!" I bellowed at her.

She looked up at the sky, which was becoming painted with the scarlet of sunset. "Well, it *is* evening," she said. "But that's when you take OFF your clothes, not put them on!"

"I'll help you," said Madison.

Oh, was I suddenly cheered! My luck was holding all the way. Madison and Teenie were hitting it off and Madison would keep her out of my bed.

Despite the determination of the crew to run my life, this was not turning out badly after all.

I supposed myself to be miles from my enemies and safe.

Totally unsuspecting what the future held in store, I went below to dress for dinner.

Chapter 2

In the ornate dining salon, Teenie and Madison laughed all the way through dinner.

He had helped her dress. He had found a door curtain with a nautical design and had draped it around her so that it looked like an off-the-shoulder evening gown of sorts.

He was showing her which spoon and which fork to eat what with, while the Chief Steward looked on indulgently and saw to the service.

Eventually they got down to the coffee and were so stuffed they had to stop laughing. It was a relief.

"You were talking about outlaws, this afternoon," said Teenie to Mad. "I just remembered that the place where I lived in New York, Tudor City, was once upon a time an outlaw hangout. Used to be known as 'Corcoran's Roost.' Paddy Corcoran, the notorious bandit, used to live there until they caught up with him."

"Really?" said Madison.

"Absolutely. And every Saturday night you can see his ghost dragging basketloads of heads he cut off, right through the park. I've run into him myself."

"Fascinating," said Madison. "You know, I can't

knock off work entirely despite my mother's insistence I take a vacation. I should continue to do research on outlaws. I wonder if there were any in Bermuda? We'll have to go ashore and hunt around for markers and things."

"Oh, that would be fun," said Teenie. "I just love outlaws, too. I can be all kinds of help, getting the locals to talk and looking under rocks and things."

Oh, that really sounded good to me. They were hitting it off very well indeed and that let me out. Thank Gods!

After dinner we went to the music salon and Teenie got some of her Neo Punk Rock records and they danced.

I retired early. It had been a pretty active day.

For three lovely days we sailed onward to Bermuda, a white ship upon an azure sea, a veritable picture book of contentment.

The combination of no sex, no marijuana, plenty of exercise and a stern taskmaster—the sports director—to see that I did it began to build me back to the world of the living.

I considered Madison so valuable that I went into a panic at the very thought of losing him. He and Teenie seemed to want nothing more than to romp all day. Although I had no evidence of it, I could only suppose that they were also romping all night in Madison's or Teenie's cabin.

My prospects seemed marvelous. Sailing along, getting back my health, I gloried in one single fact—oh, Gods, it was wonderful: NO WOMEN! My bed was utterly empty, my time was my own, and the smile on my face grew and grew.

The elderly stewardess who seemed to be taking care of Teenie's room, the afternoon of the third day, gave me a valuable tip. She said, "Your niece is such a dear thing. I think she will be lonely when her boyfriend leaves the ship."

"Leaves the ship?" I croaked in sudden alarm. "What gave you that idea?" Gods, what a disaster that would be: Teenie would be right back in my lap and bed!

"I couldn't help but overhear them talking in the steam bath," she said. "He was a bit despondent that he was letting somebody named Bury down and wondered if the dangers might not have been exaggerated. He was also asking the purser about flights from Bermuda to New York."

"Thank Gods you told me," I said.

"The owner is who we work for," she said, probably expecting a tip. And, unaccustomed as I was to doing such things, I gave her one.

What a disaster that would be! Madison was keeping Teenie out of my bed, and Madison in the hands of the fiend, Krak, would babble his silly head off! If Madison went away, I would be attacked from within and without!

Trained as I was, it did not take long to solve it. In the radio room there was a radio-telex machine. Each night in the small hours, all by itself and unattended, it chattered out the news from the wire services, making several copies for distribution to the owner and guests. Morgan probably had had other uses for the machine, such as manipulating the family financial empire. And I had another use, too.

I carefully made a feeder tape at midnight that very night, and when the news came chattering through, I adroitly added the item to the text before the machine turned off. The item was:

*MAN KILLED BY MAFIA THOUGHT TO
HAVE BEEN MISTAKEN FOR J. WALTER
MADISON. A NOTE TO THE VICTIM'S
WIFE STATED "WE APOLOGIZE. WE
THOUGHT YOUR HUSBAND WAS THAT
NO-GOOD (BLEEP) J. WALTER MADISON
THAT WE HAVE A CONTRACT OUT ON. IF
YOU WANT SOME MONEY FOR YOUR
OLD AGE, HELP US FIND THE LOUSE SO
WE CAN TORTURE HIM AND FILL HIM
FULL OF HOLES." POLICE ARE BAFFLED
AS TO THE WHEREABOUTS OF MADI-
SON AND STATED TODAY THEY WOULD
ASSIST THE CORLEONE MOB TO FIND
HIM IN ORDER TO PREVENT OTHER
ERRORS.*

The following morning at breakfast, I made very sure he saw it. "Well, you're in the news yourself," I said.

He read it. He went white. He didn't finish his powdered eggs.

The reaction was just what I wanted. And it had come in the nick of time. Bermuda was in sight.

Chapter 3

Bermuda is a pretty place. It sits in a startlingly clear, azure sea, its bays so blue they hurt the eyes. The beaches are pink. The strangely architectured houses, of different pastel shades, are constructed to catch rain-water on their roofs and help make up for scarcity.

We did not go down the long channel to Hamilton but anchored at the port nearest the sea, St. George.

The hills looked inviting and I lost no time in going ashore. I walked up and down the main street—one might say, the only street—hoping to buy some yachting clothes. A couple of inquiries promptly verified a thing I had heard: that Bermuda had the highest cost of living in the world. I did not buy any yachting clothes.

But something else happened. I was standing near the boat landing, reading a historic plaque and looking at a replica of an original building, when I became aware of someone watching me.

Covertly, I examined him. He had on a three-piece business suit of charcoal gray, an odd costume on this island of white shirts and shorts. The fellow's jaw was blue-black despite evident recent shaving. He was of very heavy build. What was he? A cop? I couldn't decide, other than that he certainly was no Bermudian.

I sauntered up the street and found a bench where I could sit down. I pretended to be very interested in the view. But out of the tail of my eye I watched this man. Apparatus habits are never lost. He seemed far too inter-ested in me. He went over to a bar and went in and I knew he was watching me through the window. I pre-tended not to observe this.

Teenie and Madison had not come ashore with me. Madison was having a case of jitters. He believed he ought to go down and sit in the bilges until we were at sea again, saying, "The Corleones might use Interpol to locate me—after all, Interpol is composed of Nazi crimi-nals and the Nazis had Italy as an ally and the Corleones might get a lead—even though I realize it would be an awful step down from the Mafia to Interpol." Teenie had stayed behind, arguing with him.

Apparently she had gotten bored with trying to coax him out of his funk, for here she came now, in a bikini and ponytail, standing on the foredeck of a yacht speedboat which was bringing her ashore.

She leaped off onto the dock and walked up the street, looking for bicycles to rent, judging from what she asked a young black boy. He pointed in about six directions at once, stuck out his palm for money and when he didn't get any, pointed straight up with his forefinger.

Teenie evidently didn't see me sitting on the bench: she was in the glaring sun and I was in the dark shade; I was quite some distance away. She went up the street past the bar into which the black-jowled man had gone.

He came out and fell into step beside her. She was chattering away, talking about bicycles, and he was nodding.

They progressed up the street a little further and I could no longer hear what they were saying. But their heads seemed closer together.

They went past a hotel. They stopped. The man was saying something. They turned around and walked back to the hotel and went in. This was very curious because a hotel does not rent bicycles.

They were in that place for about an hour. I drew back even further out of sight. I watched the door. They came out. Teenie seemed very cheerful. They walked up the street and entered a record shop. They were gone for a while and when they came out Teenie was carrying a foot-high stack of records.

They went further up the street to a dress shop. They were gone for an awfully long time. They came out. Teenie was in a cycling costume and a black man was following with about a five-foot stack of dress boxes and the records.

They went further up the street and entered a bicycle shop. After a while they came out and were followed by a second black man who was pushing, with some difficulty, THREE bicycles.

Teenie took one of the bikes, a racing model, got on it and, with a wave to the black-jowled man, rode off deeper into the island.

The black-jowled man looked all around and then led the two porters and their burdens down to the dock, signalled the yacht for a boat and sent the purchases aboard.

He came back up the street, looked in the direction Teenie had vanished, gave a short, barking laugh and went back into the bar.

It was, on the surface, a very insignificant occurrence. My first conclusion was that the black-jowled man liked very young meat, had made a proposition, been accepted and had then paid a very high price. I tried to add up how high that price had been, considering the altitudinous cost-of-living index of Bermuda. Pretty high. Well, maybe Teenie with all her new education was worth it. That black-jowled man had certainly seemed pleased.

That evening Teenie came to dinner in a silver evening gown, silver slippers and a silver ring to bind her ponytail. Madison had found the bilges were not comfortable and he sat at the table gloomily muttering that he wished we were at sea where it was safe.

"Oh, Maddie," said Teenie, digging into her *jumbo prawns au Biscayne,* "stop glooming. The Mafia aren't going to get you here. They don't need any Mafia in this place: the whole economy is built on robbery. From its earliest days, according to all the signs, Bermuda has been a hangout for privateersmen and pirates and bootleggers and you name it, Maddie. I went swimming this afternoon at the nicest little beach you ever saw and an old gray-haired man there told me all about it. Of course, I couldn't understand a lot of his Italian . . ."

"Italian?" said Madison, dropping his prawn. "They aren't Italian here. They're English! A very few speak some Portuguese, but no Italian! Are you sure about this?"

"Of course, I'm sure," said Teenie. "Don't you suppose a native New Yorker like me knows words like *assassino* and *mano nera*?"

Madison was chalk white. "Who was this man?"

"Oh, a nice old fellow. He wanted to know if I was from the pretty yacht and I said yes. And then when he was showing me how well he could swim, he asked me if there was a good-looking young man aboard with brown hair. And then he showed me a seashell and asked me if it didn't look like a *mano nera*, a black hand, the symbol of an *assassino* . . . wait. I have it here in my purse. He said I could give it to you if I wanted."

Madison stared at it. He was very white. He said to me, "How long are we going to stay in this port?"

I shrugged. "We're just cruising. I should imagine when we have fresh provisions, we can sail."

"You're all the time talking of doing research on outlaws," said Teenie. "I've heard the King of Morocco is a crook to end all crooks. Why don't we go there?"

"That's clear on the other side of the Atlantic," I said.

"Smith," said Madison, his hand shaking as he held the seashell, "I know I owe you a very great deal for saving me in New York. But could you do just one more favor and sail?"

"For Morocco?" Teenie said. "It's the grass capital of the world!"

"I'll inform the captain," I said. I was very pleased. We would be an awfully long time at sea and Madison was now fully convinced he had to come along.

We sailed about midnight, heading out through the long narrow channel dotted with lights, our wake phosphorescent beneath the stars. The lights of Bermuda fell behind and before us stretched the broad Atlantic at its least tumultuous latitude, according to Captain Bitts. It would be a leisurely and pleasant cruise.

I would regain my health and vigor. What a blessing to not be bothered with women! That daily stint I had been on had worn me to nothing. What a glorious world it would be if I never again touched a woman!

Hugging that splendid thought to me, I went below to my sleeping cabin. I disrobed and climbed into bed. I stretched out, luxuriously alone and undisturbed.

A door opened!

I had never noticed it before.

It must be the door to the adjacent suite!

TEENIE WALKED IN!

"Hey!" I said in panic and alarm. "What are you doing here?"

"Oh," she said, "the Chief Steward says he's wise in the ways of the world. He has known all along that I am not your niece. They moved me this very evening to the suite next door where I would be handier to you. They always think of the owner's comfort."

She had on a wrap. She was untying it as she stood in the middle of the floor.

"Whoa!" I said in alarm. "You can't be that hard up. This very afternoon I saw you go into a hotel with a man!"

"Oh, him," she said with a gay laugh. "What an amusing lecher. He owns all the hotels in Bermuda, you know. I only went down on him and he had an absolutely awful time trying to (bleep). He liked it all right because I am a real expert, but all it did for me was get me heated up."

She dropped her wrap off and stood there.

Then she took the clip off her ponytail and shook her hair out. She walked to the bed. "Move over," she said. "You don't think I'm going to sleep in there alone, do you?"

She climbed into the bed beside me.

"Wait a minute," I said. "What about Madison?"

She laughed gaily. "Oh, Madison is a very sweet boy. But the trouble is, he loves his mother and wouldn't think of being unfaithful to her. The thought of having intercourse with any other woman drives him up the wall."

"You're lying."

"Ask him," she said. "The only reason he tolerates me around is that he thinks of me as a kid. If Madison wasn't that way, what do you think I'm doing here in your bed, Inky?"

I blinked. There was logic in what she said. Then I saw the flaw in it. "The ship is loaded with other men. Why pick on me?"

She looked at me with her too-big eyes. "Inky, I will level with you. This equipment of yours is too great to be neglected. I am absolutely determined to be faithful to you. I will only go down on the crew to keep in practice. But you get me for a snack in the morning, a piece in the afternoon and a full-scale banquet all night. How's that?"

"NO!" I cried.

"Inky, the sports director this evening told me you were concerned I might kill myself. So if you don't like my program for you, I will have no choice but to throw myself overboard."

I shuddered. That would bring on a rap for murder.

"No," I said.

"No what?" she persisted. "No overboard or no tail?"

"No overboard," I said.

"Ah, that's better. Now that we have things clearly understood, you seem a little limp. So I'll just slip next door where I happen to have a prepared bhong, bring it in, light it . . ."

My head was spinning. What had I done to be punished like this? Factually, after that parade of women in the apartment, I never wanted to see another one again.

She was pushing the bhong mouthpiece between my teeth. "Suck it in, old boy," she said. "Now hold it like I taught you. Now another puff. This is Panama Red and it's pretty jolty. I think I'll have one, too."

She exhaled the smoke into my face.

After a while, she lifted the sheet and looked. "Ah, that's better, Inky."

A puff of marijuana smoke floated upward. Her voice was clear, above the hiss of the sea. "Now, just lie there and I will show you some of the things I learned."

A porthole cover was swinging gently. "There's a certain little muscle that can go round and round. . . ."

A curtain undulated. "Oh, this white slavery is great. . . ."

Another puff of marijuana smoke blew out the port. "Ooooooooh! Inky!!!!!"

Now and then, months later, when I had lots of time to think, I would look back on that night and wish forlornly that I had been my usual alert self, for those hours, I am sure, opened the door to all the Hells I was going to walk through afterwards.

If I had just said NO! louder. But I didn't.

Marijuana can make one awfully blind!

Chapter 4

Forlornly, I sat in the owner's salon and stared at the two viewers.

I was pooped. The sports director had been absolutely raving. "Do you realize," he said, "that if you insist on getting stoned at night, you have to exercise twice as long and hard to get rid of it the next morning? So get running before I have a dead owner on my hands!" He had worked me half to death and here, in the afternoon, I was barely able to sit in the overstuffed chair.

Teenie, apparently, was breaking in her new bicycles, and Mad, for some reason, had cooped himself up in the library with an eye on the door, muttering about Mafia that might have sneaked aboard. I was terrified I might have to go swimming with her: my muscles were so gone, I would have drowned!

Heller was in his office at the Empire State Building. He and Izzy were going over Florida ground plans.

"I don't see why you need such big alligator tanks," Izzy was saying.

"Those aren't alligator tanks. Those are spore tanks," said Heller. "The spores grow very fast but there have to be an awful lot of them and it takes tanks that big."

"Well, alligators will get into them," said Izzy. "I don't see any alligator strainers."

"These posts," said Heller. "They're a laser screen. They put an invisible curtain around the tanks. Nothing can get into them. The belts here take the spores up this ramp where they are dried and then they go into this hamper. At timed intervals they are blown up the stacks, reach the stratosphere and get carried by the upper winds. They clean up pollution, convert it to oxygen, and when they run out of food they perish."

"I don't see the fort," said Izzy.

"Fort for what?" said Heller.

"Indians," said Izzy. "You got to have some kind of fort for the settlers to retire into when the Indians burst out of their reservation."

"Oh, we don't need a fort," said Heller. "We're handling that problem with alligator cavalry."

Izzy put his glasses on more solidly. He looked very closely at Heller. Then he said, with decision, "You're joking with me again, Mr. Jet."

"No," said Heller. "Would I pull jokes on you, Izzy?"

"You have sometimes. It's very trying, Mr. Jet. I lie awake wondering if I laughed in the right place. It costs me sleep."

"No, listen, Izzy. This is one time I'm not teasing you. Look." He unrolled a big layout. "J. P. Flagrant just roughed out these spreads and sent them in."

The layout said:

"Well, I will admit sales have boomed since he came on. But who bought Bullroar for such a huge price?"

"That was another stroke of Flagrant genius," said Heller. "He sold him to King Charles of England because it was such a short distance to fall off."

"Is that why the corporation is now 'By Appointment to His Majesty'?" said Izzy. "I thought I was just making progress in taking over governments."

"Oh, that, too," said Heller. "So now do you believe it about alligator cavalry?"

I pushed the viewer away. There was no point in getting all confused trying to figure out when Heller was serious and when he was joking. I knew that the spores were serious enough. But they wouldn't hurt Rockecenter: they'd just give industry an excuse not to check any pollution they sent into the air. That would sell even dirtier fuel and make Rockecenter even richer.

I turned my attention to the other viewer.

The Countess Krak was walking down a hall in an apartment building, carrying a plastic shopping bag.

She went out the main entrance door.

I freaked! I had been so engrossed with Heller, I had missed what she must have been doing! That condo scene was unmistakable! It was where Madison's mother lived!

Bang-Bang opened up the door of the old cab and the Countess Krak got in. Bang-Bang started the cab up and drove away.

"Any luck?" said Bang-Bang.

"Oh, he was the man, all right. But she's too naive to live, Bang-Bang. She thinks her son was a sensitive child. She thinks he's dead."

"Well, Jet did find an empty on the dock, that had been fired only minutes before. I think that plain-wrapper whirlybird was trying to arrest him for speeding, all right, and hazed him into the drink. And maybe they fired a shot into him as well. Or maybe they fired the shot, hit him and he went over the edge."

"Well, we're not going to get anything more out of Mrs. Madison."

I flinched. Had the Countess Krak killed her?

"I think Jet's right," said Bang-Bang. "It leads straight to Bury."

"She did mention," said the Countess, "that just before he left that day, he had a call from a Mr. Smith."

My blood congealed. Thank Gods, Mrs. Madison had never seen me personally that I recalled. But this was too close!

"There's a million of those in New York," said Bang-Bang.

"Somebody from Bury's office," said the Countess Krak. "I wish Jettero weren't so set about not taking this Bury on."

"It would mean a frontal assault on the whole Rockecenter outfit, including the government," said Bang-Bang. "The casualties would be unacceptable."

"Bang-Bang," said the Countess Krak, "pull up beside the next phone kiosk you see. I'm going to phone Swindle and Crouch and ask for Mr. Smith."

He stopped by a delicatessen on East 45th Street and she made the call.

"Smith?" the Swindle and Crouch receptionist said. "We have no Smiths."

The Countess Krak went back to the cab. "The other address I got was 42 Mess Street. Drive down there, Bang-Bang."

This was certainly hard on my exhausted nerves.

Bang-Bang bounced off assorted vehicles and got them to 42 Mess Street.

It was now just a deserted loft. The Countess stirred around through the papers on the floor. It had all manner of scrap Whiz Kid releases. But the furniture, the phones, the news lines all were gone. The place had degenerated to an empty ruin.

As they drove back uptown, the Countess Krak said, "Well, so far as we can tell, J. Walter Madison is dead and we have shut down the operation, at least there in that place. But we do know one thing for sure."

"What's that?" said Bang-Bang.

"Madison's mother states that Madison worked directly under a Mr. Smith from the office of Swindle and Crouch. That office doesn't have a Mr. Smith. Somebody knew Madison was dead or missing and closed 42 Mess Street before anybody else suspected he was gone. I've got the hour and date of the last press releases they issued. That was probably this same Mr. Smith that called his mother. So the one thing we know for sure is that somewhere in this mess there is a man who is using the fictitious name of Smith."

Bang-Bang said, "That's not very much." I disagreed. I thought it was absolutely, HORRIBLY TOO MUCH!

"It's enough to keep me looking," said the Countess Krak.

Oh, Gods, was I glad I was at sea!

But wait. I couldn't stay at sea forever. Even though I had no place to go, I knew that sooner or later I would have to make a stand.

If the Countess Krak was allowed to go on running around loose, one day she would connect it all up to me and then, no matter where I was, I would be a goner.

It was her fault, after all, that I was at sea.

And only because, through incompetent help, I had not nailed her before.

If I were ever to get out of this, I would have to over-come all odds, forget past failures and finish off the Countess Krak.

That was as vivid to me as the ache which plagued my bones.

I was not just sitting here, helpless.

I glared at the two-way-response radio. With it I could issue an order to Raht.

If I gave him a wrong order and he missed, she would kill him and then I really would be helpless. So I had to be very careful if I told Raht to do anything.

So the question remained: What could I tell Raht to do that would GUARANTEE her end? I must think of something.

Chapter 5

Day followed day as we made our way across the smooth and picturesque sea. It was progressing toward the end of April, a calm part of the year, and we were in the calmest part of the Atlantic. The water was blue, the sky was blue, the yacht was white, the clouds were white. Captain Bitts, when I commented to him that I saw no ships, informed me that this was the most unfre-quented belt in the whole ocean. Even the whales had a chance, he said, and sure enough, on the fifth day we saw one—a monster—much to Teenie's delight.

And that wasn't all that was delighting Teenie. That very night she plagued me with questions about how could whales possibly do it? Was their equipment in proportion to the rest of them?

"They lay eggs," I said.

"They do not," she said. "They are mammals. They do it just like we do."

"No you don't, Teenie," I said. "I am exhausted. Go to your room and sleep just this one night. Between you and the sports director I don't know whether I'm going or coming."

"Well, all right," she said. "But just let me settle this one question of zoology. I found this book in the library and it simply did not show the vital elements. On such subjects I am quite an expert, you know: it was my major at Bassar. To complete my education, I must establish the relative proportions of whales."

"Oh, Gods," I said. "What now? Teenie, will you PLEASE go to bed and stop pestering me!"

She was standing there with the end of a white-edged ruler thoughtfully caressing her lower lip. "If I could establish *your* relative proportions, I could get some idea of that of whales. So if you will just let me measure you, I promise faithfully to go to bed."

Oh, Gods. "Well, (bleep) it, go ahead then," I said, "but don't be all night."

Her robe fell on the floor as she said, "Oh, fiddlesticks, Inky. I can't do it. It wouldn't be fair to whales. You're just a dishcloth."

The starburst chandelier glowed dimly in the ceiling. "To keep my part of the bargain and go to bed," she said, "you'll have to cooperate. Take a few puffs of this Hawaiian. That won't hurt you."

A cloud of marijuana smoke rose up.

The ruler was lying on the floor. I said, "Wait! Wait! You have a bargain to keep!"

The stars shone through the open port. "Ooooooh!" groaned Teenie in a shuddering voice as marijuana smoke poured out.

The curtain was hanging very still. I said, my breath short, "You didn't keep your part of the bargain!"

The ruler was lying there on the floor. "Oh, I'm keeping it," she said, and her hand reached for it and picked it up.

A bowl of fruit in a silver basket shone in the light from the nightstand. "Oh, hell, Inky. You're not co-operating at all! You're just a punctured balloon."

My hand was dangling down toward the floor. "Teenie, please go to bed."

The bhong was sitting on the table. Her fingers applied a lighted match to it. "Just another puff or two, Inky, and I'll be able to finish it and complete my bargain."

The ship's wake hissed as it purled by. "Oh, Inky, aaaaaaahhhhhh!" came Teenie's shuddering moan.

She was in my bathroom, combing her ponytail at my mirror. "Aren't I being a good girl these days, Inky? I'm not even scratching your face the way I used to." She admired herself in the glass. "And I'm putting on some fat now that I'm not eating out of garbage cans." She was fixing the rubber band around her ponytail. "I don't even bruise you anymore. You should appreciate me, Inky."

I yelled at the ceiling, "(Bleep) you! GO TO BED!"

The basket of fruit, minus half its contents, gleamed in the dim light. "Oh, Inky!" she said reprovingly. "Strictly dishrag again."

The bhong teetered on the side table. Her hand steadied it and, with the other, she applied a match. "Well,

I can remedy that! Just a couple more puffs, Inky, and then I can apply the ruler and go to bed."

A horizontal beam of sunlight coming in through the port pried at my eyelids. I woke with a start.

The bedside clock said 7:00 A.M.!

Teenie's head on the other pillow didn't move. Lying on her side, turned away from me, she was sleeping with a smile upon her lips.

I shook her shoulder savagely. "Wake up, (bleep) you!"

She turned her head in my direction. An oversize grin sprang to her oversize lips.

"Oh, you (bleep)!" I snarled.

The sun was doing a crazy circle just above the horizon.

The bowl of fruit exploded.

Her hand picked up her robe and ruler from the floor. "Inky, how can a girl keep a bargain like that when you just keep attacking her?"

She gave her ponytail a fluff. "I would have completed the measurements and gone to bed but you just never gave me a chance."

Her hand was upon the doorhandle to her room. "Now I will never know if whales have the correct proportions." She passed through and slammed the door.

"Have a nice sleep?" the steward said a few minutes later as he opened all the ports and began to air the marijuana smoke out of the room, a thing he had to do each morning.

I had a bath and breakfast and in no good mood went topside. Madison was by himself in the squash court, batting one of these balls that come back on a rubber band. The very sight of him made me furious.

FREE

Send in this card and you'll receive a FREE POSTER while supplies last. No order required for this Special Offer! Mail your card today!
❑ Please send me a FREE poster.
❑ Please send me information about other books by L. Ron Hubbard.

ORDERS SHIPPED WITHIN 24 HRS OF RECEIPT

SCIENCE FICTION/FANTASY:

___ Battlefield Earth paperback	$7.99	_____
___ Battlefield Earth audio	$29.95	_____

MISSION EARTH® series (10 volumes)

___ paperbacks (specify volumes:_____)(each) $5.99	_____
___ audio (specify volumes:_____)(each) $15.95	_____
___ Final Blackout paperback	$6.99	_____
___ Final Blackout audio **SPECIAL** $11.95	_____
___ Fear paperback	$5.99	_____
___ Fear audio **SPECIAL** $9.95	_____
___ Slaves of Sleep & The Masters of Sleep hardcover $19.95	_____
___ Slaves of Sleep & The Masters of Sleep audio $19.95	_____
___ Ole Doc Methuselah hardcover	$18.95	_____
___ Ole Doc Methuselah audio	$24.95	_____

___ L. RON HUBBARD PRESENTS WRITERS OF THE FUTURE® Volumes: (paperback)

❑ Vol IV $4.95   ❑ Vol VI $4.95   ❑ Vol VIII $5.99
❑ Vol IX $5.99   ❑ Vol X $6.99   ❑ Vol XI $6.99

_____

NEW RELEASES!

___ Writers of The Future Volume XII	$6.99	_____
___ Typewriter in the Sky hardcover (Fantasy)	$16.95	_____
___ Typewriter in the Sky audio	$16.95	_____

CHECK AS APPLICABLE: **SHIPPING*:**   _____
❑ Check/Money Order enclosed.   **TAX**:**   _____
(Use an envelope please)
❑ American Express ❑ Visa ❑ Master Card   **TOTAL:**   _____

*Add $1.00 per item for shipping and handling. ** California residents add 8.25% sales tax.

Card#:_____

Exp. Date:_____Signature:_____

NAME:_____

ADDRESS:_____

CITY:_____ STATE:_____ ZIP:_____

PHONE#:_____

Call us now with your Order 1-800-722-1733
http://www.bridgepub.com

© 1997 BPI. All Rights Reserved. MISSION EARTH and WRITERS OF THE FUTURE
are trademarks owned by L. Ron Hubbard Library.

Name: _____

Address: _____

City: _____ State: _____ Zip: _____

NO POSTAGE
NECESSARY
IF MAILED
IN THE
UNITED STATES

BUSINESS REPLY MAIL

FIRST CLASS MAIL   PERMIT NO. 62688   LOS ANGELES, CA

POSTAGE WILL BE PAID BY ADDRESSEE

BRIDGE PUBLICATIONS, INC.

ATTN: MEPB

4751 FOUNTAIN AVENUE

LOS ANGELES, CA 90029-9923

The sports director had not come up to tear my muscles and limbs apart yet. I stalked over to Madison.

He looked fresh and handsome, a very collar-ad of a man, the kind girls are supposed to pant after and scream about. Teenie, liar that she was, had obviously been maligning him.

"Why don't you do something about Teenie!" I snarled.

He looked at me with those sincere and honest brown eyes of his. "But I do do something about Teenie. I race with her with her new bikes against a miniature car. She's even tried to teach me how to skateboard and I have a scraped knee to prove it. I swim with her. I dance with her and try to show her the latest steps. I resent your implications, Smith. I'm doing all I can to bring her up and help you make a lady out of her."

"You know (bleeped) well what I mean," I grated. "Madison, are you a mother lover?"

"Smith, time after time I have noticed that you have no real idea of PR."

"Jesus, Madison," I said, "Don't try to change the subject on me."

"I'm not changing the subject. It just proves that you are ignorant of the whole field. I'll have you know that the whole popularity of Sigmund Freud came about because he married into a New York advertising firm."

"Good Christ, Madison! What does that have to do with it?"

"It has everything to do with it," said Madison. "The whole fields of advertising and PR would be helpless if it were not for Sigmund Freud. If I went against his teachings, I could be thrown completely out of the field—excommunicated!"

"I can understand that," I said. "I myself have every

reverence for Sigmund Freud. But I cannot possibly see—"

"Smith, once again, I have to point out that you are NOT a professional PR man. If it got out in the field that I was not following the orders of a Freudian psychoanalyst, I would be absolutely ruined—financially, socially and in every other way."

"Madison . . ."

"Smith," he said, "I am not being fair to you, ignorant as you are. I was very well brought up. My mother is quite wealthy and the children of the rich, you know, must all be psychoanalyzed. It is a caste mark, so to speak. When I was five, I had nightmares. My analyst prescribed that I must sleep with my mother. This was many years before my father committed suicide, so that has nothing to do with it. I am simply carrying out the accepted prescription."

"You mean you make love to your mother?" I said, aghast.

"Tut, tut," said Madison. "All little boys love their mothers. The psychoanalyst was simply prescribing what was natural."

He had conned me clear off the subject! "(Bleep) it, Madison! We're talking about Teenie. Are you or are you not going to start making love to her and get her the Hells off my hands? Don't tell me that you're allergic to sex with girls!"

He looked at me. The paddle fell out of his fingers. His jaw dropped. "Girls? Sex with girls? Oh, good heavens, Smith, that's obscene!" He went pale green. He staggered to the rail.

The sports director, when he came up to torture me, gave Madison a Dramamine and sent him below to his bunk. "I can't understand it," he said. "Flat calm sea, the ship stabilized like a billiard table and I have a sea-sick passenger throwing up his boots. Shows you what a mental problem can do. That fellow needs to be psycho-analyzed."

"He has been," I said bitterly, "that's the trouble." And I settled down to hours on exercise machines to get rid of the pot.

Chapter 6

It was the twelfth day out of Bermuda when we sighted the low sand coast, the white mosques and hills of Casablanca. For the last day or so we had seen the occasional ship north and south bound on the frequented routes. The sea had become somewhat more choppy and I was very happy of the chance to get ashore.

We were piloted and tugged to a fuel dock and I looked around. What on Earth were we doing here? The name might sound romantic but Casablanca looked aw-fully dirty and threadbare to me.

Madison was up and at it promptly. "I've got to study this king," he said. "He sounds like a real first-grade out-law. His name is Hussan-Hussan. When his father got independence from the French, they say Hussan-Hussan murdered him. He also murdered the man who had effected the real revolution and took the credit. He is held in power by the United States and he banks all the mineral receipts of the country in Switzerland in his own name. He keeps the majority of the population, who are Berbers, in total repression and perpetuates the minority rule by the Arabs with violence and force. He's worse many times over than South Africa in racial subjugation and yet he gets away with it all. I've read all I can find in our library. Now I've got to find if he is a true outlaw and, if he is, study his approaches. So I'm going to be quite busy."

He grabbed a taxi and was gone.

Teenie trotted down the gangway dressed in ponytail, sandals and shorts. A dock policeman sent her back to get a bra. She trotted down again and she was gone.

I wandered up and down the pier. The town certainly didn't look very inviting. Dust and Arabs with dust on them whining and begging through the dust. They were trying to sell me anything from donkeys to their sisters.

We were finished fuelling and moved to another dock. It was just as dirty as the first. Arabs hopefully spread their wares on the pier, thinking we were a cruise liner. When nobody came off to be robbed, they spotted me sitting in a deck chair and shook their fists and went away.

I wondered where Charles Boyer was. Or maybe Humphrey Bogart. It didn't look like the kind of place either one would frequent.

Suddenly a cab came tearing along the railroad rails on the pier. It braked to a halt. Teenie leaped out. She came tearing up the gangway and dashed into the ship. She went tearing up the ladder to the bridge and then shortly came tearing down.

She saw me. She was holding a yellow card.

"Oh, Inky!" she said. "The nicest thing has happened. I had to come back to tell you. I am flying down to Marrakech. I also had to get a landing card as a sailor because I don't have any passport."

"Where," I said, "is Marrakech?"

"It's only about 140 miles to the south and in the interior. And they have beautiful scenery and cloth and camels and everything. Real sheiks. I'm going in a special plane and will be back tomorrow morning."

"Hey!" I said. "You can't go travelling in the desert in sandals and shorts! At least pack a grip!"

But she was running down the gangway. She wasn't even carrying a purse! Well, great, I told myself. At least this is one night I'll have some rest instead of exercise.

Then suddenly I looked at the cab. The shadow in it? Yes, it was the black-jowled man from Bermuda! What the Hells was this? How did he get here?

Teenie got in and the black-jowled man closed the door and off the cab sped.

I went over to town and ate something called *couscous*, which consisted of balls of some cereal. Pretty tasteless, even though it was the national dish. The Turks should have taught these Arabs how to cook.

Madison dragged aboard about ten, all disillusioned. He found me in the salon listening to something besides Neo Punk Rock.

"He's not a real outlaw," said Madison. "He doesn't take from the rich and give to the poor. He takes it from the poor and gives it to himself. He's just a cheap crook, really. And he's got lousy PR. Every time I mentioned his name to anybody, they spat at me. Hussan-Hussan isn't even worth helping. I'm going to bed."

Shortly, I followed his example. I had a beautiful, untroubled night's sleep. I woke up early, feeling fine. To make matters even better, the sports director wouldn't let me run because I'd get too much dust in my lungs.

Teenie didn't get back in the morning. She showed up around 2:00 P.M. A cab drew up and the driver hailed the deck. A couple of sailors went down and started unloading the cab.

There were several baskets. There were many boxes.

A second cab drew up and out stepped Teenie. She had on a red fez with a long tassel. She was wearing a gold-embroidered short jacket over a red silk shirt. She had on scarlet shorts and was wearing scarlet Moroccan leather boots. She had loops and loops of gold chain around her throat.

She leaned into the cab she had just gotten out of and somebody inside handed her a valise.

The black-jowled man!

He glanced upward at the deck of the yacht, saw me and then leaned back. The cab drove away.

Teenie came prancing aboard, counted all the baskets and bales which had now been brought to the deck and then spotted me. She came dancing over, grinning enough to split her face in half.

"Well, how do you like it?" she said to me, turning around.

"Gaudy, to say the least," I said. "Listen, who the Hells is that black-jowled man?"

"Oh, him," she laughed. "He owns all the airlines that fly in and out of Morocco. He saw the yacht come in and he came over to take me down to Marrakech and get me to go down on him again. He really is crazy about it. He likes to watch the mountains down there while somebody does that to him."

"And he bought you all these things?" I said, ignoring the fact that this was the second version of who he was. She could never tell the truth.

"Of course," she said. "All kinds of goodies. You wait. I was thinking of you."

Good as her word, when I retired that evening, she came waltzing in, in a filmy new negligee and with a box. She opened the box and told me to open my mouth, and into it she popped a green cube of candy, soft like jelly. It was very good.

"Nice, eh," she said.

I agreed that it was very good candy.

"Have another one," she said.

I ate a second piece of candy.

She did something very strange. She went back to her room and got a new radio, came back to my bed-chamber, put it in the middle of the floor and tuned it in to the local radio station and simply sat there, listening to the singsong, whiny discords that pass for music to Arabs.

"What are you doing?" I said. The music was torturing my ears. She didn't answer. She was just weaving back and forth to the crazy music. I said, "Well, at least give me another piece of candy."

That got her. "For Christ's sake, Inky. You want to kill yourself?" She glanced at her watch. "You've got another five minutes until it hits."

"What hits?" I said, startled.

"Well, why the hell do you think I went to Marrakech? To get hash, that's what. And all for you."

"Hash?"

"Hashish, idiot. It's condensed marijuana. They make the best hashish in the world in the Moroccan mountains. It packs a hell of a wallop. You go eating any more of that candy and you'll overdose and go into panic. So just be calm, Inky. It takes about an hour to get into a real trip when you eat it, so be patient and listen to this nice music."

"You (bleepch)!" I started to climb out of bed.

The walls suddenly shot fifty feet away from me. The ceiling went through the floor. I was in 1492 discovering Columbus.

I started to giggle.

"Ah, that's better," said Teenie. "Now just watch and I'll show you a waterfall. Look at the muscles of my belly moving. When I showed them this in a nightclub last night in Marrakech, it got them all so hot I had to go down on the whole orchestra."

She was fifty feet away, then two feet away. Her voice was a mile away and then right in my ear.

I was giggling insanely. I could not stop.

"Well, I'm certainly happy you're happy about it," said Teenie. "That was an awful lot of trouble I went to, but it sure looks like it was worth it. In fact, I'm starting to giggle myself and I only had one piece."

For three solid hours I was giggling.

The Arab musicians came out of the radio and did a tap dance.

A camel walked in and said "Hello."

Everything was terribly funny.

Later I was to remember that. Those giggles were a mask for stark tragedy that right that moment stalked. That's what makes the memory so awful. When later I found out what was really happening, I could not possibly imagine how I had ever laughed about it, even under the influence of hashish!

Chapter 7

When I awoke we were at sea. I wondered where we were going.

"I'm glad you decided to lay off pot," the steward said as he shaved me. "It's so much trouble airing out the room."

Little did he know!

When I left the breakfast salon, I walked up to the bridge. Captain Bitts was sitting in a pilot chair, basking in the morning sun, while a watch officer and steersman handled the ship. I walked all along the bridge, looking at all the instruments and gyros. Words like *Fathometer* and *Repeater 1* and such didn't mean very much to me. All the chrome and brass and dials added up to confusion.

Bitts rose as I approached. "Where we going?" I said.

"Don't you know?" he said, somewhat astonished. "You ordered it about 4:00 A.M."

(Bleep) that hashish! "What did I order?"

"Oh," he said, "you're running a check on us. Don't worry, we're going right where you said."

I looked at the low, sandy coast to starboard. It was backed by mountains—the Atlas? But it sure didn't tell me where I was going. It just told me that we were running along a rather strange coast.

"Pretty uninhabited," I said, hoping he would then volunteer information.

"Oh, it will get lively shortly," he said. "Half the shipping lanes of the world converge straight ahead."

I didn't want him to think I didn't know what I was doing. It would undermine his confidence. "So when do we get there?" I asked.

"Oh-eight-hundred hours Thursday," he said.

"Thank you."

"Always glad to help."

Maybe Teenie would know. I went down ladders and aft to the race track. It was not all that big and pretty tightly banked. Teenie was on a racing bicycle, bent low, pedalling like mad, ponytail streaming in the wind of her passage. The *swoosh, swoosh, swoosh* as she went round made me dizzy. Whipping my head made me aware that I had an ache there.

She didn't look like she was stopping. I yelled, "Teenie, where are we going?"

Swoosh, swoosh, swoosh. "Don't bother me," her voice whipped by. "I'm trying to clock twenty miles."

"Teenie," I called, "where is the ship going?"

Swoosh, swoosh, "Ask Madison. You're disturbing my rhythm."

I left. Madison was up in the squash court. He had a glove and was playing handball against the backboard.

"Madison," I said.

He jumped. It made him hit the ball too hard so that it struck against a ventilator, ricocheted sideways, flew out into the air and then down into the sea.

"Don't do that!" he said. "I thought for a minute you were the Mafia."

"Madison," I said, "there are two places we mustn't go: one of them is the United States and the other one is Turkey."

He was mopping his face with a towel to remove the sweat. "Turkey?" he said. "But this is a Turkish yacht."

"Not the same thing," I said. "They want me in Turkey just like they want you in the U.S. Shotguns and things. So where are we going?"

Madison sat down in a deck chair and the deck steward handed him a tall drink of water and threw a bathrobe over his shoulders. "Well," said Madison, "it's like this. He took on the whole country single-handed after the king banished him. And he got so immortal that in his last fight, when he was dead, they tied his body on a horse and the enemy, just seeing it, fled in complete rout."

"Who?" I said.

"You see, I've got to make this trip pay off," said Madison. "I've got to learn all I can about notorious outlaws who became immortal. It might come in handy in PR, you see. And now I've got a chance to view some of this firsthand. Hussan-Hussan was a bust. So I've got to make up for lost time."

"Madison," I said patiently, "where are we going?"

He looked at me in some alarm. "Do you feel all right, Smith? Maybe you should get more exercise."

"Please, Madison. How did we get to going where we are going?"

"Heavens on Earth," said Madison to the sky, "he's suffering memory lapses. Oh, this is bad, Smith. You have to remember what you have written yesterday in order to alter it today. It just proves you'll never make a real pro PR man."

"Madison," I said in a deadly voice.

"Oh, all right, all right. I'll refresh your memory if you can't make it on your own. At 3:00 A.M. Teenie came tearing down to my cabin, scared me half out of my wits: I thought the Mafia had boarded us. But she said you were demanding to know who I wanted to research next and I told her and she went back to tell you, and so here we go."

"Here we go *where?*" I said.

"Oh, dear, you don't even remember when I've jogged your brain. All right. El Cid. Rodrigo Díaz de Vivar, eleventh century. The national hero."

"Of what country?" I said.

"Spain," he said.

"Spain is a big country," I said. "WHAT PORT?"

"Oh, you want to know what PORT we're going to. Well, why didn't you say so? Although, for the life of me, I can't see how you forgot ordering it. Teenie was all over the ship at an ungodly hour telling everyone you were absolutely disgusted with Casablanca and wouldn't spend another hour in the place. Frightful row, leaving so quickly. So we're sailing to investigate Charlton Heston— I mean El Cid."

"In . . . ?" I said.

"Valencia, Spain," he said, exasperated. "Don't you ever go to the movies? Listen, when all this blows over and we go home, I'm going to introduce you to my analyst. You need help, Smith."

The sports director was there, dragging me away. "You don't look too good," he said. "That's strange, because the steward said you didn't hit the pot last night. You need a few laps."

"That's what I seem to be suffering from," I said. But I jogged anyway. It really bothered me. True, I hadn't liked Casablanca. But, Gods, I had sure better be careful of that hashish!

Had I only looked, I would have seen Fate jogging along beside me, and had I then really inspected the apparition, I would have seen that it had begun to bare its fangs.

PART
FIFTY-SEVEN

Chapter 1

We went through the narrow and heavily trafficked Straits of Gibraltar and into the Mediterranean Sea. The water got bluer, the sun brighter and the clouds whiter. We turned northeasterly and began to draw a creaming wake along the Costa del Sol of Spain.

Suffering from too much exercise after too much hash and seeking to avoid too much sun, I went below to my salon in the late afternoon.

I got the viewers out of a cabinet and set them up.

Suddenly I realized my time was all askew. It was only late morning in New York.

The Countess Krak was sitting in a chair facing the Whiz Kid double. Thank Gods he didn't know me or of me, for he had on a hypnohelmet. Beyond him, through a window could be seen the yellowish landscape of lower Manhattan so she must be in the Empire State Building.

Numerous texts had been spread out and one was stamped, as I could see in Krak's peripheral vision, *Massachusetts Institute of Wrectology.*

I was startled. She must be using a hypnohelmet for its designed purpose: speed training.

She clicked it off and lifted the helmet from the head of the double. She snapped her fingers and the young man woke up.

"Now do you think you can pass your final exams?" she said.

"I don't know," he said. "I lost so much time fooling around on that job. I'll have to get real high marks to overcome the lack of classroom work."

"What do you think you'll do when you graduate?" she said.

"Oh, I'm sure about that," he said. "Twoey has to have new designs for pig troughs and every night he's pushing me to get through with school so I can begin useful work on his farm. He's also rooting around for ideas on how to raise the standard of living of pigs. I'll be busy all right. I never dreamed there was so much civil engineering connected with pigs. Opened a whole new world for me."

"What are you going to do if the media hits you when you go back to school for your exams?"

"Duck," said the double. "But if Jettero ever needs me for public appearances or anything, all he has to do is say the word. I'm not forgetting how he rescued me from that crazy psychiatrist! One minute there I was about to be turned into a vegetable and the next there I was in a van looking at Jettero. And Jesus, was I ashamed of myself right then for ever daring to think I could pose as *him*. And I know darned well you didn't tell me to think that when I had the helmet on."

"No, I don't have to do that," said the Countess Krak. "Jettero can stand on his own."

"He certainly can," said the double. "What a guy!"

I suddenly seethed. All that (bleeped) adulation for Heller! Couldn't people see what a sneaky, rotten (bleep) he really was? Him and his Royal officer ways. It made me feel nauseated.

"Well, all right," said the Countess Krak. "I've got

to go tell my class of microwave engineers to go to lunch and I suggest you do the same."

"I'm real grateful to you," said the double. "If there's anything I can do for you or Jettero my whole life, you only got to say the word."

I gritted my teeth. The two-way-response radio was lying there. Wasn't there some kind of an order I could give Raht? Something that would make these people suffer for all the horrible things they had done to me?

I couldn't think of anything.

The "dress for dinner" gong went. The steward got me into a white evening jacket and black tie. He was all chattery.

"Clothes in Spain," he said, "are very good and very inexpensive. And while Valencia isn't Madrid, I think we can find some proper yachting togs all the same. So when we get in, what say you and I go ashore in the morning and outfit you more fittingly."

"And I won't have to exercise?" I said.

"I have influence with the sports director," he said.

And so it was that after a rather professorial dinner where I got told all about El Cid and a very harrowing night wherein Arabs danced with camels on the head of a pin, I found myself, the following day, walking the busy streets of Valencia, Spain, stopping in at shops and getting rigged out to look more the part of a yacht owner.

I suspected that the steward was probably getting a commission, but shopkeepers were so insistent that I looked *magnifico* and *terrifico* and *fantastico* in this or that and were so impressed that I owned *el yate grandisimo* newly arrived, I couldn't refuse very much. The cost was not that great and I landed back aboard with a taxicab full of boxes.

I wanted to show Teenie that she wasn't the only one

who could run off and come back with clothes, but she and Madison weren't there. They had gone off to a library.

That evening, right after dinner, we were suddenly inundated with a *flamenco* troupe. The Chief Steward explained to us that while this was not Andalusia in southwest Spain, the flamenco was very good and, indeed, as I sat in the yacht's music salon, the stamping heels, swirling skirts, castanets and guitars soon got me shouting and clapping with them. The girls were black-eyed and pretty and although the men certainly looked like they carried knives, they didn't object when the ship's officers and Madison were forced into the dance. Teenie had a stamping contest with a young Spanish dancer and seemed to win or so they said. I got into it at last.

Later, I was exhausted in my bedchamber but Teenie was all fired up. She kept cavorting around the room. "Oh," she said, "I've got to get me a mantilla and a comb and some castanets and some of those skirts with flounces! When you whirl, you can show everything clean up to your neck!"

"You're an exhibitionist," I said.

"Of course," she said. "And you wait until I eat enough to get some flesh on me. Hey, speaking of eating, how would you like some candy?"

We fought. I lost.

At dawn, no less, the steward woke me up. "You'll be late!" he said, rushing about, laying out new clothes. He shaved me and pushed me into a cold shower and rushed me into my clothes so fast, and I was so groggy, I didn't get a chance to ask him what I was being late for.

Somebody pushed a roll and coffee at me as we got into a car. We sped off.

Finally I asked, "Where are we going?"

Madison's eyes glowed. "We're on our way to the out-law hangout of El Cid!" he said.

We drove north along the coast. Suddenly the (bleepedest) biggest castle-fortress you ever saw stretched away to our right. I looked to the left. All along the mountaintops ranged the hugest fortifications I have ever seen. It was all in ruins but the white stone, the pillars, the steps which mounted to the structures perched upon the crags were *impressive!* It seemed to go on for miles.

"This is a 'hangout'?" I said.

"Yes, yes!" cried Madison. "The hideaway of El Cid! Get out of the car!"

"You want me to climb that?" I gaped.

They didn't pay any attention at all. They were up and away. I was being pushed from behind by one of our guides.

All day long, except for a picnic lunch eaten with the threat of eagles stealing it, I dizzily tried to walk with closed eyes so I wouldn't get dizzy and fall. A guide finally put a rope around my neck just in case.

At dinner, back aboard, I could hardly lift my fork. I desperately wanted to get to bed and cool my aching muscles with deep slumber.

A folklorico troupe suddenly appeared and performed for us on the sundeck. The Chief Steward kept waking me up. "These are the true dances of Valencia. This was Moslem for so long, the culture is stamped deep. Listen to the Arab scale they use in their music."

Teenie and Madison had to learn some of the dances. And when they found that Teenie could ripple her belly muscles in time to their refrains, they accepted her utterly.

In the bedchamber later, Teenie kept waking me up. "Oh, I've got to have some of those bangles! And did you see those gauze trousers? No? That's just it; they're so thin the audience can watch what you do with everything you've got. Oh, I've got to get some. Inky, for Christ's sakes, are you going to sleep on me? Now eat your candy like a good boy!"

And that was about all I could recall of that night.

But the next morning, the steward didn't seem to be in any rush and I blessed my luck.

I had Madison for company in the breakfast salon.

"You know what I found out?" he glowed, as he chomped his bacon and eggs. "That El Cid was an absolute PR masterpiece!"

"Don't talk so loud, Mad. My head hurts."

"Oh, you'll really love this," he said. "You're so amateur when it comes to PR that you just plain won't believe it. But El Cid was the total creation of PR men. In the eleventh century, too! You see, when he went outlaw against the king of Castile, he was really trying to set up a kingdom for himself right here in Valencia, totally separate from Spain. But his PR figured, hey, that's not so good for his immortality so they rewrote the whole script. They tailored it up so he looked like a *Spanish* national hero and he's been one ever since! Man, I wish I knew the name of his PR. What an expert he must have been!"

Such enthusiasm did not fit my mood. Trying to hold my head in a position where it would not hurt yet still not fall off, I went down on the dock, intending to limp off somewhere beyond the reach of sports directors—maybe to a cool, quiet park.

Teenie was standing at an ice-cream cart, probably intending to top off her breakfast with an *helado*. I stepped quickly out of view between two buildings. She might have ideas for more excursions.

Suddenly a cab came roaring up. An arm from the back seat suddenly pointed at Teenie. The cab screeched to a halt beside her.

A burly figure leaped out. The black-jowled man! He went right up to Teenie. He was shouting, but because of dock noise, I couldn't make out what he was saying. But he was angry!

Teenie took a bite of the ice cream, not looking at him. The man gave the ice-cream cart a shove.

I was amazed. Where had this man come from? And why was he so upset at Teenie for eating ice cream?

He had dropped his voice and I couldn't hear what he was saying. But he was shaking his fist at her! She just kept on eating ice cream.

He kept on talking. She offered him some ice cream. He pushed it away. She put her arm around his shoulder. He pushed it off. She gave him a kiss on the cheek and he grabbed out a handkerchief and wiped off the resultant sticky goo.

She was talking soothingly.

The ice-cream man apparently hadn't been paid yet. He was standing there with his hand out. He looked cross over having had his cart shoved. Teenie put her arm around the black-jowled man again. She was saying something in his ear.

Suddenly the black-jowled man reached into his pocket and pulled out some *pesetas* and paid the ice-cream man. Teenie took the black-jowled man's handkerchief and wiped the last of the ice cream off her hands. She was continuing to talk as she did so.

The man looked around helplessly. Then he opened the door of the cab. Teenie got in and they drove away.

Unease stirred me. But then I shrugged. I shouldn't have. In my stupidity, I assumed that there was simply no understanding teen-agers. Or middle-aged men who would fly all over the place just to get another crack at unripe tail.

Little did I know what Fate was building up for me. Had I even guessed, I would have run until there was no more wind left in me.

Looking back on it, I am utterly amazed that I never even came close to fathoming what was really going on!

I was at RISK!

Chapter 2

Sitting in the owner's salon that afternoon, I came out of a brief doze with a start.

I thought I was seeing things!

Right there on the viewer was a green ring. That's all that was in the picture: a green ring. Like a smoke ring somebody had blown except that it was green.

I looked at the second viewer.

A green ring!

Oh, I knew that hashish would do me in. I was now seeing things! Yet I hadn't eaten anything but lunch.

I looked back at the first viewer.

Another green ring.

I looked at the second viewer.

Same thing!

I noticed something. I wasn't giggling.

I held my head in my hands. Maybe it wasn't the hashish. Maybe that blow on my forehead had altered my vision. Maybe this was the beginning stage of going blind.

A horrible vision of Teenie leading me around on a leash and beating me with a white cane rose to plague me. It was her fault for leaving the skateboard there.

I glanced back at the viewers. Heller's face was on one, Krak's face was on the other. Now I knew I was having visions. They were both wearing sun helmets.

I shut my eyes tightly.

Krak's voice. "Finished!" She sounded jubilant. I knew she meant me. Nothing else would give her such joy.

"Absolutely finished!" said Heller. He sounded so happy he could only be referring to my eyesight.

Experimentally, to prove him wrong, I cautiously opened one eye. Bang-Bang was on the viewer, full face. He was wearing an old marine fatigue cap that said *LT. RIMBOMBO* on it. My time sense was gone. Bang-Bang had left the marines years ago. "That'll really knock 'em dead," he said.

Another voice. Izzy's face on the viewer. He was wearing a war surplus steel helmet. Now I WAS seeing things. "What I'm afraid of is retaliation." I shut my eye. I was in no state to retaliate.

But I hadn't closed my eye quick enough. J. P. Flagrant's face. He was wearing an Indian war bonnet! Now I knew my vision was crazy. "What mean retaliation, paleface? Red brothers smoke plenty wampum. Do peace dance. Ugh."

Izzy's voice, "That's kind of you to try to reassure me, but they might get the idea it's a smoke signal to massacre everybody and hit the warpath yet."

There was something not quite right about what he was saying. Suddenly I sat up straight and stared at these viewers. Where the Devils were these people?

Now there was another face on Heller's viewer. Some businessman? "If you really approve it, Mr. Floyd, I'd like to tell my men. They worked pretty hard."

"It's great," said Heller. "I'll go with you and tell them myself."

"No, no," said J. P. Flagrant. "Please don't be premature." He pulled back a sleeve of his beaded leather hunting coat, disclosing an expensive watch. "The celebration is not due to start for another hour. We've got to launch that stack with a bottle of champagne. You can't kick off Beautiful Clear Blue Skies for Everyone, Inc. with just a casual thank you. There are fifty alligator farm buyers here in addition to all the contractors and workers. I've got the press coming in on a bus and two hundred Seminoles are going to yell themselves hoarse with tribal dances." He was fumbling in a bullet pouch. "I've got your speech all written for you. And another for Mr. Epstein. . ."

"Oy!" said Izzy. "Not me!"

"Just the first half?" said Flagrant.

"No!" said Izzy in a panic.

"It's a great speech," said Flagrant, separating it out. "It starts, 'We are gathered here in solemn conclave to celebrate, today, the greatest engineering marvel of the age. Fifty million spores a minute—fifty million are being rocketed into the sullied stratosphere of this, our noble planet. . . .' You still sure you don't want to give it?"

"NO!" said Izzy.

"All right. Then I'll hand it over to Chief Ratty War Bonnet and he can give it and nobody will know the difference."

I breathed a sigh of relief. They were in Florida to kick off the spores project. The rings had been spores being blown violently aloft through a five-hundred-foot stack.

They all walked down a path and Krak looked back. Yes, there was the vast area of vats and belts. And there was the stack. The rings were flying out of the top of it at regular intervals.

"I'm certainly proud of you," said the Countess, putting her arm through Heller's. "That's one we can mark off the list and we're that much closer to going home. Now, if we can just push along with these fuel things, we'll be through in no time."

I groaned. If they wound up a success, they would certainly ruin Rockecenter. And Lombar would comb the planet to find and kill me.

I looked at the two-way-response radio. I could think of nothing to tell Raht.

I turned the faces of the viewers to the wall. I could not stand to witness a celebration. It was too much like an Irish wake: the corpse being me.

Chapter 3

About three o'clock in the morning, Teenie came waltzing into my bedchamber. I stared. She was wearing a black hat, a red jacket and pants trimmed in gold, white stockings and black shoes. A bullfighter's rig!

"Inky, Inky, wake up!" She gave me a punch with a feathered stick that had a sharp end. "You won't believe what I have got!"

She raced back into her bedchamber and began to drag in boxes and open them. Gauze pants, veils, curl-toed slippers, headbands, bangles. A flamenco skirt, fla-menco petticoats, mantillas, combs, castanets, ivory fans, flamenco shoes, on and on. And then she opened a jewel box. A gold necklace!

"Teenie," I said, "what the Hells is this all about? Tell me truthfully. Who is that black-jowled man?"

"We had to fly to Madrid to get some of this," she said. "Private plane. We just got back."

"Who is that fellow?" I demanded. "Why was he so angry with you?"

"Well, actually, he's a Spanish nobleman. A duke. He owns half of Spain. And he was so angry with me because I ran out on him in Casablanca."

"Teenie, are you going to tell me the truth for once? What was a Spanish nobleman doing in Bermuda and Casablanca?"

"Oh, he travels all around and, just by accident, he saw the yacht in the harbor when he was flying home from Morocco where he married Hussan-Hussan's sister, a princess."

"Oh, my Gods. Now you're going to tell me that a man who just got married is interested in rolling you in the hay."

"Well, you see, I promised his wife in Marrakech and I am ashamed to say I didn't keep my promise but sailed off."

"Teenie, stop flying around trying on clothes and give me a straight story for a change. Let's start at the beginning."

"Well, that's where I am starting. You see, he told his wife how wonderful it felt when I went down on him and she demanded that I teach her. I couldn't have the wedding breaking up, could I? But it's all right now. She was in Madrid and I spent the whole evening showing her exactly how to do it and she did and oh, man, is he happy now. Eyes rolling right back in his head. So it's all handled and we can sail. Oh, look at these pants." She had her own off and had slid into the gauzy fabric. "You can see right through them. Look, Inky!"

She sure looked weird with a bullfighter's hat and jacket on, wearing Arab invisible gauze pants. I had to laugh.

"That's better," she said. "And now, as a reward, just take a couple puffs on a bhong and go back to sleep."

"No."

"Oh, come on, Inky. Don't be a sourpuss." She rushed off and came back with a bhong.

I took a puff. It tasted slightly different.

She was getting out of her clothes. "Wait a minute," I said. "If you've been fooling around with sex all night, you don't have to harass me."

"Oh, that was just a warm-up," she said. "No fun, really. I just did it so they'd have a happy married life. Move over."

"Wait a minute," I said. "This bhong tastes . . ." A heavy-headed sort of glee took hold of me. Everything seemed suddenly marvelous.

"Of course it tastes different. You're smoking fifty-fifty, marijuana and hashish. Here, let me have a puff."

A night that was two years long ensued. I woke up. We were at sea. Teenie was gone. I found, as I lay there, I was having trouble with dates. This was either July or September in either 1492 or 2186. The steward had the ports open and was blowing the place out.

"What's the date?" I said groggily.

"May first. 'Wake me early, mother dear, for I'm to

be queen of the May,' as the song goes. If you opened a port before you went to sleep, you wouldn't keep breathing it all night, sir."

"Where are we going?" I said.

"Just where you ordered, sir," he said.

"Let's not get me into that again," I said. "Please tell me."

"Where the young lady's fiancé wanted to go, sir— Marseilles. I must say, you are very indulgent of him. I personally consider the French a bunch of pigs."

"It seems rougher," I said, feeling the slight lift of the ship.

"It *is* rougher, sir. This upper part of the Med is always a (bleep)!"

I looked out the port. There seemed to be a rather heavy sea running. It made me feel queasy to look at it.

I got dressed and went on deck. I didn't want any breakfast. There was quite a wind.

Madison was crouched down in a deck chair under the protection of a ventilator. He looked up from an old book. "Hi, Smith. I really appreciate this chance."

"Of what?" I said gloomily.

He raised the book to show me the title. "The Count of Monte Cristo was a pretty wild kind of outlaw. I've often wondered if he was real or just the product of some master of our craft. One has to be able to separate truth from fiction."

"Since when did PR start doing that?" I said.

"It's a new idea I had," said Madison. "And we're going to get to the bottom of it."

I didn't want to get to the bottom of anything this morning. The stabilizers lagged a little bit and the ship had a definite pitch.

"In Marseilles harbor," said Madison, "there is a prison called the Chateau d'If. The Count of Monte Cristo was imprisoned there as a young sailor, according to this author, Alexandre Dumas. From thence he rose to a power amongst nations and was, in fact, an outlaw beyond compare. He is quite immortal. I want to see if there actually was a cell there with a tunnel like the one described. And it was terribly nice of you to send Teenie down to ask me. She certainly is a sweet, innocent child, isn't she?"

That did it. I went to the rail.

"Always face downwind," the sports director said, wiping me off. "You should have told the steward you felt queasy. Once you're really seasick, Dramamine doesn't do a (bleeped) bit of good. You get rid of it too fast. A few laps around the deck now and you'll feel fine."

It wasn't a very successful voyage to Marseilles. In the first place the French, while very glad to gouge any port dues they could, were unable to understand why we wanted to visit the Chateau d'If.

Through an interpreter, for none of us spoke French, the port director told us that if we weren't terrorists, he had no right to let people from the yacht wander around the town or harbor. There was a slim chance, though. If we could prove we were heroin smugglers, the port was wide open to us.

Madison was kicking the edge of a desk despondently. Teenie said we might as well go back aboard. She had some new pop records she'd got in Madrid and we could lie in bed and listen to them. That made me desperate. I beckoned the director into the next room. Through the interpreter I asked for a black fluorescent light. When I got it, I bared my chest and turned it on. They stared at the glowing letters, *Rockecenter Family Spi.*

The interpreter told them what it said.

Suddenly the port director was on his knees, kissing the cuffs of my pants. He was muttering and moaning.

"He says," said the interpreter, "you should have told him this at once. He had no idea you worked for the man who controls the world's illicit drug traffic. His slight against the Rockecenter name is unforgivable. He will now have to resign his post and end his days in disgrace."

The French are so emotional, so extreme! "No, no," I said, "it will be enough if you just let us come ashore and walk around and also visit the Chateau d'If."

The director began to weep with relief. He muttered something.

"He wants to assure you," said the interpreter, "that the illegal heroin traffic is maintained at its highest peak and hopes you won't report otherwise."

"I'll take his word for it," I said.

The port director got the interpretation and seized my hands, kissing them. He said something else, pleadingly.

The interpreter said, "He wants you to come to dinner at his house this evening. He has a beautiful wife and daughter and insists you spend the night and sleep with them both."

I opened my mouth to protest and the interpreter quickly shook his head warningly. "Please don't refuse him. You will insult the French national honor. It would put him in a terrible position. He would have a nervous breakdown."

Wearily, I had to let Teenie and Madison visit the Chateau prison while I went to dinner.

All in all, Marseilles was a terrible experience. I left

sharing wholeheartedly the opinions of my steward about the French.

The wife was fat and the daughter had a harelip.

Things like that tend to color your attitude.

Chapter 4

We sailed the following morning. The sea was rough and I lay stricken in my bunk. The captain and the sports director came in.

"I am making a ship inspection," said Captain Bitts, "to make sure the French haven't stolen us blind." He gazed at my stricken face. "The Chief Steward tells me you went to the port director's home. Have you still got your wallet?"

Miserably, I fumbled under my pillow. I nodded, yes.

"Well, all right, then," he said. "We've only lost four fire hose nozzles. We were lucky." He was about to leave when he turned back, frowning. "You didn't drink any French wine, did you? They make it by squashing the grapes with bare feet and they often have athlete's foot. I wouldn't want the owner coming down with athlete's foot of the stomach."

"The port director served wine but I didn't drink any," I said.

"The port director!" he said, startled. "Jesus, you didn't sleep with his wife and daughter, did you?"

I nodded miserably.

"Well, (bleep) my eyes!" said Captain Bitts. "Sports,

rush up to my cabin and get my medical kit. Steward, have you bathed him?"

The steward looked pretty agitated. The Chief Steward frowned at him. The two of them grabbed me out of bed, thrust me under a shower and began to get to work with antiseptic soap.

"Burn the sheets and the clothes he was wearing," ordered Bitts. "We can't risk an infested ship. Nothing will kill French lice but fire. They carry typhus."

The medical kit arrived. The captain got out syringes and needles that looked like they had been designed as bilge pumps. He filled them. They held me down. He shot me in the butt with three kinds of antibiotics and a heavy preventive dose of neoarsphenamine. It hurt!

As I was queasy, he finished up with a suppository of Dramamine. "If you're not up and around in a few minutes," he said, "I can give you an injection of Marezine for that motion sickness."

Another injection? "I'll be up right away!" I said.

Dressed in some new clothes, I wanly made my way to the breakfast salon. To my surprise, Teenie and Madison were at the table gobbling down omelets.

I pretended to eat so the waiter wouldn't tell the captain I better have that injection. This (bleeped) crew knew everything that went on.

The omelet gobbling was getting me. I decided to distract them. "How did it go at the prison?" I said.

"Wonderful," said Madison. "They opened every door in the place for us. They almost gave us the prison. What did you tell that port director, Smith?"

"It's a state secret," I said.

"Well, it must have been something remarkable," he said. "We saw skeletons that have been there since

Napoleon's day. Of course, the place is full of tourists now that couldn't pay their hotel bills, but we found everything we went to find."

"So what did you locate?" I said, afraid that he'd start on another omelet.

"Nothing!" he said. "Absolutely nothing. We thought we had found an opening between two cells, but it was new works, being done by a couple from Des Moines who had had their passports stolen. So we have irrefutable negative evidence. There never was a Count of Monte Cristo!"

"That doesn't sound very successful," I said to cover up the fact I wasn't eating.

"Oh, but it IS, it IS!" said Madison. "Here is this internationally known outlaw, totally immortal, name on the tongue-tip of every school child and movie director, who never existed at all! Don't you see? It's the PR triumph of the ages! Total notoriety and not a single spark of fact to sully it anywhere. It means you can create even the flesh and blood of fame without the slightest vestige of reality. What a PR that Alexandre Dumas was! God, they don't make them like that anymore."

"Tell him about the other lead," said Teenie.

"Oh, yes," said Madison. "Every officer and guard we talked to about immortal Frenchmen would kiss their fingertips and say reverently, 'Napoleon!' They looked so ecstatic that, if you don't mind, Smith, we'll drop off at Corsica and visit his home. It's right on our way."

Anything to get away from the sight of all that food. And getting to another port and calm water was irresistible. I went quickly to the bridge.

Captain Bitts was sitting in his pilot chair looking at

the sky and tumultuous sea. I said, "Could we stop off in Corsica?"

"I wondered where we were going," he said. "It really doesn't tell a captain much when an owner staggers aboard and says, 'For God's sakes, sail!' Any particular port?"

"Napoleon's home."

"I think that would be Ajaccio, if memory serves me right. A bit more than halfway down the Corsican west coast. But wait a minute. That place is French. I don't think you'd better go ashore. I don't want to lose an owner to some (bleeped) French whore. I already lost four fire nozzles."

I promised I would stay aboard. He went into the chartroom to plot his course and I left quickly before he noticed I was looking as bad as I felt. He might give me the Marezine injection.

It didn't do me any good. The sports director shortly had me doing laps.

We came to anchor in the port of Ajaccio the next day. Thankfully, I stood on a steady deck and looked at the dramatic silhouettes of the mountains, jutting ruggedly to the sky. Rose, crimson and violet granites made splashes of color amongst the luxuriant vegetation.

We weren't permitted to use our own boats because it might deprive the inhabitants of francs, and Teenie and Madison went ashore in a puffing tug.

I did my laps and exercises obediently and after lunch went down to my owner's salon. I thought I was up to watching the viewers.

It was early in the day in New York but Heller was in his office reading texts, flipping the pages too fast for me to see what they were.

The Countess Krak came in, dressed in a severe black suit, her blond hair in a bun on the back of her head. She looked like a school teacher except considerably more so.

"My microwave engineers are doing fine," she said. Then she walked around the desk, put a hand on his shoulder and looked at what he was reading. She could follow it; I couldn't. "Why, Jettero," she said. "What in the world are you doing with a textbook on primitive electronics?"

"They think that's the way things are," he said. "And if you put any truth down on an examination paper, you'd flunk."

"Examination? You don't have to take any college examinations. Izzy has that all fixed up. Exam papers will be handed in at Empire for you."

"Oh, no," said Heller. "It's one thing to do class attendance for me or even hand in quizzes. But I couldn't accept a diploma until I had been examined for it and passed. It's only three days to examination week. I've got to bone up."

"Oh, Jettero. You're too honest to live! Their science reeks with incorrect premises. I battle them every day with these microwave people. The errors are so stupid even I can catch them and I know little enough."

"You've got to say what the professor said," he replied. "I'd flunk if I didn't. And I need that diploma or nobody will believe me."

"Hi, hi, hi," said another voice. "Anybody home?" It was Bang-Bang. "Come on, Jet. I've got the M-1."

The Countess Krak looked at him. He was standing there with a rifle. "Who you going to shoot?" she said.

"No, no," said Bang-Bang. "Got a lot of candidates

but no time. Jet here has got to graduate from the ROTC and he never once has been to a drill. He don't even know the manual of arms."

"Teach her," said Jet. "And she'll teach me. I've got to finish this crazy text on quadratic equations."

Bang-Bang stared at the Countess Krak. His jaw was dropped.

"Go ahead," said Heller. "It won't take her long. She already knows a manual or two."

"WHAT?" said Bang-Bang.

"I have a few minutes," said the Countess Krak. "Show me how it goes."

Very diffidently, Bang-Bang tightened the rifle strap and began to go through an army manual of arms. Right shoulder arms, order arms, inspection arms, parade rest, calling the orders and counting the movements by the numbers.

"I've got it," said the Countess Krak.

"You've got it?" said Bang-Bang, incredulous. "You haven't touched the rifle!"

"Well, why?" said the Countess Krak. "It looks pretty primitive to me."

"Oh, yeah," said Bang-Bang. "That's the army way and it is pretty primitive. Here's the real way to do it. Marine Corps."

He went through a manual punctuated with very sharp slaps of strap and butt.

"I've got it," said the Countess Krak.

"Oh, come off of it, Miss Joy. Don't try to snow me. I haven't had my first drink of Scotch today."

The Countess Krak took the M-1 from him. She examined it. "Seems a little light," she said. She studied its working parts. Then she checked its balance.

Suddenly, very fast, she went through the army manual. Then, without pausing, she went through the Marine Corps manual.

Bang-Bang stood there, popeyed.

"Now, a *real* manual," said the Countess Krak, "would go like this."

And despite the restrictions of the office, she sent the rifle through a manual of arms that was so spinning and so ornate that the weapon was a blur except at those instants when it came to split-second positions, dead still. And then she went into a Fleet marine dress parade manual. The swirling weapon made loud swooshes as it spun and the slaps were as loud as pistol shots. She finished.

"Jesus Christ!" said Bang-Bang. "I ain't never seen nothing like that before in my life! And done by a beautiful woman, too!"

"A captain by the name of Snelz taught her," said Heller. "So she could be smuggled in and out of a ship."

"Snelz?" said Bang-Bang.

"Yes," said Heller. "He was a Fleet marine once."

"Oh, that accounts for it," said Bang-Bang. "Miss Joy, could you show me how that last manual you did goes?"

The whole thing made me very uneasy. I had forgotten she had been taught to handle a rifle. I wouldn't put it beyond Snelz to have taught her how to shoot it, too. Gods, supposing she took it into her head to go gunning for me? She was deadly enough already without this.

Oh, I didn't like the way things were going. Miss Simmons was out of the running. The spores project was completed. Heller was going to take his exams and get a diploma. The Countess Krak was training microwave engineers for some purpose I could not fathom.

Without me right on the ground to trip them up, they might very well succeed!

I could feel the assassin's blade going into my back. For that was my lot if they did.

I looked at the two-way-response radio. I wished fervently I could think of something to order Raht to do. I couldn't, but I must.

My only choice right now was to stay good and lost, keep out of Turkey and the U.S. and hope that my training and brilliance would come up with something which would stop this juggernaut of disaster. I couldn't dawdle forever. I would be squashed.

Little did I know that that malign Earth God, Juggernaut, already had his foot far more than halfway down on the back of my neck right that minute!

Chapter 5

They came back in the pink glow of evening. From their chatter at dinner, I made out that they had been at the *Maison Bonaparte* and the *Musée Napoleonien* and hadn't learned a blessed thing about Napoleon except that the island depended on tourism and didn't like tourists.

"What can you tell about an outlaw from his baby clothes?" Madison said. "Things have certainly become decadent. Corsica was once synonymous for bandits, but now they are running the restaurants and hotels. The criminal fraternity is always tight-lipped, though."

"You'd have thought we were the fuzz," said Teenie, getting around her second pheasant under glass. "Every time Maddie would get the interpreter to ask, 'Where was the main hideout of this great outlaw, Napoleon?' they'd just clam up and glare. As soon as I get around two or three helpings of ice cream, I've got to put in library time."

I gaped. Teenie in a library? She could barely read. But sure enough, she grabbed her radio and turning it on full blast to pop from Radio Luxembourg, dived into the library and began to burrow in the books.

I looked in at this extremely novel sight of Teenie trying to read. She was tapping her foot to the pop music and moving her lips painfully as her fingers slowly traced the lines of a page. She found she was reading *Hull Maintenance.*

Shortly, she yelled for the Chief Steward and he came in and seeing what she was pointing at, he indulgently unlocked some glassed cases nobody had looked into since the yacht was built. She stared at a set of the *Encyclopaedia Britannica* and recoiled, dismayed, from the size of the books. But bravely, she persevered. "What letters come before and after *N,* Inky?"

Accommodatingly, I found the entry "Napoleon" for her. She sweated at it. It was pretty hard work. She had to take two breaks to get cream sodas and strawberry bubble gum to fortify herself. Beads of sweat bedewed her laboring brow.

Finally she looked at me. "What's 'exile' mean, Inky?"

"Banishment," I said.

"Vanishment?" she said. "Aha! I've found the hideout! Where's Captain Bitts?" The Chief Steward picked up a phone.

The grizzled mariner appeared. "Are you lost in a fog again, Teenie?" he said, laughing.

"Bittie," she replied, "I haven't even got a foghorn and I'm clean off the chart."

He sat down on the arm of a chair in front of her. "I don't see how that could be, Miss Teenie. The way you had me mauling the chart drawers just before we left Bermuda, I should have thought you would have memorized every port in the world."

This was news to me. I could credit her pestering him in his bedroom but not in the chartroom. Since when had Teenie become enamored with geography?

"That's just it," she said, "these (bleepards) don't mention a port. They're talking about a whole different street map. It says this outlaw Napoleon exiled to . . ." she consulted the volume, "the 'Isola d'Elba.'"

"*Isola* means 'island' in Italian," said Bitts.

"Oh," said Teenie.

Bitts was pointing to a large globe of the world which hung as the centerpiece of the library. "It's right there," he said.

"What's that thing?" said Teenie.

"It's a globe of the world," said Bitts.

"No (bleep)," said Teenie. "You wouldn't try to con me, would you? All those charts you showed me were flat."

"The world is round, Teenie," said Bitts. "That's what Columbus proved."

"Now, let's not change the subject," said Teenie, waving a cautionary finger at him. "I know (bleeped) well where Columbus, Ohio is. I got arrested there when I was seven."

Bitts gave the Chief Steward a signal and that portly worthy hit a switch. The big globe lighted up with internal lights. Bitts took her cautionary finger and guided it over to the colored surface. "This is the Mediterranean

Sea. We're in that. Now, this is Corsica and this is Ajaccio where we are anchored. Now," and he made the finger trace, "if we go down through the Straits of Bonifacio, northerly up the east coast of Corsica, we come to . . ."

"The Isola d'Elba," said Teenie in triumph. "It's just on the other side of Corsica! Well, I'll be popped! Hey, Bittie, why didn't you tell me it was all on this big blob? Look here. Bermuda. Morocco. Italy. Rome. Sicily. Greece. Turkey. For Christ's sakes, Bittie. Why'd you let me wear my eyes out on all those flat charts when here it is, plain as bubble gum!"

"I'm not at my best at four o'clock in the morning," laughed Captain Bitts.

I was shocked. After that workout she had given me the night we sailed from Bermuda, she'd been doing things with Captain Bitts! And just before me, she'd been messing around with that black-jowled lecher! There was no end to her appetites! She was impossible!

"You leave that blob lit," she told the Chief Steward. "And you leave those cases unlocked. You guys have had me in a spin with your flat charts and travel guides. Who cares if you're liable to get ptomaine poisoning in Antone's Restaurant. That isn't the kind of education I'm looking for." She peered closely again at the big globe. Then she grabbed up the encyclopedia volume and went tearing out yelling, "Hey, Maddie, Maddie! I've found the (bleep)'s hideout!"

"She's a sweet child," said Captain Bitts, fondly.

"Yes, Mr. Bey," said the Chief Steward, "you are indeed fortunate to have such a charming and innocent niece. I just love her girlish enthusiasms. So refreshing."

I thought they must be talking about a different Teenie than the one I knew. Her enthusiasms were a lot too strong for any mortal man.

But in looking back, I am amazed that, with all my training and experience, even then I did not begin to even guess what her enthusiasm was really centered upon right then. Had I done so, I might very well have escaped.

Instead, when she came back, I tamely gave my assent to sail for Elba.

"They're not French, anyway," said Captain Bitts. "The island's Italian. They're civilized and me and the crew will get a chance to go ashore. The rest of Europe used to say, 'Death to the French.' Now it's the French who say, 'Death to Everybody.' If it's all right with you, I'll sail right now and get out of these froggie waters."

Chapter 6

The sea was beautifully calm after we passed through the Straits of Bonifacio between Corsica and Sardinia, just south of it.

Bitts had said, "You'll notice the difference when Corsica gets between us and the prevailing westerly winds." And I certainly did. We were now in Italian waters and I believe that was the first time I had ever seen anything Italian calm.

The chief town, Portoferraio, was a pretty place, white buildings with red roofs standing about the blue harbor. Teenie and Madison went tearing off and I was very happy to have a walk on solid land and exercise my Italian.

The ancient Etruscans used to mine iron there and

the name means "Smoky Place," probably from the smelters. But I think some English wag must have exiled Napoleon there because it was as close as they could send him to Hells. But the gag would have failed for it is now a pleasant resort: the industries are tourism and Napoleon.

The "Ogre of Europe" exile residence was right in the town, on the beach: the Palazzina di Mulini. I wandered around in it: nice place, not the least bit like a jail; my idea of prisons was more like Spiteos, not this palace. No wonder he had escaped! No electric caging.

Teenie and Madison had been there already. When I asked about them, one of the guards said, *'Ah, la bellina fanciulletta Americana! L'innocente.'* And I thought he must be out of his mind. He had called her "the pretty little American girl" and commented on her innocence. He was holding up two joints she must have given him as a tip. It never ceased to amaze me how people failed to see through the little (bleepch).

They had gone on to Napoleon's summer resort, the Villa San Martino, four miles southwest of town where there was a museum of Napoleonic artifacts and paintings. Some exile! A palace and a summer resort yet! But the man must have been a complete psychotic to want to escape from all this. He should have seen Spiteos!

It was too far to walk, I was not about to pay a fortune for a cab, so I idled around town and drank expressos. How calm, how soothing, to sit at a sidewalk table in the sun of early May, far from the travail and turmoil of Hellers and Kraks and Hissts and Burys.

"Hello, Inkswitch."

I knew I shouldn't have hit the hashish the night before. The hallucinogenic effects were obviously recurrent. I could have sworn that was Bury's voice.

"Mind if I sit down?"

It WAS Bury's voice.

I dared look to see if the hallucination was also visual. There he was, three-piece lawyer suit, snap-brim hat, drawing up a chair.

He looked at me. "How are things going?" he said.

"What are you doing here?" I said. Maybe the hallucination would vanish.

"Oh, just seeing to an arms cache for Hatchetheimer. He had some idea of blowing up the Vatican and needed supplies. I came in by hydrofoil." He made a gesture toward the harbor.

I put it to the test. I could hallucinate Bury easily enough but not a type of vehicle I had never seen before. I craned my neck. Yes, there was an odd kind of vessel at the landing: it looked like an aircraft fuselage on stilts without wings. It had *Octopus Oil* on the side of it.

"So, how is everything?" said Bury.

"Oh, fine, fine," I said, wrenching myself out of it.

"That fellow with the fuel threat all handled?" said Bury.

"Oh, yes!" I said. "Absolutely."

"That's a nice yacht you have there," said Bury, looking out to the anchored white and gold ship. "I haven't seen the *Golden Sunset* since a conference the Man and I had aboard her with the Morgans. How's Madison?"

"Oh, he's fine, fine," I said. "Never better. Wrecking people's reputations all over the place. Splendid man."

"And you handled the fellow with the fuel?" said Bury. He certainly was carping on it.

"Utterly," I said. "Smashed, mangled and dismembered. Incapable of even lifting his little finger."

"I see," said Bury. He rose. "Well, I've got to be

pushing off. Time, tide and court calendars wait for no man."

He gave his snap-brim hat a tug, looked at me and then walked off to the hydrofoil. Very shortly its engines started up. It moved away from the landing and then suddenly it surged forward in a cloud of white spray, stood up on its stilts and went skimming out of the bay at a hundred miles an hour.

The thunder of its engines died and the town went back to sleep.

I sat there with my skull spinning, my expresso long since cold. I couldn't figure it out. Had Bury known I was here or had it just been by accident? He could have gotten a description at the harbor office—all Italians talk too much. There weren't too many foreigners in town, for the season was quite early.

Marseilles! I had identified myself to that port director as a Rockecenter Family Spi. He must have blabbed that I had been there in the *Golden Sunset!*

The warm sun turned chill. I just then began to realize that I had told Bury an awful lie. Far from ceasing to be a fuel threat, Heller was more a menace than ever!

(Bleep) Heller! He was always getting me in trouble. Intentionally and with malice aforethought!

It was not duty alone anymore that dictated the necessity of getting rid of Heller. The universe was simply too small to hold the two of us!

I consoled myself that Bury would not find out Heller was free as a bird now to wreak his evil will upon this planet. Bury would probably think that Madison and I were taking a well-earned breather. . . .

And then it hit me. If challenged, we could say that if Heller raised his ugly head again, we were just doing research to find new ways to stop him.

Yes, that was it. We could say that while we realized the man with the new fuel was, to our best knowledge, incapacitated, we also realized he could resurge and if he did, we must have ammunition.

I wished I had thought of that while Bury was sitting there. But I had been too startled. One doesn't think well when his heart is beating five feet above his head.

Maybe I should send Bury a radio and say, "While to the best of our knowledge and belief the new-fuel man is out of the running, our dedication to duty is such that we are diligently pursuing new ways of blackening his name and impeding his progress. . . ."

No, Bury might misunderstand. The right thing to do was get a grip on this: (a) to actually find data to help make Heller into an outlaw, and (b) think, think, think of some way to throw a terminal explosive charge into the heart of the Heller operation. Then if the matter came up with Bury, to be able to say blandly, "Oh, there was no reason to worry you: we have it all under control." Yes, that was the best plan.

I felt much better. I pushed any nagging doubts to the back of my mind and returned to the ship.

I was even more relieved when a glance at the viewers simply showed Heller boning away for his exams: he was going over Army G-2 lecture notes about "Psychological Warfare for the Intelligence Officer." The Countess Krak was out shopping—the condo butler, Balmor, in tow—apparently trying to find a graduation present for Heller and, amongst all the items offered, which she seemed to feel were "primitive artifacts," not having much luck. No threat there.

Teenie and Madison came aboard in time for dinner. All the exercise had made them very hungry and they were demolishing *roast turkey au Philadelphia* at an appalling rate but it didn't detract from their intense interest in their day.

"Actually," said Madison, "Napoleon didn't get very far at that. You can look from Elba, where he was exiled, straight over at Corsica where he was born. He killed several million people and yet it only got him that short distance."

"Well, he wasn't a real outlaw," said Teenie learnedly, around a mouthful of turkey. "They didn't hang him."

"I can't really understand why he's a national hero to the French," said Madison. "He wasn't French. He was a Tuscan, an Italian. But there's something to be said in his favor. He sure was a great PR. Here he was, a foreigner, attacking the French from the inside while disguised as their general, killing millions of them, and they made him their emperor for it. Now that puts him up into PR ranks pretty high. What a genius to pull one off like that. I'm sure glad we followed this up. Gave me lots of data on what people will fall for."

Teenie had gotten a banana split and was attacking it. "So you think this was pretty successful, do you, Maddie? All right. You gimme your outlaw list and I'll get right to work on it with my research staff."

I thought I had better get busy on this myself. It would look good when I next saw Bury. "I'll give you a hand," I said.

"You sure will," said Teenie. "In fact, you're the research staff. Who the hell else knows big words like 'exilated'?"

Chapter 7

The next name Teenie chose was Spartacus. The man was a Roman gladiator who had headed up a revolt of slaves and had come within an ace of putting down the whole empire. She decided that there was not enough about him in the encyclopedia and that we had better go to Rome. It said that at the end of the revolt they had crucified six thousand surviving slaves all along the Appian Way.

She called the captain. "Bittie," she said, "how about sailing along this Appian Way so we can look at the bodies."

Captain Bitts smiled. "The Appian Way was a truck route. If you want to go to Rome, we have to stop at its port, Civitavecchia, which is just down the coast from here. It's quite a ways from the city but there's trams and things."

"They don't give Spartacus's address," said Teenie. "But maybe this guy, Crassus, that licked him, is still around. Do they have city directories in Rome where . . ."

"Teenie," I said, "Spartacus, it says here, died in 71 B.C. That's two thousand years ago. More. And it only mentions Crassus once. You're dealing with ancient history."

"Oh, (bleep)," said Teenie. "The way people move around, you can't keep track of anybody. I tried to locate an aunt in Chicago once and (bleep) if she hadn't moved five times. I wouldn't have run her down at all if I hadn't seen in the papers they'd just put her in the city jail."

She looked at the globe, did some tracings with her finger and then said, "All right. We'll go to Civita-whatchacallit and take it from there."

"We'll be alongside at dawn," said Bitts. "We're cleared into Italy and all we have to do is sail. So I'll up anchor and away. Have a good night's sleep. When you get a look at Rome traffic, you'll need it!"

Well, I didn't get a good night's sleep. You would have thought all that walking would have tired Teenie out. But after two pieces of hashish candy and other things, I was giggling and doing other things until past midnight.

True to his promise, when I awoke, Captain Bitts had us tied up alongside a dock in Civitavecchia. It was early. The steward had left a port open the night before and it was the din that had awakened me. I looked out. I had a vista of the dock, a forest of cargo booms and funnels and a locomotive stopped nearby which just then gave another blast on its whistle and almost caved in my eardrums. The Italians are an industrious people and especially when it comes to making noise.

I was about to draw back when a flash of color caught my eye. It was Teenie in some scarlet running shorts and a bikini bra. She was at a peddler's stand looking at guidebooks. She was apparently having an argument against his efforts to sell her lottery tickets.

Once more I was about to draw back when I saw a shadowy figure beyond Teenie. A hand reached out and seized her arm.

The black-jowled man!

There he was in his three-piece suit!

He glanced toward the ship and then he yanked Teenie into the dimness behind the booth. They seemed to be having an argument. He had his face very close to Teenie's and he was scowling as he talked.

Then she said something.

He looked at her. And then he did an astonishing thing! He went down on his knees and raised his hands in supplication.

She kept shaking her head. Then she raised a finger in admonishment. He looked at the ground under his knees in dejection.

Teenie kept on talking. Then she started to walk away.

The black-jowled man grabbed at her wrist. She stopped. She spoke.

He looked at the ground again and then he nodded slowly.

She walked back to the ship. The black-jowled man got up, staring after her. He dusted off his knees.

Teenie yelled something to the port gangway sentry who yelled something up to the deck. Then one of our own sailors appeared and Teenie yelled something at him.

She turned and went back to the black-jowled man and they went off down the dock and out of sight.

At breakfast, I was astonished to find Madison. I should have thought he would be off to Rome. I said so.

"Oh, Teenie has gone there," said Madison. "She left word that she might be absent a day or two. I don't think she'll find much about Spartacus in Rome anyway. He was defeated way to the south, in Lucania, when he was attempting to cross to Sicily. Besides, I've got to get my notes together on Napoleon. What a man. He did such a thorough job, France has never amounted to a hill of beans since. Just a little foreign runt, too. What a PR triumph!"

We saw nothing of Teenie for two days. She came back in a small truck. It was stacked with glittering trunks and luggage. She bounded up the gangway in a silver sequin hunting outfit topped with a plumed hat.

I was on the deck and she bounced up to me. "Look at my silver boots!" she said, lifting one sideways so I could see it better. "Ain't they the screaming most?"

"Teenie, what on Earth is in all those trunks and bags?"

"Oh, them," she said, glancing down where the crew was bringing them aboard. "They're mostly empty. I didn't have anything to put my stuff in. A couple are full, though. That's what delayed me: The (bleeped) *modiste* didn't have a single model the same size I was and I had to stand around getting measured and measured and fitted and fitted. And she kept putting big hems in, saying how I'd grow. Well, maybe I will. Man, do they have great food in them deluxe hotels! I thought all wops ate was spaghetti and I haven't even seen a strand of it! The greatest chow you ever chomped. Am I in time for supper? Boy, am I starved!" She started to rush off. Then she halted. "Those black grips are yours. You didn't have any luggage either." She rushed off.

She appeared at dinner in a black silk evening gown, obviously created by one of Rome's finest couturiers, the effect spoiled somewhat by the rubber band on her ponytail.

"What about Spartacus?" said Madison.

"Who? Oh, yes. Spartacus," said Teenie. "Well, it seems we have to go to Naples to find out."

So I told the captain to sail for Naples, but Teenie didn't seem to have her mind on outlaws. She came into my bed salon in a negligee of absolutely transparent sea green, put a new phonograph down in the middle of the rug and sat before it.

"This is the greatest gadget, Inky," she said. "It runs on batteries and it plays a record upside down or vertical or any way at all with a laser beam. No chance for a roll to slide a needle out of a groove. And now I can play my records without a single scratch."

It had two detachable speakers she set up some way apart. "I got some yowley new singles, too. Just wait until you hear this one!"

She turned it on full volume. The drums pounded. The guitars yelled. The bass boomed. A tenor and a chorus sang:

> I'm sneaking up on you.
> I'm going to get you, you, you.
> You're going to get yourself in my clutches!
> Look at these claws, claws, claws!
> Yay, yay, the trap is set, set, set!
> So stick in your foot, foot, foot!
> So stick in your neck, neck, neck!
> Stick, stick, stick in, stick in, stick in
> Your naked neck in, neck in, neck in!
> So stick in all of you! You! You! Woohooo!
> Oh, I'm going to get you, you, you!
> I'm sneaking, I'm sneaking, I'm sneaking
> Up on yoooooooooooooooooouuuuuuuuuuuuu!
> WATCH OUT!

The last part of the song almost made me jump out of my skin.

"Ain't it flowy?" said Teenie with dreamy eyes.

"It's terrible," I said. "It doesn't even rhyme."

"Oh, but the sentiment," said Teenie. "I just love a sentimental song. Here's a bhong I fixed for you. Have a puff."

I took one puff.

Suddenly the whole room went up in a spiral of bright pink. As I tingled from head to toe, I still retained wit to ask, "What was in that pipe?"

"Hash oil," said Teenie. "The absolute jet plane of Mary Jane. It's the very best in Rome. Fifty (bleeping) bucks a gram! And I got a whole bottle of it!"

The sea-green negligee slid to the floor. I had enough wit to know what would happen now. But all I could do was giggle.

And horror of horrors, the music did sound wonderful, even the shouted, "WATCH OUT!"

Oh, Gods, if I only had!

Chapter 8

In Naples, another teeming forest of cargo booms with tugs and trains running about under them like wild animals, we found no trace of Spartacus. But Teenie got on the trail there of somebody called Garibaldi who had helped wrest a lot of Italy from the age-long domination of Austria and gotten shot for his pains. And this took us to a place where he had once landed—Palermo, Sicily.

Of course, in Palermo, one had access to a whole island full of bandits and outlaws that not even the Italian government could cope with. This was the ancestral home of the Mafia. In a hired car, Madison, Teenie and myself drove all over that very extensive island. And one could imagine, from that rugged and sometimes barren terrain, how it could breed so many hit men. It was no surprise to be told that it had been largely settled by pirates.

We even took an excursion to the eastern end of the island where Mount Etna smokes into the sky. The name itself means "I burn" and judging by the number of eruptions and lives taken by it, it is well named.

The thought of driving the last twenty-one miles above the town of Catania just to get to the top made me quite dizzy and it took quite a few "grouches" and "spoilsports" from Teenie to get me up there.

At the top she was very intent. It was a brilliantly clear day and she stood with the high velocity, smoke-tinged wind whipping at her ponytail and, with Madison's help and a map, spotted the Italian mainland to the northeast, spotted Malta to the south and then a dim haze which might have been Tunisia to the southwest. She tried in vain to see Corsica. She stared to the east and squinted her eyes hard trying to see Greece. And then cupped them, squinting, trying to see Turkey. But, of course, even from ten thousand feet, they were under the horizon, Greece being over three hundred and Turkey over six hundred miles away.

"Well, I'll be a son of a (bleepch)," she said. "Old Bittie wasn't lying. The world *is* round after all!"

All the way down through the lava flows, down through the beech forests, down across the vineyards and back to Catania, she kept marvelling about it. "Why don't we fall off?" she said. "What if we skidded or something? How come the water doesn't run out of the ocean?"

Madison tried to explain gravity to her by holding up a couple of oranges as we bounced along. She held the oranges. She even made the driver stop the car. But she couldn't get the oranges to snap together the way Madison had said. She thought he was lying.

We made the ninety miles back to Palermo in time for a late dinner aboard and you would have thought it would have left its mark on her. It didn't. She explained to me that hash oil cured anything and that is the last I remembered.

The next morning at breakfast she unfortunately found the town, Corleone, just south of us. "Hey," she said, "isn't there a Corleone mob?"

I flinched visibly.

Madison assured her that there was indeed a Corleone mob. They controlled the unions and shipping lines and every U.S. port, gambling and prostitution, and if it wasn't for them, Faustino "The Noose" Narcotici, *capo di tutti capi*, would be a happy man indeed. The Corleones were death on drugs.

"Prostitution?" said Teenie. "I didn't know there was a whore's union. Hey, Inky, how does this fit in with your white slavery racket? Do you have a closed shop or don't you?"

"The Corleones," I said stiffly, "are people you leave very much alone."

"Hey," she said, "that sounds dangerous. Maybe we better get the hell out of here while we still have our scalps. Where is your list, Maddie? We better get them screws churning."

She got the list and promptly marched off to the ship library. The sports director wouldn't take my word for it that I hadn't had any pot last night and he worked me until my muscles screamed.

Despite all the warnings and urgency at breakfast, when I left the gym and came to lunch, we were still in Palermo and there was no sign of Teenie at the table.

"She went ashore about nine," the Chief Steward said. "She was wearing a pair of horn-rimmed glasses with no lenses in them and said she was going to the University of Palermo. Her fiancé went with her."

I dawdled through the afternoon. We still lay in port. I didn't want to go ashore: this talk about Corleones had made me a bit nervous.

I looked at the viewers. Heller was busy taking examinations at Empire University. Maliciously, I thought that if Teenie was so suddenly interested in universities, maybe she should be sicked on to him. Longingly I fingered the two-way-response radio. I just couldn't figure out how to get Teenie back to New York without my being later hit for rape of a minor.

The Countess Krak had both Balmor and Bang-Bang in tow, still looking for a graduation present. She went into a store and, for a bit, my attention lagged. Then suddenly I found myself staring at a handful of rifle shells!

"Yes, ma'am," came a clerk's voice. "Those are Holland and Holland .375 Magnum cartridges."   .

"They knock an elephant flat," said Bang-Bang. "One boom, one dead elephant."

"I was thinking of other game," said the Countess Krak.

Any lethargy I felt up to that instant congealed into panic.

Those huge, gleaming brass cases with their lethal slugs had only one message for me.

POW! POW!

I almost shrieked. Then I realized that it was a knock on the door. Sanity returned.

I was only too glad to shut down the volume and throw a hasty blanket over the viewers.

"Miss Teenie is back," came the Chief Steward's voice. "And I think she needs your help."

I hastily left. Anything to get away from those deadly viewers.

She and Madison were in the library. Her unlensed glasses askew, Teenie pointed at a tower of books Madison had worn himself out carrying.

"Those (bleeped) professors," Teenie said, "are supposed to be so educated and half of them don't even speak English. We had to buy those at a bookstore. They got plenty of pictures but I didn't notice until we were halfway back to the ship that they're all in Italian! So it's up to you, Inky. You're the only one that can sling the spaghetti around. Start translating." She sank into a chair and began to inhale the cream soda that a steward brought, reducing the bottle tide at an alarming rate. "Whew!" she said. "It's good to wash the catacombs out of my throat."

"We stopped by the catacombs on the way to the university," Madison said. "They have the corpse of an American consul there who knew Garibaldi."

"Corpses, corpses, corpses," said Teenie. "Jesus, they even got them hanging from pegs on the wall! Cold and rattly. Corpses all around staring at you with sightless eyes."

I chilled.

"But get on with the translation, research staff," said Teenie. "Start winding that spaghetti around so it spells Brooklyn."

The top one was a volume of the history of the Corleone family! Timidly, I opened it and found myself staring at a photograph of "Holy Joe." Shades of Silva! Yes, there was the date of his assassination! Yikes! There was a photo of Silva!

I put the book quickly aside. I picked up the next. It had a flashy cover, a bust head in a helmet.

"Now, that's the one we're interested in," said Teenie. "Alexander the Great."

"Quite an outlaw," said Madison. "His mother, Olympia, poisoned his father, naturally, and the boy went on to rape the whole known world. He had a psychoanalytic problem but, no matter, he was one of the greatest outlaws of all time. Just a barbarian from Macedonia and he could do all that."

"You already know about him," I said.

"No, no," said Teenie. "We haven't dug into his private life at all. We haven't any idea how he got such good PR when he was such a bum. Crazy, too. Thought he was a god. But we need a few more details and then we'll be able to split for Macedonia."

"Wait," I said. "That's awfully close to Turkey. If the Turks get their hands on me, I'll be shish kebab."

"That's why we got the books on the bottom," said Teenie. "When we finish with Alexander, we can go look into 'Chinese' Gordon."

"To China?" I said.

"No, no, Inky. Jesus, are you ignorant. 'Chinese' Gordon made his last stand in Egypt. And you can see right there on that globe that you can go from Macedonia to Egypt without hitting Turkey. I'm looking forward to riding a camel up the pyramids anyway. So start chewing alphabet about Alexander so we can get out of this place. A tough-looking Mafia type was asking after you on the dock and we don't want to have to stick you in those catacombs with all those dead eyes staring at you for the rest of eternity."

We sailed just as soon as we could get a pilot and tug.

That evening, as we headed for the Strait of Messina that separates Sicily from Italy, I was not waiting up to see the whirlpools that had almost sunk Ulysses. I was in my bedchamber and the record player was going full blast.

Teenie was sharing a joint and weaving to the throb of a new record she had bought. She was giggling. The heavy-rhythmed song went:

> *Go on home!*
> *To bed.*
> *Go on home!*
> *To bed.*
> *To me.*
> *Go on home!*
> *To bed.*
> *To me.*
> *To Oh, Boy!*
> *Push it home!*
> *To me.*
> *To Oh, Boy!*
> *Push it home.*

Stupid (bleep) that I was, I thought she was giggling because she was high on pot!

PART
FIFTY-EIGHT

Chapter 1

In a leisurely way, through deceptively calm seas, I was being sailed onward to my doom.

Fate is sometimes like a headsman who is in no hurry: he gets the victim on the platform, adjusts the condemned man's neck just so, artistically hones his axe and sends an assistant off for a mug of beer so he can enjoy the scenery and gloat before he delivers the sizzling swoosh that will sever forever the desirable connection between skull and torso.

There is no doubt that the scenery was beautiful. We rounded the bottom end of Greece, passing through the Cyclades into the legendary Aegean Sea. The azure waters were lapped by the cooling breezes of late spring; the white cotton-puff clouds rose in majesty above the fabled isles of song and story. The white yacht drew a gentle wake but it was a fatal mark in my history.

Over to the east of us lay Turkey, but it was further than a hundred miles and out of sight—and, unfortunately, out of mind for me. Our course lay between the two continents of Europe and Asia. As I was well-oiled on pot at night and distracted by exercise all day, Asia, where catastrophe awaited, might as well have been on another planet.

Four cruising days were consumed, days like drops of lifeblood running out unseen. I had found that the yacht, at low speeds, did not bob around at all even in a moderate sea and Bitts was nothing loathe to drink beer in his pilot chair and yarn with his watch officers about Jason and the Golden Fleece and experiences they themselves had had with girls and ouzo on one or another island that we passed. Teenie herself seemed to find this very educational, for she was up there two or three times a day.

I gave attention to my own duty. Every day I checked up on Heller and Krak. There was seven hours' time difference now and it was three or four in the afternoon aboard the yacht before they were very active in the morning in New York.

Only once did I hear a mention of the yacht. They were at breakfast in their condo sunshine room because it was pouring rain outside.

"I'm sorry you lost the ship," said Heller. "It was very nice."

"The Turkish navy had more use for it than I did," said the Countess. "You've been cured completely of your silliness about other women and I have no slightest idea of ever running away from you again. Besides, we're finishing up here very swiftly and we'll be going home in no time at all. So, who needs it?"

I did. Without it, I would be in the clutches of Turkish authorities at best or full of holes from Nurse Bildirjin's father's shotgun at worst. Little did I know how much worse it was going to get.

Macedonia, where Alexander's father, Philip, had ruled, is at the north end of Greece. We sailed into the Gulf of Salonika with Mount Olympus, home of the Greek Gods, rising in snow-capped majesty to our port. We threaded our way through the fishing craft off the

city of Katerini and, turning northeastward, sailed grace-
fully into Thessalonica, the second major port of Greece.

They found us a nice, clean berth, bombarded us
with welcomes, and Teenie and Madison rolled up their
sleeves to hunt down the haunts of Alexander the Great.

They pushed me into accompanying them and in a
wheezing car, left over from World War II, we rattled off
to the site of Philip's capital, Pella, twenty-four miles
northwest of the modern city.

The archaeologists had been busy and that was all I
could say for it. In an otherwise pastoral scene, they
had laid bare foundations and several floors. I will admit the floors of the former residences were interesting:
in later homes on Earth, you find paintings on the
walls but in the time of Alexander the Great, they put
the pictures on the floors! They were pebble mosaic,
many-hued, heads of lions, scenes of the hunt and they
WALKED ON THEM!

I right away told Teenie and Madison that this was
very significant psychologically. It was obvious to me. I
tried to explain it to them. "Greek Gods," I said, "dwell
in the sky. Now, you can get the idea of baby Alexander
trotting around here in his diapers and he sees all these
Earth scenes *under* his feet, so of course he thinks he's
a god in the sky. Simple. An obvious case of spacio-
psychological mispositioning of the medulla oblongata,
leaving him with no option but to conquer the world."

They didn't get it.

"That doesn't explain why his mother poisoned his
father," said Teenie, working a camera she had mysteri-
ously acquired and framing a shot of a particularly silly-
looking lioness who was busy chomping a luckless man
and laughing about it.

"Well, that's just it," I said. "I've been reading these

books and she didn't. Philip was assassinated by a young
man who thought he had suffered injustice at Philip's
hands. I gave it to you in the notes I made for you,
Madison."

"Oh, I read them," said Madison. "It's just more
natural that Olympia would poison her husband. Besides,
it makes better headlines. I can see it now in the *Athens
Times,* 18 point quote Outraged Queen Slips Hubby
Arsenic unquote."

"It isn't factual," I protested.

"Factual?" said Madison, sweeping his hand to indi-
cate the ruins of the ancient city, "what does FACT have
to do with it? Alexander was 99 percent a PR creation.
The legends of his life have almost nothing to do with
fact. He was one of the most romanced-about outlaws in
history. PRs, according to your own notes from those
very books, were sweating for centuries to dream up new
copy about Alexander. And as for the poison story, even
that is too close to the truth to make good newsprint. She
had plenty of reason."

"Oh, come now," I said.

"Open your books!" said Madison. "Every time Philip turned around he was marrying some new woman. He
practically had bedsores from so many nuptial couches.
And when he finally married a skirt named Cleopatra—
not the Egyptian one—his wife Olympia got fed up,
grabbed Alexander, jumped into her chariot and left the
kingdom in a cloud of horse biscuits. One marriage too
many. A man that marries at all should be in a padded
cell and a man that commits bigamy ought to be tied
down and tortured by the most fiendish psychiatrist available."

It spoiled my day. I went over and sat down under

an olive tree. He had expressed my own beliefs and plights altogether too well.

It was right at that moment that the true significance of the threat in Turkey hit home. I was already married twice in New York.

The thought of marrying another in Turkey was more than I could bear and when I remembered that Nurse Bildirjin was a sadist who put her knees into chests while a patient's skull was being drilled, I began to shudder. And when the fact that she was also underage wriggled into my mental torture scene, I began to be quite ill.

When we returned to the ship for lunch, I ate very little and begged off from further excursions in the afternoon. They left without me.

Slumped in the owner's salon, I was not cheered the slightest bit to hear from the lips of the small, bald-headed Mr. Twaddle, the Assistant Dean of Students at Empire, that Heller had passed all his examinations with flying colors.

"Wister," said Twaddle, standing up and removing his pipe, "I posted a notice to see you personally because I am utterly astounded! You are very close to a first ever. One hundred percent across the boards in a vast array of subjects. It's really quite astounding what we at Empire can do with a student. I look at these grades from that military college and compare it to these grades for your senior year here and it's hard to believe my eyes. What a diligent student! Goodness gracious, how you have reformed! Shows what constant application in class will do under our superlative faculty. And amazing, you never missed a single day in attendance."

"I find it somewhat astonishing myself," said Heller. The dog! He'd never set foot in those classrooms after the first few days! That Izzy had arranged it all!

"So that puts your class average at the top as well. So I am pleased to tell you, and wanted to do so personally, that you are graduating as a Bachelor of Nuclear Science and Engineering next week, Magna Cum Laude."

"I appreciate it," said Heller.

"Oh, don't thank me. There's another note here from Miss Simmons. She's usually an absolute tiger on students. Hard to understand. She's the one who called it to the attention of the faculty that you should be given the highest possible honors. Here's her note. She says, 'I am eternally grateful to this student for the way he has promoted relations between my students and myself. Without what he has done, it would be a joyless world.' She even made a speech at faculty meeting, telling them she had never been more satisfied."

"I'm glad to hear it," said Heller. "It was touch and go there for a while. But after a time she began to come around."

I mourned the loss of my ally.

"Now, there's one more thing," said Mr. Twaddle. "You finished your senior year as an ROTC officer. According to your enrollment in the ROTC, you should be sworn in to the United States Army as a second lieutenant and go on active duty."

"Sworn in?" said Heller.

"Take the oath of allegiance and all that," said Mr. Twaddle.

"That would be..." Heller stopped. I knew the quandary this was putting him in. As a Grade X Royal officer of the Voltar Fleet, he would incur the death penalty if he swore allegiance to some alien force. I became very alert. If this happened, I had him!

Mr. Twaddle raised a hand to silence him. "Your ROTC studies were for G-2, Army Intelligence. Your diploma is for nuclear science.

Colonel Tanc sent over a new Army ruling. Here it is, right here. As there is no war in progress at the moment, the Army has no need of more intelligence. Unless war is declared, any nuclear engineer is permitted to apply himself to his trade in a civilian capacity. So the news is that your induction into the Army has been deferred. And you can accept all those high-priced industry offers that will be raining on our students come graduation day."

"Wonderful," said Heller.

My heart sank. There went my last chance. Heller would be as busy as a hurricane getting out new fuel and wrecking Rockecenter and Lombar. This was BAD!

Gloom deepened around me.

The reality of the mess I was in was reaching me.

Suddenly the thought hit me that Bury would be on my trail when Heller's villainous determination to save this planet reached his ears. A better, cleaner fuel would be just wonderful for five billion Earth people but would be death for Rockecenter and that's what counted.

I couldn't stand any more. I dragged myself to my bedchamber and lay down.

I must have dozed. I awoke to find Teenie rummaging in my closets.

She saw I was awake. "Inky, do you have an alpenstock?"

"What's an alpenstock?" I said.

"A thing you climb mountains with. I'm getting all ready for tomorrow. Maddie and I are going to drive down and climb Mount Olympus if we can."

"For Gods' sakes, what for?" I said.

"For Gods' sakes," she said. "They tell me that's where all the Greek Gods live. Zeus and the rest of 'em. And Alexander thought he was a god and maybe he went up there, too."

"Hey, no," I said. The thought of so much exertion made exhaustion run through me. "It's nine or ten thousand feet high, snow-capped, a whole series of peaks. It's dangerous. You might get dizzy and fall. For Gods' sakes, don't let yourself be killed!" That was all I would need to drown me in the soup I was barely swimming in. "Besides, I think all those Gods packed up when people stopped sacrificing goats so they could eat. I doubt you'll even find a busted laurel wreath."

"Oh, that isn't my only reason. I want to get a bird's-eye view of the sea out there and the islands. And I want to try to see Turkey. It's only about two hundred and twenty-five miles due east and nothing between it and us but water. Hey, what the hell's the matter with you, Inky?" She yelled louder. "Steward, you better come in here with a bucket! Inky's gotten seasick in port!"

Chapter 2

The first inkling I had of real trouble came the following afternoon.

I was stricken in my bed, as I had been since yesterday. There was a tap on the door. The wireless officer looked in. "Is Miss Teenie here?"

"Why do you want her?" I croaked from my bed.

"It's just that her radio traffic is piling up and I haven't seen her all day."

"Radio traffic?" I blinked. What the Hells was Teenie doing getting radio traffic? From whom and why? "I'll take it," I said cunningly.

"No, no," he said. "It's always marked confidential."

The elderly stewardess heard the commotion. She came up the passageway carrying a laundry bag. "Miss Teenie won't be back until supper," she told the wireless officer. "You know better than to come down here and bother Mr. Bey. He's ailing."

The man saluted and withdrew, carrying the mysterious sheaf of messages in his hand, unread by me.

The next event was less mysterious but more shattering. About four, I heard a rumbling on the dock beside us. I raised myself on a shaky elbow and looked out the port.

DEMONSTRATORS!

They were carrying signs, shaking fists, marching round and round beside the ship!

TURKS GO HOME!
TOOLS OF YANKEE IMPERIALISM
DOWN WITH TURKEY!

I always knew there was bad blood between the Turks and Greeks. It began with the Persian Wars. And although Alexander had conquered Asia Minor, as centuries passed, the Asians had gotten their own back and the Seljuk Turks had conquered all of Greece and held it right up into modern times. It looked like the bad blood had spilled over at the sight of our Turkish flag.

But this was a mystery. We had been made quite welcome here, strictly red carpet. And now this!

The dock guards were just standing around doing nothing.

Then here came a car. It nosed through the demonstrators. It stopped by the gangway.

Suddenly the demonstrators realized it was stopping at the yacht.

They converged on it!

Teenie and Madison and an interpreter leaped out. Stones flew!

Teenie and Madison struggled toward the gangway through the mob. The interpreter went sprinting off. The car driver jumped out and ran.

Suddenly from the yacht came white streams. Fire hoses! Our sailors were knocking demonstrators down left and right.

Teenie and Madison made the deck.

Demonstrators picked themselves up and fled, chased by the violent jets.

Captain Bitts's voice rang out and the fire hoses went off. I stared at the dripping, deserted dock.

Teenie and Madison came in my door. They were wet. Madison was bruised.

"Black PR," said Madison. "Somebody has uncorked the bottle. As an expert myself, I know the signs. Who would ever have thought I would be at the receiving end of a black PR campaign."

Captain Bitts was at the door. "I hope that didn't alarm you," he said. "This happens to a lot of yachts, especially when they have Americans on board. It happens most often right after a visit to an American consulate but nobody here was there to renew passports. Are you all right, Mr. Madison?"

"Wet," said Madison.

"Better than in a hospital," said Bitts. "I'm glad they weren't carrying guns."

The wireless officer was behind him, shoving a message in his hands. Bitts read it. "Local VHF," he said, "from the harbor master. He's requesting that we sail as soon as possible to avoid further damage to his port."

"Black PR," said Madison. "The only people who are that expert at it is the U.S. State Department. Don't even bother to ask if the harbor master did that on the orders of the American consul. I know because that's how they work."

"A government shouldn't attack its own citizens," I said. "That's psychotic!"

"Of course it's psychotic," said Madison, "but whoever said the American government was sane? You mark my words, the American consul this very minute is handing out press releases to the Greek papers saying we're Turkish saboteurs. I'm the pro, Smith. You aren't."

"How do you know this?" I demanded.

He lifted his hand. He was holding a soaked placard all crumpled up. On one side, in Greek, it said, *TOOLS OF YANKEE IMPERIALISM*. On the back, in English, in very small letters it said, *Printed in the USA*.

"Whoever would have thought," repeated Madison, shaking his head sadly, "that I would be the target of a black PR campaign. Me, the expert. Well, let me use your radio teletype, Captain Bitts, and I'll start up the machine guns. If they want war, I'll give'm war."

"What do you intend to do?" I gasped, appalled at the idea of being caught in the line of fire.

"Do?" said Madison. "Well, hell, Smith. You can see you aren't a pro. I'll throw a torrent of press releases into the Russian Tass news agency, exposing a Yankee plot to get Turkey and Greece involved in war to sell

both sides munitions and then I'll hire a hit man to assas-
sinate the Greek Premier, have a Turkish flag hanging
from the rifle and CIA credentials in his pocket. So that
when the second hit man I hire kills him, I can release
through Tass . . ."

"Hold it!" I wailed. "You'll have Russia and the
U.S. involved in atomic war next."

"What's wrong with that?" said Madison.

"We'd be in the middle of it!" I screamed.

"Oh, I can tell you aren't a pro, Smith. I'm the one
that got the bruises here. They want trouble, I can
deliver. Count on me, Smith. Now, Captain . . ."

Yikes, he was dangerous!

Teenie had a hand on Madison's sleeve. "Maddie,
you're all wore out from failing to climb Mount Olympus. Get your pinkie off the panic button. All we have
to do is sail. Not all ports are hostile to the Turks. Egypt
has been governed by Turkish officers for ages, you told
me so yourself. And if they start a beef in Alexandria,
Egypt, you can have your atomic war. Okay?"

"All right," said Madison grudgingly. "I just don't
like some punk in the State Department to think he can
out–PR me. It's a matter of professional pride. I am
going to send a radio telex to the Greek papers, though,
and picture-transmit them this placard. They'll tell the
American consul they got it and he'll order them to hold
all press and somebody in the State Department will get
fired. The American government is too goofy to live. Trying to black PR me. I'll get on it."

"I'll tell the harbor master we're sailing, then," said
Captain Bitts.

"And lay your course for Egypt like we discussed,"
said Teenie.

"Aye, aye," said Captain Bitts.

Teenie and I were left alone.

My head was churning, my nerves were raw. There was some loose end I hadn't grasped. Then I had it. If they sailed for Alexandria, Egypt, direct from here across the Aegean Sea, they'd get awfully close to Turkey. I said so with a sudden yelp.

"Nonsense," said Teenie. "I helped lay out the course myself. I'm an expert now, you know. The closest we will come to Turkey will be the Greek island of Chios, the home of Homer. And if we leave in a couple of hours, we'll pass by there tomorrow night in total darkness."

"For Gods' sakes," I begged. "Don't let me fall into Turkish hands."

She smiled an enigmatic smile. She said, "Now get this loud and clear. If it even looks like you're going to, Inky, I will handle it. Trust me."

I fell back on my pillow. I pretended to be mollified. But, oh, how well I knew the chanciness of life. I was going to have to be awfully alert if I was going to live through this.

Danger was in the wind!

Chapter 3

We fled through the night and when the day dawned we were far out in the Aegean and the only sign of Greece was a rocky reef on the starboard being beaten by the waves as we passed it by.

A swell was running and up ahead lowering clouds spoke of rain.

Steadfastly, I kept to my bunk as we plowed to the southeast. The slight lift of the deck from time to time was, to me, a threat: the ship at any moment might really start to roll.

I ventured on deck in a bathrobe. It was strange: nobody was hounding me to exercise. Some subtle change had come over the ship: A sailor hosing down a deck did not smile or speak.

The vast dome of the sky lay upon an empty circle of sea. I crept up a ladder toward the bridge, fearfully peering off our port bow to be sure there was no sign of Turkey. I did not enter into the enclosed pilothouse but stood in the wing.

A movement caught my eye: the switch of a ponytail.

Teenie. She was sitting in the captain's pilot chair looking forward through the bridge windows. There was no sign of Captain Bitts. It was very strange: had she taken over the ship?

The steersman glanced my way and I retreated.

I knew it would not be until night when we would come close to Turkey but still, it made me nervous just to feel that it was there to the east, waiting like some monster of the deep to devour me. Eerie. The feeling was almost palpable. In imagination I could hear the snap of its teeth that would be followed by a grinding sound as it chewed me to bits.

I went back to my bedchamber. A feeling of dread was crawling in my bones.

Enemies.

I had enemies, that was sure.

I began to doubt Madison's theory of why we had had to leave that port. I knew down deep it must be some foe of mine who thirsted for revenge.

Idleness permits the world to fill with hostile shadows. With sudden resolution, I decided to think this thing through. I must take an orderly approach to still the queasy fear.

I got a piece of paper, a pen and, knees under me on the bed, began to make a list.

Who was behind this Thessalonica attack? I began to write.

The unknown assassin? Lombar had set him on me to kill me if I failed. Had he slipped across to Greece to do us in?

The Countess Krak? It went without saying that she would murder me most painfully if she really knew I had stolen her yacht and, all the time, had been behind these assaults on Heller. Gods knew, she was capable of anything!

Heller? Did he have connections I didn't know about? Even though he and Babe Corleone were estranged, had he set some *Mafioso* upon my trail from Palermo on?

Torpedo Fiaccola? No, the diseased necrophile was very dead. Gunsalmo Silva? No. He was dead, also. So that made two I could scratch from my enemy list.

Meeley, my old landlady on Voltar? Ske, my old airbus driver? Bawtch, chief clerk of Section 451? No, I had given them counterfeit money and they would have been caught and executed by now. The two forgers who had falsified the "Royal proclamations" the Countess Krak had somewhere and was counting on? No. They were not only on Voltar, they were also dead at my orders.

The Countess Krak? Had she somehow set in motion this attack upon the yacht?

The ghost of the old man with fleas that I had killed at Limnos? That island was over there not too far away

and it was well known that ghosts existed mainly for
revenge. When I became a ghost, if I did not get
promptly routed to some Hell, I knew I would want
revenge. Yes, that old man with fleas was a likely can-
didate. He had been a Greek with Turkish connections
and hadn't he already gotten some revenge by infesting
me with fleas? I put a heavy underscore below his name
on the enemy list.

Adora Pinch Bey and Candy Licorice Bey, my two
bigamous wives in New York? No, they couldn't have
organized that demonstration in Thessalonica, for their
skill in spectacles was all confined to the sexual sector.
Furthermore, they did not speak Greek.

Mudur Zengin, head of the Piastre National Bank of
Istanbul? He had been very hostile the last time I saw
him and now, with all these yacht expenses, he must be
running very short of my funds. His bank had guaran-
teed the Squeeza credit-card bills and maybe he couldn't
pay them anymore. He might be doing it to get revenge.
He had the power and the connections to cause a commotion in Thessalonica.

Aha! Nurse Bildirjin's father! He must have been
tearing around for months waving a shotgun, slavering
to ventilate the man who had impregnated his daughter!

He was a prominent physician in Turkey. These
medical types stick together and he must have Greek
connections galore! He must have heard I was in Thessalonica!

And yes! How easy it would be for him to go into
a conspiracy with all those women that Ahmed, the taxi
driver, and Ters, the old chauffeur, had violated just so
they could blame it all on me. These two offenders I had,
of course, blown up, but the women were very much alive.

Maybe some of those violated women had become pregnant! Nurse Bildirjin's father, as a medical man renowned and powerful in Afyon, would be in a position to know this.

A thought struck me. I had not looked closely at those Greek demonstrators. Were they really those Turkish women in disguise? Well, I didn't have to know that.

In a sudden surge of enlightenment, I thought I knew what this was all about.

THEY WERE TRYING TO DRIVE ME HOME!

I drew a huge circle around Nurse Bildirjin's father. Certainty congealed. He had connived with the women and the Greeks to drive me out of Thessalonica. He was hoping to get me back to Turkey where he could work his will on me.

THAT WAS IT!

I shuddered. I would not only be shotgunned to death but, by the law of the Qur'an for adultery, I would also be stoned to a pulp!

I stared at the list. My eyes focused on that ringed name. Oh, Gods, I must be very alert indeed!

I spent the rest of the day praying that never again in my life would I set foot in Turkey.

It would be the most painful method of suicide ever devised!

Chapter 4

Cowering in my room, I stared hauntedly at the port-hole. Darkness had fallen.

The atmosphere was very strange. No one had come down to tell me to go to dinner. No one had come near me with any food. It was just as well. The ship was moving with the slightest hint of a roll under the impact of a following swell.

Rain had begun to fall as we moved into a belt of storm. Black drops glistened on the black pane like tears. I tried to see through it but only got a sheen of porthole light reflection on the surging waves of passage.

I glanced into a mirror. My cheeks were gaunt and gray. It was the first time that I noticed the scar: healed now, it gave me a ferocious frown. I felt very far from ferocious. I felt hunted and forlorn. Out there in that blackness, near to hand now as we passed it, lay Turkey and inevitable doom were I to so much as set a toe upon it. I could almost hear the boom of a shotgun and the lethal thud of agonizing stones. This scar would be nothing if I fell into those hands!

I turned back to the porthole and peered out.

A sound behind me!

I whirled, repressing a scream.

It was Teenie.

She had on an old bridge coat on which stood bright globes of rain. A battered officer's cap hid her ponytail and shadowed her oversized eyes. She was looking at me, saying nothing.

She walked toward me. She put out her hand and pushed my chest slowly. I backed up toward the bed and sat down on it.

"You look awful, Inky."

"I'm worried about Turkey," I said, swallowing hard.

She shook her head. "In a few hours, that will all be over. There's no reason for you to be upset. Everything is being handled. You should learn to trust people, Inky.

And most of all, trust me. I may very well be the only friend you've got."

I flinched. According to the very best Apparatus textbooks, that is what you say just before you slide a Knife Section knife between somebody's ribs. But I showed no sign of what I thought.

She reached into her pocket. "The best thing for you to do is simply go to sleep and awaken to a better day when we're sailing free and clear near Egypt." She was pushing something toward me.

I knew it. Hashish candy!

For some reason, Teenie wanted me helpless!

"Take it," she urged, when I did not.

I stared at it. THREE pieces! It would knock me out like a brutally wielded club.

Oh, I was thankful I had told myself to be alert and wary.

I was wearing a bathrobe with large sleeves which partially covered my hands. I was adept at this sort of thing. I took the first piece and went through the motions of putting it in my mouth. I chewed and swallowed. But the candy had simply dropped into my sleeve no matter how my jaw bulged: it's done with the tongue.

I took the second piece. I made the motions of putting it in my mouth and chewing it. "Um, um," I said. "Delicious." But the second piece was in my sleeve.

The third piece went the same way.

"That's better," said Teenie. "Now, soon you'll simply go to sleep and it will all be over. It's still six hundred miles to Alexandria, but by dawn Turkey will be far astern. So just be a good boy and sleep."

She went to the door. She looked back. "I'm spending the night up on the bridge just to be sure everything gets handled. Don't worry about a thing." She left.

I went to the door. Yes, her footsteps, heard above the engine throbs, were receding.

I went to the bathroom, dropped the three pieces of hashish candy out of my sleeve and flushed them down the electric toilet drain.

I went back and lay upon my bunk. The look in her oversized eyes, the expression on her too-big mouth—yes, she was up to something. Apparatus training tells.

The ship, as it progressed, was lifting to a swell. Two hours I lay there staring at that black, rain-streaked porthole glass. I glanced at my watch from time to time. This was one night I would not sleep. That I vowed.

Suddenly, I was aware of something: a change! For the last few minutes, there had been no ship pitch. We were travelling like a billiard table. I was not enough of a sailor to be able to figure out what this meant but I was sure it must mean something. The rain had not stopped, as witness that streaking black window. So what was the meaning of this?

Far away, somewhere in the ship, I heard a faint staccato of bells.

A vibration ceased.

THE ENGINES HAD STOPPED!

Chapter 5

Through my rain-streaked port glass, I could see something coming out of the night.

A craft of some sort!

I could see the glow of a light in its bow. The port

running light gleamed red as blood. A white light in the stern told me it was not a third the size of the *Golden Sunset*.

It was approaching. Like shadowy Demons, sailors, seen by the port lights from our ship, were hanging fenders along its rails. It was going to come alongside! Yes! Somebody had thrown a line aboard!

What was it? A patrol craft? I could not tell.

Somebody, a dim shadow, was standing by its pilot house. He was even with this very deck.

A port light flashed across his face.

THE BLACK-JOWLED MAN!

Oh, Gods! What was this? My wits spun!

Quickly I grabbed my bathrobe tighter about me. I sped out of my cabin. Barefooted, I came to the deck. Like a shadow myself, I melted behind a big life-jacket box.

The pelting rain struck at me. I peered out.

The craft came against our hull with a thump.

The black-jowled man came to its rail.

Another figure came out of a door on this deck and, in the darkness, went to our rail opposite the black-jowled man. They were only about five feet apart.

A flashlight winked in the hand of the black-jowled man. It fell upon the face of the person at our rail.

My blood froze.

TEENIE! Those eyes and mouth were unmistakable even under that battered cap and in the rain.

"You didn't have to start a riot, you (bleep)!" she said. "You almost got me hit with a rock and then where would you have been? We were sailing anyway the very next morning. Jesus, I'm mad at you!"

"That's not one-sided!" snarled the black-jowled man. "You didn't have to go to Thessalonica at all. It

was time to show you the party can get rough! You've
been wandering all over the globe! Delay, delay! What
have you got to say to that?"

"I got to say I never would have had any bullfights
or clothes, you cheapskate. You know what I think? I
think right now you're trying to con me. I don't think
you have any idea at all of giving me what I deserve."

"Delay, delay, delay! You deserve to be shot! You
weren't supposed to take a joy ride. You were supposed
to deliver him into our hands!"

My heart stopped beating. Then a sickening wave of
awful comprehension rushed through me. Those songs!
Marijuana becoming hashish and hashish becoming hash
oil. Her interest in charts, her efforts to see Turkey from
the mountaintops. The search for outlaws, each one inex-
orably closer to Turkey! She had been shanghaiing me
aboard my own yacht to return me to a place where I
would be murdered!

He had begun to swear at her. She said, "Keep your
voice down. You earlier threatened to pay the captain to
finish it off. Well, let me tell you something, buster, Bitts
and me are in cahoots. We're just like that!" And she
raised two fingers parallel. "This yacht ain't going to
move a foot unless I tell it to. And you know what I
think, you (bleep)? I think you're going to try to get me
in and then you're going to wave your dirty hand and tell
me to get lost. That's what I think you're going to do."

"You wrong me," said the black-jowled man. "I keep
my word."

"The hell you do," said Teenie. "Remember that
Rome jeweler's? You said we could go back and pick up
the necklace and what did you do? You just plain forgot!"

"I didn't!" said the black-jowled man. "I picked it
up myself the day after you sailed. Here it is."

He fumbled in his pocket and brought out a box.

"That ain't going to do you any good now," said Teenie, waving it back as he extended it across the gap. "You probably had him put in fake stones and hope I can't tell in this light. No sir, Mac. I don't trust you worth a (bleep)."

He put the box back into his pocket, with an angry thrust.

She raised a cautionary finger at him. "Now hear this, loud and clear, buster. I'm not moving this yacht into Turkish waters until I get my ten grand."

"Jesus," said the black-jowled man.

I was seething. Rage had begun to take over. So that was her price, was it? Ten grand for delivering me to my death!

Teenie stepped back from the rail. Above the hiss of the rain her voice was plain. "Ten grand in my little hot hand, buster, and then and only then will I give the word."

"Jesus," said the black-jowled man. "I haven't got ten grand aboard here."

"See?" said Teenie. "You were trying to pull a con. You weren't going to pay me at all! Oh, I'm used to dealing with the likes of you. I was brought up on birds that would rather do a double switch than eat."

"Listen," said the black-jowled man. "Izmir is right over there. Our agent will have the cash. I can get it in two hours. And if I pay you, will you order this yacht to Istanbul? You know (bleeped) well, we've got to get our hands on him."

"All right," said Teenie. "We'll stand by right here off Chios."

"No, not all right," said the black-jowled man.

"How do I know you won't just sail away the moment I leave? I think you better step over that rail and come with me."

"All right," said Teenie. "I'll tell Bitts."

She passed within three feet of me in the dark. She went to the bottom of the bridge ladder. She yelled up, "Stand by right where you are off Chios. We're going into Izmir. I'll be back in a couple of hours."

"Aye, aye," came down from the darkness.

She sped back past me.

"You sure you've got him safe?" said the black-jowled man before he extended an arm to help her over the rail.

"You bet he is," said Teenie. "Drugged to the gills and I'll keep him drugged. He thinks he's on his way to Egypt. You want to go down and see him?"

"We've wasted enough time. Jump."

Teenie landed on their deck. Lines were cast off. The screws of the craft churned. It was swallowed in the rain and dark.

Oh, the perfidy of women!

I was sick to the core with her treachery.

I HAD TO ACT!

Chapter 6

TWO HOURS!

But two hours can become two minutes if one doesn't rush.

There was a rift in the rain. A momentary luminance of moonlight spread its green horror across the scene.

There was a loom of land a mile or two away. That must be Chios, the Greek island almost up against the Turkish shore.

I yearned toward it. Oh, Gods, if I could only reach it, I would be out of their tentacles.

The rain closed in again. But I had had an omen. Some God, if only for a moment, had plucked the veil aside.

ACTION! I had to get into action quick! Even now the hurled stones for adultery were halfway through the air. Suddenly I realized that the stones of the demonstrators had been another warning from the Gods. It had been another omen and I had not seen it!

I would not miss it now!

Swift as a cat I raced below. Did I have time to pack? The hand grips that Teenie had bought me in Rome lay upon the closet floor. Anything that had to do with Teenie was bad luck. I flinched from them. No, I did not have time to pack. I would abandon my things.

I grabbed some clothes at random and began to hurl them on: running shorts, a business jacket, a straw hat, scuba slippers.

Wait, wait. I had to get some sanity into this. I could not leave behind my two-way-response radio, my money or my passports. The wastebasket had one of these liners they put in. They were waterproof. I dumped the perishable things in it, tied the top of the bag and lashed it firmly to my belt.

I was ready to swim for it.

Wait, wait. I wasn't armed.

I opened the drawer where I had thrown the guns I

had brought aboard or purchased in ports. My hand went out instinctively to grasp the biggest caliber there. Then I recoiled. If I had to shoot the crew, the sound of shots might be heard for miles. A silenced gun, that was what I needed. But the only thing there that had a silencer was an old American International Model 180. I had bought it, as I am wont to do, in an idle moment from a furtive street peddler in Palermo only to discover later that it was only .22 caliber. Its virtue was that it was fully automatic, a machine gun. He had sold me the whole case, somewhat battered, that contained it. Anxiously I looked into the four drum magazines. Yes, they were loaded!

It was all disassembled. With shaking hands and many a slip and misfit, I got the ugly short thing assembled. I snapped a flat drum on top of its barrel. I slid the silencer in place. It would not make much impact but with 1200 rounds per minute rate of fire it could hold off a lot of men. I picked up the drums. I tried to find someplace to put them. A life jacket! I hurriedly cut a slit in one, tore out the stuffings and thrust the magazines in.

I flung the rifle over my shoulder and put on the life jacket. Then I had to take the life jacket off and free the rifle. I put the life jacket back on and put the sling back on. . . . It was all too heavy! I would go down like a stone! What to do?

Suddenly I thought of Madison. I could not leave him aboard. If they seized the yacht, it would be in the papers. He might be mentioned. Krak would hear he was aboard, come over and interrogate him and then kill me! I could not leave him behind. He might drown swimming two miles.

A speedboat. I would force Bitts to land me in a speedboat!

I raced to Madison's cabin.

He was peacefully asleep.

I put my hand across his mouth so he would not cry out.

I must think. I had to tell him something.

"Madison," I said in a hoarse whisper, "don't scream. We have to flee for our lives. I have just discovered the Mafia bribed the captain to make eunuchs of us and sell us into slavery."

His eyes flared wide with terror. That was what I wanted.

"Get dressed! I've got to seize a speedboat and get ashore to a Greek island. Quick! Quick!"

"Oh, I knew it," wept Madison. "Ever since Palermo he has been laughing behind my back whenever he beats me at poker."

"Hurry, hurry. The slavers will be here in minutes."

He grabbed up clothes and began to stuff them into a grip.

"There is no time to pack," I whispered.

"I can't go naked!"

"Then put some clothes on!"

"That's what I'm doing."

"You're packing."

"I've got to pack. You can't give press conferences dressed like a bum. Not even to slavers."

I knew he would not change his mind. I unlimbered the rifle and stood at the door, listening in an agony of suspense for footsteps that might come.

He finished packing. Then he took an athletic suit out and put it on. He saw I was wearing a life jacket and got one from under the bed. He glanced out the port. It was black but he could see the rain on it. He grabbed a couple of raincoats out of the closet. He wrapped one around his grip and tied it tightly. He got into the other one and put on the life jacket over it. He was still looking around.

"Don't delay," I whispered urgently. "What are you looking for?"

"Something bulletproof to go over this," he said.

I hurried him out of the door. He dashed back and got his grip.

I pushed him to an upper deck. I whispered in his ear, "No matter what happens, stand here."

The rain was coming down.

Like a lethal cat, the machine gun ready, I mounted the bridge ladder.

There was no one there!

I heard voices above me.

The signal bridge!

I crept up the next ladder.

Captain Bitts and two sailors in oilskins were standing at the foot of a signal mast. They were trying to hoist lights up to its yardarm.

Signals! They had suspected I was trying to escape! Some lanterns were strung at intervals on a line going up. They were going to signal the shore!

"The God (bleep) block is jammed," said Bitts to a sailor. "See if you can free the other halyard. We can't flop around here all night dead in the water with no drifting lights." To the other one, he said, "Are you sure you told the electrician what panel was blown?"

"He said it's a short from the rain. He don't wanna go up there until morning."

"Then help free this God (bleeped) halyard!" said Bitts.

I spoiled their little game right there. I levelled the machine gun. "Hold it!" I said. "Stand right where you are or I'll blow you to pieces!"

"Jesus Christ!" said Bitts, staring at me.

"You got a right to be surprised," I said in a deadly voice. "You didn't know who you were dealing with! Get a speedboat in the water at once or get a bellyful of lead. You're going to land me, and right now!" I pointed toward where I had seen the dark bulk of shore.

He was standing there with the two sailors. Their hands were on the halyard. The lanterns suspended above them cast eerie pools of colored light around them. Bitts seemed to come awake. "NO!" he said. "It may seem flat calm here but a speedboat couldn't live in that surf over there! You'd drown!"

He thought he had me. He thought he could trap me aboard. But I had picked up a lot of knowledge strolling around this ship. "That won't work," I grated. "You've got rowing inflatables forward that can live in any surf. Throw one in the water and drop a ladder to it!"

"Listen..." said Bitts.

"Shut up! No arguing! One more word and I shoot!" I cocked the machine gun.

"Wait," said Bitts. "I think you ought to know..."

I lifted the muzzle of the machine gun to point over their heads.

I pressed the trigger.

The black powder of the .22s sprayed a fan of orange blaze! The deck flared with the light.

The staccato spits of the silenced weapon were hardly heard above the falling rain.

SNAP!

CRASH!

The bullets, fired high, had severed the lantern halyard!

The heavy-glassed lights came smashing down upon the men.

One hit Captain Bitts!

Even as he fell, a second and a third lamp hit from aloft. One burst into flame!

The two sailors, skidding on the deck, had leaped aside.

I knew they would flee and alert the ship.

"Freeze!" I cried, levelling the gun at them.

They froze, staring at me white-eyed, bathed in the oil fire's light.

A torrent of rain struck through the tableau.

The running rivulets of fire went out.

"Get an inflatable over the side!" I barked at them. "Move, or I'll fill you full of lead."

They moved but one hesitated over Bitts. He bent down. I knew he was looking for a gun.

I fired a second burst! The orange flame-fan arced above their heads.

They sped to the forward ladder and started down. I followed them. One was unwinding a pilot ladder from the gutter and dropping it over the side of the hull. The other one got a rowing inflatable out of a locker.

I looked anxiously through the rain. Was that craft coming back? I saw nothing but rain.

The sailor put a line on the inflatable.

"You can't fool me," I said in a deadly voice. "Put the oars in it."

"Don't you want the motor?" he said blankly.

I knew right then the motor wouldn't run. They were trying to trap me. And even if it did run they could follow the sound. "Oars!" I barked.

"They're strapped inside it," he said. He threw it over the rail. It was a long way down to the water.

The other sailor had a flashlight. I snatched it from him and shined it down. The inflatable had struck and the water had triggered its gas bottles. It opened out with a sizzle barely audible in the hiss of rain.

I had not realized there was any sea at all. The stabilizers were holding the yacht steady. The inflatable was bobbing up and down in surging waves.

I must be brave. I was about to go over the rail when I remembered Madison again. He was right there. I sent him down first.

Carrying his wrapped suitcase, he descended. With a foot, he got the inflatable against the hull. It was surging up and down. He got in and held it to the ship. I tossed the flashlight to Madison.

I menaced the two sailors with the machine gun.

I backed down the ladder.

The inflatable seemed to be leaping up and down, rising five feet up and then falling away.

I took my life in my hands.

I jumped.

I landed in a clutter in the bottom of the craft.

The sailor on the deck gave his rope a toss.

We rebounded off the hull and bobbed outward from the ship. A gust of rain washed over us, carrying us further away.

I looked back.

The ship was a misty, light-sparked shape in the night.

I had escaped!

Now I only had to get ashore in Greece!

Chapter 7

The sea was black, the rain was black, the sky was black. I felt that I was being drowned in a hurricane of ink!

Gone was all sense of direction, gone was any stability, and, a couple of minutes after I had gotten into the boat, gone was anything I had eaten in three days!

It is a nauseating fact that I was very seasick.

"Row!" I cried between retches.

"Row where?" said Madison.

"Row anyplace, but for Gods' sakes, get me ashore. I'm dying!"

The only advantage in being in all this was that the rain was so heavy it was washing my face clean. I felt I had the whole Aegean for a bathtub and the sky as well.

"You better bail," said Madison. "The water is up around my knees."

Maybe it would be far better to just drown and get this over with. I felt like I was in an automatic washing machine with the lights off. I might as well pull the plug and go down the drain.

A vague haze of moonlight came through a temporary rift of cloud. Madison was trying to do something with the oars.

The water, smashing around in the craft, was up to my chest. That was because I was lying in it.

"Bail!" said Madison urgently.

There was no bailing can. I only had my straw hat.

I used it. As fast as I threw water out it rained back in.

"There's a fast current running here," said Madison above the hiss of the downpour. "Did you see how fast we sped away from the ship? Or maybe it's the wind. No, there isn't any wind. Yes, I think there is some wind. . . ." He was holding up a finger to test it. A wave knocked his hand down. "No, there isn't any wind. It's the waves. Yes, I think it is the wind. . . ."

"Oh, Gods, make up your mind!" I yelled, trying to bail with my straw hat.

"I'm much better with a typewriter," said Madison. "Give me a nonbouncing desk and I could handle this. Eighteen point quote STORM unquote 20 point quote STORM SUBSIDES unquote 22 point quote MADISON SAVED. . . ."

I thought the inflatable was going to sail up into the air, flip like a pancake and come down. Then it slid and slithered from one mountainous crest to the next and then, for variety, tried to be a pancake again.

"Wait," said Madison. "I think I hear surf."

I stopped bailing. It was all running out of the holes in the hat anyway. I took time out to retch.

The faint haze of light, cast by the moon far above this holocaust, grew stronger for a moment.

"There's land over there!" said Madison.

He promptly put his back to it and even though he caught crabs now and then and even though we spun entirely about occasionally, we seemed to be making progress.

To my right I heard a snarl. I knew what it was at once. The monster who had been waiting for days had decided to attack full force and swallow me at last.

I saw a faint but nearby glimmer of white. It could be nothing but teeth.

"Hold on!" cried Madison. "I'll try to surfboard in!"

Up we rose. Down went the bow of our craft. And suddenly we were going at sixty miles an hour! Through white-frothed blackness!

Then we tripped.

With a roaring ferocity, the surf devoured us!

Down I went in the churning maelstrom.

Abruptly I realized that the life jacket was not a life jacket anymore. It was a death jacket. Full of magazines, it was taking me straight to the bottom!

I tried to get rid of it. The machine gun across my back was holding it on!

I felt myself surging forward in the depths.

Now something was strangling me!

I struck something on the bottom. A rock?

Something was towing me!

Oh, Gods, the sea had decided to take me off to its cave where it could eat me at leisure.

It was too much for me. I passed out.

A bit later, I opened my eyes. There was a roaring in my ears.

Something was over me, outlined against the luminous sky. This was where the sea would boil me alive and have me bit by bit for snacks.

"Goodness," said a voice. "I'm glad you're still alive."

The sea doesn't talk English and it wants to see everybody dead. I was reassured.

I raised my head. The roaring wasn't in my ears. I could see the waves in the faintly luminous glow. They were roaring and thundering away but I was at least ten feet up the beach from the water.

Something was still strangling me. I tried to pry it off. The boat painter! It had gotten wrapped around my neck. When I pulled at it impatiently, the boat nearby gave a jerk.

"Thank heavens I didn't have to go diving for you," said Madison. "When I pulled the boat further up out of the water to get my suitcase, you were tied to it. You're lucky."

"Don't talk to me of luck!" I said. I got myself untangled. Then I became aware of the firmness of the ground. It was only moving a little bit under me. I felt it again. It was moving less. I put both my hands against it and pushed. It wasn't moving at all. Maybe I *was* lucky.

"I don't know if they followed us," said Madison.

That brought me around very swiftly. At the moment the clouds were thinner but there was still rain. I couldn't see the yacht or any lights but then, actually, I didn't know where to look except out into the sea. We might even have come around some point.

I looked behind us. A hill loomed.

"Come!" I said. "We've got to find cover! If they send anyone after us, we must not get caught in the open."

I got up and took a step forward. Ouch! I was barefoot! The scuba shoes must have come off.

Nevertheless, I must walk!

Stumbling and stubbing, I led the way up the hill through underbrush. We climbed and climbed. At last I came limpingly onto a flat area. At first I thought it was a road, for it seemed to be paved. The luminescence from above the rain brightened the scene for a moment. It wasn't a road. It seemed to be a wide floor, half an acre at least.

Aha! A ruined city or the fragments thereof. Greece abounds with them. I thought I knew where we must be now. There is an ancient excavated city from the Bronze

Age at the southeast end of Chios and it is on the side of the island which faces away from Turkey. Emboriós, I think its name was. I felt encouraged. I was sure that I had landed on the island where Homer had written his famous poems. The odyssey I was engaged upon might not satisfy Ulysses but it certainly contained a lot more horror than I was comfortable with.

I went further up the hill, Madison trudging after me. I came to a rocky prominence. In spite of rain, I caught a whiff of goats. Perhaps there was some shelter here along the face of these cliffs.

I took the flashlight Madison had retained in his pocket and played it cautiously ahead of me. I found a faint path. It ended in a shallow cave.

It was very low and it was very plain that goats used it, but it was shelter from the rain. I crawled in and Madison followed.

I turned the flashlight on my feet. Blood! I knew I could not walk any further: I had no shoes.

I glanced apprehensively down through the dark where the sea must be, far below. They would be after us, I had no doubt. Black Jowl had meant business. Kidnapping from Greek soil with no witnesses around would not cause him a second thought.

I gloomed. Maybe I was not safe after all!

PART
FIFTY-NINE

Chapter 1

Lying in the stinking cave, licked now and then with gusts of rain, I wondered what the future held for me. Something awful, I had no doubt. I was right.

Music!

> *Home, home on the range,*
> *Where the deer and the antelope play,*
> *Where seldom is heard a discouraging word*
> *And the skies are not cloudy all day!*

Jesus! On the Greek island of Chios, drenched in rain, with the ghost of Homer haunting around, how could a western ballad get in here?

It was Madison. He had taken a small portable radio out of his suitcase and had it on Radio Luxembourg.

"Turn that thing off!" I wailed.

"I was just trying to liven things up," he said. "It's kind of dull."

"As soon as it gets daylight," I snarled, "you won't find it dull. I'm going to have to sell our lives as dearly as possible!"

"Maybe I can find some blues," he said. "But I do think country western is a more suitable soundtrack if you're going to start shooting."

The radio said, "We now have a request from our armed forces in Turkey, 'Join the Big Round Up in the Sky.'"

"Oh, Gods, turn it off," I begged.

He did.

Wait a minute. Radio! I was suddenly hit by a brilliant idea!

I untied the sack from my belt and spilled its contents out on the floor. I picked up the two-way-response radio.

Oh, thank Gods! Raht answered!

In rapid military Voltarian, I said, "Listen and get this straight. Put a message through to the base. Order Captain Stabb to take off in the tug and pick me up quick!" Hope was surging in me. That flat space back there might serve as a landing place. Stabb could whisk me to the depths of Africa or someplace safer than here.

Raht said, "Got the message. But where are you?"

"I think I'm on the southeast end of the Greek island of Chios."

"You *think*," said Raht. "If a spaceship is going to pick you up, you better be sure where you are and right down to a pinpoint. They're not going to wander all over the place trying to locate you. They'd have to kill any inhabitants they ran into if they made a mistake. You're risking a Code break."

"Look," I said, "I have not got much time. They are running a race with dawn. Pinpoint me with that radio."

"It's not that accurate at such ranges. Tell you what. I'm not at the office but I'll rush over there. I can put your carrier beam on the grid analyzer if you transmit to it. Hold on. I'll get right over there." He clicked off.

"What language were you speaking?" said Madison. "It didn't sound like any lingo I ever heard."

I masked the flashlight and looked at him. He knew too much already. If the Countess Krak ever got her hands on him, I was dead for sure!

Before I could stop him, Madison took the flashlight and began to paw around in the mound of papers I had spilled out of the sack to get my radio. "Well, look at all the passports!" he said. "Inkswitch, Federal Investigator; Achmed Ben Nutti, United Arab League; Sultan Bey... I don't see any here for Smith." He looked up. "What is your real name, anyway?" He looked back at the papers. "And what's this writing?" I had used a blank Apparatus gate pass to scribble amounts of money on: the printing was three-dimensional, of course, and it plainly said, *Coordinated Information Apparatus, Voltar Confederacy.* It even had the logo the Fleet called the "drunks." "Three-dimensional printing?" he said. "That's out of this world, man."

At first I hadn't stopped him because I was thinking of something else: about what to do with him. Then I hadn't stopped him because the gesture of doing so would have alerted him to the fact that he was into something secret. And when he hit the gate pass blank he had gone beyond mere stopping. Code break. Madison would have to be shot.

Then, much as it was unlike me, I stayed my hand as it reached instinctively toward the machine gun. Madison was too valuable. Madison could wreck men's lives and start wars and raise Hells in a way Voltar had never heard of: PR. Lombar was always looking for ways to ruin people and this was one he had never heard of.

Despite my condition, decision was swift. When the tug picked us up, I would simply order Captain Stabb to take Madison back to base, put him in detention and ship him off to Lombar with a note. Maybe it would make Lombar less brutal on me if I gave him such a gift. It would not only get Madison safely beyond any Krak interrogation—which would be extremely fatal now that he knew my other names—it would also put me in good with Lombar Hisst.

I had to dissimulate. But I am trained in that. I forced a chuckle. "Your instincts as an investigative reporter will get you in trouble yet, Madison," I said. "Just don't spread it around and you'll find out all about it someday."

"Oho!" he said. "I smell a story! Eighteen-point Mystery Man Tells All."

He sealed his fate right there.

Chapter 2

After a tense interval that seemed hours my radio went live. Raht's voice: "I'm in the New York office now."

"What the Hells was the delay?"

"This analyzer hasn't been used for years," said Raht. "I couldn't find a power pack. But it's operating now. Just hold down your transmit plate and I'll get it into the computer."

I did. There was a pause. Then Raht came on again. "It's a good thing I checked before I called the base. You're not on Chios."

"You must be making a mistake," I said. "I am definitely on Chios, right beside the ruins of Emboriós. Check again, you idiot!"

There was a pause. "I rechecked. You're not on

Chios. I have the Voltarian grid map of this planet right on the scope. You're at 43-17-4.1052 exactly."

"That doesn't tell me anything. Give it to me in Earth geography."

"Let me get a blowup of an Earth globe, get it to the same scale and superimpose... Here it is. You're 340.2 yards up from the beach and 9.1 miles west by south of Karaburun."

"WHAT?"

"You're just across a narrow strait from Chios. You're on the Turkish mainland."

Oh, GODS! I had gotten turned around in the rain and dark! And ruins were a dime a dozen in this land!

The ground under me went suddenly hot.

"Raht," I pleaded, "please, please tell them at the base to send that tug quick. I've GOT to get out of Turkey!"

"All right," he said. "I'll relay the message. But don't go running off. They'll have my head if they make a fruitless trip. I'm gone."

Madison said, "Who is that you're talking to?"

I was numb from shock of finding where I was. "New York," I said.

"On that little thing?" said Mad. "It's not much bigger than a cigarette lighter."

I didn't answer him. He'd find out all about real electronics soon enough. On Voltar. I was more interested in that blackness out there. I couldn't see much but I had to be alert for the tug.

I hoped they didn't direct their blueflash this way when they settled down on that expanse of pavement. It was around a shoulder of the hill but still, I must take care to protect my eyes with my arm. I didn't care if

Mad got a pupil full of it. He'd be knocked out soon enough anyway, for shipment.

It seemed like hardly any time at all before I saw a haze of light. But wait, there was something wrong. The whole terrain was getting gray.

IT WAS DAWN!

With a sudden sickening I realized I had been too late! They couldn't make it in the short span of darkness that had been left.

I moaned softly.

The intensity of morning twilight increased. Bushes began to take on detail. The waves in the surf below were no longer just white streaks.

It stopped raining. There were clouds but even these were thinning.

The ships!

The *Golden Sunset*, two or three miles away, was growing distinct. It was obscuring nearly all of another craft beside it. I could not make out the kind of vessel the other was. A fishboat? A yacht? A patrol craft? All I knew for certain about it was that it wanted me! And here I was pinned down, hidden it is true, but trapped in Turkey, the very place I must not be.

To my left, lying out in the water, three islets emerged from the twilight. And then directly before us but some miles away there seemed to be a bulk of land.

Suddenly a random shaft of sunlight moved in under the scudding clouds. It was from directly behind us.

The sun rises in the east, I told myself. My cave in the cliff was facing due west. I was looking across the narrow strait at Chios. Any hope I had that Raht might be wrong collapsed. Even the sun said I was in Turkey.

There is something discouraging about having a

thing you already know pounded home with sledge-hammer force.

Chios was only a few miles away. A wild plan to swim for it folded up like a popped paper bag.

MEN!

They came from around an outcrop on the beach. One, two, three, four, five, six ... BLACK JOWL!

They were working north along the beach. They must have landed in a quieter cove to the south, not choosing to dare the pounding surf opposite me where we had landed.

THEY WERE SEARCHING!

Scattered out they would examine the shore and then the slope above it with their deadly eyes.

Black Jowl was carrying a hand radio. He would pause and speak in it from time to time and look out toward the ships. Oh, Gods, on those ship radios he would be in communication with all the world. What was he ordering? A general mobilization of the armed forces of Turkey? Maybe at any moment now fighter planes would come screaming out of the dawn sky: I keened my ear for the clank of tanks, the scuttle of infantry. I scanned the horizon: maybe the Turkish navy would show up. After all, I had entered the country without passing through immigration: they would use that as a crime to turn me over to Black Jowl and then stand back laughingly as I was stoned alive. That is, if they did not kill me on the first frontal assault.

I looked to my machine gun. I upended the barrel. A stream of water came out. Never mind, it would still shoot. I braced myself on my elbows and drew a bead on Black Jowl. Then I paused. It was only a .22 caliber weapon and while I had heard that a .22 would travel a mile, I didn't think it had a very lethal impact at long range. I had better wait.

A shout rose up above the distant boom of surf. The men raced forward.

One was pointing.

Our inflatable!

Oh, why hadn't I pushed it back into the sea?

Black Jowl came and stood before it. He talked into his radio, looking at the ship.

How had they known the inflatable was there? And then I realized they had followed us in on radar last night. Probably the thing even had a radar target on it!

The men fanned out. I knew what they were looking for: footprints!

They found the trail! Probably blood from my broken feet. No, that would have been obliterated by the rain. But they seemed to be following something.

I cocked my machine gun.

Suddenly the black-jowled man shouted something to the rest of them. They halted.

The black-jowled man was talking into his radio. I could not hear what he was saying due to the hiss and boom of the sea. Oh, if I only had a listening device. But then, I didn't need it. From his gestures to the men it was very plain that he knew I was up there on that cliff.

But it was puzzling. They did not come charging up. They were just standing there three hundred yards away, looking first to the cliff and then to the black-jowled man.

His communication seemed very lengthy. I could guess what it was: he was ordering a full frontal assault by the combined forces of NATO! Then women with stones would act as the mop-up squad.

Then something very peculiar happened. Black Jowl

removed his radio from his mouth and made an arm signal to his men.

They picked up the inflatable, punched the gas out of it and folded it up. Black Jowl was making sure I did not escape by sea!

Carrying the craft they filed off to the south. They vanished around a turn of the beach. Very soon, in two boats, they came into view again.

They headed for the ships.

I watched as they crossed the water. I looked up at the sky for any fighter planes.

At long last they boarded the vessels.

Sometime later the yacht, still obscuring the other ship, got under way. Both of them sailed northward. For Istanbul?

My radio went live. It was Raht, of course. Nobody else had a matching unit for this frequency. "Officer Gris?"

"Yes."

"I got a message for you here. Just sit tight. You'll be picked up about sunset."

"Thank Gods."

He clicked off.

"Another name?" said Madison. "Something *Gris?* That sure is a funny language. Sounds like Chinese but it's not Chinese as Chinese is in tones and I used to have to order my laundry in Chinese. It sure isn't Russian. Sort of liquid and lilting. I don't think I've ever heard some of those vowels. And that *S* isn't really an *S.* One does it by actually blowing one's breath. It sounds more like *HIST.*"

"Shut up!" I snapped at him.

But never mind, he'd be meeting Lombar Hisst soon enough, the poor fool.

Something was bothering me. Sunset? It wouldn't be dark yet at sunset for this was late spring and the twilight was long even in these latitudes. Raht must have meant AFTER sunset. Yes, he was so (bleeped) inaccurate: he had probably just omitted the word *after*.

Now, if I could live through today without discovery, I thought all would be well.

Little did I know the forces of evil that were at that very moment churning in the world. And that I was at the very center of the vortex!

Chapter 3

Throughout a long and worried day I suffered.

The goat cave stunk a bit more than even I could stand and that's saying something for an officer of the Apparatus.

Although we had hundreds of square miles of water to look at if you included both the strait and the Aegean beyond it, visible to the north, we didn't have a single drop to wet our parching throats.

About noon the rain clouds cleared away and the sun, moving westward, began to pour into the cave. It made things worse.

Madison kept turning on his radio and getting rock music. I recognized the Hoochi-Hoochi Boys that Nurse Bildirjin adored. They were singing Turkish with English slang.

Get stoned with me,
You oughta get stoned with me,
Can't you see I'm dead without you.
Take my joints,
I'll never puff them.
Grab my bhong . . .

"SHUT IT OFF!" I screamed at him.

"I'm sorry," he said. "I just thought I ought to soak up some of the local folk songs. I'm in a culture lag. One minute you're talking a language nobody ever heard before that I know of and the next, I'm getting pop music in English and Turkish. What did those Turkish words mean?"

"Oh, shut up!" I begged him. I was getting feverish. You don't smoke marijuana continually as I had been for weeks past without acquiring a throat that is very sensitive to lack of water. What I wouldn't give for an ice-cold Seven Up. Almost instantly I saw, actually SAW, the green can before me, eight times as big as life, frosted with dewy drops. I steeled myself. I did not reach for it. It vanished.

As the afternoon wore on, the sun, glancing off the water, made my eyes burn and raised the shelter's temperature—and its stink—beyond endurance. I kept reaching for the cans of Seven Up but they continued to vanish.

Finally the sun was very low, boring into the cave in a last determined effort to get me. It won. I sank into a faint.

A hand was shaking me. "I think somebody is calling that other funny name you've got—Gris, Gris."

I stared up groggily. It was Madison. I felt annoyed. "For Gods' sakes, if you're going to say it, say it right.

What you are trying to enunciate as an English G is pronounced halfway between *HA* and *TH* with a throat rumble."

"No, no, listen!" said Madison. "Somebody is calling it."

I sat up. Yes! There it came from afar, "Officer Gris! Officer Gris!"

I scrambled to my feet. It was still daylight. The fools must be flying the tug around in daylight! They'd get us all exterminated for a Code break!

I started to rush out. Madison was thrusting something at me. My sack of money and papers. I grabbed it.

On flying feet I rushed from the cave. My feet didn't fly very long. I stepped on a stone. Agony!

Limping, I made my way along the goat path. I rounded the shoulder of the cliff. I came to the flat area. I stopped.

There sat the huge, bulletproof, 1962 Daimler-Benz, the red eagle blazing on its side!

There was Ahmed the taxi driver.

There was Ters the driver.

BUT THEY WERE DEAD!

I had killed them with a bomb!

Thirst and repeated shocks had caught up with me!

Now I was not only having delusions, I was also being haunted by ghosts.

Ters gave his evil laugh.

I fainted dead away.

Chapter 4

When I came to it was dark.

I was lying on the fatal car bunk.

We were rolling along.

"He's come to." It was Madison's voice. He was in back with me. Ahmed was in the front seat beside Ters who was driving.

By the dim light coming up from the bar I could see Madison opening a paper sack. He uncapped a Coke and handed it to me. I propped myself on an elbow and drank thirstily.

"This is a nice car," said Madison. "A real antique. What's the eagle on the side stand for?"

"Folly," I said.

Ahmed in the front seat turned. "Glad you're awake. Have you been ill?"

He must still be alive. I could hear his voice. "Shock," I said.

"It'll do that to you," said Ahmed. "But you'll have time to recuperate. It's almost 225 miles to Afyon. Ters and I will take turns driving, we'll take it easy and we'll get you safely home."

"Oh, no!" I cried. "Don't take me there!"

"Why not?" said Ahmed. "Oh, by the way, I have a message from Doktor Muhammed Ataturk."

I stiffened. He meant Prahd Bittlestiffender, the young cellologist I had kidnapped on Voltar. "Is he after me, too?" I said.

"No, no," said Ahmed. "Of course not. We're all your friends, remember? The young doktor was the one who sent us out here to get you after Faht Bey turned your request down."

So that's how it was. It made me nervous. "What was the message?" I asked fearfully.

"Well, it's about Nurse Bildirjin, the young Turkish girl at the hospital. He said not for you to worry even for one second. He said to tell you he has everything fixed up."

Ters gave his evil laugh.

I concentrated on the message. Madison was pushing a sandwich at me. I followed it with a second Coke.

My wits began to work. Evidently Prahd had done an abortion on Nurse Bildirjin after all. Maybe her father had never even found out.

I felt optimistic, even reassured. Maybe this was going to turn out all right after all.

I fell asleep.

It was well after dawn before I awoke. They had evidently made more stops for they had more Cokes. Drinking one, I saw that we were rolling into Afyon.

They drove down some back streets and then into a broader road.

"Hey," I said, "you're not taking me to the villa. Where are you going?"

Ters, who was driving, gave his evil laugh.

He braked suddenly in front of a mosque.

He honked his horn.

Instantly the car was surrounded by a mob!

With horrified eyes I saw Nurse Bildirjin. She was very swollen with child.

HER FATHER! He was elbowing forward. HE WAS CARRYING A SHOTGUN!

With screams surging in my throat, I scrambled around trying to locate my machine gun. IT WAS GONE!

There was Prahd, his straw-colored hair standing up at all angles. He opened the car door and I cringed back. He got in. He looked at me with his bright green eyes.

"You tricked me!" I cried. "You lured me to my death!"

He closed the car door to shut out the mutter of the threatening crowd. "You are unduly alarmed," he said. "I have been trying to contact you for months. Thank Gods you came back in time. It would have been a terrible scandal if the baby had been born first."

"Born FIRST? Born before what?"

"I made a bargain for you. It is all arranged. The first part of the bargain was to start my pay. Is that agreed?"

Oh, (bleep) him, I couldn't officially start his pay. He was officially dead by my action on Voltar. But he had me on the spot. "All right," I said. Later I could delay it but right now this was an emergency.

"Next," he said, "is letting me take some time off from altering the identity of criminals and permit me to begin a campaign to cure prevalent diseases in Turkey and that you will finance it."

Who cared about this riffraff? And I could welsh on this. "All right," I said.

"The third part of the bargain I made," he continued, "concerned all these wives you violated. Many of them got pregnant, you know. The penalty is being stoned to death."

I flinched. I looked out the car window fearfully. Yes, some of those women were in the crowd! They had stones in their hands!

"I studied the Qur'an," said Prahd. "All their law comes from it, you know. And there's a thing called *kaffarah*. Instead of suffering the legal punishment, one can escape it by private atonement. So I arranged that you would create a fund to feed the poor of each one of their villages for the next century. That will make the resulting children sort of holy and cared for."

The next century! Gods! Well, I could get out of that some way. Demand that it was only for the one-eyed poor or something. "All right," I said. "But what about Nurse Bildirjin and her father?"

"Oh, that was the easiest one of all," said Prahd. "All you have to do is marry her."

I knew I was going to faint again. But this was no time for fainting. I could recall too vividly her bony knees when he'd operated on my head! Madly I scrambled through my wits to find some way to overcome this threatened catastrophe. I had it!

"What if I was already married?" I cried.

"Well, I've been studying the Qur'an. The faithful are allowed four wives. And the same number of concubines." He smiled brightly. "So it doesn't matter what else you've been up to."

The whole world seemed to tilt before my eyes and then came straight. It hit me like a thunderbolt. Adora Pinch Bey and Candy Licorice Bey couldn't get a Moslem for bigamy. I was safe from them! Oh, my, would I be careful to say my daily prayers.

Still, life would be Hells around that vixen Bildirjin. But I nodded.

I reached for the door handle. Then I saw the tattered state I was in. A pair of grimy jogging shorts, a sea-wrinkled suit jacket, bare and bleeding feet. I grasped at a reprieve. "I'll have to go home and get dressed first."

"No, no," said Prahd. "A Moslem marriage is not all that formal. It's even unusual to do them in a mosque but Nurse Bildirjin wanted it extra legal. Your clothes don't matter. Everything is waiting."

He opened the door and pushed me out. The silent crowd glowered at me. They were waiting for a signal from Prahd. He told them it was all agreed to. I heard some stones being dropped and people frowned. Nurse Bildirjin's father uncocked his gun.

I limped into the mosque on bloody feet, a martyr to my duty as an Apparatus officer.

Chapter 5

A Moslem marriage is pretty businesslike. They don't consider women have any souls so the religious angle is almost absent.

Nurse Bildirjin was dressed in a white silk cloak and hood. The costume helped to hide her swollen belly but it was pretty obvious nonetheless. Her black eyes were looking at me with complete indifference.

A Turkish religious master was present, a *khoja*. He was just there to see that nobody messed up his mosque.

Nurse Bildirjin's father had two copies of a contract. This was an exchange of a promise to be faithful and all that.

Somebody was pushing a pen into my hand. I lifted it to sign. Then I saw the sum on it! The *mahri*, or dowry to the wife, was specified.

"A HUNDRED MILLION *LIRA!*" I screamed. That was a million U.S. bucks!

"Of course you'll want your child to have the best of care," said Prahd. "And a nice villa for Nurse Bildirjin to vacation in. You're founding a family, remember."

"As a matter of fact," said Nurse Bildirjin's father, shifting his shotgun to the other arm, "I have the bank orders right here. You have to pay the dowry at the ceremony, you know."

I hesitated.

The crowd ran out to get the rocks they had dropped.

I signed the contract and the orders on the Piastre National Bank of Istanbul. Gods, what would Mudur Zengin think and do now?

I was aware of Ters and Ahmed at my side. They were signing the marriage contract as witnesses!

"Now, that was easy, wasn't it?" said Prahd. "That's all there is to it."

He might think it was nothing. I felt like I had just been wrapped around and around with heavy chains.

"Now put your bride in your car," said Prahd.

I didn't want to touch her. I was afraid she would bite. I walked out of the mosque. As I glanced back, I saw that she was following me. The *khoja* was shooing the crowd out. They came to gather around the car again.

My feet were killing me. I felt a fever burning through me. But I carried on. I got into the car.

Madison was sitting there writing in a notebook. Big as she was with child, there wouldn't be room for Nurse Bildirjin if the bunk remained raised. I clicked the latches to lower it.

Half the rear seat cushion was out of position. I took hold of it to adjust it.

My fingers touched something.

Fevered as I was, I went cold as ice.

Under that cushion, exactly where I had put it months ago, was THE BOMB!

I lifted the cushion.

There it lay.

The latch which should have clicked over at the end of the time limit had not moved to connect and fire it!

Something had blocked it from thrusting home. It must be being held suspended by a piece of dirt or lint!

I had been bouncing over rotten roads all night sitting on a defective bomb that could go off any minute!

A thin scream surged into my throat.

I picked it up.

I could not toss it out the window. It had enough explosive to blow this car to bits.

I slowly backed out of the car holding it, not knowing if the last thing I would see in this universe would be its lethal flash.

"A BOMB!" cried Prahd. "Run for your lives! He's going to blow us all up!"

There was the wind of sudden passage as the crowd fled. The thunder of feet died away.

I kept backing. Oh, Gods, I better not stumble. The time delay was all run out. There was just that little lever left to fall in place. It could not be reversed.

I did not know what to do with it. The standard action would be to throw it into a bunker and run.

I didn't have a bunker.

Yes, I did!

The mosque door was open. Its walls were thick.

I backed toward the door.

Carefully I turned.

I measured the width of the door.

I threw with all my might!

The bomb flew into the door.

I turned to sprint away.

My lacerated feet betrayed me. I only ran ten paces before I fell.

WHOOOM!

The walls of the mosque flew outward like a suddenly inflated balloon!

The minaret toppled sideways and fell.

Rubble started to patter down as clouds of smoke rose into the sky.

I had been skidded by concussion another twenty feet.

Finally, a voice. Prahd's. He was picking me up. "I don't know why you have to do these things," he said. "It's good nobody was in there. They could have been killed. I thought when I gave you new equipment you would get too interested in other things to have time to blow things up. But I see I was wrong."

People were coming back, staring at the ruin and glaring at me. Then I noticed something very odd. The *khoja* was smiling broadly. It alarmed me.

"What's he so happy about?" I said. "I just blew up his mosque!"

Prahd was getting me over to the car which Ahmed seemed to have moved some distance away before the blast. "You see," said Prahd, "they know you here. When I arranged this and said who the husband would be, he wouldn't let you enter the holy place. He said the roof would fall in. But I persuaded him that if it did, you would build him a new mosque. And sure enough, the roof fell in. He's happy because he has been wanting to build a much more ornate one for years."

The world was spinning. What did a mosque cost? I got into the car. Nurse Bildirjin pulled her white silk cape sideways away from me. I wondered why. I looked down. My feet!

"I'm bleeding," I told Prahd. "You'll have to take me to the hospital."

"That's right where we're going," said Prahd.

We drove off and came at length to the World United Charities Mercy and Benevolent Hospital. It was amazingly groomed up: it was all landscaped and even now volunteer peasants were at work cutting the grass of *their* establishment. They saw who it was and stopped work to stare at me as I got out and limped up the steps. They were completely silent. What ingrates! If it hadn't been for my brilliant idea to alter the identities of criminals these peasants would have no hospital at all! Riff-raff!

I went through the lobby, thinking I was going to an operating room. But Prahd was simply taking me to his office.

I sank down in a chair. "I'm in terribly bad shape," I said. "This horizontal scar on my forehead needs attention, too."

He looked at it. Then he got out a bottle of antiseptic and swabbed my feet. It really stung! He picked up some rolls of Earth-type bandage, sprinkled some reddish powder on them and wound them around my lacerations. He evidently was not going to do anything extensive. When he had finished that he stood back.

"Hey," I said, "what about this forehead scar?"

"It makes you look like you have a ferocious scowl," he said.

"I know," I said.

"Well, people need some kind of warning. I think we'll just leave it that way."

I was about to protest. He could get rid of it without

half trying. The door opened. Nurse Bildirjin walked in. I blinked.

She was dressed in her usual hospital uniform, let out a bit to accommodate the swollen belly.

"You just married me," I said. "Aren't you going home with me?"

"And break up the beautiful relationship I have with Doktor Muhammed?" she said. "Don't be silly. We were just making sure the baby had a legal father."

"And a million bucks," I grated.

"Of course," she said, smiling sweetly.

It was really from that moment that I began to suspect that I was being had by the young Doctor Prahd Bittlestiffender.

"I am going home," I said.

Little did I know that my travail had barely begun!

Chapter 6

The villa was sitting there against the mountain in the spring sun. It was a sort of shock to see it so peaceful and serene. But then, in its history it had witnessed three thousand years of the agonies of men. From Phrygia, through Rome and up to now, more than one pair of bloody feet had walked through its gate.

Madison and I got out. I looked around. I saw that Utanc had a new car: an awesome red Ferrari, a vehicle that represented an awful lot of bucks, at least a hundred thousand.

The staff was peering timidly from around corners, very nervous.

Musef waddled forward. Gods, he was fat on all this good food—he must be three hundred and fifty pounds! Torgut was right beside him, swinging a hefty club. They were both grinning like a couple of apes.

"Welcome home!" they both cried.

At least my bodyguards were glad to see me. They might not be in wrestling shape but they could certainly make the staff step. Torgut had only to point his club and three staff dived to grab Madison's bag.

Well! This was more like it!

I limped across the yard into the patio. The fountain was plinking away.

Utanc's door was open.

Her eye was applied to the crack.

The two little boys had evidently been caught in the open. They rushed feverishly to her door. She let them in and then closed it.

"You want anything, you just yell," said Musef. "It won't take us any time at all to beat it out of these people. We got lots of practice."

"Who's he?" said Torgut, pointing at Madison with his club.

"This fellow won't be with us long," I said. "But he's not to know it. I'm disposing of him later. Don't let him wander around or get into things and don't let him reach a phone."

"We hear and obey," said Musef, grinning.

"What are they talking about?" said Madison. "I don't speak this lingo."

"They're telling me that the Mafia has been prowling around," I said in English. "There's lots of them in this valley. You can hear them howling at night."

"They didn't seem very serious about it," said Madison.

"Oh, that's because they enjoy killing them. These two men are my bodyguards. They're the champion wrestlers of this province. I told them to look after your safety and not let you go wandering about getting yourself shot." I pointed to a guest room. "So why don't you just go in there and have a bath and get some sleep. The staff will see that you get fed. And don't be alarmed if we keep the door locked. We don't want the Mafia to get you."

"Got it," said Madison. He went into the room. Two staff carried his grip in. I winked at Musef and he locked the door.

Well, things were going much better. Maybe I could work this out after all. At least I wasn't going to be stoned to death and I could probably even wriggle out of paying the *kaffarah* to the violated wives.

I went into my room. I handed the American International machine gun to Musef and told him to clean it and its magazines before it rusted to pieces. I got out of my clothes and gave them to Karagoz and told him to go out and burn them.

I shaved with a proper spin razor.

I got into a shower and scrubbed the goat stink off.

The careless bandages Prahd had thrown on my feet got wet so I took them off. I scrubbed the lacerations with soap. I wondered if I would get lockjaw from the goat droppings. Well, I had my own medical kit now. When I had dried myself I worked proper Voltar antiseptic into the wounds—ouch, but it stung! I covered the open ones with false skin.

I dressed in black pants and a poinsettia-pattern sport shirt. But I couldn't stand the tightness of boots and got into some curl-toed slippers that were loose.

The waiter served me some ice-cold *sira* and the fermented grape juice was the first thing that had scaled my throat in weeks. It was followed with some *iskembe corbasi*, a soup of tripe and eggs. I began to feel better.

But just as I was beginning to believe that things would work out all right, the axe fell.

Karagoz came into the dining room. "There's a very polite fellow at the gate. He says he wants a word with you that will make you very happy."

In that mood of feeling things would now work out, I said carelessly, "All right. I'll go out and see him." I didn't even pick up a gun!

I limped in my curl-toed slippers out to the twin pillars. I didn't see anyone. I stepped further toward the road, looking up and down. Nobody.

I turned around to go back in the gate.

He was standing beside the left-hand pillar.

THE BLACK–JOWLED MAN!

Unarmed, in the open and helpless, I stared. Then I said, "How did you know I was here?"

He moved forward, blocking my escape back through the gate. "Oh, we've been in communication with your friends. About dawn yesterday, I got a radio from Doktor Muhammed Ataturk that you'd be here today for sure. That's why we thought it wiser not to look for you in all that underbrush. Besides, you had a machine gun then. I see you don't now."

Prahd! He'd been helping these people to round me up!

"I know who you are," I said. "You're acting for Mudur Zengin of the Piastre National Bank of Istanbul!"

"No, no," he said. "Mudur Zengin is a friend of

yours, though I can't understand why. When your concubine bought the yacht in New York, he helped execute the purchase with a mortgage by his bank. And he's been advancing money for its bills to Squeeza credit. Of course, we've seized the yacht now that it is in Istanbul and Mudur Zengin is quite cross."

"Then who the Hells ARE you?" I demanded.

"Perhaps I better introduce myself," he said, taking out a card from his wallet.

I looked at it.

FORREST CLOSURE
International Mortgage Division
GRABBE–MANHATTAN BANK

"Hold it," I said. "I don't owe you anything. I don't have a mortgage with you on anything. You have gone crazy."

"Oh, I am afraid you do," he said.

I decided to let him have it. "Grabbe-Manhattan Bank is owned by Rockecenter! I don't think you know who you're talking to!" I assumed a very haughty mien. "I am a Rockecenter family spi!"

He smiled. "Change it to you *were*. The City of Miami suddenly stopped ordering fuel oil. Octopus instantly investigated and found that they were getting an unlimited supply of electricity from Ochokeechokee, Florida. They showed some photographs around and identified Wister as the engineer. Mr. Rockecenter couldn't believe it! You can't have inexpensive energy flying around wrecking things! He sent Mr. Bury to find why the cheap fuel man had not been stopped and Bury found that you had kidnapped Madison, closed his office and gone on a happy yachting cruise. Mr. Bury

even confirmed it by travelling himself personally to
Elba to see with his own eyes. And there you and Madison were, thousands of miles off the job. Obviously you
had both been bought: a yacht like that costs a fortune.
So, no, Mr. Inkswitch/Sultan Bey, you are no longer a
Rockecenter family spy. You've been fired with malice
aforethought and I'm afraid you have no protection
there. Quite the contrary. You could be charged with taking bribes if you ever set foot in America again."

I was reeling under these blows. The secret sign tat-
tooed on my chest was worthless. But I rallied: "That
doesn't explain this silly nonsense about a mortgage!"

"Well, oddly enough," said Closure, "when this
mortgage thing occurred, we did not know Sultan Bey
and Inkswitch were the same person. All that we were
led to believe was that one Sultan Bey owned a villa, the
total land of a mountain and thousands of acres of prime,
arable, poppy soil. And when you had us approached to
mortgage it for a mere two million dollars, we, of course,
leaped at the chance. So we rushed it right through and
granted you the mortgage."

"Hold it!" I said. "I didn't take out any mortgage
like that."

"Oh, I am afraid you did," said Closure. And he dis-
played the papers.

I gripped them. My Gods, the land involved com-
prised not only the thousands of acres of prime opium
land Voltar held but THE ENTIRE EARTH BASE!

And right there at the bottom was my SIGNATURE.

Oh, Gods, I could be vaporized for this!

Black Jowl was still talking. "You see there is an
embarrassing point in all this. For you. The amount was
so trifling and the security so huge that we trusted you

and never gave it a second thought. And then we found out that you didn't own it!"

Of course I didn't own it. It belonged to the government of Voltar!

"Now really," said Closure, "we are being very nice to you. If we had exposed this crime we could have had you and your yacht rounded up wherever you were because you were still under the Turkish flag even if you were at sea. The state would throw you in prison and I need not call to your attention that a Turkish prison means death."

Oh, how well I understood that!

"And we are really a very humane institution and we didn't want you to have to suffer that."

I blinked. This was the first time I had ever heard of Grabbe-Manhattan being humane! I became wary.

"So we contented ourselves with simply hounding you homeward. The young woman was cooperative, within the limits of her own greed."

"Wait a minute," I said. "That yacht was worth more than two million! If you seized it, that cancels the debt."

"Oh, I'm afraid not. It was mortgaged and you had very little equity in it. And this land mortgage is overdue. You made no payments on this mortgage. You are overlooking something. If we got the Turkish government to cooperate in this, they could prefer charges. They would have no choice but send you to prison for mortgaging a property you did not own. But don't be so disturbed. We have a perfect out for you. Now that you are here and in reach of funds and friends, you can get out of this entirely."

"How?" I said in desperation.

"Why, all you have to do is buy these lands and villa

and mountain out of your own money and turn them over to us and we will stamp this document paid and you will be in the clear."

So that was why they had hounded me home. They had not dared kick up a fuss or they would lose these properties. But my position was completely impossible. I could not tell these bloodsuckers that the property in question belonged to the Voltar Confederacy. It would be a Code break beyond all Code breaks. There was no possible way to acquire it for them even if I would. The doors of the Turkish prisons yawned.

But he was dealing with an officer of the Apparatus. He was threatening the Code break of all time! If they ever found out what was underneath that mountain... Yikes! Voltar would execute me. Even a temporary solution was better than none!

I looked up at the secret spot on the gate where I had installed the alarm bell that would alert the staff.

In a steady voice I said, "I know when I am beaten. Come in and I will make the final arrangements."

Under cover of steadying myself, I pushed the bell.

Black Jowl, all smiles now, walked forward through the gate.

I led him across the yard toward the patio.

Cat-footed, Musef and Torgut came behind him.

A flurry.

THONK! went Torgut's lead pipe.

Black Jowl crumpled without a sound.

I whispered to Musef, "There is an old Phrygian tomb under my bedroom floor. Dump him in my sleeping quarters, tie him up and leave him. I will do the rest."

They carried him in there and lashed him up. They left.

How incautious I had been to go around unarmed!

I put a Beretta and a gas bomb in my pockets. Then I approached him.

I went through his pockets. I found his office phone.

I carried him through the closet into my secret room.

I opened the tunnel door and dragged him by the heels down the passage to the hangar.

A security officer came up. "Throw him in a detention cell," I said. "And do not let him speak to anyone."

He made a motion to two guards. They bore Black Jowl off. I heard the cell door clang.

I went back up the tunnel, through my secret room and out into the yard.

I gave the card to Musef. "Call this number," I said. "Tell them that you have a message from Mr. Forrest Closure. Say that things are proceeding very well but that it may take another week or two to finish things off."

He touched his shoulders and nose in a sign of obedience. He went away. He came back shortly. "They accepted that," he said.

I had bought time. I did not know exactly what I was going to do. I had a week or so to handle this. I must think of something.

I was halfway down the chute to the very worst of Hells, but actually, at that moment, didn't know it.

Chapter 7

The beauties of spring were on the villa garden: appearances are so deceptive. The shrubs and flower beds were all in bloom, the songs of birds filled the air, the fountains plashed in a peaceful undertone.

The raucous snarl of a jeep blasted through the calm. Faht Bey, the base commander, came roaring through the gate. He sprang out, his overpoundage quivering with rage down to the last ounce. He saw me.

"Bombed mosques!" he roared. "A stranger dragged into detention! WHAT NEXT?"

He came to stand before me. He raised his hands in supplication to the sky. "Oh, Gods, we were doing so great without him!"

It was irritating. He hadn't said "Hello" or "Did you have a nice trip?" I was not his senior, exactly, but I was his Section Chief and Inspector-General Overlord for Voltar's Earth base here at Afyon. I decided to put him in his place. I used the name the police knew him by on the planet Flisten. "As you were, Timyjo Faht. You forget to whom you are speaking! Have a care!"

"Listen," he said, "the space freighter *Blixo* is arriving tomorrow night. Is there any chance of your going home on it?"

He had opened a new vista of horror. Suppose I returned to Voltar and they then discovered the Earth base had been foreclosed on over my signature? Faht Bey obviously didn't know about it yet but unless I handled it, he would soon enough. And then he'd have every possible weapon he needed to bring an abrupt end to my career. I decided to be polite. "I am sorry for the commotion. It was all in the line of duty."

He glared at me. "Your idea of duty can get too (bleeped) confused with your personal appetites! I would give a year's pay to get something on you that would end your career forever, Officer Gris. And the next insane idea you get that threatens this operation is going to be reported to Lombar Hisst in the most painful detail. There isn't a single person in this area that would befriend you. And I have had too much more than enough!"

He stomped away to his jeep and drove off.

If he only knew it, he already had adequate grounds to put me under arrest. His crack about my having no friends left bit deep.

Mournfully, I wandered back in to the patio. I was getting depressed.

Utanc's door opened. There was a rush of slippered feet. As I started to walk around the fountain to my room, my way was barred.

Utanc was on her knees before me.

She raised her beautiful black eyes to me. "Master, I have sinned. I was by the gate and could not help but overhear what that man said. When I signed your name to that paper, I had no idea what I was doing."

"You forged that mortgage?" I roared.

She nodded. "When you cut off all my credit cards, I did not know which way to turn. I had some small expenses I could not meet. And when I asked their advice at the Grabbe-Manhattan branch in Istanbul, they told me I should ask you to sign a mortgage paper. I was far too frightened of you to ask you to do so and I signed your name to it. I did not understand it would bring disaster upon you."

Suddenly I realized that Grabbe-Manhattan had taken advantage of this shy desert girl from the Kara Kum in Russia.

From her side she drew a curved knife. Reaching up, she extended the hilt. "Kill me."

I looked at her, stunned. The idea of those beautiful

black eyes going dead made my own blood run cold. I cried, "NO!" and thrust the knife aside.

She dropped it to the patio pavement. She seized my hand in both of her own. "O master, do you forgive your slave?"

I looked down at her. Suddenly all the love I had ever felt for her surged up in me. I thought of her dances, the joy I had taken in her. "Yes," I said.

"O master, I do not deserve it. I have been thoughtless and wanton. I value your love. I will, I vow, mend my ways and try to be worthy of you."

Gently, I lifted her to her feet.

I heard a car door slam, but at that tender moment I only had attention for the beautiful Utanc.

There was someone at the patio door. A voice, "Who is this?"

I turned.

TEENIE!

Behind her, in the yard, staff was unloading a small truck full of baggage.

In the door she stood holding two grips. Her oversized eyes were round with surprise and her too-big mouth agape.

She dropped a grip.

She pointed at Utanc. "WHO is *this?*" she repeated.

I stood very tall. "*This,*" I said, "is the woman I love. The only true love I have ever had. The only woman I will ever love."

Teenie's eyes got rounder. She looked from Utanc to me. "You mean ... you mean you don't love me even a little bit?"

I looked at her, this scrawny traitor with her silly ponytail. With all the contempt I could muster, I spat upon the floor!

Teenie seemed to deflate. She dropped the other grip. She groped forward and clutched the fountain rim for support. She sank down on it. Unaccountably, she began to cry.

I glared at her. Her tears were plashing into the fountain pool. Brokenly, she said, "I guess I made a mistake."

I really snarled at her. "You're (bleeped) right you made a mistake, you little (bleepch)! You sold me out!"

She looked at me bewildered. Then she shook her head. "Oh, you poor, dumb jerk. You're the one that blew it. You skipped out just when I had it all handled."

"You were delivering me into their hands!" I raged. "I heard you with my own ears."

"Oh, you dumb (bleepard)," said Teenie. "The trouble with you is nobody dares tell you anything. If they did you'd find some way to mess it up!

"When Grabbe-Manhattan approached me in Bermuda, they told me they also owned the Squeeza credit card company and even though the Piastre National Bank was paying the bills, Grabbe-Manhattan could end our credit in ports at any time and leave us high and dry unless I brought you home to Turkey.

"So I took all the time we could while I tried to sell the yacht. The Crown Prince of Saudi-Yemen had seen it in Atlantic City and when I found him on the radio, he agreed to buy it. We were delivering it to him in Alexandria. The price was five times what you paid for it. It would have cleared off all your debts with Mudur Zengin.

"Captain Bitts thinks you're insane. He tried to tell you about the deal and he also tried to tell you we were just outside Turkish waters and the storm would take you, not to Greek Chios, but straight in toward Izmir.

And you knocked him out! He's got a terrible cut on his head.

"When he realized he didn't have an owner aboard to sign the papers, he radioed Mudur Zengin. And Zengin didn't know about the Grabbe-Manhattan mortgage and he thought we'd be seized as pirates if you were not aboard so he told us to come into Istanbul.

"Grabbe-Manhattan put a lien on the ship, grabbed it, sold it themselves to the Crown Prince and pocketed the profit.

"You dumb jerk! You blew it!"

I knew how she lied. I snarled, "You're the one that blew it! You didn't have to come near Turkey!"

"Oh, Jesus!" she said. "You don't understand anything! The sale of the yacht would only have cleared off your debts to Mudur Zengin. We wouldn't have had a dime to operate. When we landed in Alexandria, we would have to have capital to buy a whorehouse and get a new start in life.

"That dumb fishboat Closure had could only make half the speed of the yacht. As soon as I got back with the dough, we would have told Grabbe-Manhattan to go to hell and split at twenty knots!"

"You expect me to believe that!" I snarled, getting madder by the second.

"You better believe it," she said. "We're two of a kind, you dumb jerk. Both of us are rotten to the core. We're so screwed up with psychology and crime we got no idea which end is up. But at least we can stick together! There ain't any hope otherwise. And you blew!

"I had a hell of a time getting the dough out of them. And I didn't blow. I came back here for you!"

Utanc spoke unexpectedly. "You can't have him! He's mine!"

Teenie suddenly looked at her. Then her lip raised with scorn and she looked at me. "Where the hell did you find that thing, Inky? Some garbage can?"

Utanc drew herself up. She let out a whoof of disgust. She went to her room, went in and slammed the door.

I glared at Teenie, my rage mounting. "Now look what you have done, you (bleepch). Why don't you get the Hells out of my life? I would kill you slow, slow, slow if I could. I've hated you from the first moment I ever laid eyes on you! I should have slaughtered you ages ago. And now you've wrecked my life and sold me for a lousy ten thousand bucks. I hate you!"

She went white. She reached into her purse and pulled out a wad of bills. "It was for you! Take it, you (bleep)!" And she threw them at me with all her might.

It was too much. I hauled off and slapped her with all *my* might.

Her feet went off the floor. She hurtled sideways, slammed against the wall and went down. She lay there for a moment, then she raised her head. Blood was running from the side of her mouth. Pure hatred burned in her eyes.

"You'll be sorry for that, you (bleepard)," she said. "I'm going to leave here and get back to New York and then you'll wish to God you had never been born!"

Fear hit me. She could make that rape of a minor charge stick. Extradition would follow.

I had to get rid of her. I didn't dare kill her. If I failed to produce her in a reasonable time I could also be hit for murder because of that injunction.

Inspiration! There was a way I could put her on ice and yet return her if they tried to say I had killed her. She did not speak the language and could do me no harm.

I WOULD SEND TEENIE TO VOLTAR!

The *Blixo* was coming in. Madison was going.

I glanced around. There were no witnesses.

"If you want to cry on somebody's shoulder," I said, "Madison is in there." And I pointed to my own bedroom.

She glanced in that direction. Then she got to her feet unsteadily and went through the door.

I was right behind her. With my heel I kicked the door shut. At the same moment, I pulled the gas bomb out of my pocket.

She didn't see Madison. She turned.

I pushed the gas bomb into her face.

She crumpled.

Working rapidly, using heavy cord, I tied her feet and hands together.

I went out into the patio. The truck was gone but they had piled her baggage by the door. Working quickly, I dragged it into my room and out of sight. There was quite a bit of it.

Two big black suitcases looked like the ones that had been in my closet on the ship. I opened them. My clothes and guns and viewers! She had packed up and brought my things. I left them there.

I picked her up and took her through my secret room and down the tunnel. I dropped her and made four more trips to get all of her baggage and so leave no evidence.

I called the security captain.

"Put this girl in a detention cell with her baggage. Hold her with no communication. She is a passenger for the *Blixo*."

They hauled her away and, down the corridor, the cell door clanged shut.

I went back to the patio.

The money was still lying on the pavement. I gathered it up and put it in my wallet.

Having no crystal ball or ways to read the horrible future to hand, I thought, with satisfaction, that that was the end of Teenie.

PART SIXTY

Chapter 1

I paced in the yard of the villa in Afyon, Turkey, for hours, trying to take stock of my situation.

Actually, it was pretty desperate. In a week or two Grabbe-Manhattan Bank was going to wake up to the fact that its Chief of International Mortgage Division, Forrest Closure, alias Black Jowl, was not being heard from.

As I had been fired as a Rockecenter family spy I could expect no help from that quarter. They even wanted to charge me with taking bribes!

The mortgage papers he had had on him were not the originals. Those were still on file at the bank. They could still tell the Turkish government to charge me with mortgaging land I didn't own.

Rockecenter had seen a chance to acquire enormous tracts of prime opium land that the base usually leased out to Turkish tenants. He had no inkling that in this usual bank tactic he had also gotten his hands on the Voltar base.

If Faht Bey found this out, he could have me seized and shipped home for execution as the author of the Code break of all time.

Lombar would never forgive me for messing up Rockecenter, for it would cut off the I. G. Barben Pharmaceutical drug supplies that were vital to undermining Voltar.

Oh, Gods, how was I going to get out of this?

My professors at the Apparatus school always used to say, "Take care of the details and the big problems will take care of themselves." It was good advice.

I would take care of details.

It was, I suddenly realized, dusk. A chill wind had begun to blow.

Musef approached. "Master, that man you put in the guest room has been asking if it's safe for him to walk around. I think he's getting suspicious that you mean to rub him out."

Ah, that was one detail I could take care of.

I went to my room and located a small bottle. I called on an intercom to the kitchen and had them bring me a large pitcher of *sira* on a tray with two glasses. Into one glass I put a heavy dose from the bottle. It was liquid chloral hydrate, the time-honored knockout drops bartenders use. I filled the glasses.

I went to Madison's door and unlocked it and, bearing the tray, went in.

He was standing at the barred window which looked out on the room's private garden. "Oh, hello, Smith," he said. "What's the chances of getting out of here and walking around? I feel pretty depressed and some exercise will do me good."

"Well, well," I said heartily. "I was thinking the same thing. All that riding isn't good for one. Tell you what. I've ordered us some dinner and afterwards I'll take you out of here and you'll see some country that will knock your eyes out. So just sit down while they get it ready and have an appetizer."

I gave him the glass of *sira*. He sat down in a comfortable chair and took a sip of it. "What is this stuff? It tastes kind of bitter."

"Fermented grape juice," I said. "The ancestor of real wine. Not even intoxicating. So drink up. Down the hatch." I set him an example and drained my glass.

He swallowed half of his. "You know, Smith or Gris or whatever your name is, I've been thinking. I maybe didn't do all I could have done. I really hate to let Mr. Bury down. He's a fine man, Mr. Bury, and I owe him an awful lot. I've got strong employer loyalty, you know. I never give up on a job until I'm actually fired. And you know, he didn't fire me. He didn't tell you I was fired, did he?"

"I had to get you out to save your life," I reminded him severely.

"Well, yes," said Madison, drinking the rest of the sira. "But I'm not at all sure I did all I could have done for that client, Wister. For instance, I had one grand idea I never got around to carrying out. I was going to get him to rob the U.S. Treasury in Washington and pull the whole FBI in pursuit. A blow-by-blow escape. But I didn't have the time. Then there was the idea where he stole Alaska and sold it back to the Russ——"

His head slumped. His glass fell from nerveless fingers.

I moved like a cat. I packed all his clothes and things into his grip.

I threw him over my shoulder and grabbed the suitcase with my free hand.

I sped to my secret room and down the tunnel. I called the guard captain.

"Another one for transshipment," I said.

"You been busy," said the guard captain.

I ignored the compliment. "Hold him in a detention cell. Ship him and that girl to Voltar on the Blixo." I dropped Madison. I raced back to my room.

I got out some despatch paper. I wrote:

> *Lombar Hisst*
> *Chief Executive of the Apparatus*
>
>   *I am sending you an extremely valuable*
> *man as a personal present. His name is*
> *J. Walter Madison. You will be utterly*
> *amazed what he can do.*
>
>   *Soltan Gris*
>   *Section Chief 451*

I marked it URGENT and IMPORTANT and put it with outgoing despatches.

Little did I know that when I sealed that envelope, I also sealed my own doom.

Foolishly, I thought, that is the last I'll see of J. Walter Madison.

Chapter 2

Details. I was taking care of details all right. But by the following afternoon I had made no real progress on the real problem I faced.

The night before I had conned Musef and Torgut into believing the three people that had entered were now buried somewhere in the countryside. Late at night I had had them back up the old Ford Station Wagon to the patio door and I had carried out, with many a grunt and groan of effort, three big sacks I had blown full of air. I had put them in the back and driven off. Then an hour later I had returned with the sacks deflated and told them, "I've dumped those corpses where nobody will ever find them. So you just forget you ever saw those people."

They grinned delightedly. "We hear and obey, Master. You sure are a smart chief."

But sitting here the following afternoon, I did not feel very smart. How in the name of all the Gods was I ever going to get out of this mess?

I glanced at my watch. It would be early morning in New York. Possibly Heller and the Countess Krak were up to something I could exploit by wrecking it.

I got out the viewers Teenie had brought back and was rather surprised that old splotches of dried *sira* and such had been cleaned off of them.

Their batteries were fine.

I looked at Crobe's. He was simply sitting in a detention cell right here, waiting shipment out on the *Blixo*.

Heller's was blank. He was still asleep.

Only the Countess Krak's was live and interesting. She was pouring together Bavarian Mocha powder and hot water. Then she got some chilled tomato juice and put some Worcestershire sauce and Tabasco in it.

She put it all on a tray and went to a bedroom. She set it down and opened the shutters. A flood of dawn light struck through horizontally, almost flaring my viewer out.

She turned and approached the huge pillared Etruscan bed. "Wake up, lazybones," she said. "You told me to be dressed for hiking today and be up before dawn and here you are still snoring."

"Ouch," said Heller, putting an arm across his eyes. "Can't you even let me recover from a hangover?"

"Your graduation party is over. The guests all went home. You're a working man, remember?"

He took the tomato juice and sipped it.

"I told you you shouldn't let Bang-Bang talk you into trying Scotch."

"The cat drinks it," said Heller.

"Well, Mister Calico is a very industrious cat. And speaking of industry, when are we going to get busy and get off this planet and go home?"

"I've got a right to take it easy. After all, that whole year in college about wore me out!"

"Oh, nonsense. You never even went to class. And now that you have this precious degree of Bachelor of Nuclear Science and Engineering, what are you going to do with it? They'd laugh at it at home. I never saw so many errors as their science has. Can't exceed the speed of light indeed! They ought to ride in a real spaceship."

"My, you seem bitey this morning."

"Well, you would be, too. I leave you at twelve midnight singing 'Auld Lang Syne' with fifteen students you never met before that party. You told me to be up at dawn in hiking clothes without fail and then, to my recollection, you never even came to bed!"

"Did I say that?" said Heller.

"You certainly did. And you made a big point of it. 'Without fail,' you said."

"I must have been drunk," said Heller.

"Those girls were drunk enough," said the Countess.

"Oh, is that what this is all about," he said, drinking his coffee.

"No, that's not what this is all about. I'm not jealous anymore except sometimes. I'm just peeved that you wasted so much time getting a degree you don't need. The best-looking and most competent combat engineer of the Voltar Fleet getting a diploma as a *Bachelor* of Nuclear Science and Engineering is just plain ridiculous. Being a bachelor is what I'm trying to get you home and cure you of."

"I need the degree so I can sign articles on fuel for professional magazines. They won't listen to you unless you have a degree."

"So when are you ever going to get time to write any articles swinging by your heels from a chandelier and leading the band?"

"I don't need any more time now," said Heller. "I finished them."

"When?" she challenged.

"Last night after the party." He was pointing.

She looked at a table that was set up. It was piled high with half a dozen manuscripts.

"Oh!" she said in a very cross way.

She walked out of the room.

Heller took a shower and got dressed in hiking clothes. He packed a little bag, putting in some keys, papers and a book. He went out on the terrace and found her.

"Don't be cross," he said.

"You tricked me into getting cross with you. You led me on."

"It was just a joke," said Heller. "I'm sorry."

"Getting off this planet is NO joke," said the Countess Krak. "It is psychotic. It scares me half to death."

"It's also a pretty planet," said Heller. "Now come along like a good girl. I have something you will find fascinating."

He went to the elevator. She picked up the cat and followed him.

They got into the Porsche.

He sped up the ramp. He began nudging the Porsche crosstown.

Krak was sitting there a bit gloomily. She said, "I'm sorry I was cross with you, Jettero. But you did lead me on. I'm just so anxious to get home. I have such wonderful news waiting for us."

There she was, pushing, pushing, pushing. The one thing she mustn't do. If they succeeded, they would get me executed for sure.

Heller was steering through the early morning streets. He reached sideways into his bag and handed her a book.

"It was my fault," he said. "Jokes don't go too well with breakfast hot jolt. But cheer up. That book will interest you. It's about Prince Caucalsia."

She looked at the book. It said *The Devil's Triangle* on the cover. She looked through the index. "Is this another joke? I don't see his name here."

"Well, no," said Heller. "Their history doesn't really go back twelve thousand years. But if you will open the map in the front you will find some islands off the Florida coast called the Bahamas. They have electronic and radio phenomena there. Also electromagnetic disturbances. And their fathometers record a pyramid on the sea floor."

"Is that odd?" said the Countess Krak.

He shot the car onto the Bruckner Expressway. "Not terribly. But there's another thing reported by ships and planes: time lapses and distortions. Ships vanish. Planes fly into other time or lose time on their instruments. The only thing I know of that would do that is a very small black hole. Voltar sometimes stores them in pyramids."

"Yes?" said the Countess Krak, getting interested.

"So I think that's where the continent sank. I think Prince Caucalsia's energy plants went down with it and they're still running under the sea."

"And they would cause all that?"

"Only thing I know of that would," said Heller. "Time distortions from captive black holes."

"Isn't that where you sent that Coast Guard ship?"

Heller laughed. "Actually, it went much further east. And they got home all right. The only danger they ran was being sent to a psychiatrist and I wouldn't wish that off on anybody."

"So you think this is where Prince Caucalsia established his colony," said Krak.

"Best guess so far," said Heller. "I'd write an article about it except that it would be the Code break of the century!" He glanced at her. She was looking through the windshield gloomily.

Heller began to sing the nursery song:

> If ever from life you need fly,
> Or a king has said loved ones must die,
> Take a trip
> In a ship
> That will bob, dive and dip,
> And find a new home in the sky.

Krak joined in:

> Bold Prince Caucalsia,
> There you are on high.
> We see you wink,

> *And we see you blink,*
> *Far, far, far above the Mo-o-o-o-o-n!*

They both laughed.

"Now I've got my girl cheerful again," said Heller.

"I'm just an old nagging grouch," she said, putting her head on his shoulder. "I don't know what a handsome guy like you is doing with such an awful scold as me."

"You're not a scold," said Heller.

"Yes, I am," said the Countess.

"Let's fight about that," said Heller.

They both laughed but for the life of me I couldn't see the joke.

She looked out the window. "Where are we going, anyway?"

"I'm taking you to a den of vice," said Heller. "And don't worry. It has everything to do with our getting off this planet. It's an old abandoned roadhouse in Connecticut."

(Bleep) them both! While I didn't have any idea what he was up to now, I knew it boded no good. I had better watch this very carefully.

Gods, how I needed an idea to wreck them!

Chapter 3

They boomed along the New England Thruway past New Rochelle, Port Chester and Stamford and then Heller turned off and drove into Norwalk. He stopped at a supermarket and bought some hot dogs, marshmallows, buns and other things.

They drove on, on a state highway.

"Just look around," said Heller, waving his hand at the hilly countryside all decked out in green. "Those purple flowers on the shrubs are rhododendrons. The trees are maples and evergreens, and all these wild flowers, who knows? Summer is about to arrive and this is the fanfare. Like it?"

"Oh, it is pretty," said the Countess Krak. "Nowhere near as lovely as Manco, of course, but very nice."

"You think the planet is worth saving, then," said Heller.

"Not at the cost of our marriage," said the Countess Krak. "These primitives drive me spinning. They get the simplest things wrong."

"Oh, they're not all bad," said Heller.

"Well, why can't they take care of their own planet? How is it my Jettero has to come along and work his fingers to the bone? It's not our planet. It's theirs. Why don't they do something effective?"

"They're just a little deficient in technology, that's all," said Heller.

"A little crazy, you mean. Those engineers in my microwave class at first didn't see anything wrong at all with letting somebody like Rockecenter suppress new developments so he could make money and stay in power. And psychology, why do they let their children be taught they have no souls and are just the victims of their emotions and can't control themselves? Admittedly, they're in bad hands, but why do these people stand for it?"

"Part of their training," said Heller, "is that they can't do anything about it and, having seen the muzzle ends of some of their control forces, I can see how the people would feel that way. They're caught up in an 'agree or get shot.'"

"Are we ever going to invade this planet?" said the Countess.

"Oh, not for another hundred and eighty years if this mission succeeds. And by then they could be sailing very smoothly. It wouldn't be much of an invasion: more like an alliance. They'd simply join the Confederation. The danger is they could make the planet uninhabitable and the Grand Council would launch a shooting invasion now just to save the place. I don't want that to happen to them."

"Well, I don't think we ever ought to touch them," said the Countess Krak. "Do you realize that a primitive culture like this can backfire on a higher level civilization? It could corrupt Voltar."

"Oh, I think you're overstating it," said Heller. "What could these people possibly do to the Voltar Confederation?"

"Plenty," said the Countess Krak. "Sexual perversion, trying people in the press, rotten courts, crazy suits, power attained through economic dominance by a few, psychology, psychiatry, drugs and more drugs. They're dangerous, Jettero. I believe we should leave them severely alone. Quarantine the place."

"Oh, dear," said Heller. "You do seem out of sorts today."

"I'm worried. I have an awful feeling something dreadful may happen to us. A sort of cold feeling like we're always being watched by somebody who means us no good."

I quickly averted my eyes from the viewer. What she had said made my hair stand up on end. How had she guessed that that was exactly the case? Was she a witch or something? By the Gods, that woman would have to be gotten out of the way before much else could be done.

"Look," said Heller, "we're making real progress. The spores project is working great and cleaning up the air. And just two days ago, Izzy got Chryster into production on gasless cars. Very shortly, with luck, we will have done everything we can do from the surface of the planet. Then I'll get the tug and we'll finish the job."

I freaked. Gasless cars? That would ruin Rockecenter completely!

And what did he intend to do with *Tug One*? Oh, Gods, this was much worse than I thought!

I prayed fervently for some idea that would ruin this pair forever.

"I'm sorry that I seem out of sorts," said the Countess Krak. "It is a lovely day and I don't want to spoil it for you."

"Well, never mind," said Heller. "I have somebody you will enjoy meeting. Not all these inhabitants are bad."

He swung off the highway abruptly and drove along a road that was hardly more than a trail. Shortly, the abandoned service station came in view.

Chickens flew noisily out of the way of the Porsche and Heller brought it to a stop.

The old blind woman came out of the house. She stood wiping her hands on her apron. "And how are you, nice young man?" she said. "I see you've brought your sweetheart today."

How could she tell? Krak's footsteps? Her perfume?

They had to go into the house and have a cup of coffee.

"They paying your rent regular?" said Heller.

"Oh, yes," said the old blind woman. "And it makes

a big difference. Didn't you see I have three times as many chickens now? Quite prosperous."

She and the Countess Krak chattered about nothing the way women do and after a bit Heller went out and opened the garage. There sat a battered jeep!

I realized suddenly that during all the times I had not watched my viewers, he must have come up here. It made me nervous to think that he could have wandered around without my being aware of it. What else had he been up to?

He put the Porsche in the garage and he and the Countess and the cat got in the jeep, bade the old blind lady good-bye and drove back to the highway.

They drove for a while and then Heller slowed. He looked ahead. The deputy sheriff's car was sitting there in the speed trap. Heller drew up alongside it.

"Well, if it ain't the whitey engineer," said Ralph.

"Hey, will you look at that dame!" said George.

"Dear," said Heller to the Countess, "may I present Ralph and George? They're deputy sheriffs of the Maysabongo Marines."

"Wow!" said George.

"Jiminy!" said Ralph, hastily taking off his cowboy hat.

"We're just going down to check the place out," said Heller. "So don't be alarmed if you see some smoke."

"Well, I should think so!" said George.

"Jesus, I wish I had a job like yours," said Ralph.

Heller drove the jeep up the road and plunged it off the highway onto the almost unmarked trail.

"You do slaughter 'em," said Heller.

Krak was laughing. "But what's this about Maysabongo Marines?"

"They get a hundred a month extra duty pay for

looking after the place and George's uncle, who is the sheriff, gets two hundred. Extra duty pay. Nobody is liable to bother this area."

They skirted around full-grown trees and at length topped a rise and drove into the valley. Heller ran the jeep over to the flat area the tug had used and looked around, evidently checking for unwanted debris.

"Where's this den of vice?" said the Countess.

"Right over there in that stand of trees." He drove the short distance to it.

"A house!" said the Countess.

"A roadhouse," said Heller. And he told her about the Prohibition era and how the bootleggers used to bring contraband booze up the creek until two highways and a dam ended its career.

They got out and the cat immediately began exploring. Heller went up the stone steps and unlocked the door. "The place is really a fort," he said. "Stone walls, armored doors, bulletproof glass. There's probably enough gangsters buried around here to start a ghost regiment." The Countess Krak walked into the dance hall area, looking at the yellowed paper lanterns. "The place is cold."

"I'll open up all the doors and let the breezes blow through," said Heller. And proceeded to do so.

"Why did you want this place?" said the Countess.

"Landing area," said Heller. "And something else." He beckoned and they went into the bar. He pressed a catch and the end of it opened. He went down the ladder and she followed him.

He played a light on some chiselled letters, *Issiah Slocum, Hys Myne, 1689.* Then down the galleries.

"The first idea I had," he said, "was to find this lost mine and then pretend to open it and get it in operation.

I didn't think I'd have enough finance. So I was going to make gold and then pretend I'd mined it here." He went down a gallery and lifted a tarpaulin. There lay the boxes the tug had carried as cargo.

"So why didn't you?" said the Countess.

"Well, for one reason, we have money to burn. But the main reason is, there's a missing box. For some reason, Box #5 disappeared on Voltar or en route. It contains the pans necessary to do the molding. Nothing on this planet is strong enough. It would just melt under the bombardment."

"Didn't you ever find it?"

"I've sent two or three notes to Soltan. I asked him to reorder it."

"Do you still need it?"

"Well, yes. But not for gold. I want to make a setup for fuel rods. They take the same kind of pan. I wanted to give the setup to Izzy and they could have rods they would just feed into city mains and get billions of megawatts of power direct."

"I should think he would have reordered it and sent it," said the Countess.

"You sit down over there if you can find a clean place," said Heller. "I want to look through this stuff."

He rummaged around. He put some meters on some metal sheets. Finally, he said, "All sorts of goodies here but nothing that will help. However, this will amuse you."

He went over to a place in the floor and lifted a board, revealing the top of a small sack. He reached in and pulled out a handful of something and went over to her.

"Some weeks ago when I was last up here, I ran a small batch of these." He opened his palm and shined the flashlight on it. It flared!

"Oh, what are they?" said the Countess.

"Diamonds," said Heller.

She picked one up and looked at it against the flashlight. "Oooooo!" she said. "That's beautiful!"

"Thought you'd like them," said Heller.

I was suddenly sitting on the edge of my chair. Slavering. She was looking at what must be a pure blue-white of ten carats!

Heller dumped the rest of the handful in her purse. "Take them along. Diamonds are just coal. I was testing pan hardness by compressing carbon blocks. There's a limit to the amount of this sort of thing you can do. You'd flood the market which, on this planet, is pretty tightly controlled."

She was still looking at the diamond when they went back upstairs.

Heller built a fire in the kitchen range and made some hot dogs. They ate them. Then he showed her how to toast marshmallows on pieces of wire with the front door of the firebox open.

He wound up a Victrola and put on some jazz records from the 1920s and they danced.

Later, Heller locked the place up. They went back and picked up the Porsche.

Driving back to town, the Countess was petting the cat who seemed to be sleeping off an overdose of hot dogs.

"Did we get what we went after?" said the Countess.

"No," said Heller. "I thought there might be something I could use so I looked again. But there isn't anything there I can substitute for really hard pans and make fuel rods. They were all in Box #5."

"How do you communicate with Soltan?" said the Countess.

"He gave me an Afyon address," said Heller. "I'll

cable it again when we get back. We really need Box #5 ."

I smiled thinly to myself. I was doing better than I thought. I really was slowing him down!

But it didn't solve my own problems. I would have to do more. AND FAST!

Chapter 4

In came the *Blixo*, roaring out of the night.

I went aboard the moment they had a ladder up.

"Well, well," said Captain Bolz, "and how is the filthy rich Officer Gris?"

"Problems," I said.

He massaged his hairy chest. "We all got problems. It's a good thing other freighters come in here. I had to go through a whole refit on Voltar. I'm weeks and weeks off schedule. The widow in Istanbul will be absolutely wild. But I've got things to cheer her up. Bar silver but mainly me." He started getting into his shore clothes.

"How are things on Voltar?" I said.

"Hells, I don't know. I'm just a captain of an Apparatus freighter. His Majesty don't tell me anything at all." He laughed at his joke. "You better ask that catamite, Twolah. He came aboard so beaten down he must know half the secrets of the government. Didn't have any trouble with him this time. He just sort of hid in his cabin."

"I have three passengers for you," I said.

"Straight up or suspended?"

"Crobe you've carried before. I'd keep him locked up. The other two don't matter. Neither speaks Voltarian. But the girl, Teenie Whopper, I'd keep away from the crew. She's worse than Twolah."

He stopped tying his shoe and pushed a set of blank forms at me. I had recovered my identoplate from Faht Bey and began stamping.

He put the forms away. "This is a very fast turnaround," he said. "I'm way off schedule. So get your business done with Twolah and get him and your passengers aboard. I'm off to Istanbul for a very fast trip and when I return here, I'm gone."

I followed him down the ladders and then turned and gave the guard captain loading orders for the passengers and the necessary stamps.

"I'll be glad to see that girl go," said the guard captain. "She's sitting in her cell swearing like a pirate, demanding we give her one phone call. The adjectives she's using on your name would melt the stone! You want to see her and calm her down?"

"Gods, no! Tell her to open up one of her trunks and have a nice smoke! What about the man?"

"The Madison fellow? He's no trouble. He's just sitting there saying he knew it would come to this. And that crazy Crobe hasn't said anything at all."

"Well, get them shipped," I said. "I'm supposed to see a courier."

"He's right over there. He didn't even arrive in irons this time."

Twolah, nicknamed Too-Too, was cowering by a ladder. He had a bag. I beckoned for him to follow me and took him into an empty cell.

Too-Too wasn't so much beaten down as bursting

with secrets he was afraid the wrong people would get out of him.

He leaned close to my ear. His perfume hit me in a wave.

"He's done it," said Too-Too.

"Who has done what?" I said impatiently.

"Lombar. He has totally subverted the Grand Council with drugs. The court physicians helped him. They've got everybody hooked and Lombar controls all the supplies." He drew back and gazed around to make sure he was not being overheard. He leaned forward: "He has even hooked His Majesty, Cling the Lofty!"

My eyes flared. Oh, what news this was!

"He's going on to hook the population," whispered Too-Too. "In all but name, Lombar Hisst is in virtual control of all Voltar."

It was electric news. I suddenly realized that shortly I would become the Chief of the Apparatus!

"He said to give you this," said Too-Too.

He slid a paper into my hands. I unfolded it. It was made of words and letters cut from newssheets and pasted on a page.

It said:

KILL THE (blEepArd)!

I looked at Too-Too. "What about Captain Tars Roke? Heller had the communication line to him."

"Captain Tars Roke has been dismissed as the King's Own Astrographer. He has been ordered to join the Fleet on distant Calabar. Forget him."

A surge of absolute joy raced through me!

"The rest of the message," said Too-Too, "is to be sure the opium and heroin and amphetamines keep coming and that means to do nothing that would disturb I. G. Barben."

That meant nothing must dislodge Rockecenter!

My joy took a little sag. I thought of my present relationship there. My problems were not all solved.

This was going to be tight!

I stamped the papers he had brought.

My mind was on other things.

"Don't I get my reward?" he said. "You know, the big guard and the fat woman . . ."

I pushed this loathsome catamite from me. "You'll get your reward when I am Chief of the Apparatus," I snarled.

I had other things to think about.

I had to work out how to handle these matters. I had to solve the problems which were hammering at me. And I had to solve them fast.

Chapter 5

In my secret room I tensely crouched over a sheet of paper. I had to make a plan. I was well aware that what I determined might well alter the course of billions of lives. I could not make a mistake: they had to lose, not me.

Black Jowl.

I wrote his name down.

What was I going to do with him?

Then I had it!

I would kill Heller. Then blow up Chryster Motors in Detroit. Then blast Ochokeechokee, Florida, off the face of the map, thus solving Miami not buying fuel. Then kill Izzy Epstein and Bang-Bang Rimbombo by blowing up the Empire State Building. I listed them. I did not want to overlook any.

Then I would call Bury and I would say, "See? Madison was going too slowly. But now I have eradicated the fuel man and all his works." I would add modestly, "I'm sure you've read it in the papers." Then I would say, "So please get my rating restored as a Rockecenter family spy, for I have done my job and then some." And he would say, "Inkswitch, how proud we are of you. Of course your rating is restored."

Then I would go to Black Jowl in his cell and I'd say, "On your feet, buster. You're talking to a Rockecenter family spy and you only got to phone your office to verify it." And he of course, in a whipped sort of way, would tear up his mortgage on the Earth base.

I'd let him cringe a little before I booted him off the property. Yes, that would be nice, so I added it to the list.

I sat back proudly to eye my masterpiece.

Then my eye caught a flick of movement on the viewer. A knife was being drawn through a piece of meat. THE COUNTESS KRAK.

I shuddered.

I looked back at the plan before me. I sheltered it so it could not be visible from the viewer. There was a flaw in my master plan.

The moment anyone drew a bead on Heller, he himself would be in the telescopic sight of a sniper rifle in the hands of the Countess Krak!

I thought about this for a time. Yes, it was a definite flaw.

In order to successfully gun down Heller, it was vitally necessary to get rid of that witch.

I thought and thought. I paced back and forth. I had been unsuccessful in this before. I must not be unsuccessful now.

Suddenly a basket caught my eye. There were many communications in it, untouched, unread, an accumulation of my long absence. The germ of an idea began to penetrate my mind.

I went to the basket. Right on top was a card from Widow Tayl.

Yoo-hoo, wherever you are.

Why don't you write?
I can feel him kick. He's almost ready to arrive. Looking forward to a happy marriage.

Pratia

To Hells with her. When I was Chief of the Apparatus, I'd have her exterminated. I threw the card on the floor.

There were some overdue Voltar bills. I threw those on the floor.

The next one made my hair rise. It was deep in the pile but the date stamp on it was not two hours old! It was from the unknown assassin Lombar had assigned to kill me if I failed! It said:

KILL OR BE KILLED
IS THE LAW.

It was signed with a blood-dripping dagger.

It made me very nervous. I had long since ceased to try to figure out who this must be. But it did look like it was connected with the *Blixo* for that time-date was an hour after its arrival.

How cruel it would be if, just as I was on the verge of total success, almost ready to become the head of the whole deadly organization, this assassin might make some kind of a clown blunder and kill me in error!

Oh, I had better look very busy indeed!

What I was looking for wasn't in there. My eye strayed. THERE IT WAS!

A messenger had slipped it under the door, probably in the last few minutes. HELLER'S CABLE!

He said that he was sending it. Yes, there were two other cables, much older, lying there in the dust.

I opened the last one:

> *SULTAN BEY, ROMAN VILLA,*
> *AFYON, TKY*
>
> *PLEASE EXPEDITE REPLACE-*
> *MENT OF BOX NUMBER FIVE.*
> *IT IS DELAYING THE MISSION*
> *COMPLETION. JH.*

The other two older cables said much the same thing. But I did not want to know what they said; I wanted to be sure he knew and she knew that they had been sent.

I knew I had this thing solved now.

But I only needed one thing. I did not have it yet.

I went to bed and rolled and tossed restlessly. I rose early and puttered about, cleaning guns.

When they got up in New York, I sat tensely at the viewers, watching, listening, lying in wait.

I prayed for luck. I did not have all that much time.

I loaded both viewers with the strips I had run out of in New York. I must be able to backtrack in case, while I was eating, they said the thing I was looking for.

Evening came. The *Blixo* took off.

I spent another feverish night. I paced through another wasted morning. I had only a week or so before someone noticed Black Jowl was gone. Heller and Krak were just delaying so as to spite me. I needed just a few magic words.

My afternoon came and they got up.

And then at their breakfast I GOT MY KEY MESSAGE.

Heller and Krak were at a breakfast table on the condo terrace surrounded by greenery.

"Dear," said Heller, "I'm sorry to have to be running about so much, but this afternoon Izzy wants me to go with him to Washington. Wonderful Oil for Maysabongo is going to take options on every drop of fuel in the United States, all reserves. Izzy doesn't know how to calculate capacities and I am pretty close to the Maysabongo ambassador from last fall."

"ALL the fuel?" said the Countess Krak. "Where will you put it?"

"We don't have to put it anywhere," said Heller. "You can buy options to buy anything. If we have the option to buy it at a certain price, then, if we do buy it, they have to sell it to us at that price. So we're purchasing a six month's option. The companies are so money hungry and the option sellers so eager that it is no trick. They don't think we'll ever complete the purchase and they'll just be in pocket half a billion for the options and still have their oil. Anyway, we're going down there and brief the ambassador. And then we're going to fly over to Detroit tomorrow afternoon and I'm going to test drive one of the new gasless cars to give it an okay for the production line. I'll try to be home about midnight tomorrow night and if not then, certainly by the next morning."

"No women in Washington," said the Countess Krak.

They both laughed.

"I'm leaving on the one o'clock plane," said Heller.

My prayers had been answered. This time I would not miss!

I reached for the two-way-response radio. I called Raht. He was at the New York office.

"At 2:30 this afternoon," I said, "you are to make a phone call." And I gave him the number.

"That's the Royal officer's condo," he said.

"Precisely," I said. "But he won't be there. His woman will have returned from the airport. I want you to say that you have an urgent personal message from Officer Gris. Then you are to give it to her. The message follows: 'I cannot possibly send you the replacement for Box #5 as I am afraid Jettero might hurt himself with them.'"

"Is that all?"

"That's all," I said.

"Wait a minute," said Raht. "That message sounds fishy to me."

"It will make sense to her. Do what you're told!"

"Listen," he said, "I know how your mind runs. I've seen that female. She must be one of the most beautiful women in the Confederacy. She compares to Hightee Heller, the dream girl of poor Terb. Are you absolutely sure that this isn't going to hurt her in any way?"

"No, no," I said easily. "Of course not. It's just a sort of code message and she'll be delighted to have it."

"I hope so," he said. He clicked off.

Who the Hells cared what he thought. He was paid to do his duty just like I was.

At 9:30 P.M., my time, I was glued back to that viewer. She had seen Heller off at La Guardia Airport and at 2:00 P.M., her time, had returned home to the condo.

At 2:30 the butler Balmor came into her study where she was grading student papers and said, "Madame, there is an urgent phone call for you. I have switched it to your line there."

In a panic, maybe thinking something had happened to Heller, she picked the instrument up.

Raht gave her the message flawlessly.

"Who is this?" she demanded.

But Raht had hung up.

She rose. And then she said the very thing I knew she would. "Heavens, what have I done?"

I laughed with glee. It was working. She thought the hypnotic suggestion she had given me was still in place and that it was blocking my shipment of Box #5.

She walked back and forth a couple of times. Then she reached for the phone. I couldn't believe my luck. She was falling for it. She believed, of course, that the only way she could handle that was with another hypnotic session. And the only way she could deliver that . . .

"Give me Airline Central Reservations," she said. She got it. "What is your next direct connection to Istanbul?" They told her there was no direct connection. Due

to schedule changes, the best they could do for a reservation left at ten o'clock tonight and had a six-hour layover in Rome.

"I'll take it," she said. "Make the reservations on
through to Afyon, Turkey. The name is Heavenly Joy
Krackle."

They gave her the flight numbers. I hastily wrote
them down.

I was really laughing. She hadn't used the Squeeza
credit card, saying she would pay cash.

Then she said, "Please make the ticket round trip."

I grinned with glee from ear to ear. That was one
round trip that wouldn't be used.

The Countess Krak was never going back!

Chapter 6

She wrote a brief note to Heller and gave it to Balmor. She gave instructions about the cat. And then she
began to pack.

Suddenly, I got to worrying. Supposing the assassin
missed on Heller?

If the Countess was killed outright, I would have no
bargaining power.

Suddenly, INSPIRATION!

I knew exactly what I had to do and I did not have
much time.

I rushed through the tunnel door, across the hangar
and to the room of Captain Stabb.

"How fast can you get the line-jumper in the air?"
I said.

"Ten minutes," he said. "What's up?"

I realized I would have to be very clever to get this
pirate to cooperate.

"We're laying the stage to rob a chain of banks,"
I said.

"Well, it's about time," said Captain Stabb.

"Now, on this planet, bank robbers have to have hostages."

"Really?" he said.

"Yes sir," I said. "They have to have hostages. But
I've got a new wrinkle. We're going to take the hostage
in advance."

"Hey," he said. "That saves trying to find somebody
alive after you've picked up the whole building."

"Right," I said. "So we're going to take a hostage
who is connected to billions. And then we are going to
do a series of actions that will make us all rich beyond
belief."

"Hey, wonderful," he said. "It's been pretty dull
around here. Without you to order it, that Faht Bey
wouldn't let us take off."

"Well, he will now. Tell me quick, which one of
your men can best impersonate an Earthman?"

"Jeeb, the second engineer."

"And he has no compunctions about stabbing somebody in the back?"

"Let's not make jokes," said Captain Stabb. "Piracy
is a serious business. Of course he can do a little thing
like that."

"Then get aloft at once," I said, "put him down just
north of the international airport in Rome, have him buy
a ticket and, without fail, be on this flight."

I gave Stabb the rest of the instructions. I gave him the necessary money and equipment the man would take.

"When you have done that," I said, "come back here for me. We will leave again tomorrow night. So, on your way!"

I called Faht Bey and told him it was at the orders of Lombar Hisst. They cleared the line-jumper out and it was gone through the mountaintop illusion and into the night sky.

I went back to the viewer.

There must be no mistakes!

I watched her as she finished packing her grip.

COUNTESS KRAK, I'VE REALLY GOT YOU THIS TIME!

And Heller would never blame me if I missed on him.

But I wouldn't miss on him either.

They would both pay, and dearly, for all the trouble they had caused me!

And I toasted myself in *sira* as the new Chief of the Apparatus!

I had the heady sensation one has when he knows he is going to win for sure!

Chapter 7

I consulted the base tables and references.

I did my calculation very precisely.

She would leave New York at 2200 hours Eastern Standard Time tonight. That was 0500 tomorrow, my time. She would arrive in Paris, Charles de Gaulle Airport, 1100 Paris time the next day. That was noon, my time.

She would arrive in Rome, Leonardo da Vinci Airport, 1510 Rome time, 1610 my time.

She would leave Rome at 2100 hours tomorrow night. That was 2200 hours, my time.

She would never arrive in Istanbul.

The flight from Rome was on a Mediterranean Airlines plane. It would be Flight 931. The plane was a DC-9 Series 10. It had a wingspan of 89.4 feet, a height of 27.5 feet, a length of 104.4 feet. It was powered with two Pratt and Whitney jet engines mounted on either side of the fuselage in the rear under the tail. The speed was maximum 560 mph. The weight of the plane was 98,500 pounds plus a payload of 19,200 pounds.

It would probably have a pilot and copilot, possibly a navigator as it would be flying over water. It would probably have three flight attendants. It would be carrying up to ninety passengers.

Captain Stabb and the line-jumper returned before dawn and I hurried to the hangar with my figures.

Stabb was climbing down from the cabin of the bell-shaped ship. He was all smiles. He came over to me. "Got him landed. And we also got him on this two-way-response radio and this viewer. He's carrying the Mark V camera as a lapel button." He handed me the viewer.

Yes, there was a view of the waiting room of the Leonardo da Vinci Airport lobby in Rome. It was off vertical. Jeeb was evidently taking a snooze on a waiting room seat.

I gave Stabb my figures. "These jet engines have a

thrust of 14,000 pounds each. That's a total of 56,000 horsepower. Seems like quite a lot."

"No problem," he said.

"All right," I said. "Get some sleep. We'll be leaving here tonight as soon as it is dark."

"I can't wait," he said, grinning.

I raced back to my room. I had to make sure the Countess Krak was boarding that New York plane.

Yes, there she was, checking in. And sure enough, she had her shopping bag. I knew what it contained.

"Your flight will be called in half an hour, ma'am," said the clerk. "Have a pleasant trip."

I grinned. Oh, this was wonderful. Time and again I had tried to nail the deadly Countess Krak and each time she had gotten the best of me. But this time I would not fail!

Some little kids were tearing around the lobby. One of them bumped into her. She put out her hand and patted him on the head and he looked up and smiled.

I sat there tensely and watched. I had to make sure she actually got on that plane and didn't try to reach Heller in Washington, for I knew he would scream his head off saying "NO!"

She bought some candy and some magazines.

Then her flight was called.

I eagerly watched her board.

She settled herself in the reclining seat and fastened her belt.

The engines muttered. The plane was taxiing to take off.

With a blasting roar, runway lights flashing by, it sped into the air.

I let out a sigh of relief.

But still I watched just to make sure.

After twenty minutes my screen began to dim. Then it went out.

She had gone beyond the two-hundred-mile range of the activator-responder which had remained on the Empire State Building.

All my viewers were inactive now. With Crobe well on his way to Voltar, with Heller out of range in Washington and with the Countess Krak winging over the Atlantic, there were no images for me to watch.

She would be eight hours and fifty-five minutes actual time in the air before she arrived in Paris. She had a two-hour-and-fifteen-minute layover in the French capital. In eleven hours and ten minutes actual time she would be landing in Rome. Five hours and fifty minutes after that she would be taking off on Mediterranean Airlines Flight 931 from Rome. Well before it left, I would be taking off from Afyon.

It would be twelve hours now before I had a chance to pick her up on Jeeb's camera in Rome about a thousand miles away. And it would be nearly sixteen hours before I left.

I lay down in my bed and tried to sleep. I couldn't. All my dreams were coming true.

The Countess Krak was winging straight into my spider web. And soon there would be one less foolish butterfly in the universe.

And all my problems would soon be solved.

Chapter 8

At about six o'clock that evening, my time, she came on the screen of Jeeb's lapel camera.

I was sitting at dinner, too excited to eat, the viewer parked on the table before me, the two-way-response radio beside it.

She was walking along a row of shops in the Rome airport arcade. She was dressed in a dark blue tailored suit. Her hair was a fluffy gold beneath a wide-brimmed floppy hat. A couple of young Italian men stood suddenly stock-still and watched her pass them.

She was window shopping and the Italian wares as always were quite ornate: model cannon, silk scarves, tapestry wall hangings.

Jeeb must be lounging inconspicuously on the concourse. He had spotted her, for as she passed him, he turned and kept her centered. I had given him a passport photograph which wasn't very good and I had had some qualms that he might not recognize her. Those qualms were now at rest. Good man, Jeeb.

Two young boys rushed up to the Countess Krak. They had notebooks open. They wanted her autograph, obviously thinking she was a movie star. She laughed and signed them.

They passed Jeeb, marvelling, looking at their books. "Cristo," said one in Italian, "I thought Lauren Bacall was dead."

"Naw, you don't know nothing. That's her daughter."

The first one looked back. "Oh, yes. I remember now. But she's prettier than her mother."

The radio came live. "Officer Gris?"

"Right here," I said.

"Have I got the right woman? She's prettier than the photograph and she signed some funny name for those kids."

"That's the woman," I said.

"Good. Had me blinking for a minute."

"Carry on," I said. "But be very careful. She's deadly and very deceptive."

"I'll watch my step," he said. He clicked off.

She had gone in a shop and Jeeb moved so as to keep her in direct view through the door.

I could faintly hear her voice above the concourse clatter and chatter. I turned up the volume.

She was buying silk scarves. I hadn't realized she could speak Italian now. She must have gotten coaching from Heller.

She had a green one and was holding it up to the light. It was a very elegant scarf. "I will take it," she said, "it matches his eye color. Put it in a nice box. It's a present for a doctor friend of mine."

Prahd. She was buying a present for him.

She was looking at other scarves. Then she found a long cravat that was light tan. It had a pattern of antiques guns. It was pre-tied. "And I'll take this one for another friend so wrap that as a present, too."

She meant it for me. I shuddered. Guns to shoot me and a noose to hang myself. Oh, the implication was very plain. It was a good thing I was acting!

When she had her wrapped gifts, she went to a restaurant and ordered and began to eat her dinner.

Jeeb, clear across the airport café, was eating his and

keeping an eye on her. He annoyed me a little bit by
choosing such a fancy dinner for himself with my money.
I would speak to him about it when this was done.

Right now it was coming up to deadline for my own
departure.

I went to my room and dressed in a warm, electric-
heated ski suit and boots and hood. It can get pretty cold
at thirty thousand feet.

I looked at myself in the mirror. The jet black of the
costume would minimize me as a target in case there was
shooting.

I buckled on some guns. I put some other items in
my pockets I might need. This time I didn't forget the
control star which would bring the Antimancos to heel
if they got out of line.

I picked up the radio and viewer.

I went down into the underground hangar.

The line-jumper crew was all ready and eager to go.

I clambered up the ladder to the cabin.

COUNTESS KRAK, I'LL GET YOU THIS
TIME!

Chapter 9

The line-jumper leaped up through the illusion of
the mountaintop and out into the inky night.

The two Antimanco pilots were hunched silhouettes
in the glow of their instruments and screens.

Captain Stabb sat beside me on the crew bench.
Behind us the other engineer crouched.

We were swiftly at seventy thousand feet and racing at two thousand miles an hour through the night, west-bound for Rome.

Through Jeeb's camera viewer came the call, "Flight 931, Mediterranean Airlines for Istanbul, boarding now at Gate Five."

Captain Stabb looked at me, his beady eyes glittering in the reflection from the viewer that lay between us. "I wonder if there's anything in her cargo hold."

"It's the woman we want," I said. "The banks come afterwards."

"We might just be lucky," he said.

"That's the hostage there," I said, pointing at the Countess Krak standing in the line to board. "The one with the two gold wrapped packages under her arm."

"Is there anything valuable in them?" he said.

"I'll leave it to you to find out," I said. "But getting the hostage is the thing."

"Don't worry," he said, "we're experts at this sort of thing. I could tell you some tales that would curl your hair."

I was not interested in having my hair curled. All I wanted in my hands was Krak!

We flew and very shortly, far below, with the aid of the viewscreen, I could see the lights of Rome.

Stabb was looking at his watch. He stood up on the seat to see over the pilot's shoulders. "Got the airport runway on their screens."

He looked back at the viewer. The passengers were boarding. Now we would see if our luck was still holding.

The passengers were taking their seats. Jeeb was holding back. The Countess Krak put her presents in an over-head rack and sank down into a window seat on the left of the aisle. She was about at the center of the plane.

There were not all that many passengers. I tried to count them and estimated forty. The night flight to Istanbul, scheduled to arrive there at dawn, must not be all that popular. They were businessmen and tourists and women and kids. A coach flight.

LUCK!

The seat directly behind Krak was empty!

The lapel camera moved. Jeeb was settling himself just behind the Countess Krak.

"That's wonderful!" I said.

"Good man, Jeeb," said Stabb. "Didn't you see him bribe the counter clerk?"

I groaned a little bit. He was certainly spending my money!

One of the Antimanco pilots said over his shoulder to Stabb, "Give us the word so we can identify it when it taxis out."

Stabb was watching the viewer. The mutter of plane engines was coming from it. "Now!" he said.

"Got it," the Antimanco replied. "It's moving on my screen."

Presently, watching the viewer, Stabb said, "Taking off!"

"Verifies," said the Antimanco pilot.

Shortly, the other pilot said, "He's heading easterly. That's the one!"

Captain Stabb had out his map and turned a subdued flashlight on it. "Now it has the width of Italy to cross. Then it's over the Adriatic Sea. Then it would hit the coast again over Lake Scutari on the border between Yugoslavia and Albania and then over the Dinaric Alps. But I elect for the sea. It will be over that stretch of water for more than half an hour. All right?"

"Excellent," I approved.

He waddled ahead and bent over the pilots, showing them the map.

I looked back at the viewer. I could only see the top of the Countess Krak's head.

The Antimancos were watching their viewers. Captain Stabb came back. "They've got about a hundred and fifty miles to go," he told me. "Then they'll start over the sea." He turned to the engineer behind us. "When I give the word, blanket their radio."

The engineer nodded and looked down at the device he had on the floor.

Tense minutes ticked by.

"They'll be over water in three minutes," an Antimanco pilot said.

"Start dropping down," said Stabb. "Blanket their radio," he told the engineer.

The line-jumper was dropping so rapidly the viewer tried to float.

"Range two miles and closing," said an Antimanco pilot.

"Pace their speed exactly when we hit," said Captain Stabb. "We don't want shore radar to see anything odd." He turned to the engineer. "Stand by tractor beams."

"Range two hundred yards and closing," said an Antimanco pilot.

I looked at the viewer. All was calm aboard that flight. An attendant up near the door was getting a pillow for a child.

Captain Stabb grabbed Jeeb's radio. "NOW!" he barked.

The viewer showed that Jeeb's lapel camera was rising up.

Jeeb reached over the seat. He shoved the back of the Countess Krak's head forward with his left hand.

He raised his right and savagely struck a paralysis dagger into her shoulder.

The Countess Krak tried to rise up.

The flight attendant screamed.

"Range zero!" barked an Antimanco pilot.

"Tractor beams!" roared Stabb.

The airliner's back was gripped and slammed up against the line-jumper underside. There was a lurch.

I looked down. The engineer had thrown the hatch open. The back of the airliner's fuselage was visible, held to the line-jumper's bell.

"Maintain that ship's speed!" shouted Stabb.

I looked at the viewer.

BEDLAM!

People were trying to get out of their seats. Children began to scream.

Jeeb backed down the aisle.

"Cutters!" shouted Stabb.

The engineer went down through the hatch.

A pilot was coming through the airliner flight deck door.

"Can I shoot?" shouted Jeeb into his radio.

"Fire away!" I shouted back.

Jeeb raised a glass blastick and let drive. The pilot fighting his way toward him and three people around him dissolved in electric fire!

"I've got it!" shouted our engineer.

I looked down. He had opened a large circular hole in the top of the airliner.

Captain Stabb was instantly scrambling down the ladder the engineer had used. Stabb dropped through and out of sight.

The bedlam increased from the viewer and I could hear it coming up through the hole.

Stabb moved into sight in the viewer. His huge arms were flailing out left and right, knocking passengers back. A child got in his way and he hurled it screaming at the flight deck door.

Then Stabb had something in his hand. He wrenched the door wide open.

The copilot struck at him. Captain Stabb's club smashed his face to bloody pulp.

Stabb was in the flight deck for a long minute while the screams went on. A businessman sought to tackle Jeeb and Jeeb fired again.

The view went clear.

Stabb came out of the flight deck. He was holding the pilot recording box on which they record last minute occurrences before they crash.

Another child, struggling up, got in his way. He smashed its skull with the box he held.

Stabb came opposite Krak's seat. A man clawed at him and he smashed him with the box. The captain was looking in the rack for the gold wrapped packages. He found them and tore one's wrapping off. He looked at the silk scarf and threw it away. He ripped up the other one, found another scarf. He tossed it aside in disgust.

Several passengers were still moving. Systematically, Stabb battered them to death. Then he and Jeeb began to rip watches off wrists and wallets from pockets. They emptied a bag full of baby clothes and threw their loot in.

Then Stabb bent over in the center of the ship and lifted up the Countess Krak. He threw her over his shoulder and walked back toward Jeeb. The Countess Krak's hair was hiding her face. Her arms trailed, limp.

Stabb made a gesture and Jeeb went up the ladder. Jeeb appeared at my level. He put the bag of loot aside and reached back. He picked Krak off the captain's shoulder and tossed her on the floor.

Stabb came up.

"We still over the sea?" he shouted.

"Miles to go to shore," an Antimanco pilot shouted back.

"Stand clear!" roared Stabb. "Engineer, let go the tractor beams!"

I looked down through the opening as the ladder was pulled in.

The airliner suddenly fell away from us.

It went over on one wing. It began to spiral down.

I felt very heavy and then realized we were climbing at a rapid rate.

An Antimanco pilot called, "There's islands below us. It says on the map they're called the Palagruza."

That wasn't so good. I didn't want it crashed on an island. "Track that airliner carefully!" I ordered.

I looked down through the open hatch. It was black. I could not see anything. Suddenly it snapped closed. I got up and looked at the screens.

They had the airliner in clear view with nonvisible light bands. It was swooping, its engines still going.

"It won't pull out," said Stabb. "I wrecked the controls."

It seemed to be heading in a general, floppy way toward a large island. I held my breath. It had to crash in the sea and leave no traces.

Suddenly it went into a vertical power dive and did not come out.

It struck with a huge explosion of spray just offshore of the larger island.

I sighed with relief.

I turned my attention to the floorboards.

There lay the Countess Krak. She would be out for another three hours, at least.

I did not want to touch her. I began a gesture to Captain Stabb. "Tie her hands and feet and tie them well."

The Countess Krak was deadly no more. She was in my hands!

PART
SIXTY-ONE

Chapter 1

We returned to the Earth base in the mountain at Afyon, Turkey, well before dawn.

We dropped through the electronic illusion that even radar reflected as part of the mountain's peak. We came to rest on the hangar floor.

I did not want to touch the Countess Krak. I signalled Stabb to pick her up.

He threw her over his shoulder and clambered down the ladder. "We got our hostage," he said to me. "Now, when do we start robbing the banks?"

"I have to make sure they have gold shipments in them," I said. "I'll get my lines out and let you know first thing."

"Where do I put the hostage?" said Stabb. "We want her in a safe place."

"Oh, I've got one," I said. "Follow me."

I walked into the prison block and all the way to the end. Here lay the big cell I had built for Crobe, completely escape-proof even for the Countess Krak.

I worked the combination lock on the outer door. I unlocked the inner door. I threw on the lights. The place was filthy: it had never been cleaned up. And Crobe didn't care where he did what he did.

There was a flooding lever that would wash the

place out. I reached for it and then I stayed my hand. It
served the (bleepch) right.

I stepped in. A horrible stench. I gestured toward
the bed.

Stabb walked in and threw her on it.

We withdrew. I securely locked the inner door. I
closed the outer one and spun the combination.

I looked through the small square port. What a
delight! There she lay, tousled and defeated—my prisoner. At last I had removed her as a menace!

When I thought over her list of crimes against me,
I was appalled that I had let her live so long. What an
oversight!

A puckish whim hit me. I could not spit on her. But
I could make sure that when she woke she would be
chilled to the bone.

I reached over and pulled the flooding lever.

Sprays jetted out from the walls in a blinding rush.
Their force was driving filth off the walls and along the
floor and into the drains. I had not intended that. I only
wanted the place soaking wet.

I tried to shut the lever off but it was an automatic
set. That (bleeped) construction chief had done his work
too well when he had fitted out this place. The jet sprays
ran their course. The water vapor hung in the cell. A hiss-
ing sound started up. The water was followed by jets of
drying air! That was not what I intended at all! I wres-
tled with the lever but it was moving back at its own
speed.

Upset, I looked back through the small port. I could
not believe my eyes! It was nearly time for the paralysis
dagger to wear off but the cold water had revived her.

She was looking at her bonds.

Then she did something with her wrists. A turning twist.

Her hands were free!

She grabbed at her ankles, and faster than I could follow she had her feet untied!

Belatedly I reached for the clamp which would pin her to the bed. I closed it. I stared back into the room.

The clamps came down but they closed on a bed with nobody in it!

She was standing, dishevelled, in the middle of the floor.

She saw my face at the port.

Her mouth framed, "You!" She pointed. Straight at me!

I reeled back. No telling what that finger could do to my wits.

Far down the corridor, I looked back at the door.

Oh, she was dangerous! Part of her theater training must have been as an escapist. She had made nothing of those bonds.

I would have to handle that port. Somebody else might look in. Nobody knew the combination to that cell but me. Nobody had a key to the inner door but me. Still, I must not take any chances.

I went into the hangar and found a square of cloth and some tape.

I sneaked back up the passageway, staying very low so she would not see me.

All in one motion, I taped the cloth over the port.

I withdrew to a safe distance. The cell was soundproof and escape-proof. I would forbid anyone to go near her or to even take her meals. Ha! Maybe she would starve to death.

Then I recalled that I had thrown a whole case of

emergency space rations in there for Crobe, enough for a year or two.

The air port.

My wits cleared. When the time came to kill her, it was all right. My cunning design had taken care of that. Nobody could get out that air shaft. But poison-gas capsules could be dropped down it from outside the mountain.

I felt easier.

When I had killed Heller and no longer needed her for a bargaining pawn, a capsule or two could be dropped down and that would be the final breath of the Countess Krak.

Only then did I permit myself to feel I had done well.

The way was wide open now.

All I had to do was kill Heller.

And all my problems would be solved.

I went to sleep congratulating myself on how clever I had been.

I dreamed I was at a banquet, attended by a thousand Lords. It was the banquet of my inauguration as the Chief of the Apparatus, loyal servant of the redoubtable Lombar Hisst who now controlled all Voltar.

Chapter 2

The following morning I woke up and had a bright idea. I didn't have to go near the cell to keep an eye on the Countess Krak. All I had to do was get Raht to ship me the activator-receiver for her bugs.

No sooner thought of than done. I picked up the two-way-response radio off the bedside table and called Raht.

"For Hells' sakes, Officer Gris," he said, "don't you ever think of anybody but yourself? It's one o'clock in the morning here."

"Time means nothing when duty calls," I said. "Get down to the Empire State Building and ship me the woman's activator-receiver."

"Why? Isn't she in New York?"

"We won't be needing them anymore," I said. "So step lively and get them out by International Spurt Express to me. I don't want them lying around. Possible Code break."

He groaned. He clicked off.

I spent a happy day. I idled around. I checked up on Black Jowl. He was just glooming away in his cell. He didn't see me. I didn't go near Krak. It was enough to know she was in there. I issued strict instructions: Nobody was to lift that cloth.

What I was looking forward to was watching Heller's arrival back in New York. His viewer was still blank. But when he arrived and got Krak's note, he might make calls about the plane and he would find it had crashed. It would crush him.

I would order Raht to kill him. Crushed like that, Heller would be an easy target.

With him dead, I could wipe out Chryster, Ochokee-chokee and the Empire State Building. Rockecenter would be jubilant. Then I could release Black Jowl and tell him to get lost. I would then kill the Countess Krak.

I would put Faht Bey in his place with the information that I would shortly be his supreme chief. I would threaten his life if he didn't keep the opium and heroin and amphetamines coming. And then I would go home. How proud Lombar would be of me!

Heller's viewer stayed blank.

I had dinner.

The viewer was still blank. Heller was overdue in New York. Maybe that fool Raht had made a mistake and shipped me the wrong unit.

I called him on the radio. "My viewer is blank!" I said angrily. "Can't you ever do anything right? You shipped me the wrong unit!"

"I shipped you the one with *K* on it. It went out on International Spurt at 3:00 A.M. You should have it tomorrow. His is still on the antenna."

"Then you turned his 831 Relayer off. My unit here is as blank as a piece of clear glass!"

"If his relayer is off, you can't get a picture?"

"That's right. So it's off. Now get down there and check it!"

I tossed the radio aside. Oh, when I was Apparatus Chief, I'd get rid of an awful lot of riffraff!

An hour later he called back. "The 831 Relayer is on. If he's in New York you ought to be getting a picture."

My screen was blank. A riffle of unease went through me. Where was Heller?

Then I remembered something. "You told me you had him bugged."

"I do. But it's just a locational bug, not an audio and visio bug."

"Well, (bleep) you to Hells, if you've got a bug on him, why are you denying me the information about where he is?"

"My bug receiver must be busted."

I groaned. Oh, Gods, why was I served by such riffraff? "How do you know it's busted, you idiot?" I said.

"Have you tried to repair it by fiddling with it and banging it? Turning its switches on and off?" Cripes, I had to think of everything!

"I know it must be busted because when I looked at it a few minutes ago it said he was over the North Pole. Before that it said he was in Chicago."

"That's impossible!" I snapped. "Now listen carefully and do what you're told for once. Go to his condo or down to his offices at the Empire State and hobnob with or bribe some of his staff and find out where Heller is! My life may depend on it. Get going!"

I found, when he clicked off, that I had begun to sweat. It would be like Heller to take it into his head to simply come kill me to pass the time.

Two awful hours went by. Then suddenly the radio went live.

"Hey," said Raht, "all Hells have erupted around his office. I didn't even have to bribe anybody. The staff is standing around in the halls crying and wringing their hands. The airline called the condo and the butler, Balmor, phoned Epstein. You told me you wouldn't hurt the woman. She's dead!"

I was thinking coolly. "How?" I said.

"Flight 931 out of Rome for Istanbul crashed with everybody lost. It's in the papers. What did you do?"

"How could a plane crash possibly have anything to do with me? I don't build these flimsy primitive death-traps they use. How would I know it would crash?"

"Are you sure you didn't blow it up or something?"

"What nonsense!" I said. "These jets fall out of the sky all over the place. It practically rains planes."

"Well, all right," he said.

"Now, listen. It's not our job to worry about what

happened to one of their flying coffins. You've GOT to find the man. I have orders for you."

"What now?" he said.

"You are to kill him."

"WHAT? A Royal officer? You must be out of your mind! That carries a death penalty just to threaten it, much less do it!"

"You have no slightest choice," I said. "Kill him or I'll kill you, if I have to blow up all of New York City to do it!"

"Gods!" said Raht, impressed.

"You'll look silly praying to them with your head blown off," I said. "So find that man! Where is he on your location bug now?"

"I told you it was broken."

"Look at it, (bleep) you!"

"See? It's totally out of whack. It says he is over Scotland."

My blood congealed. Chicago, North Pole, Scotland . . . Heller was airborne. He might be en route to Turkey!

I swallowed my heart. Then I made myself be calm enough to think and speak. "You get next to some of those people. You find out what flight he's on. We may have to waylay him. Report to me every hour."

I clicked off. Water was actually dripping from my palms.

After an agonized hour, my radio went live again.

"I got it," said Raht. "His butler, Balmor, phoned him in Chicago before he phoned the office. The Royal officer chartered a jet at the Chicago O'Hare International Airport and took off immediately for Italy to begin salvage operations in the Palagruza Islands in the

Adriatic Sea. The crash was spotted just off one. He is going to try to recover his girl's body."

My hair stood on end. What else might he discover?

"Listen," I said, trying to keep my voice steady. "Grab a plane at once. Get to that area. And at your first chance, kill him!"

Raht clicked off.

Only Heller's death stood between me and total victory.

I did not have much time. Black Jowl might be missed. At best I only had another five days.

I prayed that my prayers be heard.

Heller had to die!

Chapter 3

I went to bed. I tried to sleep. It was no use. Something was nagging at me. Then I had it!

I grabbed the two-way-response radio. I buzzed it.

"What's up now?" Raht's voice, irritated.

"When you go to the salvage area, take the Royal officer's activator-receiver and 831 Relayer with you."

"Do you know where I am?"

"How in all the Hells could I know where you are? I can't work this funny locator rig on top of this radio and you know it."

"You want me to turn around and go back?"

"Yes!"

"Then you'll have to talk to the pilot of this

commercial jet. I'm halfway over the Atlantic on my way to Italy."

"You're being impudent."

"I'm trying to carry out the order you gave me. Listen, would you mind clicking off? The little kid in the next seat is listening in."

I clicked off. Well, at least he was on his way to kill Heller.

Somehow I sweated through the night. Somehow I managed to live through the next day. Tenseness and anxiety were my lot. By late that night, I was a rag.

My radio went live, startling me half out of my wits.

"I'm at the Italian naval base in Taranto," said Raht.

"Have you done it?" I said.

"How can I have done it? He isn't here."

"Then what are you doing there, you idiot?"

"I'm calling you to report progress. Don't you want reports? I assure you, it would be a great pleasure not to talk to you at all, Officer Gris."

"Keep a civil tongue in your head. If he isn't there, what are you doing there?"

Raht said, "I traced him down from Rome. I just missed him. He's working with the airline company and the Italian government. He came down here to get them to take a naval tug and crane and divers to the site of the crash. They have to go around the heel of the boot of Italy and north up the Adriatic Sea. It's a trip of about 300 miles. I just missed them."

"Well, get after them!"

"That's what I'm trying to do. I've got to go back to a town called Termoli on the Italian coast that's near to the Palagruza Islands and rent a fish boat to get out there."

"What weapons do you have?"

"Well, you can't carry guns on a plane but I have a blastick."

"That will do just fine. Get on it!"

"It's about 160 miles to Termoli. I'll have to drive all night."

"Then drive all night!" I said angrily. "Radio me back when you have done it."

He clicked off.

I tried to go to sleep. Heller was about 700 miles away. It was too close. I rolled and tossed and sweated.

I suffered through the next day. No word from Raht.

Krak's activator-receiver had come in on the morning plane but for some reason wasn't handed to me until near evening. Nervously, I set it up and turned it on.

For a moment, I didn't know what I was looking at. It was simply a page of print.

Then I remembered that I had furnished Crobe a whole library in waterproof bookshelves to get him interested in psychology and psychiatry. I had also given him forty other books, a set entitled *Voltar Confederacy Combined Compendium Complete, including Space Codes, Penal Codes, Domestic Codes, Royal Proclamations, Royal Orders, Royal Procedures, Royal Precedence, Royal Successions Complete with Tables and Biographies, Court Customs, Court History, Royal Land Grants, Rights of Aristocracy, Planetary Districts of 110 Planets, Local Laws, Local Customs, Aristocratic Privileges and Various Other Matters.*

The Countess Krak had found these books, obviously.

I came out of my daze. I thought, well, it would do her plenty of good to study up on psychology and psychiatry. It would bring her into a realization of how wonderful they were.

The viewer was out of focus. I sharpened the image. I began to read what she seemed to be studying.

SECTION 835-932-N

PROCEDURES REGULATING TRIALS AND EXECUTIONS OF GENERAL SERVICE OFFICERS

A scream surged in my throat. I choked it back.

Her finger had appeared on the page. It was travelling down the fine print.

(1) **Executions in the field**
    (a) **By duly constituted conference of officers**
    (b) **By a senior when it is not feasible to return culprit to a base for trial**
    (c) **. . .**

The viewer began to swim before my gaze. Her finger had gone back to (a). I had not realized that the officers of this base could put me on trial. I had always been a little shaky on these regulations and depended on the fact that nobody else knew them well either. If Faht Bey and officers here took it into their heads to try me, they could also execute me for such things as flagrant Code breaks.

She was now onto another part of the section.

OFFENSES CARRYING DEATH PENALTIES

(a) **Capital Crimes under military statutes:**
    (1) **Threatening to kill, murder or ordering the murder of a Royal officer.**
    (2) **. . .**

The room swam around me. Raht had mentioned it

but I had thought he was just talking! There it was in the Penal Codes!

Her finger was travelling on:

(34)   Kidnapping . . .

A scream rose in my throat and got out.

I reeled away from the viewer.

Gods, that woman was dangerous!

She was sitting in there trying to find legal ways to bring about my death!

I raced down to the hangar. I found the guard captain. "Don't go near that prisoner in the special cell! Don't even look in! She has a dreadful disease that blinds you if you even glance at her."

"Oh, have you got a prisoner in there? You didn't log her into the detention cells if you have. When you came back a few nights ago, you must have bypassed the guard office. That's irregular, Officer Gris. What's her name?"

"Incognito," I blurted.

He was making a note. "Miss or Mrs.? I wish you wouldn't keep messing up procedures. We can't keep our files straight if you just keep rushing people into cells without logging them."

Then I had an inspiration. "The person I put in there can't be logged. She is a nonperson, executed years ago. She has no legal rights of any kind."

"Oh, one of those," he said. He lost interest. But I knew he would report it to Faht Bey.

I sighed, because my injured feet remained unhealed. I resented walking.

I went through the long tunnels and finally came

into Faht Bey's office. He looked up from his desk and flinched when he saw me. I resented being flinched at.

"The other night when I returned in the line-jumper," I said, "I put a prisoner in the special cell. She is not to be looked at or communicated with. She is a nonperson without rights. She is actually a menace to the State."

He grunted and made a note. "What about the other one you have locked up? He's not a nonperson. I have his card here. He's Forrest Closure of the Grabbe-Manhattan Bank."

My pulse skipped several beats. "Have you talked to him?"

"No. Should I talk to him?"

"NO!" I said. Oh, Gods, if Faht Bey found out his whole base was mortgaged, maybe they would convene an officers' conference on me!

"Why are you holding him?" said Faht Bey.

"Reasons of state!" I said emphatically. "I can't tell you any more than that."

"Are you sure?" said Faht Bey.

"Of course I'm sure!"

"I think you're up to something, Officer Gris. Raping women, blowing up mosques. We're supposed to lie quietly here and do what we're supposed to do. You know, of course, that heroin supplies continue to vanish. We inventoried two days after you came back, just to be careful. And we're out a lot of kilos. If I had any proof, Officer Gris, I'd convene an officers' conference on somebody I am looking at."

"What would I do with heroin?" I yelled.

"Run a drug ring on the side," said Faht Bey. "You seem to have quite a bit of money we didn't give you."

"Special funds came in on the *Blixo*," I lied.

He raised his eyebrows and shifted in his chair. "This Forrest Closure," said Faht Bey, "could be a messy thing. Grabbe-Manhattan is connected to I. G. Barben Pharmaceutical. They could cut off our amphetamines. I can't make heads or tails of why you would order him put in a cell. In fact, I haven't the least idea of what you are up to. I am responsible for this base. Now let me tell you this: If I find any evidence that you are cooking up another catastrophe for us, I will convene a conference on you and take my chances with authorities on Voltar. My guess is that they are as sick of you as we are. Have I made myself clear?"

I limped out.

Things were pretty touch and go.

In just three or four days now, Grabbe-Manhattan was going to realize that Forrest Closure should be reporting back in. They would send somebody here and, of course, talk to Faht Bey, and the base commander would know he was dealing with the biggest threat this base had ever experienced.

What would Faht Bey do? He would tell them that I had no title to this base and he'd feed me to the Turkish authorities. And in addition to whatever the Turks did to me, I would also have a conference convened on me and be sentenced to death.

My only possible hope was Heller's assassination. And soon!

Only then could I make things come out all right.

Chapter 4

The following day, I was feeling pretty haggard. I was bolstered somewhat by the fact that I had Lombar's order to kill Heller and so could not be tagged for that. But I had all these other things threatening me and if I also failed to nail Heller, then to the list of enemies I could also add Lombar.

Amongst other things, my feet had not healed. Walking around with cuts in goat droppings is not conducive to health of the heels. The wounds were festering.

I had Ters drive me to the hospital. Nurse Bildirjin, my third wife, passed me by without so much as a glance as I waited in the lobby.

I got tired of it. I found Prahd washing his hands after an operation.

"The free clinic is closed for the day," he said.

"Hey, wait a minute," I said. "I might die of blood poisoning. I can't even wear boots."

"Then you can't kick anybody," he said. And he would have walked out of the washroom.

I blocked his way. "You can't treat me like this."

"I'm not going to treat you at all, Officer Gris. You owe me an order starting my pay. You have not made arrangements for funds to start campaigns against prevalent diseases. And you have not paid the *kaffarah* to the villages of the wives you messed up. And your marriage-dowry bank order bounced. When you see fit to go up to Istanbul and straighten up your affairs with Mudur

Zengin and keep your bargains, I might have time to talk to you."

"How can I go to Istanbul with my feet rotting off?" I demanded.

"Steal some crutches," he said. "Nobody around here would even lend you any." And he simply walked out.

I was NOT going to Istanbul and face the rage of Mudur Zengin of the Piastre Bank. The way my luck was running in that direction, he would probably have me arrested for getting dirt on his floor.

Riding back home, I pondered this. It seemed quite logical that when I had killed Heller, getting back in Rockecenter's good graces, I could do my future business with Grabbe-Manhattan. Until then, I would let it ride. To Hells with those (bleeped) wives, anyway. And who cared if the riffraff had disease?

In my bathroom, I soaked my festering feet in Epsom salts and was hopeful it would help.

My radio went live. RAHT!

"Have you killed him?" I shouted.

"That's what I'm trying to tell you," said Raht.

"Then tell me!"

"That's what I'm trying to do. Do you want this report or don't you?"

I swallowed my rage. "Give me the report!"

"That's better. An agent's report should be precise, not rushed and all tangled up. You almost took my ear off. Now, let's see, where was I? Yes. I arrived at Termoli but they didn't have any fish boats. All available craft were out at the site of the crash. So I went up the coast to Pescara, a bigger town, and I got a boat.

"Pescara is about 120 miles from the Palagruza where the plane crashed, and it took us some time to get out there. The Adriatic is pretty stormy, lots of waves and tides.

"The plane went down in about a hundred feet of water. The Italian navy was trying to raise it with a tug and crane. It was pretty buried on the bottom in yellow mud and sand and lying upside down.

"A plane like that weighs forty or fifty tons and the crane they had just wasn't up to it.

"The Royal officer was helping them. They tried to pump some kind of foam into it but it was so broken up the foam just floated away. So the Royal officer went down in scuba gear and they began to send up bodies.

"Did you know there were a lot of kids on that plane? Well, anyway, they had to get another craft up to take the bodies. They had a priest there making the sign of the cross as each one came up. I counted thirty-five. The airline people said there were forty-nine on the plane including crew. But the crash had opened the side of the ship up and fourteen of the bodies, they figured, must have floated away. They spent a lot of time trying to find them and couldn't.

"The Royal officer had helicopters searching the sea and beaches, but they only found some bits of wreckage. So he went down again and they started passing up cabin hand baggage. They found a couple scarves identified as having been bought by the woman in the Rome airport and I think that was the first time he began to believe she had been aboard, because he started caving in.

"Finally the navy got some cutting tools up from Taranto and they opened up the baggage compartment and he found her suitcase. He seemed to lose interest after that.

"The authorities are trying to investigate the crash. The pilot recorder is missing..."

"(Bleep) you, Raht," I snarled. "Did you kill him or didn't you?"

"Now I know how you got poor Terb tortured and murdered. No planning. That place was completely swarming with Italian navy. If I had fired, I would have had to cross 120 miles of water in a slow boat with patrol craft on my tail. In order to do a job like this, you have to have the subject in some secluded place where nobody can witness it and you can get away."

"So you didn't kill him."

"Not yet. I'm just giving you a report."

I knew I would have to give firmer directions. "Where is he now?"

"Leaving the area. That's why I'm giving you this report."

"Raht, if you don't do this job, you're through. I'll kill you myself! You missed your opportunity!"

"There WAS no opportunity!" he snapped.

"Are you going to kill him or aren't you?"

"Of course I'm going to kill him. I think he is heading back for New York and I'll be right on his heels. The moment I get him alone, he's dead. But I need help."

"What kind?" I said suspiciously.

"When he's back in New York he'll be on your viewer again, right?"

"Right," I said.

"The first moment you pick him up, you've got to tell me. And you've got to tell me, if you can, where he is going. All I have to have is just a few minutes in a secluded place. I shoot, he's dead. And I can get away."

Delays, delays. I couldn't afford them. But there was hope. "I'll help you," I said.

He clicked off.

Then I cheered up a little. I had tried several times

to get the Countess Krak and had failed. But now she was my prisoner and simply by dropping a couple gas pellets down her air chute, I could kill her.

I decided it would be the same with Heller. Even he couldn't survive with me directing the assassin every step of the way, right up to the final fatal shot from a well-planned ambush.

Chapter 5

I could not be absolutely sure Heller had gone back to New York. Raht had said nothing about him getting on a New York plane. He might come here to Turkey instead.

Nervously, I wondered if I could do anything to prevent that catastrophe.

I went out and checked the alarm bell at the gate. Musef and Torgut were alert, armed and ready to gun down any intruder.

In my secret room, I ran a check on the floor tile which, if pressed, sounded a general alarm to the hangar and assembled the whole base in battle order. It was fine.

I checked Krak's viewer. She was eating space emergency rations and studying the *Voltar Confederacy Combined Compendium* section on "Royal Proclamations." I knew she was thinking about those two forged Royal documents I had foisted off on her. I wished I knew what she had done with them. But never mind, if she tried to present them they would execute her.

Still, I thought I had better make sure her door was

safely closed. I went down to the hangar and up the tunnel to the detention cells. From afar I looked at the outside of her door.

Even if he got here, Heller would never suspect I had her. They hadn't even written her name in the log.

I wondered if I had left any other clues lying around.

I ran into Captain Stabb. "We're all keened up for those bank robberies now," he said. "If it's in Europe or Africa, we can use the line-jumper. But if you're going over to America, I think it's better we take the tug. So we checked out her water and air today. She's got fuel enough to make it to the fifteenth Hell and back twenty times over."

"If you take *Tug One*," I said, "the assassin pilots will be tagging us with their two flying cannons."

"They won't touch us unless we try to leave the planet. By the way, we cut out your share of the wallets. It's in here."

I followed him into their stone-walled sleeping rooms. With a shock I saw they had laid out on the table the valuables of the passengers and crew. Evidence!

There were wristwatches, rings, travellers checks, money and I.D. cards!

"Devils," I said. "We can't have this stuff lying around. It would connect us to the crash!"

"Well, we were just waiting until you came down. We'll pry the stones out of the jewelry, melt the gold. . . ."

"And throw the watches away," I said.

He shrugged.

"And don't try to forge those travellers checks," I warned him.

He frowned.

I was about to take it up further when my eye lighted on something.

Krak's purse!

Talk about leaving evidence around! I grabbed it.

"Here, here," said Stabb. "You can't do that. There's a lot of money in it."

"If that Royal officer came in here and found this, he'd shoot us to bits!"

"Is he going to come here?"

"He might."

"I thought he was going to be killed."

I said, "That's in progress this very minute."

"Oh, well, then. Why worry?"

"He might come here first."

"Oho!" said Captain Stabb. "In that case I'll order my men to go armed even in the hangar. You don't have anything to worry about, Officer Gris. We'll shoot him on sight. Okay?"

I was somewhat mollified.

By giving up my share of the loot and the money, they agreed to destroy the evidence and let me take Krak's purse away.

Back in my room I went through it.

MY SQUEEZA CREDIT CARD!

After all the trouble that had caused, I had it back! It cheered me up for hours.

I regarded it as a portent, an omen of good fortune. To me it looked like things were really on the mend.

Chapter 6

Just as my nerves were about to snap like overtightened wires, Heller showed up on his viewer.

What a relief!

He was debarking from a Pan Am plane at John F. Kennedy Airport in New York. It was very early morning there.

He was walking very slowly. At immigration they had to ask him twice for his passport. At customs the stone-faced official had to open his bag himself.

Heller walked out to the lobby. His name was being called and he went over to the message desk.

The chauffeur from the condo was waiting for him there.

"Did you bring the bag?" said Heller.

"Yes, sir," said the chauffeur. "And the Porsche is in the parking lot."

Heller reached into his pocket and came up with a banknote. He handed it to the chauffeur. "You better catch a cab back. I'm not returning home."

"Sir, I do not mean to intrude, but do you think that is wise? We all think you would be much better in familiar surroundings."

"That's the trouble with them," said Heller in a dead voice. "They're too familiar."

"Sir, Mr. Epstein said..."

"I know, I phoned him from the plane just after I phoned you. I know you all mean it kindly. But all

I want is to go off by myself a little while and try to get over this."

My luck was holding! This was exactly what I needed!

Hastily, I called Raht on the radio. "Where are you?"

"I'll be at JFK in about an hour. I'm on TWA from Rome via Brussels." I could hear the background roar of the plane engines.

"He's going to be off by himself. Call me the instant you land."

"Will do," said Raht. He clicked off.

My attention went back to Heller. He was following the chauffeur across a parking lot. The Porsche was sitting there.

The cat!

He was at the window.

The chauffeur unlocked the door and the cat sprang for Heller's chest. Heller petted it and put the cat on his shoulder.

"At least he'll be some company for you," said the chauffeur. "He's just been moping around the house. I put his food and things in the back like you said."

Heller got in, took the keys and started the car. The chauffeur saluted and Heller drove away.

"Well, cat," he said, "I guess we've got to get used to her being gone." There was a catch in his voice. My screen went misty.

Oh, this was ideal. Heller wouldn't be alert at all! He was even driving kind of slow and wooden. I had planned much better than I thought. I had depressed him beyond belief. He would be a sitting duck!

He was driving north up the Van Wyck Expressway. It did not tell me yet where he was going.

He passed the turns that would take him into New York and drove straight on.

He entered the Whitestone Expressway and shortly crossed the Bronx Whitestone Bridge. He continued north on the Hutchinson River Parkway. At Exit 6 he turned into the New England Thruway.

Suddenly I understood. I could not believe my luck! He was heading for the roadhouse in Connecticut! I was sure of it!

Despite old blind ladies and deputy sheriffs I would have to pilot Raht in there.

Well, I could do it.

I grabbed a map. The whole trip up there from JFK Airport was only about forty-five miles.

He turned off the expressway and went through a town. He went along the state highway and turned onto the cow path. He came up to the abandoned service station and the old lady came out.

"Where's your sweetheart today?" she said.

Heller couldn't answer her. My viewer misted.

He got the jeep out and put the Porsche in the garage. He transferred his baggage and drove off.

I had realized before that this old highway, long since grown over, was the same one which used to serve the roadhouse. And sure enough, he drove along over brush and between trees and came to the creek with the broken wooden bridge. He put the jeep in four-wheel drive, went through the creek bed, pulled up the far bank and was shortly stopped under the huge maple trees.

He unlocked the door, carried his baggage in and with very slow movements, quite unlike him, began to straighten up one of the old bedrooms so that it could be used for sleeping quarters.

My radio went live. "I've cleared in," said Raht.

"Oh, are you in luck," I said. "Now listen carefully." And I gave him very explicit directions to rent a car and where to go. "And when you get in sight of the abandoned service station, leave your car and continue on foot. The old lady will come out. She carries a shotgun for intruders. Shoot her. Then proceed on foot." And I gave him the rest of the directions to get to the roadhouse. "When you get across the creek, hide under a bush and call him. He is certain to come to the door, thinking it is one of the deputy sheriffs. When he does, shoot him."

"I've got all that," said Raht. "There's something else. I want you to give me the direct order, very explicit, to kill a Royal officer, by name. I have a recorder on right here in the terminal. In that way, if this ever comes to trial, it's your responsibility."

I almost laughed to myself. The order came from Lombar Hisst and he controlled Voltar, even the Emperor. I said, "I am Officer Gris. You, Agent Raht, are ordered to kill one Jettero Heller, Grade X Combat Engineer of the Fleet." I added the date and time.

"Now one more thing," said Raht. "If I do this I want ten thousand dollars cash. I'm not in this business for my health. You've had me on lowered allowance and pay for months and I mean to get my own back."

I almost laughed. He had just made it worth ten thousand to me to shoot him the next time I laid eyes on him. "Of course," I said. "I'll tell you what. I'll make it twenty thousand. How's that?"

There was silence at the other end. Then an excited, "It's a deal! But I'm not going to rent a car. I'm going into town first to steal one and also get a silenced rifle. It'll only add an hour to my schedule. I want to make awful sure of this. All right?"

"I hope it's a big caliber," I said.

"Will do. Officer Gris, you've made my day!"

He clicked off.

I polished my hands one against the other.

Heller dead!

This I was going to ENJOY!

Chapter 7

Heller was sitting in the main room of the old bootleggers' roadhouse in Connecticut. The door was open but the light was dim.

He was holding in his hands a handkerchief with the initial *K* on it. His head was down. He must be feeling very bad.

The cat seemed to sense his mood and was just sitting on the floor, looking at him.

Two hours had gone by and he had not moved.

My radio went live. Raht's muted voice. "I'm on the other side of the creek. I can see the roadhouse."

"Be very silent," I said. "He has good ears. He's sitting in the main room and the door is open. What kind of a rifle do you have?"

"Sako Safari Grade .300 Winchester Magnum. Thirty-two hundred feet per second muzzle velocity, more than a ton and a half foot-pounds of impact."

"Excellent," I said. "It will blow his head off."

"Yes. And just to make sure, I've got specially loaded explosive bullets. The rifle is silenced."

"Did you get the old blind woman?"

"I sure took care of her," he said. "You're on the level about that twenty thousand now, aren't you?"

"Indeed so," I said. "Now listen, just angle around until you can see in the door and let him have it. Shoot to kill, first shot."

"Got it. Be sure and tell me if he hears anything or moves."

"I will," I said.

I watched the screen carefully. Heller was just sitting there. A perfect target.

Minutes went by. Then my radio went live again. Raht's voice was a barely audible whisper. "I am under a bush about twenty-five yards from the house. But I can't see in the door. Trees are in the way. Is it all right if I call to him and get him to come out on the porch? The second I see his head, I can fire."

"Do it," I said impatiently.

I tensely watched my screen.

Then I heard a faint voice through my speaker: "Hey, whitey engineer!" Oh good, he'd think it was a deputy.

Heller's head lifted. He was looking toward the open door.

The call repeated: "Whitey engineer!"

Heller put the handkerchief in his pocket. He reached around to the back of his belt and drew the .45 Llama automatic. I hadn't realized he was armed or would be suspicious.

He got up.

He went to the door.

He didn't see anything and stepped further out on the porch.

BLAM!

An explosive bullet crashed into stone to his left.

Raht had missed!

Heller went down on one knee. He was looking at a bush.

He raised the .45 and, without sighting, fired!

There was a yelp of pain!

Then a blast of fire from the bush.

BLAM!

The visio on my screen went dead!

There was the sound, metallic. The pistol dropping to the stone. Then the thud of a body falling.

BLAM!

My speaker was dead.

I sat there for an eerie moment.

No visio.

No sound.

Gradually it was borne in upon me that Heller had been hit in the temple, destroying the visio. Then he had dropped his pistol and he himself had fallen. And Raht, taking no chances, had fired again, hitting him in the head and destroying the audio bug.

I sat very still.

I could not believe my luck.

HELLER WAS DEAD!

Chapter 8

I sat there in a daze.

For all these long months he had made my life a mess of assorted Hells.

And he was gone.

I had expected to feel surges of jubilation. Instead, I was sort of numb.

A fantasy that his ghost might come and haunt me passed through my mind.

I shook it off. Psychologists and psychiatrists were all agreed men had no souls. They were just animals, just a bunch of cells. There was no life after death. Thank Heavens for that! It sort of steadied me.

Maybe if I shared this news the expected joy would come.

I got to my feet. They were festered and painful. I picked up the radio and limped down the passageway to the hangar. I found Stabb.

"I've got good news for you," I said. "The Royal officer has just been executed. He's dead!"

Stabb's beady eyes flared. "You don't mean it!"

"Fact," I said. "He's just had his head blown off."

Stabb gave a bark of joy. He yelled to his crew. He told them and they cheered.

"Oh, Gods," said Stabb, "that should happen to every condemned officer in the Fleet! Them and their high-and-mighty ways. How can an honest pirate do his job with (bleepards) like that around! So he's dead, is he? Well, let's get cracking on the bank robberies, now that that is off your mind."

My radio went live. "Officer Gris! I've got the blood staunched now. He got me in the leg. I'm in bad shape, Officer Gris. I can't walk. You've got to get me out of here."

"Oh, I think you can manage it," I said. "We've got other things to do than cover up your bungling."

"Officer Gris," said Raht, "I don't think you understand. When I was looking for bandages, I looked down a shaft and there's all kinds of equipment here. For

Gods' sakes, come over here with the tug before we have a Code break to end all Code breaks. Voltar is written all over these boxes."

"Well, set the place on fire," I said. "Burn it all up and get out of there as best you can."

"I don't think these diamonds will burn."

Stabb was suddenly alert. "Diamonds?" he said.

I was suddenly alert as well. "How many diamonds?" I said.

"I can't carry them out. I got them as far as the front porch and I can't get them any further. They're spilled all over the steps."

I looked at Stabb and Stabb looked at me. We nodded in sudden accord.

"The moment that it's dark here," I said, "we'll take off in the tug. You stay right there and wait for us. We'll take care of everything." And you, too, Raht, I added to myself.

Right that moment it was 5:00 P.M. where we were. We could take off at 8:00 when night was thick. We would follow the sun's shadow around the Earth and land in Connecticut.

"I'll try to hold on through the next five hours," said Raht in a faint and pain-filled voice. "Promise not to abandon me if I go unconscious and can't answer."

"Don't worry," I said, "we'll soon be on our way!"

Stabb's men were scrambling to get *Tug One* ready to lift off.

I hobbled back toward the tunnel.

A black-uniformed assassin pilot pointed his red-gloved finger at the tug. "You're going to take off in that?"

It was an unnecessary question. The Antimancos were swarming over it.

"Just remember this," said the assassin pilot, pointing at the two flying cannons on the other side of the hangar, "if you try to leave this planet, we will blow you out of the universe. Those are our orders. They have not been changed. The locational bugs are in place on your ship and we will be right behind you."

"Wait," I said, staring at the deadly assassin ships, "you could get some nutty idea we're trying to evade you when we aren't. You take it easy with those things."

"You are not our senior," said the assassin pilot. "You just make sure you don't do anything that might give us 'nutty ideas.' Your tug is completely unarmed. Just one shot from either one of our ships and you're finished. We haven't had a kill in months and we're hungry."

He went off to alert the other three pilots and get ready to fly.

Faht Bey was barring my way. "What are you up to now?"

"I'm just carrying out orders," I said.

Faht Bey looked at the assassin ships. All four of the pilots were now in conference below them. "If they have reason to finish you off, what do I do with Forrest Closure? You can't keep a representative from Grabbe-Manhattan here forever"

"Don't you dare let him go until I return!" I said in sudden alarm. "I've got this all solved now, so don't mess it up."

"YOU are telling ME not to mess things up?" he said. "Officer Gris, if I had the slightest excuse I'd convene an officers' conference on you this instant."

"You would be sorry," I said. "I am of vast service to this base. Just a short while ago I removed the Crown inspector that was going to execute every one of you!"

Faht Bey walked off.

I went to my room. Gods, my feet were hurting. Maybe I was developing gangrene. Or possibly lockjaw. I felt my jaws experimentally. No, they hadn't locked yet.

I got into the black ski suit.

Musef and Torgut were at the door. "Any orders?" said Musef.

Suddenly I realized I had good news for them. "Remember the DEA man that you had a fight with last fall?" I said. "He's dead."

They beamed like rising moons. They grabbed each other and began to do a circular dance, the combined seven hundred pounds of them shaking the floor. Their whoops were earsplitting.

Utanc came to the door to see what the noise was. Alarmed, she saw I was buckling on my guns.

She sped forward to me and threw her arms about my neck. "O Master, you are going into danger!"

"It's nothing," I said.

She kissed me tenderly. "O Master, I would die if anything happened to you. Come back safe!"

I was touched.

Eventually my room cleared of people. I had one further problem. Should I kill the Countess Krak now or when I came back?

I had a little time. I had two poison-gas grenades. All I had to do was walk outside and up the hill to the vent hole hidden behind a rock, drop in one or both of those grenades and that would be that.

There was only one thing really wrong with it. The thought of walking on these feet over the rough terrain was more than I could measure up to.

I went in and looked at her viewer. It had no image on it. She must have lost track of time in that place and was asleep.

And then I was seized with an uneasiness. Suppose, while I was gone, she would get out: I'd come back to the base and find her waiting there, ready to stomp me into the pavement.

I picked up a poison-gas grenade. I hobbled out into the yard. My feet were terribly bad. I did not think I could make it up the hill.

Ahmed was sitting in a car talking to Ters. I beckoned and Ahmed came over.

"Listen, Ahmed," I said. "There's a gray rock up on the hill there. Just behind it you will find a hole. A badger made it and his noise is interrupting my sleep. Here's a gas grenade. You pull the pin and drop it in. Will you do that for me?"

"Of course," he said. He took it and raced off.

I went out further into the yard where I could watch.

Ahmed went out on the highway and trotted up the hill. He went to the gray rock and pointed, looking down at me in the yard. I nodded.

I saw him pull the pin.

He reached over and dropped the poison-gas grenade in the hole and darted away.

There was an immediate explosion. White vapor rose into the air.

Ahmed was coming back down.

"Thank you," I said fervently.

I went back into my secret room.

Her viewer was blank.

I waited for a thrill of exultation.

It didn't come.

I said aloud, loudly, "COUNTESS KRAK, YOU'RE DEAD!"

I threw the viewer across the room. It broke. I was finished with it at last. I looked at the shards of glass that now spattered the floor. I went over and stamped on the speaker.

It hurt my foot.

Rage shook me. Even in death she was able to injure me!

I stamped harder.

It hurt more.

I jumped on it with both feet!

I found that I had begun to scream.

That wouldn't do. I was the winner, wasn't I?

I found that I was coughing and my throat burned. That wouldn't do either. SHE was the one who had been gassed, not me!

Carefully, I steadied myself down. I must do something to get my mind off it.

I had other things to think about anyway. She was *finished!*

I began making further plans. We would pick up the diamonds and other things in Connecticut. Then we would flash down to Ochokeechokee, Florida, and bomb the spores plant. Then we would move to Detroit and wipe out Chryster. And after that we'd blow the Empire State Building sky-high.

Then I would contact Peeksnoop at National Security Agency and get connected to Bury or Rockecenter, tell them the fuel man and all his works were no longer a menace to them and be back in their good graces. And finally I could tell Black Jowl to tear the mortgage up.

I would then go home to glory and reign supreme as the Chief of the Apparatus.

Feeling steadier, I went down to the hangar magazine to collect weapons and explosives. I planned that my last days on Earth would end with a big BANG!

*Is this the
end of Earth?*

Read

MISSION EARTH

Volume 8

DISASTER

About the Author
L. Ron Hubbard

L. Ron Hubbard's remarkable writing career spanned more than half-a-century of intense literary achievement and creative influence.

And though he was first and foremost a writer, his life experiences and travels in all corners of the globe were wide and diverse. His insatiable curiosity and personal belief that one should live life as a professional led to a lifetime of extraordinary accomplishment. He was also an explorer, ethnologist, mariner and pilot, filmmaker and photographer, philosopher and educator, composer and musician.

Growing up in the still-rugged frontier country of Montana, he broke his first bronc and became the blood brother of a Blackfeet Indian medicine man by age six. In 1927, when he was 16, he traveled to a still remote Asia. The following year, to further satisfy his thirst for adventure and augment his growing knowledge of other cultures, he left school and returned to the Orient. On this trip, he worked as a supercargo and helmsman aboard a coastal trader which plied the seas between Japan and Java. He came to know old Shanghai, Beijing and the Western Hills at a time when few Westerners could enter China. He traveled more than a quarter of a million miles by sea and land while still a teenager and before the advent of commercial aviation as we know it.

He returned to the United States in the autumn of 1929 to complete his formal education. He entered George Washington University in Washington, D.C., where he studied engineering and took one of the earliest courses in atomic and molecular physics. In addition to his studies, he was the president of the Engineering Society and Flying Club, and wrote articles, stories and plays for the university newspaper. During the same period he also barnstormed across the American mid-West and was a national correspondent and photographer for the Sportsman Pilot magazine, the most distinguished aviation publication of its day.

Returning to his classroom of the world in 1932, he led two separate expeditions, the Caribbean Motion Picture Expedition; sailing on one of the last of America's four-masted commercial ships, and the second a mineralogical survey of Puerto Rico. His exploits earned him membership in the renowned Explorers Club and he subsequently carried their coveted flag on two more voyages of exploration and discovery. As a master mariner licensed to operate ships in any ocean, his lifelong love of the sea was reflected in the many ships he captained and the skill of the crews he trained. He also served with distinction as a U.S. naval officer during the Second World War.

All of this—and much more—found its way, into his writing and gave his stories a compelling sense of authenticity that has appealed to readers throughout the world. It started in 1934 with the publication of "The Green God" in Thrilling Adventure magazine, a story about an American naval intelligence officer caught up in the mystery and intrigues of pre-communist China. With his extensive knowledge of the world and its people and his ability to write in any style and genre, he rapidly achieved prominence as a writer of action adventure, western, mystery and suspense. Such was the respect of his fellow writers that he was only 25 when elected president of the New York Chapter of the American Fiction Guild.

In addition to his career as a leading writer of fiction, he worked as a successful screenwriter in Hollywood where he wrote the original story and script for Columbia's 1937 hit serial, "The Secret of Treasure Island." His work on numerous films for Columbia, Universal and other major studios involved writing, providing story lines and serving as a script consultant.

In 1938, he was approached by the venerable New York publishing house of Street and Smith, the publishers of Astounding Science Fiction. Wanting to capitalize on the proven reader appeal of the L. Ron Hubbard byline to capture more readers for this emerging genre, they essentially offered to buy all the science fiction he wrote. When he protested that he did not write about machines and machinery but that he wrote about people, they told him that was exactly what was wanted. The rest is history.

The impact and influence that his novels and stories had on the fields of science fiction, fantasy and horror virtually amounted to the changing of a genre. It is the compelling human element that he originally brought to this new genre that remains today the basis of its growing international popularity.

L. Ron Hubbard consistently enabled readers to peer into the mind and emotions of characters in a way that sharply heightened the reading experience without slowing the pace of the story, a level of writing rarely achieved.

Among the most celebrated examples of this are three stories he published in a single, phenomenally creative year (1940)—FINAL BLACKOUT and its grimly possible future world of unremitting war and ultimate courage which Robert Heinlein called "as perfect a piece of science fiction as has ever been written"; the ingenious fantasy-adventure, TYPEWRITER IN THE SKY described by Clive Cussler as "written in the great style adventure should be written in"; and the prototype novel of clutching psychological suspense and horror in the midst of ordinary, everyday life, FEAR, studied by writers from Stephen King to Ray Bradbury.

It was Mr. Hubbard's trendsetting work in this field from 1938 to 1950, particularly, that not only helped to expand the scope and imaginative boundaries of science fiction and fantasy but indelibly established him as one of the founders of what continues to be regarded as the genre's Golden Age.

Widely honored—recipient of Italy's Tetra-dramma D'Oro Award and a special Gutenberg Award, among other significant honors—BATTLEFIELD EARTH has already been translated into 12 languages, and easily ranks as the biggest single-volume science fiction novel, at 1050 pages, in the history of the genre.

The MISSION EARTH dekalogy has been equally acclaimed, winning the Cosmos 2000 Award from

French readers and the coveted Nova-Science Fiction Award from Italy's National Committee for Science Fiction and Fantasy. The novel has sold more than five million copies in six languages, and each of its 10 volumes became international bestsellers as they were released. Beyond that, L. Ron Hubbard recorded 21 consecutive international bestsellers.

His literary output ultimately encompassed more than 260 published novels, novelettes, short stories and screenplays in every major genre.

For more information on L. Ron Hubbard and his many acclaimed works of fiction visit the L. Ron Hubbard literary Internet sites at: http://www.bridgepub.com, http://www.authorservicesinc.com and http://www.battlefieldearth.com.

"I am always happy to hear from my readers."

L. Ron Hubbard

These were the words of L. Ron Hubbard, who was always very interested in hearing from his friends and readers. He made a point of staying in communication with everyone he came in contact with over his fifty-year career as a professional writer, and he had thousands of fans and friends that he corresponded with all over the world.

The publishers of L. Ron Hubbard's literary works wish to continue this tradition and would very much welcome letters and comments from you, his readers, both old and new.

Any message addressed to the Author's Affairs Director at Bridge Publications will be given prompt and full attention.

BRIDGE PUBLICATIONS, INC.
4751 Fountain Avenue
Los Angeles, California 90029